To KILL the LEOPARD

To KILL the LEOPARD

Theodore Taylor

Harcourt Brace & Company

New York   San Diego   London

Requests for permission to make copies of any
part of the work should be mailed to:
Permissions Department,
Harcourt Brace & Company,
8th Floor, Orlando, Florida 32887.

Library of Congress Cataloging-in-Publication Data
Taylor, Theodore, 1922–
    To kill the leopard/Theodore Taylor.—1st ed.
      p.   cm.
    ISBN 0-15-124097-3
    1. World War, 1939–1945—Fiction. I. Title.
PS3570.A9549T6   1993
813'.54—dc20   92-36464

Designed by Lydia D'moch

Printed in the United States of America

First edition
A   B   C   D   E

For Gloria Loomis
Agent. Adviser. Dear Friend.
With love, TLT.

Acknowledgments

For research assistance and advice on the Royal Navy and wartime London I'm especially indebted to Doris Spriggs, Middlesex, England; for the same on Lorient, France, to Admiral Yan Bordelet, Ret., and Raymond Bernard, former German prisoner of war. Marine Baumeister Manfred Krutein served in Lorient and aboard U-boats. Captain David Bryce, USN (Ret.), advised on combat sections; Captain John Taryan on the merchant marine. Pam Strayer straightened out my French. Hank Searles and Bansie Vasvani rescued me from editorial sins. Last but not least, thanks to Lucy Poshek for manning the word processor, always a thankless job.

To KILL the
LEOPARD

Book One

LORIENT

"U-boote sind die Wölfe zur See:
Angreifen! Reissen! Vernichten! Versenken!"
(U-boats are the wolves of the ocean:
Attack! Rip! Destroy! Sink!)
                    —*Admiral Karl Dönitz.*

LORIENT, FRANCE—JANUARY 1941

Horst Kammerer sat on the foredeck of the *U-122*. He watched an artist paint a large snarling leopard on the front of the new submarine's conning tower beneath the spray deflector. A worklight illuminated the cat in an attack leap. Two smaller leopards would go on the port and starboard sides of the tower where numbers were always stenciled in peacetime.

The *122*, an IX long-range type, was in the huge, nearly completed concrete pen, a sea-level fortress at Keroman in Lorient harbor, nestled safely away from British bombers with five other boats. Midships she swarmed with activity as workmen prepared her for patrol.

The bunker's gray concrete walls and thick steel-reinforced roof were still damp. Machinery noises echoed in the tunnel-like U-boat garage. The stink of the boats mixed with the acrid fumes of welding torches and the odor of new mortar. Foul, oily water lapped around the *122*'s hull.

"Rudmann, do you know about the *Felis panthera pardus?*" Kammerer asked, his breath silvery at the edge of the light.

"No, sir," Rudmann replied. A fine brush detailed the glaring black pupil of the leopard's eye. His hands were gloved.

As a civilian, five-foot-one Rudmann, who wore grandma spectacles, had painted posters and murals in Berlin. Recruited in late 1939 to decorate U-boats, he now held the rating of chief petty officer. In civilian life he was well known for his circus renderings, and he was quite bewildered serving in the Nazi navy. The wool great-coat uniform swallowed him up.

"I researched the leopard before choosing it, Rudmann." Rudmann changed brushes to begin applying spots around the head.

"Its small prey are birds, lizards, and monkeys. Larger prey is up to donkey size, like antelopes. But I discovered it is especially fond of domestic dogs."

Rudmann was nervous. The U-boat commander watched his every stroke. "I didn't know that," he mumbled quietly.

"I like to think of enemy ships as donkeys. Stubborn but dumb."

"Yes, sir," said Rudmann, making a mistake. A splotch of black spread into the left eye, staining the iris. His hand began to tremble. His grandma glasses fogged.

Kammerer caught it. "Relax, Rudmann."

"Yes, sir."

"I thought about using the black panther as my symbol, then decided the color wouldn't stand out against the gray of the hull. The orange coat and black spots of the leopard are more striking."

"That was the right decision, Herr Kapitän. I've done fifty-six boats so far and keep busy repainting. The sea scrubs them away, as you know." Rudmann talked with a slight lisp.

Kammerer laughed. "You should try to mix sea-proof paints."

"Yes, sir."

"Did you know that this will be the maiden combat patrol for the *122*?" Her first effort after coming out of the Baltic had been aborted due to engine trouble.

"I wish you happy hunting."

"Thank you, Rudmann. My specialty is killing tankers. Admiral Dönitz tells us, 'Destroy the tankers! Destroy the tankers!' England needs four big ones each day just to survive. So I try very hard."

Karl Dönitz was *Befehlshaber der Unterseeboote, BdU*, a leader respected, even revered, by almost every U-boat sailor. He was their *Löwe*, their lion.

Rudmann shivered. It was not the cold dankness of the bunker. The shiver indicated that he hated death and destruction, something that Kammerer and the admiral obviously enjoyed.

In Operations at the nearby Kernevel headquarters a blackboard kept score on tanker kills. So far 136 British, Norwegian, Danish, and Panamanian-registered oil carriers, the latter mostly owned by American companies, had been posted in red chalk.

Kammerer continued, "So that's what I'll be aiming for, Rudmann. To date, my personal score is five. Not bad for only two combat patrols, eh?" He'd commanded the smaller VIIC type on those two sorties.

"No, no sir..." Flustered Rudmann added, "I mean, yessir."

Oberleutnant Joseph Graeber approached the commander, holding a clipboard. "The transmitter is fixed," the first officer said. "I'm satisfied; Heinze is satisfied."

Kammerer signed off; then he said to Graeber, "How do you like it?" nodding toward the leopard.

The First studied the artwork. "Looks menacing enough."

"That's exactly what we wanted, isn't it?" Kammerer answered, sounding quite pleased with himself. Graeber smiled and excused himself, going aft.

Kammerer fell silent, thinking about the two months ahead in the North Atlantic, brutal this time of year. But the crew was well rested after a thirty-day leave. Many of them had returned to Germany on the *BdU Zug*, the admiral's own four-car express train. It ran from Lorient to Le Mans, where a Brest section joined it, then on to Paris, Rotterdam, Bremen, and Hamburg. The train sometimes carried spare parts and technicians. It was mainly used for officers and crew on leave. Nothing was too good for the *Unterseeboote* men. A few of them were from Kammerer's last boat; the others, like Graeber, were new. But all seemed enthusiastic, and Kammerer felt good about the hunting prospects.

Arms folded, brown eyes locked on the main leopard,

Kammerer didn't look German though he was as Teutonic as the Brandenburg Gate. Black haired and olive skinned, he looked Italian or Arabic. If anyone cared to ask, he said, "Blame it on my French mother." Giselle was from Auch—she was dark haired and olive skinned. His high cheekbones, skier's body, and curly black hair appealed to many women, who found him boyish. At twenty-nine his looks were deceptive.

By 6:15 Rudmann's feet were two nonexistent stumps and his hands were totally numb. He asked the officer-of-the-deck to call Kammerer to view his leopards.

A moment later Kammerer smiled widely, then said, "Perfect, Rudmann." He shouted to Graeber to have all crew members report to the foredeck to look at the boat's new insignia. They came on the double. Smaller leopards now adorned each side of the conning tower.

Soon Rudmann was basking in applause and almost forgot his chilblains. Admittedly the leopards were among the best insignia he'd painted thus far, and he was proud of them, especially when Kammerer said, "I'll make sure Kapitän Godt knows." Godt was U-boat chief of staff, second to Admiral Dönitz.

Gratified by all the attention, Rudmann left the tomblike bunker at about half past six. He caught a streetcar for the center of blacked-out Lorient, intending to return to his room at the Hôtel Bisson. There was another boat insignia to render tomorrow; then he had orders to go to Saint Nazaire for a similar task. He had no desire to stay in shabby Lorient. It sat on the right bank of the Scorff immediately above the confluence of the Blavet, blessed with a fine protected harbor.

Rudmann alighted from the streetcar on rue des Fontaines and began to walk the three blocks to the Hôtel Bisson. The city was dark, though there were peeps of light from shop windows. Even with these slits, the early evening darkness was almost impenetrable. He could see no more than a dozen feet ahead.

He turned the corner at the second block and took a few steps. Grabbed from behind, he was strangled in less than a minute, and his body vanished in less than two.

As the *Résistance* members dumped it into the truck, covering it quickly with a tarred net, Gobelins said to Tramin, "That coat made him look bigger. He's a minnow." The painter of the leopard was a victim simply because he wore a German uniform.

The truck rattled off into the night, headlights blacked out to small slits.

✛ ✛ ✛

Until the German occupation, some forty-five thousand Bretons had lived in this coal-smoked town. Some fled when the Nazi motorbikes and armored cars came in from Vannes via Rennes. But most stayed. The people had been peaceful for centuries but were still fiercely independent. Just the sight of the field gray uniforms caused some to boil over.

The finest hotel, the Beauséjour, was now a residence for officers; the Bisson, Pigeon Blanc, and the Music Academy housed enlisted men. The Préfecture Naval, on Place d'Armes, was occupied, and Admiral Dönitz had seized the imposing three-story brick-and-stone Gothic château of Monsieur Bertrand, the sardine merchant, at Kernevel between Lamorplage and Lorient, to be his residence and command headquarters. Next door was his communications center.

Lorient was perhaps the finest fishing harbor in Europe; its Grand Bassin and Bassin Long, capable of handling hundreds of boats, had been gobbled up. The Nazis had grabbed the naval shipyard on the left bank of the Scorff that built fine cruisers. They had taken schools and the hospital. The Cinema Rex showed German films nightly.

Their tentacles reached into nearby Carnac and Quiberon, with rest camps complete with beer-garden decor. The crew ate, drank, and made merry; they walked the beaches, rode horses, played soccer and tennis; most of all, took French girls to bed.

Back-street cafés and bars like the Casino and Les Trois Soeurs, renamed Die Sechs Titten by its *Deutsche* patrons, rang with *"Über Alles"* until late at night. The best cafés and *all* the brothels were now off-limits to the French. Additional German-supervised whorehouses were being opened. The old roads were filled with Mercedes trucks, cars, and marching soldiers.

An eclipse had spread over Lorient. The shadow of the swastika had shut out light.

✙ ✙ ✙

Squat, burly Georges Gobelins stepped out of his old truck at dawn, two bunches of flowers in his right hand, and made his way into the Cimetière de Kerentrech along a path between the graves. He finally stopped at two headstones nestled together. Crossing himself, he first looked at the ground occupied by his wife. She'd died three years earlier after a short illness. Then he looked at his son's burial place. Claud had been murdered recently.

He came each day on his way to the Lorient fish docks to pay respects to the only family he had. He missed them to the point that his life was *almost* empty. But there was a dark space left for hatred.

Placing the hothouse flowers down by each headstone, he again felt the urge to kill. He would rid the earth of anyone who wore a German uniform. He stayed a moment longer, rage muscles working in his jaw, then trudged back up the path to the truck. After a few coughs it started. He continued to the docks. The *Vaincre* was tied up there, and Tramin, his mate, would be waiting.

Though some of the Lorient fishing fleet, colorful blue-hulled boats with red sails, were still wind powered the transition to gas and diesel engines had started long ago, and the *Vaincre* depended on gas to take her nets to sea.

Gobelins and Tramin were gone all day.

✝ ✝ ✝

Late that evening, Kammerer and Graeber were dining in the Beauséjour, on the town square, sharing a seafood platter—lobster claws, whole crabs, two dozen oysters, several langoustines, shrimp, clams, and scallops—nothing but the finest, two nights before departure.

"You'll learn!" Kammerer said. "If you don't take chances you won't sink ships. If you run scared you don't belong in U-boats." Graeber nodded but his red-cheeked farm-boy face indicated a certain wariness. He hoped not to end his career on the leopard boat.

Though he kept quiet about it, twenty-four-year-old Josef Graeber had no Nazi leanings. In fact, he disapproved of what was happening in Berlin and now had regrets about his choice of service.

On his last patrol, in a five-hundred-tonner as second watch officer, he'd had an acute fraying of nerves. By the time the four hours on the bridge were over, every far-off bird looked like an enemy aircraft. Low clouds on the horizon resembled British destroyers. He'd hidden the problem. Maybe he didn't belong in *122*.

"I've said it to the crew; I've said it to you, Fromm, Dörfmann, Bauer—everyone—we're going to make our mark on the tankers. I swear that I can sniff them out. Big, fat waddling ganders loaded with roasting material. My goal is twenty-five."

Graeber blinked.

"Oh, don't look so surprised . . ."

That was an impossible number, Graeber thought. The man was an obsessed lunatic. "I . . ."

"Have you ever seen one blow up?" Kammerer asked.

Graeber shook his head.

"It's spectacular. Lights up the whole sky if it's loaded with high-test. If you're near enough the explosion can knock you down. They burn with a roar that's like a blast furnace. And the smell!

Oh, the smell. If you're on the windward side you get both the heat and the stench. Enough to choke you ..."

Kammerer had been so busy talking that he'd barely touched the *fruits de mer*. His eyes were lighted with the thoughts of burning tankers.

An obsessed lunatic, Graeber was convinced.

Just before Sullivan Jordan left the house in Cradock, Virginia, near Portsmouth, Maureen was nursing the baby. As she sat on the overstuffed chair in the living room, the floor lamp spotlit her as if she were on a stage. CBS radio was on, and Edward R. Murrow was talking about air raids above the wail of sirens. "Now we take you into the streets of blacked-out London ..."

It was a beautiful picture. Maureen and the baby at her breast in a halo of light, and Sully knew he'd remember it for a long time. She was auburn haired and attractive, with pale, luminous skin.

She said, "At least you're still on a coastal run."

"That's right, hon," he said. "No problems." He bent down and kissed both of them. She'd just changed the baby, and he breathed in fresh talcum.

"I love you," he said, lingering a moment to look at them. Then off he went into the cold dawn, walking east along the Norfolk and Western tracks down to the Elizabeth River tank farm.

The SS *Tuttle* sailed on schedule at 1:00 P.M. She was 9,750 deadweight tons, 431 feet in overall length, 56 feet wide, and 33 feet deep. She could carry 78,310 barrels of oil in sixteen tanks. Her steam turbine gave her a maximum speed of 9.5 knots.

The Royal Navy's director of intelligence was in the frail old Admiralty Building in London's Whitehall district. Close by, on the ancient Horse Guards Parade Ground, was a newly constructed rust-colored monstrosity called The Citadel. Buried far beneath this massive, boxy bomb-proof concrete-and-granite blockhouse was the Operational Intelligence Centre (OIC), heart of the anti-submarine warfare effort.

Commander Roger Winn, Royal Navy Volunteer Reserve, limped into the OIC's Submarine Tracking Room at about 7:00 A.M. He'd spent the night above ground in his crosstown flat. On other nights he could be found in one of the uncomfortable bunks in the Citadel. Childhood polio had left him with a hunched back and gimpy leg.

Looking down on the huge ocean chart, the Main Plot, that covered an eight-foot-square table Winn asked, "What do we have this morning?"

The weary night chief duty officer, his eyes reddened by the harsh lighting, said, "That IXB that came out of Lorient three days ago puzzles me. I don't think she went south."

"Do you mean the *122*? Kammerer's boat?" Winn asked.

The duty officer nodded. Usually, Dönitz sent the long-range boats west of Gibraltar or farther down into the South Atlantic, off Africa.

"I have an idea that the good admiral is taking her out for some convoy action. First patrol. More shakedown for both captain and crew," Winn speculated.

"I'm inclined to think so, too," the duty officer said, turning away to answer a phone buzz.

Winn continued to stare at the ocean chart. It was a jumble of coded markers, pins, flags, symbols, and erasable pencil markings that changed by the hour if not by the minute. Submarine symbols, the known or suspected positions of the enemy, and elastic cords laid out convoy routes. Colored pinheads and flags denoted sub sightings, signals, and wireless intercepts. Other tiny flags indicated ships and escorts. But the grand game being played on the huge table wasn't a game.

Winn ran the Submarine Tracking Room the way he prepared cases for trial as a highly respected barrister in civilian life. He often knew when the boats departed and knew which boats were under way, but there was usually uncertainty as to where they were going. Once they got out on the high seas they disappeared, showing up suddenly off the Outer Hebrides or the Azores or Freetown. It was that damnable fissure between the time they left port and the time they fired their first torpedo that Winn wanted so desperately to close. Most often, he had to rely on his guesses—his "fictions," as he put it—as to the ultimate operating areas of the boats.

On the walls of room NID 8 (S) next door were charts of all sorts, covering everything from German U-boat construction to the date boats were sunk. On a smaller table was an exact copy of Dönitz's Kernevel grid chart of the standard *Nord-Atlantischer Ozean*. Operating areas were laid out alphabetically in numbered squares so that Dönitz could send his boats to exact attack positions within a half-dozen miles. NID 8 (S) even kept track of U-boat commanders by name.

Nearby, in another room, teleprinters chattered incessantly, night and day, with decoded German messages, direction-finder fixes, and air reconnaissance and agent reports.

Meanwhile, round-faced Winn had to answer to the prime minister's "prayers." They came in blunt memorandum form from Churchill: "Pray tell me what happened to the convoy that left Halifax on the ninth ... ?"

He had carefully explained to Mr. Churchill, an occasional visitor to this room, how he arrived at his fictions. "A combination of many things, sir." He recited interception and deciphering of enemy signals, submarine sightings by aircraft, sightings by escorts and merchant vessels, monitored propaganda, observers of friendly or neutral nations, coast watchers and agents, captured documents, and prisoner-of-war interrogations. "We have twenty-seven categories"

Churchill said, "Educated guessing."

"Precisely, sir."

The prime minister had seemed satisfied.

Not needing to say, "Let's keep an eye on *122*," to the duty officer, who was now off the phone, Winn limped along to another office.

Lieutenant Cedric Unsworth had just reported aboard for his day's work and was having a bacon sandwich with his mug of tea. He was just as sleepy as the duty officer. Two air raids during the night had awakened him. Nonetheless, he offered a cheery "Good morning" to his boss.

Unsworth was also a reserve, a tutor of economics at Oxford in prewar days. He was now putting his expertise in data collection to good use.

Winn said, "Dig out everything you have on *122*. It sailed out of Lorient three days ago."

The fair-haired economist was another disabled person in the bowels of the Citadel. A sweet-stick had punched out his left eye in a childhood accident and he wore an unsinister black patch over it. "Shall do," he said. He looked over at aide Dottie Beavers, of the Women's Royal Naval Service (WREN), as Winn limped away.

Wren Beavers moved toward the open files, arranged vertically like crackers in large square wooden boxes; she could see a bit of black tape on boats that would never sail again. The files contained information on personnel that predated the war by several years, primarily newsclips about one officer or another scissored by alert agents in Wilhelmshaven, Kiel, or Danzig. Horst Kammerer was in those files.

All sorts of information was funneled into Unsworth's submarine identification (SI) section from every office that had anything to do with the battle of the Atlantic. Organization had begun in earnest a month after the war had started. Unsworth's first black-taped envelope was for the *U-39*, sent to the bottom forever northwest of Ireland. To date, thirty-two U-boats had been wreathed in his funereal colors. Unsworth's sense of humor sometimes leaned toward the macabre. He gleefully called subs "hearses."

Dottie Beavers, new to the SI section, asked, "All right, Lieutenant, sir, how do you know that particular sub sailed that particular day?" Like Unsworth, she'd been a teacher though not at the university level. She'd taught kindergarten.

"No crystal balls," he said. "All of them are escorted out to sea by one or more minesweepers. When the minesweeper says good-bye, they send a message to the shore station. We intercept. That simple."

"I'm amazed," said Beavers. "You'd think they'd wait until the minesweepers got back to port."

Unsworth smiled. "The haughty, invincible Hun!"

"They have no idea we're listening?"

"They listen! We listen! In these files there's a history of almost every submarine they have. Aerial photography covers it from the time the keel is laid until it's launched, then commissioned. After that, we listen during the training period in the Baltic. We keep listening until it arrives at a Biscay port or up in Norway and then on till the bloody thing is sent to the bottom. Wireless is our rope to spy heaven."

Unsworth was having a marvelous time piecing together profiles and sometimes felt guilty about enjoying his work.

"Let me quickly tell you how we got the latest information on Kapitänleutnant Kammerer. Again, it's quite simple. Herr Goebbels, of the Nazi propaganda mill, likes to keep the people of the Third Reich stirred up. So when a U-boat returns to base after a successful patrol, Goebbels makes sure that newspaper reporters, radio reporters, and newsreel cameramen are there to record the joyful welcome. Our BBC monitor at Caversham joyfully records every word when it is broadcast from Berlin on the nightly news. We listen when Kammerer names and brags about the ships he's sunk and tells us about the area he's operated in. Caversham has it translated and sends it by teleprinter to us. *Voilà.*"

He passed Dottie Beavers the teleprinted copy of Kammerer's interview after his last patrol.

✛ ✛ ✛

After all these years Sully still felt an excitement when the lines were slipped. Tugs churned bow and stern if the currents or winds were too strong to go out alone. The feeling heightened when the tugs stopped tooting, and the ship's whistle sounded a good-bye blast. The broad bow would cut a white vee in the water, such as the *Tuttle* was doing now.

Under the high white stack, on which Consolidated Oil was painted vertically in red, catwalks ran from the *Tuttle*'s forepeak aft to the bridgehouse, then on aft to the afterhouse over the maze of deck piping. She looked much like all the other ungainly tankers built during World War I. There was not one thing sleek or fancy about her.

She'd plowed back and forth along the coast, over into the Gulf of Mexico, and down into the Caribbean for twenty-six years, fair weather or foul. She'd been through a dozen hurricanes without ever breaking her back, though one of them had stripped the paint off her. She just hunkered low and let the waves tumble over her.

Captain Kaarlo Ryti came out of the chartroom, located directly behind the wheelhouse, saying to Sully, "Sparks tells me the weather should hold. It'll be easy going south." Though Ryti had sailed on American ships for forty years, there were still some remnants of his Helsinki accent: *weather* became "wedder." A small, potbellied man, Ryti had first gone to sea on four-masters, in the Australian grain trade.

Then Sam ("Sparks") Bessemer emerged from the radio shack below, his artificial leg clumping. He held a slip of paper. "Another one just got it. British freighter below Dakar." Torpedoed, of course.

"Close to shore?" Sully asked.

Sparks shook his head. "Forty-five west."

That was hundreds of miles out in the South Atlantic, in the doldrums, that equatorial girdle of low pressure, where the air was hot and sultry, the wind stagnant, and the sea flat and cobalt.

"Just birds and seaweed out there," Sully murmured, exchanging a look with Captain Ryti.

"Maybe someone is near her," Sparks offered. Captain Ryti

told him to keep listening for a response. They were all in the same fraternity no matter the flag.

Matkowski, at the helm, was on his first tanker trip. This was his first day out. He listened intently. He'd come aboard in Norfolk. At twenty, he was chubby, with dark, curly hair. He was a Pole from Gary, Indiana. Sully guessed that he himself had looked just about as young and tender when he was twenty. But Sully had never been chubby. He was now thirty-three, and the sun, plus the wind, hadn't been particularly kind to his face.

Matkowski said, "Another ship sunk?" after Ryti left the bridge. Sully nodded and began to pace on the port wing. The *Tuttle* steamed on.

✛ ✛ ✛

One-Name Fong served a choice of beef stew or fried chicken in the officers' mess, and Sparks Bessemer distributed his war dispatches from the four o'clock International News Service schedule, the ship's P.M. "paper."

Ryti dined with his officers unless his presence was demanded on the bridge. Sully always ate at about 5:15, then relieved big-bellied chief mate Juho Kalevi, another Finn, for a half hour so he could dine. The engineers had a similar schedule, though the chief, John Logan, a lean New Englander, timed his meals so he could chitchat with Ryti.

So far as Sully was concerned, they were all highly competent professionals, though Bob Cheney, with his thinning, white spiked hair, needed a hearing aid. Cheney, at sixty-odd, was the oldest third mate Sully had ever sailed with. Both Ryti and Logan were also in their late sixties.

An hour later the thirty-eight tankermen settled down for the night. Friendly ivory lights appeared in the midship and afterhouse portholes. No matter what occurred in the Atlantic, Germany, and Lorient, all was still peaceful along the southern coast of the United States.

JANUARY 20, 1941

T wo hundred and thirty miles southwest of Ireland's Black Sod Bay the boat with the snarling leopards plunged along at ten knots. Heavy seas sent cold spray over the five men in the conning tower bridge, all clad in oilskins. She searched for targets en route to joining a wolfpack "rake."

Now and then, when the hatch was open briefly, icy water from the bridge cascaded down into the boat itself, spilling into the control spaces, then into the oily bilge, making it even more damp inside.

The watch this twilight was standard: four pairs of lookout eyes, plus the commander, who went on and off the bridge as required. So far as Kammerer was concerned, everyone on the bridge was a lookout, sensitive to the slightest change of view. Eyestrain was expected.

Thus far, the patrol had been routine, though the day before yesterday Kammerer had had to dive when an undetected Coastal Command Sunderland roared down on them out of the sun. But an unannounced practice dive was carried out daily anyway, just to make certain everything and everyone functioned properly. Aside from such interruptions he'd spent a lot of time in his bunk, in the *Kapitän*'s "nook," since leaving Lorient. He'd catch sleep when he could, conserving energy. He was on instant call night and day.

A white towel peeped out from the lip of his oilskins to absorb the water slosh. Kammerer's face, with a week's black stubble, was wet. It gleamed. He was easily identified as skipper by his white capcover, usually set at a haughty angle. He alone could wear the white cap, easy to spot in the conning tower on black, stormy nights. His boat commander's insignia had a proud verdigris patina from hours in salt air and spray. His body was often soaked to the skin.

In the main control room below, the clock read 1640 hours; dusk, an ideal time for attack. In the morning, just after dawn, was just as good. Ships were always visible on the horizon, while the U-boat could barely be seen in all the surrounding grayness.

Suddenly, they spotted an enemy ship ahead. It was impaled in a band of wintry twilight yellow, silhouetted beneath a thick fold of dark clouds.

Kammerer shouted to Graeber, "My God, that's a pretty picture!" Then he yelled into the speaking tube, "Battle stations! Both engines full ahead! Steer two-six-five!" For him this was a time of absolute elation.

The *122* soon increased speed to sixteen knots and raced toward the target. Her diesels throbbed. Unless the ship was making that speed or better, Kammerer figured he should nail her within four hours. Any merchantman that traveled alone these days probably could make fourteen knots. This one was unescorted, prey for any U-boat.

By now, the powerful binoculars, connected directly to the range-finding apparatus, had been mounted, and he bent to get a better look at her.

"Big empty freighter!" he shouted. Bound for America? Had she been American she would have been lit up like Coney Island in July, Kammerer knew.

Although it was somewhat of a joke, America was still legally neutral. The U-boat commanders had strict orders from Berlin, Hitler's specific orders, not to shell or sink any vessel that flew a U.S. flag. Kammerer, for one, wanted to sink *any* ship, of any nation, carrying cargo to England.

He looked into the eyepieces. An enlisted man had wiped the

lenses. "I'm betting she's British and will go about twelve thousand tons."

Graeber shouted, "I won't take your bet!" and bent to the Zeiss instrument to take a look.

Kammerer went below to personally check the target in the standard ship's silhouette book, the *Gröner*, murmuring, "Looks like a Castle liner," then returned to the bridge. The British company had sixteen ships, from five thousand tons up to twenty-two thousand. This one appeared to be 14,500, a vessel built in 1923.

They were in a stern chase, not the best of situations. Staring at her again, he yelled into the speaking tube, "Give me the target's course and speed . . ."

In a moment, Wolfgang Bauer, the warrant third officer, yelled up, "Speed 14.5, course two-six-five . . ."

Leutnant zur See Hans Dörfmann was the second watch officer overseeing communications and gunnery during surface action; Bauer's specialty was navigation. Heinrich Fromm, the engineering officer, was the most important man aboard after Kammerer. Not only was he in complete charge of the engines, he was also responsible for diving. Fromm's ability to judge the boat's sink-and-rise tendencies was sometimes the deciding factor between life and death.

Kammerer liked the chase, stern or not. They'd locked on to this fat one, and unless a British escort showed up, she was his to kill. The excitement was all-consuming. He was a human shark, hunting big game on the wild water.

Born in the outskirts of Hamburg, he had the sea challenge in his blood long before this war or before he'd even set foot on a submersible. He'd worked on a trawler during the summer of his fifteenth year, and a Baltic schooner the following year. Naval academy exams came along the last year in high school, and he passed them without too much trouble. At Flensburg-Mürwik, where only the fittest survived, he'd come in seventh in his class grades and first in physical drills. In his final year, he had his pick of duty on capital ships, destroyers, minesweepers, or U-boats. He chose U-boats, liking the challenge.

The constant damp, fetid stench of the boats—machinery vapors, diesel oil, sweat, rotting food, and toilet disinfectants—didn't offend him the way it did some of the other officers. It was part of life in the pressure hulls.

When the British were depth-charging, Schumach, the chief boatswain, who'd served with him before, had seen Kammerer staring up at the overhead, finger raised in disdain.

Occasionally in wild weather, when the boat plunged and wallowed, and giant waves tumbled over the conning tower, Schumach had seen Kammerer, harnessed with a leather belt and steel wires to keep from being washed overboard, beat his chest, yell like Tarzan, and enjoy himself. At times, Schumach and others aboard his first boat had thought their *Kapitän* was insane.

Insane or not, Kammerer *was* different. He'd always have the lights dimmed for the evening meal unless the boat was in combat, and there was a regular concert each night around eight o'clock, sometimes jazz, sometimes classical. On Sundays, such as this one, the music always ended with a boys' choir.

+ + +

Sparks said at breakfast, "Another tanker got it last night. Shell boat west of Gibraltar."

Everybody fell silent.

Sully thought about it again during the afternoon watch while walking his usual route from the rear of the starboard boat deck through the pilothouse and out to the rear of the port boat deck, then back again. Some mates stayed stationary on the bridge wings or in the pilothouse. But Sully was a walker. He took forty long strides each way. He averaged three hours of walking in good weather. Walking, thinking.

He remembered Ryti talking about a tanker he was riding

during World War I. They were headed for London. The captain was in his chair in the in-port cabin when the torpedo hit off Land's End. The fire burned out a week later. He was found still sitting in the metal frame of the chair, his skeleton charred like blackened toast.

So far, fourteen petroleum carriers of U.S. companies, flying mostly Panamanian flags, had been lost. Just two days ago, *Esso Hampshire*, registered out of Delaware and manned by British sailors, had been torpedoed in a convoy. Only one man was saved out of forty-two.

Who'd do what if they were hit? They'd kicked it around. Chief Logan said to jump into the stream of the engine-room discharge and slip back with it into the wake of the ship, as burning oil flowed to the outskirts of the stream. Sully had already made up his mind to sleep fully clothed on the boat deck in case he ever got into sub waters, life jacket by his fingertips. The idea was to avoid being burned alive.

When Sully took his usual position forward of the helm, which gave him a wide sweep of ocean to examine, Matkowski said, "Mate, I got to admit I'm afraid of these things."

Sully turned his head. "Why'd you sign up?"

"Needed the work," Matkowski admitted. Sully nodded. Freighter sailors said all tankermen were crazy, perched on enough gasoline to scorch Manhattan. "It's not all that dangerous," Sully said, "even if we're carrying high-test stock. Just be careful unloading and loading. Don't smoke or make sparks out on deck ..." This is exactly what he'd told Maureen the first time he met her.

"Riding tankers doesn't bother you?" Matkowski asked.

"Look, the nearest we ever get to being in a bomb is when we're empty or cleaning tanks. They're full of vapor. You can't even smell the stuff a lot of times. More tankers have blown up empty than full."

Matkowski didn't look convinced.

"You know what flash point is?"

"Not really."

"It's the temperature at which vapors form a flammable mixture with air."

"Oh."

Sully snapped his fingers. "*Va-room.*"

"Doesn't make sense," said Matkowski.

"Whether it does or not, there have been a good dozen explosions in ballast, all in the tropics, all while cleaning tanks."

"Will we clean tanks this time?"

Sully shook his head. "No, we'll clean 'em when we shift to light oil." They were bound for Caripito, Venezuela, to load crude, heavy oil. Light oil was refined products, such as aviation gasoline, auto gas, stove oil, diesel, lubricating oil, naphtha.

"Mate, you like riding these things?"

"Uh-huh. There's no dust, no cargo booms—we just connect the hoses and let the stuff flow in; then pump it out up north."

"Never shipped on a freighter?" Matkowski asked.

"Nope."

Sully'd sailed on both black-oil and light-oil tankers in and out of Texas City, Port Arthur, Galveston, Corpus Christi, Baytown, Beaumont, Aruba, Curaçao, Cartagena, Puerto La Cruz, and Las Piedras in Colombia. Caripito and Guiria, in Venezuela. Had he missed a couple of oil ports? Maybe.

Sully finally advised, "Take a few trips with us. You'll like it."

Though he was continually aware of the cargo gurgling beneath the steel decks, Sully's only worry was collision. Two tankers getting together. It had happened in Houston Ship Channel. *Va-room.*

✢ ✢ ✢

Kammerer said, "We're gaining on her." What he thought was a Castle liner loomed ever closer in the deep twilight.

The *122*'s twin diesels turned the props at three hundred revolutions a minute. Foam followed the slender hull in a long white ribbon. If the ship's lookouts were alert, the ribbon would be the first indication that a submarine was in the wake.

"Shall I go full ahead?" Graeber asked.

"Your decision," Kammerer said, testing the First.

Graeber would make the final surface attack.

The engines could run wide open for eight hours and not be damaged. Whatever ailments the Nazi sub fleet might have, the diesels, cylinders taller than a man, were not among them.

"Full ahead!" Graeber barked down the hatch. The yellow band of light was fading quickly and, with it, the merchantman.

The blowers and compressors throbbed as the diving tanks emptied every few minutes to keep the hull high and reduce water resistance. The whole boat rattled and clattered.

Below, the spirit of the chase had caught on. There was little thought of danger in the *Zentrale*, the main control room, the area by the torpedo tubes, or at the sound and radio listening posts. Everyone waited. Soon, darkness would blot out the sea, but *122* had already closed to eight kilometers. The target would be tracked visually. If the boat ran full speed, the enemy's propellers could not be heard by the soundman.

By nine o'clock, Kammerer had overhauled the big freighter, changing course to hit her midships. A stern hit was made only by accident.

"She's English, all right!" Kammerer yelled. Had she been a neutral, she would have turned on her lights to illuminate big painted flags on the sides of her hull. In combat zones neutrals were always lit up like store windows. But this enemy ship wanted to disappear hurriedly into the darkness.

Finally, he spoke again. "Have you checked the time of moonrise?" Graeber hadn't. He would forever after that.

Graeber called down the voice tube, "When is moonrise?"

Kammerer and Graeber glanced skyward. The heavy clouds had begun to scatter. The freighter would be backlit whether she liked it or not. Take advantage, Kammerer suggested silently.

The navigator checked the *Nautical Almanac* and called up, "Twenty forty-seven." Eight forty-seven P.M. The moon had already risen.

Kammerer changed his estimated attack to 2145, presuming the target didn't increase speed. He guessed she was full ahead already.

Moonlight was always both a blessing and a danger. An alert lookout could see the U-boat. Any ship traveling alone also had to be heavily armed, especially one this size and speed. No commander in his right mind wanted to duel with four-inch stern guns, much less the smaller calibers midships and forward.

Kammerer called down the voice tube again, this time to the *Funkmaat*, radio operator Heinze. "Check your merchant band to see if she's sending anything . . ."

"She's quiet, Herr Kaleunt."

"Keep listening."

✚ ✚ ✚

The moon rose over a cloud roll shortly after nine and began to light the sea at fifty-four degrees latitude in fleeting patches. Areas were suddenly silver, then black again within seconds. The target was now visible to the naked eye when caught in a splotch of silver. She looked ghostly.

At dusk, she'd changed course twice, simply to make U-boat attack more complicated. Now she was back on her basic track bound for the east coast of America—most likely New York—to pick up desperately needed cargo for the United Kingdom. At least this is what Kammerer thought.

Twenty minutes, roughly, to attack, and the entire boat was in battle conditions, every man at his station. Soon, Graeber shouted that the *122*'s forward tubes were ready, "bow caps" off. Outer doors were open. The tubes were "wet" and needed only the impulse from the bridge to be unleashed.

"Bridge control," said Graeber.

The attack sight, the target bearing transmitter (TBT), was "on," with the target in the center of the crosswires, aimed just aft of the midships house.

"Lined up!" Graeber called out.

Kammerer nodded.

Everything was going well. He knew that in a few seconds the attack table would be connected with the gyrocompass and the attack sight. After that, it was almost automatic. So long as the crosswires of the attack sight held the target, the apparatus would do its job.

The torpedoes were set at a running depth of twenty feet, speed of thirty knots, to tear out the bottom of the target.

"Stand by for surface fire. Fire at one thousand meters ..." The order was acknowledged from below, in the torpedo compartments. "Tubes one, two, and three ready ..."

Kammerer nodded. "Fire when ready."

Graeber intoned, "Ready," then said, "On, on, on ..."

"Fächer eins ... LOS! Fächer zwei ... LOS!"

The firing button was pushed, "eel" motors started, and the *122*, at intervals of less than two seconds, jumped as the torpedoes pushed toward the freighter. Fromm flooded the tanks simultaneously to compensate for the forward weight loss of the tin fish.

Kammerer looked at his stopwatch and counted aloud. Two orange mushrooms lit the silvery sea, quickly followed by a pair of *booms*. There were cheers from below.

"Perfect shot," Kammerer said; then he yelled, "Hard starboard!" The *U-122* had made her first kill, and he breathed a sigh of relief. The torpedoes had been erratic the last two patrols. Below, the shock of the hits rattled the boat and pounded against it like sledgehammer blows. Within a minute the sounds of the freighter breaking up could be heard in the listening room, and Heinze soon monitored her frantic *SSS SSS SSS!* She gave her call sign, GBSL, and her position. Heinze quickly looked her up in his *Schiffsliste, Teil 1*. She was the *Castle Innesberg*, 13,800 tons, of the Castle Mail

Lines, London. Kammerer had guessed correctly. To this hour, she brought the day's tally for all of Dönitz's boats to eighty-six thousand tons.

Kammerer moved in for a closer look at the target, already sliding under. He saw a single life raft, with several people aboard, on the moon-spattered surface. Kammerer switched on the spotlight. His bridge binoculars were trained on the raft. The shaft of light revealed two adults and three children in nightclothes.

Graeber said, "We'll rescue them . . . the children . . ."

Kammerer switched the light off. He said, "No." Graeber's eyes widened. He was shocked. Meanwhile, Heinze pecked out a coded quick signal to *BdU*, announcing the kill. Other boats on patrol would monitor it on the U-boat band.

Kammerer said to Graeber, "Good work," and went below, telling Bauer to continue west. Dönitz had said never worry about survivors. After all, this was total war out here on the steep *Atlantik*. Both sides knew it.

Later, over coffee, Graeber asked the *Kapitän*, "Do you ever feel remorse after a sinking?" Some commanders did, he knew. Graeber did not know this one very well. Kammerer looked over at Graeber in astonishment.

✛ ✛ ✛

The SSS (submarine attack), then the plaintive SOS, of the *Castle Innesberg* had first been heard by a listening operator at Ballycastle, in Northern Ireland, monitoring the merchant channel. Per orders he immediately notified OIC, and then teletype bells clanged at a half-dozen different Admiralty offices in London. Those privy to the ship sailings and routings were appalled. The *Castle Innesberg* had on board 106 children being evacuated to Canada. They were probably sleeping soundly when the torpedoes hit.

In the Citadel, Commander Winn read the teletype, aware of the *Innesberg*'s precious cargo; he guessed there might be heavy casualties and looked over at the plot, which showed that Kammerer was advancing steadily toward his probable rendezvous with other wolfpack submarines.

He was silent awhile, then said to the duty officer, "We have 106 incentives to destroy the *U-122.* I want it tracked as if my own children had been aboard the *Castle Innesberg.*"

Two days later the news leaked out. *The Daily Mail* headlined "106 Children Dead." Winn clipped the headline and attached it to the rim of the plot table.

✛ ✛ ✛

It was much too dangerous to keep a diary or a log, but Georges Gobelins had circled certain dates on the calendar that hung in the kitchen of his cottage on the road to Nantes, on the outskirts of town. The last seven months had been a nightmare.

On June 18, 1940, German troops had reached Brittany, and on the twenty-first, Gobelins had joined others to resist with a few artillery pieces and machine guns near Hennebont where the road from Rennes intersected. By noon the fight was over. The Germans had armored cars and tanks. The Frenchmen scattered. Six had died.

On June 22, Hitler did his little jig in the forest at Compiègne after the armistice was signed. Next day, Admiral Dönitz arrived to inspect the harbor. Twelve days later the first U-boat arrived. With Tramin, Gobelins had watched it enter port. More than two hundred Frenchmen were on the dock to welcome it. Had they no shame?

July 9 had been a special day. He'd been asked to join the *Résistance* and said yes.

But it was December 10, circled in a shaking hand, that would go into his grave with him, the day his son Claud had been shot to death, standing thirty feet from Gobelins.

✛ ✛ ✛

The *Tuttle* loaded in Venezuela and was under way again within ten hours. Time in port could be boring for Sully, but never at sea. The sea was capable of a beautiful face at dawn and unbelievable violence by noon. He treasured both. There were seldom two days or two nights that were the same. Seas and winds changed constantly. Never the same clouds at twilight as in the morning. In coastal waters, or the Gulf of Mexico, or the Caribbean, the seascape changed almost hourly.

Sully's binoculars were always busy, even when he walked his bridge pattern. He'd spot something floating in the water and focus on the flotsam. A box, a huge tangle of weed, a Portuguese man-o'-war, a giant jellyfish, or a cypress knee out of the North Carolina sounds would float by.

He'd learned the seabirds and could imitate the loud, buglelike call of the herring gull. He knew the storm petrels that danced over the surface with wings held high, flying determinedly far out on the Atlantic; he was familiar with the blue-faced boobies, frigate birds, and ospreys; and he knew the stars intimately—Polaris, Arcturus, Regulus, Achenar, and Deneb Kaitos. He'd sighted his sextant on Venus and the sun and the moon.

He enjoyed the occasional spectacles, ships lit up with aureoles of Saint Elmo's fire or the fast-moving waterspouts in the tropics. There were days and nights when the bow couldn't be seen in snow or fog or when hurricane winds made knifeblades of raindrops.

The dim glow of Norfolk was off the port beam, and Sully had been staring in that direction for a long time.

He did love sailing ships as much as he loved Maureen and the children but in a different way, which he could not define. He was suddenly jolted with guilt. That was stupid: What was he thinking of? The sea was a moody mistress, cold and arctic, wanton and tropical. Maureen was always ardent, and the children were always lovable even when they galled. He felt disloyal.

"If you want to go to sea, don't get married, Ski," Sully said.

"You are, Mate."

Matkowski was again on the helm, his nose and forehead illuminated by the compass light. Frolick was the starboard bridge-wing lookout, pacing back and forth out there in boredom.

Laden with the Caripito crude, rising and falling in relatively calm water, the *Tuttle* moved north to Bayonne at 1:50 A.M. The air was cold. There was little breeze. The heavens were a dark sieve of stars. The ship hummed and vibrated as did all ships under way. Sully always thought of them as being alive and breathing. Landsmen often thought of them as entirely rigid structures, but he felt that tankers in particular undulated as they swam along.

As usual for the dogwatch hours, only the black gang—wiper, oiler, fireman, and second engineer—was awake, down in the warmth of the engine room. Everyone else on board was asleep. All was peace and quiet off Tidewater, Virginia.

"Why'd you get married?" Ski asked.

"I was in love," Sully said. "I wanted a home life. I'd had my fun by the time I was twenty-five."

In the soft shadows of the bridge, talk was always subdued and intimate during the night watches. Though the ocean spread far and wide outside, there was a closed-in feeling on the bridge.

Sully kept looking west. Over there, about fifty miles, were Maureen and the kids. How often was she awake at night? This always happened coming north, especially any night close enough to shore to see skyglow.

"I knew I wouldn't be home often, but I didn't realize she believed that once the kids came along I'd quit. Give it up."

"Have you ever thought about quitting?"

"Ski, everybody on this ship has thought about it. The only way it works is to have your wife aboard, even your kids. I'm serious. The time I ran between Talara and Callao, that's the port of Lima, a Greek ship came in and tied up behind us. Tramp freighter. The captain owned it, and his wife lived aboard."

"Wouldn't that cause trouble, a woman with all the men?"

"If she was pretty. The Greek's wife was dumpy and had to be fifty. I saw her hanging up wash."

A white light developed off the port bow, and Sully walked

over to lift the binoculars from the sill, adjusting the knob for focus. Traffic always increased off Norfolk, with ships coming not only out of Hampton Roads but also out of the Chesapeake. He was likely in an overhaul situation with this one. "Come right five degrees."

Matkowski said, "Well, I sure don't have marriage on my mind."

"I hope not. Settle down when you're fifty."

Frolick came into the wheelhouse. It was time to switch chores again; Matkowski went to the bridge-wing lookout for an hour. He'd be back on the wheel for the final hour.

Sully returned to the port side, drawn toward that pale half-circle above the Norfolk-Portsmouth area, thinking of Maureen and the kids. The first few hours home he always felt like a stranger; Maureen told him all the things that had happened, and Danny looked different from the last time he'd seen him.

Last time, a few seconds after he'd entered the house, he noticed the small browning Christmas tree in the living room corner. He knew the gifts beneath it were for him. He'd sent theirs from Texas before sailing for New Jersey and had spent the hallowed night off the coast of Georgia. *Merry Christmas to all.*

✢ ✢ ✢

The report that Lieutenant Unsworth studied this early February morning had to do with the sinking of the *Castle Innesberg*. It was an interview with the sole survivor, the ship's chief steward. The *Innesberg* incident had predictably gotten into Parliament: *Why were children aboard a vessel that couldn't steam at seventeen knots?* Unsworth looked up and said to Beavers, "The steward swears he saw a big leopard on the conning tower of that sub. I've got a hunch she's the *122* out of Lorient. If he's correct, she got the *Innesberg* three days later." He made a notation to include the leopard insignia in the *U-122* file, Kammerer's file, with a question mark.

"She's the new one, I remember. First patrol," the Wren said.

Unsworth nodded, glad that the Germans were identifying their boats with all kinds of symbols. A leopard was appropriate. He said, "I heard Commander, Western Approaches, is very much interested in this one. The admiral's grandchildren, two little girls, were aboard the *Castle Innesberg*."

Unsworth picked up a survivor report from another ship, thinking of the terror those children experienced moments before their death.

Wren Beavers walked away, shaking her head.

About 9:30, Konteradmiral Dönitz went out on the lawn of the slate-roofed château, near the entrance to the air-raid bunker. He stood in the shadows and breathed the tangy Biscay air. Immediately, a guard came over with his rifle aimed at the dim figure. Dönitz identified himself, and the embarrassed guard apologized.

The admiral, with his receding chin and hairline, did not resemble a lion. In civvies he could be mistaken for an accountant or insurance salesman. He was quite ordinary in appearance.

"You were only doing your job," said the admiral.

"Thank you," said the private, vanishing into the darkness.

Dönitz constantly thought about his boats on patrol and wondered if they were all practicing his proven doctrine: Take advantage of background light, wind, and sea to present the smallest possible silhouette; reach a position ahead of the target, observe it carefully; and *then show no mercy*.

During the day, he could gaze from the Operations room windows toward those great bunkers that were being completed across the Ter; he could also watch U-boat traffic on the west and south channels. From his very first visit, Dönitz knew he had the perfect site from which to operate his boats. Seven months later it was all working, at sea and ashore. Here in Lorient, he felt total involvement in the war, a feeling he'd never had in Paris.

Lorient was close enough to Paris so that the officers could unwind in the clubs. Then there was his splendid *Zug*, bound to the city on the Seine several times a week to transport personnel on leave. Never let it be said that "Onkel Karl" neglected his troops.

He was not boasting idly to Berlin. There was no doubt in his mind that if the Supreme Command would allow him the necessary hulls he could cripple the Allies in a matter of months. Of course, Hitler was the problem. He meddled. In some ways, Hitler was more of an enemy than Churchill, a politician who understood sea warfare.

Dönitz looked at the shadow of the nearest bunker. The RAF could drop all the bombs they wanted and never disturb the slender boats parked inside like cars in a great warehouse. He marveled at the work of the builders, *Organisation Todt*. The gigantic buildings contained thousands of tons of steel and uncounted tons of concrete. Cranes attached to the overheads lifted whole U-boats. Except for arrivals and departures, the enemy would never see his weapons in their bays.

With boats coming off the ways in Germany at twenty a month, now was the time for Hitler to let him fight all-out, Dönitz thought. Let him control the Atlantic! Let him starve England! His goal was to destroy ten million tons of enemy shipping. He'd choke those miserable islands industrially. That's why he told his boat commanders, *"Destroy the tankers!"* Without oil, the British would come to the peace table on their skinny knees.

✛ ✛ ✛

Sully sat with a handful of dimes and quarters in a booth at the end of a water-taxi dock in New York. He waited for Maureen to return his call from their neighbor's phone, the only one on her end of Vail Place.

When the phone jangled he picked it up. He could picture her standing in the neighbor's dark, narrow hallway in a bulky sweater and flat shoes, frown of concern on her face, and maybe even biting her lip the way she sometimes did when she was worried. There was the usual wariness in her voice.

He told her he'd had a sudden change in plans and was changing ships for another run.

"Where are you going, Sully?"

"I don't know." Of course he knew. And she knew he knew.

"It won't be in a war zone, will it?"

"Don't know, hon."

"An old ship?"

"Well, it isn't new."

"Is it fast?"

"I'm afraid not."

"Bigger than the *Tuttle*?"

The *Tuttle* was discharging over in Bayonne. "Yes."

"Why you?"

"The other ship needs an experienced mate. Their second fell down an iced-up ladder this morning. Broke some bones. The office asked Ryti if they could shift me. They'll move old Cheney up to second and get a New York relief for him. Are the kids OK?"

"They're fine."

"You OK?"

"I'm fine, too. What's the name of the other ship?"

He blew out a breath. "The *Galveston*."

"She a Consolidated ship?"

"That's right."

"You never mentioned her."

"She's been sailing under the Panamanian flag."

"Didn't you tell me once that the Panamanian flags are the ones they're sending over to the war zone?"

Jesus. "Some of them." He was getting antsy.

"I hope the *Galveston* isn't one. I'll worry the whole time you're gone. Call me when you get to a port, will you?"

"I promise."

"How's the weather in New York?"

"Icy cold. It's been snowing off and on."

"It's cold here, too, but we haven't had any snow. If something happens and you don't go out on that ship, let me know, will you?"

Jesus. "Yes, hon. I gotta go. I've got to catch the water taxi, and I want a cup of coffee before I do it. My hands and feet are freezing. You take care. Hug the kids for me."

"Sully, I'm scared! I'm really scared!"

"Come on, Maureen. I'm gonna be fine. You take care. Good-bye now. I love you."

☩ ☩ ☩

As yet, no bombs had fallen into place Alsace-Lorraine, Lorient's main town square. It was much as it had been for a hundred years. In narrow streets, shops of lower-floor tradesmen were identified by sheet-metal signs that creaked in the wind. Roofs of the houses almost touched. Windows were lined with boxes of geraniums. Around the square itself were shops and hotels, including the Beauséjour and Pigeon Blanc.

On Sundays, the day to worship, mend nets, promenade, and eat good meals, church bells summoned the faithful with a thunderous chorus. Though the old priest called it a cathedral, Notre Dame de Victoire was better known locally as the church of Saint Louis. It stood on the south side of the large square, always filled for the first and second masses. Even the few prostitutes servicing the unmarried fishermen went to mass.

On festival days and on summer Sundays, in peacetime, there were sweetmeat stalls and catchpenny booths. Wagons sold hot food. There was always a carousel for children. Bands played in the roofed stand. Lorientians were fond of their town square. Georges Gobelins had often sipped an aperitif at the sidewalk tables of the Grand Café, directly over the cobblestones from the square.

Today there was silence aside from the shouts of Rudi Kuppisch. The hoarse words of the peach-skinned, barrel-chested Gestapo major were being translated to a crowd of several hundred by an interpreter.

"We have tried to deal fairly and make friends with you, but you, in turn, have committed sabotage and murder. As of today, crimes against us will be punished severely ..."

Within the last month three U-boats had limped back to port: two because of sand and sugar dumped into their lubricating oil, another with two crewmen dead—someone had tampered with the diesel exhausts. Civilian workers were suspected. Within the last week, three members of a shore patrol unit had been murdered in an alley.

The eight men to be executed, picked randomly, were in groups of four, shackled to each other and blindfolded.

"In the future, for every one of us you kill we will execute four of you." His words echoed into rue Paul Bert and des Fontaines. Soldiers from the garrison were in four squads around the quadrangle. Early light bounced off their helmets.

Gobelins listened, vowing to sooner or later rid his saddened town of Kuppisch, no matter the cost.

"I want someone to step forward and tell me what happened to the three members of our shore patrol."

Gobelins knew. He and Tramin, his fishing partner, had killed them. Tramin stood nearby. They exchanged glances. Gobelins's jug head in a beret made an almost imperceptible negative shake to Tramin.

Kuppisch repeated what he'd said and waited a moment. Gobelins's grim expression did not change as he vowed silently to take four of theirs for every single French man executed. No one could stop the *Résistance* by threats or deeds, no matter how terrible they were. If he stepped forward and admitted guilt, who would be the next leader to cave in? No, he'd have to live with his crimes forever, knowing that—indirectly—he was sending eight innocent Frenchmen to their deaths. But there was no turning back. The eight would be revenged, again and again, their names added to that of Claud. There was no turning back.

The elderly priest from Notre Dame de Victoire stepped forward. "I do not know what happened to your shore patrol, but I am offering myself to save these young men. They have done no wrong. I beg you not to shoot them. Shoot me!"

Kuppisch waited while his interpreter relayed the priest's words, then answered in his own tongue: "You are a brave man, Father, but I do not accept your kind offer."

"God help you on judgment day," the priest said.

Kuppisch ordered the executions to begin. "We will burn any bodies that are not claimed."

The first group of four were brought before the positioned machine gun as the priest interceded again. "I beg you to let me give them last rites." Kuppisch groaned and then said to the interpreter, "All right. Tell him to hurry. I have better things to do today."

Soon, Gobelins closed his eyes tightly. He thought about Claud and flinched as the burst of machine-gun fire echoed across the square. Pigeons flew up. There were screams from the crowd. Next of kin tried to break through the cordon of soldiers as the first four bodies were dragged off to one side. Gobelins fought back tears as he had the day Claud was murdered at the fishing port. Claud had protested at being drafted into a German work battalion. Gobelins's suppressed rage threatened to explode again. His whole body went stiff.

As the next group of four were lined up for their last rites and death, a slight dark-haired girl ducked between two soldiers and ran toward them, past the machine gun. She yelled, "Christian, Christian . . ."

She was caught just as she touched the last one on the right-hand side and was dragged back, kicking and screaming. The soldiers then shoved her through the cordon line near Gobelins and threw her to the pavement. Moving quickly, he scooped her up and held her tightly, feeling the sobs that wracked her body. He said to her, "Do not stay here. I'll take you home." He owed her that. Kuppisch shouted something in German, and Gobelins saw what was happening: The blindfold of the prisoner she'd just touched had been ripped away. He was a handsome red-cheeked teenager. Gobelins said to Tramin, "Claim his body," and then to the girl, "We go." He cradled her in his arms and moved steadily away from the scene. She weighed nothing.

As they heard the *rat-tat-tat* of the machine gun, her body went limp. He continued toward the waterfront, wishing he, too, could go limp—vanish from this awful place.

✛ ✛ ✛

He took her to Raphael's bar, and said to the owner, "I need the bed."

Raphael shrugged. The bed in the back room had been used many times. Giggles and moans had come from there.

Over his shoulder Gobelins said, "And bring me a bottle of brandy. Two glasses."

That, too, was not an abnormal request.

Gobelins gently put the girl down on the bare, stained mattress. She was conscious again and wept. Her small breasts quivered. No words, just sounds of hurt and anguish.

He knelt beside her, and his callused, scarred fingers gently massaged her shoulders. His hands declared his sympathy.

She was a very pretty girl, he could see, though the redness and contortions of her face hid her beauty. A girl in her early twenties, he estimated. She was dressed simply—blouse, skirt, and a cotton jacket. Her shoes were a bit worn, but a war was on.

Raphael brought in the brandy immediately. He saw that the usual use of the room and bed did not apply. "Is she ill?"

"I'll tell you later."

After a while she stopped crying. Gobelins said, "Can you get some brandy down?"

She opened her bloodshot eyes and nodded.

She choked on the first sip but did better on the second and shivered as the strong liquor settled in her stomach.

"I'm Georges Gobelins, a fisherman."

She examined his weather-beaten face. "I'm Hélène Dussac."
She took a deep breath and then looked around the storage room.
The aged, stained plaster walls hadn't been painted in years. "What
is this place?"

"It's a bar at the fishing port. A friend of mine owns it."

She half rose up on the bed. "I'll go back ..."

Gobelins said, gently, "Lie down again. Another friend will
take care of whoever that was ..."

Hélène Dussac swallowed. "My brother, Christian, eighteen
years old ..." The dam broke, and the small thin body convulsed
again.

Gobelins took her back into his arms. He babied her, murmured to her, and told her to cry it out, get rid of it somehow.

She cried for almost an hour and then fell asleep.

Gobelins did not leave her side for almost two hours, except to
urinate. He sat there and thought of the catastrophe he and Tramin
had caused by killing Rudmann and the shore patrol. How could
he make it up to those innocent eight men who'd died in the
square? Would he ever sleep again?

He was holding her hand when she awoke just before noon.

"You should have a little something to eat. I'll send out for
some soup and crackers. Then I'll take you home."

"I think we should go out in front before someone gets the
wrong idea."

He smiled at that thought. "As you say."

"Where can I wash my face?"

Gobelins nodded toward the shabby *toilette*. "I'll be at the bar."

Tramin came to Raphael's. Christian had been taken to a funeral house on Dumanoir, he said.

They went there and made arrangements for his burial. Then
they returned to the bar. Hélène told him about Christian. Gobelins
told her about Claud, who had worked the boats. He also told her
about how his late wife had battled cancer.

"Perhaps it was a good thing. I don't think she could have handled what happened to Claud. I'm not sure I can."

After he walked her to her apartment on La Coutaller, he said, "While you were asleep those two hours, I had some thoughts. Would you like to repay that Gestapo major?"

She said yes without hesitation. Her brown eyes sharpened. "I would like to stick a knife in him."

To Gobelins, she didn't look or act as if she could harm a snail. She was a snippet of a girl. So much the better.

"I understand your choice, but I have another proposition for you. You can reach me through Raphael."

✝ ✝ ✝

As Kammerer slept soundly in his bunk behind the green leather curtains, the *U-122* bore westward at eight knots, searching for random targets and awaiting further orders from Kernevel to join the gathering wolfpack. Lookouts swept the horizon 360 degrees as she rode the long swells on an angle, fishtailing and rolling enough to cause some queasiness down below.

The *U-122* was still in her shakedown mode, and drills continued daily. Kammerer was determined to bring her combat readiness to a peak within the shortest possible time.

Book Two

THE DEATH HOLE

FEBRUARY 28, 1941

leet pelted the gray water of Sydney Roadstead, Nova Scotia, as a launch came alongside the gangway of the SS *Galveston*. She was deeply laden with Bunker C grade oil, fuel for ships' boilers consigned to the Admiralty, Liverpool.

Captain Roger Ewing, master of the *Galveston*, dressed in civvies, with an old brown hat covering his bald head, stepped aboard the navy boat for the ride over to the *River Mersey*, the convoy commodore's flagship, which was a dun-hued British combination passenger freighter.

Sully and Congreve, the stubby, wiry Cockney gunnery warrant, of the Royal Maritime Regiment, boarded behind Captain Ewing, who said, "Miserable day, eh?" Sully had taken an immediate liking to Congreve, whose face was pumpkin-round and reddish. He had a rust-colored walrus mustache and rotten teeth.

The British crew seemed decent enough. Captain Ewing was undoubtedly a veteran mariner. Sully had drawn Ewing's attention to his chief mate's papers to point out that he'd never sailed in anything but tankers. This information had traveled to the crew's mess and the officers' saloon. Nowadays any new mate was viewed with suspicion. Did he know oil ships? Was he a secret drunk? Would he panic under enemy attack?

The launch sped toward the *Mersey*, threading the armada. For more than a week ships had been arriving from American and Caribbean ports prior to sailing in SC74B (a slow convoy), bound for the United Kingdom. Fast convoys always sailed from Halifax.

En route from New York, Ewing had told Sully that he'd retired at sixty-five from British Shell. He'd volunteered to go out again after his oldest son had gone down aboard HMS *Jervis Bay*, shelled by the pocket battleship *Scheer*. He was now seventy. Because Sully had never sailed in convoy, Ewing had invited him to the commodore's conference usually held ashore.

Ships rode at anchor in every direction. A pair of small rescue vessels flew green flags with diagonal white bars. Red flags above two freighters indicated they were loaded with ammo. Sully'd swept the anchorage with his binoculars. A half-dozen nations were represented. Most were fitted with guns and all had blackout screens in their portholes.

"We had a convoy a week ago with sixty ships," volunteered the coxswain.

"I do prefer the smaller ones," said Ewing. "Less chance that we go bump on dark nights or in the fog."

The fogs off the Newfoundland Banks were notorious. Blacked out ships were almost invisible until suddenly there was a bow or stern fifty yards away.

Slightly built, Ewing had a merry, ruddy face, dominated by a large purple-veined nose. Thick white crinkly brows were above his still sharp and expressive eyes. He'd shown Sully his five grandchildren, posed in a silver-framed Christmas picture, after Sully had displayed his wallet-size photos of Danny and baby Julie.

Scanning the vessels, Ewing sighed. "I'd prefer to go it alone. Who wouldn't? Too dangerous nowadays."

Slower, older ships such as the *Galveston* had to suffer in "nine-knot" turtle-paced groups. They were fine U-boat targets because they seldom made over seven knots. Clunkers that couldn't make seven were considered expendable and sailed alone, often doomed.

Even though most of Ewing's crew had made the dangerous voyage at least twice, some three or four times, and some had survived torpedoed ships, most were anxious to get going, get it over with.

Soon the launch slid up to the *Mersey*, then stood off to join a dozen more that would wait until the convoy conference was over, and return the masters to their vessels.

Ewing, Congreve, and Sully climbed two ladders to reach the spacious dining room of the old Orient Lines ship. Most of the captains had already gathered, along with armed-guard officers of the ships equipped with guns. Ewing knew a few of the masters and circled tables to shake hands. Sully and Congreve waited patiently. Coffee and sweet rolls were being served.

Finally the convoy commodore arose. "Welcome aboard, gentlemen. I'm Rear Admiral Haines, Royal Navy, Retired. I'll try to get you to England in good shape." J. C. K. Haines was also white haired and hearty. Battle ribbons from World War I and the Boer War rode below the tip of a white pocket handkerchief.

"I must tell you that fourteen vessels out of the last slow convoy were destroyed, with heavy loss of life." He warned that Admiral Dönitz was using his *Rudeltaktik*, wolfpacks, and sailing right into the lanes at night. "I can promise that we'll be attacked once we reach midocean, where there's no air cover."

Haines went on: "Our composition is standard—five ships deep in nine columns at the usual distances, a thousand yards between columns and six hundred between ships, bow to stern. And I don't want any rompers..."

A "romper," Sully knew, was a faster ship that went off on its own. Seated between Ewing and Congreve, he listened intently.

Then Haines read off the cruising speed and proposed routes subject to quick change—they would pass Cape Farewell, on the southern tip of Greenland, but avoid iceberg areas, and then proceed far south of Iceland. "Our rescue vessels will follow the convoy at close range and do their jobs as best they can. *I do not want any convoy vessels to attempt rescues.* If a ship directly ahead is hit, go around it—keep steaming."

There was immediate griping. Some masters with ships

making ten knots fumed over the slow speed of SC74B. The pace of the convoy was always set by the speed of the slowest ship. Most of all they resented navy authority.

Commander Blalock, escort commander, arose. "We'll take you to the Western Ocean Meeting Point, or WESTOMP, Newfoundland." There the Newfoundland Escort Force would deliver them to the Midocean Meeting Point (MOMP) at approximately thirty-five degrees west longitude. The next escort would be a larger force of both British and Free French combat vessels. "All of us will have only one thing in mind—your safe and timely arrival in the United Kingdom."

Captain Macomber, of the rescue vessel *Dimmock*, introduced himself. Apple-cheeked and bushy-browed Macomber said, "We're the little ships, former coastal steamers of fifteen hundred tons, and we're here to scoop you out of the water in case you're unlucky." He said they were fitted out like a hospital. They had scramble and float nets so that men drifting by were caught like fish. "We also have rescue boats. If you find yourself in the drink, blow your whistle. Even in fog, we can find you." He paused and smiled. "Having said all that, I hope I do not see even one of you on my vessel."

Finally the commodore's aide, Lieutenant Grimes, Royal Navy Reserve, arose to finish the briefing. "We hope no smoke will come from your stacks during daylight hours. It draws U-boats to us like flies to honey." He asked for blackout integrity. A submarine watch officer with a good pair of binoculars could see a cigarette flare a mile away. "Order your stewards not to dump any garbage. The submarine commander can follow it like a bloodhound trail. Good luck."

Sully drew in a deep breath.

Admiral Haines arose to say, "You'll make my job easier by keeping proper station. We lose almost as many ships to collision as we do to torpedoes. Thank you."

Lieutenant Grimes distributed sealed instructions and communications codes to each captain, and specifically instructed that the envelopes not be opened until near departure time at 5:00 P.M.

"What'd you think, Mr. Jordan?" Captain Ewing asked as they descended toward the main deck and gangway.

"I feel better about it." What else could he say?

"You've never sailed the North Atlantic?"

"No, sir."

"Well, I tell you that the weather is more a menace than the submarines. You're between the Nazi devil and twenty-foot wave troughs in the North Atlantic this time of year."

While listening to J. C. K. Haines, Sully had thought about Ryti's skipper who'd ended up a charred skeleton sitting in the framework of his burned-out chair.

As the launch bore down on the *Galveston*, which sat low in the water, Sully studied the ship he hoped to ride all the way to England. She looked particularly forlorn; no one was visible on deck or along the catwalk. Except for the thin coil of smoke from her high stack, she looked abandoned. As the launch came along the starboard side, tucking up against the gangway, Sully hesitated and thought that he might never leave her alive.

They hurried along the slippery red-leaded main deck and climbed the ladder to the midships house. Ewing stopped at the chief mate's cabin to say to Baldwin, "We'll sail at five."

The chief officer, who would get a ship of his own once they reached Liverpool, looked up from his hated paperwork. "Anything encouraging?"

"No," said Captain Ewing. "Quite the contrary. Attack is certain. Do you agree, Mr. Jordan?"

Sully felt as if he'd been agreeing all day. He nodded.

Baldwin sat back in his chair. "If we only had wings . . ."

Ewing laughed. "We may get them another way. Are we set?"

"While you were gone, they finally delivered the survival suits." Baldwin shook his head ruefully. "We asked for sixty-two. We got sixty-one." The *Galveston* had sixty-two personnel, including the gun crew.

Ewing said, "Issue them to everyone except me."

The sheet-rubber survival suits, which exposed only the face, could keep a man alive for several hours in the waters off Iceland. Otherwise, death was probable within minutes.

Ewing departed. He climbed an inside ladder up to his in-port stateroom and office.

Sully went on to his own cabin.

"Put your papers and other things in a hot-water bottle and screw it tight so you can grab it and stick it under your belt if you get hit," Captain Ryti had advised just before Sully left the *Tuttle*. He'd called it a "panic bag."

After departing the company office on Wall Street, Sully went to a drugstore to buy the red rubber bladder. He'd felt a little foolish. His mother had used one regularly for her backache, he remembered. Now it sat on top of the small built-in writing desk in his cabin, near the enlarged photo of Maureen, Danny, and the baby.

Sully stared at it for a while, then put his mate's papers and an ID card inside, screwing the black top tight. Aside from his watch and seventeen dollars, he had no other valuables to place inside.

At 4:30 P.M. Chief Mate Baldwin was on the bow supervising lifting the anchor. Hosewater scoured Nova Scotia mud from the hook.

Captain Ewing stood silently on the bridge. Sully was near Ewing, bundled against the late-afternoon rawness. In the usual departure or arrival procedure, the second mate was on the bridge, third mate at the stern, and chief mate on the bow.

Some of the other ships had already departed, according to schedule.

The log of the *Galveston* soon read:

1640—began weighing anchor.

1655—engine slow ahead.

1700—anchor home, steaming in company with other ships of convoy.

1810—took departure of Sydney Harbor, Nova Scotia.

An hour later, Admiral Haines signaled for the convoy to form into the nine prescribed columns. He ordered the "Execute" flag to be popped from the bridge halyard, emphasizing it with a long, deep baying blast from the *River Mersey*'s whistle.

✢ ✢ ✢

As the ships of SC74B steamed out and assembled, it was late night in Berlin. In the closely guarded *Funkbeobachtungsdienst*, better known as just *B-Dienst*, the Naval High Command's superb radio monitoring service, fifty-odd teleprinters clacked out message intercepts from listening posts that had been established from Hammerfest, Norway, down to La Coruña, Spain.

Long ago, *B-Dienst* deciphering experts had broken the British naval code. In May of 1940 copies of the British merchant code had been captured in Bergen when Norway fell. As of this month, *B-Dienst* was intercepting about two thousand Royal Navy messages a month. They provided information about convoy departures, arrivals, and ports of destination.

Just after the air-raid all clear sounded, the listening post at Den Helder, the Netherlands, picked up traffic from the Halifax area.

The sailor manning the teleprinter called his superior over. "Look at this, sir. Something's happening off Sydney, Nova Scotia."

The cadaverous senior-grade lieutenant, Mayer, took the intercept off the teleprinter and carried it to the decipher section. It was entered into the decryption device by one of the civilian nimbleminds.

Two hours later Mayer knew exactly what was occurring at roughly sixty degrees north, forty-five west. A ship named *Annibell* had broken down, and the convoy commodore was requesting that tugs be sent out from Sydney to tow it back to port. The convoy was designated SC74B. Mayer looked up *Annibell* in the international registry and then returned to the teleprinter. "Any more traffic on it?"

"Yessir," said the sailor, watching the machine.

Mayer said, "We know the *Annibell*. She's carried ammo in the past."

The sailor said, "Maybe she's lucky she broke down."

"Maybe so," said Mayer as he left to telex the information to Kernevel.

✢ ✢ ✢

Next morning at about 8:45 Dönitz finished breakfast in the château overlooking the sluggish Ter and went directly to the *Lagezimmer* to review overnight messages and discuss operations. He retired early, usually around 10:00 P.M., and always arrived before 9:00 A.M. His immediate picture of the war at sea was gained from the huge *Atlantik* grid chart table, sectioned in numbered squares, locating each U-boat on patrol and the latest information on convoys.

Greeting Kapitän Godt and the seven staff officers who'd been preparing for the daily briefing for more than an hour, Dönitz said, "Well, gentlemen, what interesting things happened last night?"

Hans Reichmann, senior operations officer, though Godt actually ran operations, said, "A slow convoy came out of Sydney."

Dönitz's eyes lit up. "How many ships?"

His dream was to destroy an entire convoy, and there was nothing he liked better than to direct a wolfpack. The staff knew how much he enjoyed being the master billiard player. He'd send boat after boat to group attack over a two- or three-day period and then would listen for the results, his usual sour look vanishing as the tallies rose. He'd perfected *die Rudeltaktik*, and it had worked so far.

Godt replied, "The normal for a slow one. Something around forty."

Staring at the grids, the admiral ordered a new operation. "Set up Group Dresden," he said, "south and east of Iceland."

They would begin to gather like wolves; the first U-boat would make visual or sound contact with SC74B, report its position to Lorient, and then shadow the ships at a distance until the other boats collected for the attack. When the pack was finally in position for the night rendezvous, the admiral would turn over tactical command to the senior boat officer present.

"Group Dresden it is," said Godt, nodding to the staff.

Each officer then briefed Dönitz on his area of responsibility.

The admiral went to his office shortly after ten to make his usual morning call to Grand Admiral Raeder in Berlin.

The urgent signal to form *Gruppe Dresden* and attack SC74B went out from the high-powered command radio transmitter. The nine boats to be involved were fully fueled, had their full loads of torpedoes, and were currently unemployed.

Whatever the *Unterseeboote* lacked, it was not communications. Dönitz was blessed with the finest system and the best electronic minds Germany could develop. At Kalbe, the central homeland, there was an ultra-long-wave transmitter that could be heard on the ten-thousand-meter band seventy-five feet below the surface off New York or down in the Caribbean. Dönitz never complained about the dot-and-dash business.

For the past two weeks Hélène Dussac had been thinking about Georges Gobelins. She closed the bookstore early and climbed on her bike to go crosstown to Bar Raphael. As she dodged in and out of the blocks until she reached la Rade, she wondered exactly what Gobelins had in mind. There was guarded talk of the *Résistance*

every day. It was a dangerous subject, even on the lips of those involved.

Raphael gave her directions, told her the name of the boat and where it was always tied up in the Port de Pêche, along Quai de Magasin de Marée. Soon she saw the stocky form of Gobelins. In black rubber boots and a rubber apron, he was hosing down the *Vaincre*. Tramin was aboard as well.

Gobelins spotted her and waved. He shouted to her to wait a moment as the stream of water gushed along the afterdeck and spilled over the sides. He'd off-loaded the catch earlier in the day at Bassin Long.

Finally, Tramin shut off the auxiliary pump, and Gobelins beckoned her aboard the dripping seiner-trawler, saying, "I've wondered about you."

Hélène said, "I wanted to come and thank you."

"No need," said Gobelins. "I owed that to you."

She didn't ask why he thought he owed her anything. "And I wanted to talk to you about what you said—that proposition." She glanced over at Tramin with a questioning look in her eyes.

Gobelins understood the look. "Henri is as safe as de Gaulle. As a matter of fact, I find myself holding him back."

Tramin nodded. "Georges is not as aggressive as I'd like."

Gobelins laughed heartily. "Come with me. I can offer you some black-market tea we get smuggled in from Spain that is really from Ceylon."

She followed him into the tiny cabin behind the wheelhouse. It was sparsely furnished with two tiered bunks and a table barely two feet wide. A bench lay hidden beneath it. A two-burner stove was in the corner. Blackened pots and a single frying pan indicated a probable fare of soup, bread, and fried fish. The overhead was brown with grease. Hélène slid onto the bench.

After he placed three china mugs down on the table, she said, "I've thought about it. I want to somehow get that Gestapo chief for what he did to my brother."

Gobelins looked over at Tramin. "How?"

"Stick a knife in him, poison him."

"That's nonsense. You're not capable of doing either of those things, and you know it."

"I'm a woman. I think I'm attractive."

"You are correct both times."

"I could find a way to offer myself to him, then kill him."

"Child, you are talking pure nonsense." He looked at Tramin again. "She has a great imagination, eh, Tramin?"

"Listen to her," Tramin said.

"I am listening, and what I hear is foolish talk."

Gobelins's gray eyes went back to her face. "Hélène, I know you are going through great sadness and emptiness. You have wild anger at what was done. I felt the same way after they shot Claud. I wanted to kill every German in Lorient. But as the days passed I realized I'd be gunned down as well. So I decided to do something else. I won't tell you what it is, but I have done it, working off my anger little by little. Hurt them in other ways."

"What other ways?"

"Other ways. But you are a woman, as you said, and you are attractive, as you said, and perhaps some people I know can make use of that. A pretty French girl is always useful, eh, Tramin?"

Tramin's dark wedged face indicated agreement. "There are other ways to hurt the Boche."

"Are you both in the Résistance?" Hélène asked, looking from Tramin to Gobelins.

The kettle began to whistle.

Gobelins answered, "We both have contacts with people who do not like the occupation." He poured hot water into the mugs. "If you like yours rich, let it steep five minutes."

Hélène nodded. "Are they here?"

Gobelins said, "I will give you the name of a nun in the convent. Don't talk to any of the others, just to her. But think about it for a few days. You may live to regret that you talked to her."

Tramin warned, "Maybe you haven't heard, but they are starting to use an old French punishment for people who commit crimes
against them."

"What is it?"

"If you haven't guessed, the guillotine." Tramin seemed to take
pleasure out of being blunt.

✛ ✛ ✛

"In four days, we'll be in the 'Air Gap,'" Ewing said one afternoon,
quite casually. "I hear the Germans call it *das Todesloch*, the Death
Hole. We call it the Gorge, or the Abyss. Same thing."

Sully frowned. Where the hell was the Death Hole?

Ewing read his frown. "Where we have no air protection as of
now, the absolute mid-Atlantic."

Planes from England didn't have the range for the round-trip
if they stayed above the convoys for any length of time. Even the
flying boats out of Iceland had the same problem. Coastal Command was waiting for the American bomber, the *Liberator*.

"The Germans well know about the Air Gap and have made
it their bloody battleground."

"Where is it?"

"You won't be needing a marker when we arrive there, Mr.
Jordan. You'll see oil slicks and debris on the water from the last
ships. Anything that floats. Boxes, straw, mattresses, life rings,
dead bodies. Oil! Oil! Oil! The Air Gap is like a nautical garbage
dump."

"There's no way to avoid it?" Sully asked.

"Not unless we go south of the Azores and add two weeks to
the run. I always breathe easier when we see the first Sunderlands
overhead."

He was referring to the British patrol bombers, Sully knew.

The Death Hole talk would suddenly creep in between mouth-
fuls in the mess. Sully didn't think it was deliberate, at least not
for his benefit.

Stein, who slept with a hatchet by his bunk, said, "The cloud cover lifted and left us sitting under a half-moon . . ."

Sully listened. Stein told him that there was ice three or four inches thick on the decks, lifeboats, booms, winches. Everywhere. Twenty-one ships glittered like diamonds, afire with reflection. Then the ship at the head of Stein's column got it, and as Stein's ship passed it, he could see its ice-coated bow sticking out of the water like a bloody serpent's head; little red life-vest lights bobbed everywhere, and he already knew the men floating in them were dead.

"Two minutes is all you live. No one had survivor suits," Stein continued.

Sully felt as if he didn't belong in the same room with Stein. What was *he* to talk about? The five gulls he'd seen perched on a drifting cypress stump coming north on the *Tuttle*? He wondered how some of these Brits hadn't gone mad.

For the first time in his life, Sully felt a fear he'd never before encountered. Not the kind that spurted adrenaline when his car whipped and skidded on an icy road, nor that moment when Danny was two and had wandered off along the canal lock. One fragile second he was there, the next he was gone. Sully's fear then was measured from the time he saw Danny, ran, dove, and then grabbed him, coughing and choking, from the brown water.

This fear was of a different kind, more or less constant from two days out of Cape Breton; a fear that lay like a cold, pulsing cancer in his stomach, that sometimes throbbed in his temples. He didn't know how to handle it except to hide it, which was what everyone else was trying to do.

✛ ✛ ✛

"Who sent you?" Sister Cecile asked brusquely.

"Georges Gobelins, the fisherman," Hélène replied, puzzled by the attitude of the Notre Dame de Victoire nun. She'd come to the Lorient convent to offer help, and Sister Cecile had done everything but slam the door in her face.

They were walking in the garden. The nun kept staring at Hélène as they walked. She wore rimless glasses. Her unseamed pink-hued face was oval in the frame of the starched white *cois*. Though the nun's body was hidden in the habit, Hélène guessed she was sturdy. Hélène had seen her walking around town a number of times in the past.

"What did he say about me?"

Hélène hesitated. There were too many in Lorient who were cooperating with the enemy, and suspicion ran deep, even if Gobelins had sent her.

"Well?"

"He said to say two words to you: *Sein Island*."

Sister Cecile finally smiled. "Your name again?"

"Hélène Dussac."

After General de Gaulle made his appeal last June, the fishermen of Sein Island were the first to respond. One hundred and thirty of them sailed for England within hours after the general's call to resist and join the Free French Army. When the Germans arrived on Sein, they found only women, children, old men, the priest, and the mayor. The people were dressed in black, mourning for France.

The nun said, "Gobelins is not one of us. I mean in a formal way. He sends people to us, such as you."

Hélène looked around. She felt the serenity of the convent and almost wished she didn't have to go back out on the streets. How peaceful it was behind these old stone walls.

"I must ask you again—are you certain? You realize that what happened to your brother could also happen to you. To me. To anyone involved."

"I'm certain."

"You know that General de Gaulle has denounced taking individual enemy lives. It only results in mass executions, like Christian's death, of course. Instead, he asks us to increase sabotage . . . rail lines, communications, factories. It's much more effective than shooting or knifing any sailor or soldier."

"I understand."

"How old are you?"

"Twenty-five."

"You don't look it. You have a childlike appearance, which is all to the good, as Gobelins said. Any family, husband, lover?"

"Christian was my family. Our mother died when I was twelve, and our father died three years ago. I have a boyfriend who's a prisoner of war ..."

"Is he another reason for you to join the Résistance?"

"Yes."

"How do you support yourself? Gobelins didn't tell me."

"I operate a bookstore for Max Goff. He stays in Paris most of the time. He deals in rare books there."

Hélène noticed the nun narrow her eyes when Max Goff's name was mentioned. She wondered why.

"He calls Lorient Livres an outpost of culture here. He's never made much of a profit from it, but he's kept it open just the same."

"Of course, I've seen you in the store. You have higher education?"

"Two years at the Collège de France before my father died. That was where I met Monsieur Goff. He was born here, you know."

Sister Cecile nodded.

"He doesn't know how much longer we can keep the shop open. It'll probably be until we sell off most of the stock we have now."

"I don't know what we've done to be punished, but I keep praying that times will change soon," the nun said.

"I don't think they'll change as long as the Germans are here," Hélène said.

Sooner or later, all conversations between the French always returned to the invaders.

"The reason I'm in the Résistance is that those submarines down in the harbor go out on missions of terrible destruction and death. My father was a seafarer, and I, too, have a brother. He's serving in what navy we still have afloat and free. If I can save one Allied ship, just one ..."

Walking slowly along the gravel path, back and forth, they talked on for another ten minutes. The nun said she'd had much trouble with her conscience over being a conduit to the British. "Are you sure?" she asked Hélène, once again with finality.

"Yes."

"All right, I'll inform the necessary people. You will not know who they are. I'll be your only contact. Never call me. Come here, worship, then see me. And if something should happen to you, I hope and pray you'll have a lapse of memory."

"I'll try. What should I do?"

Hélène estimated the sister was in her late sixties, but her brown eyes were clear and piercingly sharp; her voice was that of a young woman. The eyes were pinning Hélène, searching for any sign of retreat.

"You're very pretty and quite sexual. Cultivate a U-boat captain, but let it happen naturally. Be reluctant at first to even talk to him—any officer. Gradually give in. Do not ask him specific questions. Let him volunteer information."

Hélène hung on every word. She engraved them in her mind.

"Is it necessary to go to bed with him? Probably. I'm a nun, but this is war. If he wants to think you're trading sex for food, all right. That is done here every night. Then give him the idea that you're attracted to him, even if he is the enemy. You'll basically be looking for two things—when he will sail and where he will go: South Atlantic, Mediterranean, North Atlantic convoys, Arctic waters ..."

"Should I write things down?"

"Only to memorize them, then burn the paper. I can't give you all the answers. You seem to be very intelligent. Remember what you hear, even seemingly useless things. There are men in London who are expert at taking bits of information and fitting them into a total picture."

Hélène took a deep, uncertain breath. She hoped she wouldn't falter.

Sister Cecile cleared her throat, her sharp eyes searching Hélène a final time. "I'd think it unlikely that a U-boat commander would be diseased. Their medical staff must give good medical attention, n'est-ce pas? Just the same, you never know ... "

"I'll take my chances, Sister."

The nun took a deep breath. Hélène felt the woman's inner conflict. "And you do know how to protect yourself against the other thing ... pregnancy, ma fille?" she managed.

"I think so. I haven't been a virgin for quite a while, Sister Cecile."

Advice given, the nun accompanied her to the old rusting iron street gate, with its small molded replica of Christ on the cross. "You're joining a volunteer group, and you may never know who the others are. The only payment you'll ever receive is the knowledge that you might help end a war."

As the gate creaked open, the nun said, "Good luck. Visit whenever you have something to say ... God bless you, Hélène. Keep safe."

"Say a rosary for me, please."

"I already have," said Sister Cecile as the gate creaked shut. "Two days ago when Gobelins said you'd be coming to see me."

✝ ✝ ✝

Well south of Iceland, dawn came up incredibly clear. The sea was moderate. Weather conditions were astonishing for late winter. The light breeze had a frigid edge to it. Yet by 9:00 A.M. even the most critical weather observers could declare that March 9, 1941, was a surprising day. The sky was blue and nearly cloudless, and the sea was some shades darker than the sky.

But there was never a guarantee out here in the North Atlantic that such ideal conditions would last more than six hours. Usually, there were gale-force winds and huge gray-green seas, fog so thick that the bow couldn't be seen from the bridge, or snow squalls that caused blinding whiteouts. Blame it on the Icelandic Low!

Rear Admiral J. C. K. Haines had checked the barometer on the bridge of the *River Mersey* at 7:00 A.M. and now again at shortly after 9:00. He muttered to Lieutenant Grimes, "Falling, falling." He eyed the instrument as one would look at a sidewinder.

Had there been an aircraft at five thousand feet, the pilot would have clearly seen the majestic parade of SC74B: forty-four ships in the designated nine columns, five ships deep, with the fourth column from the port side minus the *Annibell*. Their wakes laid wide white gashes in the choppy water as they kept fairly good station. Some of them were almost six hundred yards stern to bow. A few of the coal burners let out poles of black smoke. The diesel tanker sparked, to the dismay of Admiral Haines.

The convoy followed Route B, the November-to-May track to Londonderry, which was the northernmost road to the western approaches to England but still hundreds of miles below Iceland.

The recently arrived camouflaged escorts appeared to be doing their jobs nicely. They cruised along the quarters of the convoy and crisscrossed astern and ahead. Blinker lights often stuttered. Though the morning was serene, they were on keyed-up alert. A February Halifax convoy had lost eleven ships at almost this exact position.

The Brits and French had relieved the joint Canadian-American escorts twenty-four hours previously.

COMCONVOY (Admiral Haines): *Thank you for looking after us so well. Best of luck and good hunting.*
COMESCORT: *Your ships behaved in top-notch fashion. Wish you a pleasant, sub-free voyage to Londonderry.*

With the exchange of messages, the Yanks and Canucks steamed toward Iceland to refuel and await a westbound convoy. The relief at the Midocean Meeting Point (MOMP) might be as far east as twenty-two degrees west longitude but always north of fifty degrees north latitude.

The position of SC74B this day was roughly 51°26′ north, 32°36′ west—in the infamous Air Gap, also called the Death Hole.

✝ ✝ ✝

Eight *Gruppe Dresden* boats were stretched in a "stripe" hunt pattern on a north-south search line, roughly twenty-two miles apart, "raking" the ocean. They moved along at ten knots on the probable path of Admiral Haines and company. The distance between the search boats varied, depending on weather, between twenty and forty-odd miles. Usually, only the time-proven medium-size boats attacked the North Atlantic convoys, but Dönitz had dispatched the *122* to see how well it would operate in *das Todesloch*. She was now roughly sixty miles west of *Gruppe Dresden*, loafing along.

At dawn, over the diesels' rumble, the slosh of the water and keen of wind, Kammerer said to Bauer, "I picked her up in the d'Angleterre, on rue Jacob, beautiful girl and—" He was cut short by the shout of the starboard bow lookout.

Kammerer raised the 7 × 50 binoculars to his eyes. The ship couldn't be seen. Hull-down on the horizon, a telltale thin black wand of smoke was clearly visible. The coal burners needed to dump clinkers every watch. Then the shovels of new coal burned with a vengeance, funnels soon belching plumes.

Graeber, routed from sleep, looked through his binoculars. The time was 0715 hours.

Graeber said, "To the left, also faint smoke trails."

"I see them!" Kammerer said. "That's our convoy!" He gave orders to send the boat on a new course, toward SC74B. "Both engines full ahead." Seventeen knots within five minutes.

Rudmann's salt-glazed leopards, though already fading, were still plainly visible. Spray splashed the tensed animals as the diesels pounded.

Word spread throughout the boat: *targets ahead*. The usual

crew excitement accompanied the sightings. The sooner torpedoes were expended, the quicker the boat would return to Lorient, beer, girls, and safety.

Dörfmann, also roused from his sleep, climbed the ladder to the bridge for a look.

Though it didn't show, Kammerer was just as excited as the torpedomen, engine ratings, and Smutje, the cook. His pulse drummed. The hunt had officially begun, not unlike the big-game hunts he'd read about. The targets were always twenty or thirty times larger than the U-boats. There was almost a sexual satisfaction, a climax, as the "eel" left the tube and exploded in the side of an enemy ship. Once, he had actually climaxed.

Though it seemed slow to those in the conning tower, and even to Kammerer, the *U-122* moved rapidly toward the pencils of smoke. They grew into mast tops. Finally there it was, always a spectacle, always breathtaking. He immediately reported the convoy's position to Kernevel.

✝ ✝ ✝

The Huff-Duff (High Frequency Direction Finder), the most recently developed secret device, was basically a cathode-ray tube that rendered a visual bearing on any radio signal up to a thousand miles away. A single bearing wasn't worth listening for because the range couldn't be established. However, a second bearing from a different location sometimes pinpointed, within fifty miles, the original transmission, depending on weather and wireless conditions.

"Gotcha, you heinie asshole," said Radioman Second Class Thomas Ridley in the new Huff-Duff *Y* listening station at Hvalfjordur, twenty-five miles from Reykjavik. His earphones were hooked to a compact Type FH4 receiver developed by the Royal Navy Signal School. It had only been in operation three weeks. Ridley didn't have enough experience to know the individual "fist" of the *U-122* sender but did recognize the high-speed grouping.

The time was 0805, Greenwich mean time (GMT).

In Kirkwall, on the bleak Orkneys and hard against historic Scapa Flow, the Home Fleet's main base, Miss Nancy Lockridge, pert blonde of the Auxiliary Territorial Services, put it rather politely. "Sir, I have an enemy U-boat signaling." She gave the coordinates. Her time was also 0805, GMT. It did not take long for Submarine Tracking to intersect the Hvalfjordur and Kirkwall bearings.

Commander Winn said, "They're on the doorstep of that slow convoy out of Sydney."

All eyes in Tracking were focused on the position of SC74B south of Iceland. Trade Plot, next door, was notified within the minute and the leopard boat's position was posted on the huge merchant ship plot.

Huff-Duff was the brainchild of a pair of scientists doing ionosphere work at the Radio Research Station, Slough. The Y stations had been established before the war from Land's End to the Shetlands to fix all traffic east of the thirty-fifth meridian. But the airwave wizardry was of little help to SC74B at the moment.

✝ ✝ ✝

Admiral Dönitz, summoned to Operations, stood almost in the center of the Situation Room. He said to Godt and the staff, "The usual procedure. Tell Kammerer to maintain contact and report to me every two hours. Order the other boats of Gruppe Dresden to close U-122 at top speed. I want them to attack just after midnight ..." It was the most vulnerable time. He looked over at Commander Reichmann. "Will they be in position by then?"

"I think so, sir."

"You think so? Don't you have a good idea of the location of the other boats?"

Dönitz's face sometimes looked as though he'd just sucked a lemon. It looked that way at this moment.

"Yessir."

"Well, just give me that exact answer. They'll be ready to attack at 0100? Correct?"

"Yessir."

Though he loved the simplicity of *die Rudeltaktik*, the true submersibles going underwater only for reconnaissance and to escape depth charges, he was always tense when the wolfpacks came together. He'd admitted to Godt that he wished there were a dozen of him. He could be in personal command of each boat, stage them around the convoys, and direct each individual attack as well as the overall onslaught.

"That isn't possible, is it, Eberhard?"

"I'm afraid it isn't, Admiral."

He ordered the steward to bring breakfast to his office, not to the château's dining room. He would eat with Godt, then go back and forth between the *Lagezimmer* and his office throughout the day and night, eventually clad in pajamas and bathrobe, as the boats reported.

Ten minutes later the priority high-speed signals from *BdU*, Lorient, went out to *Gruppe Dresden* ordering the boats to attack the eastbound convoy in the designated grid.

✢ ✢ ✢

The signals were instantly intercepted by women of the Auxiliary Territorial Services at Penzance, near Land's End, and Torquay, not too far from Plymouth. There were many other intercept stations scattered all the way to Golspie, on Dernoch Firth in northern Scotland.

Dönitz's messages were teleprinted within minutes to Submarine Tracking's most important intelligence source—the Government Code and Cipher School (GCCS) at Bletchley Park, some forty miles north of London, in Buckinghamshire. Many of the finest mathematical and most eccentric minds in England were employed on the grounds of the Victorian mansion. Dons from Cambridge and Oxford had been recruited to figure out the complex German ciphers. Hundreds of cryptanalysts worked in the stately mansion and temporary wooden huts that now blighted the gardens and lawns of the lovely estate. It was Bletchley Park that enabled Commander Winn to arrive at his best fictions.

Bletchley—the most secretive "school" on earth, known only as Station X—had provided much of the U-boat history by breaking the German code *Thetis*, used in the Baltic while the undersea craft were undergoing trials and training. This information was used daily by Lieutenant Unsworth and Wren Beavers.

This late winter morning the men and women of Bletchley were trying to break a half-dozen other Nazi codes, and many hours would pass before the *Gruppe Dresden* instructions were unraveled.

U-147, Hans Remus, and *U-105* responded to Dönitz and notified Lorient that they were closing at full speed. The others communicated likewise within a half hour.

Huff-Duff listened in. Submarine Tracking plotted them.

✠ ✠ ✠

Bauer had returned below and went to work at the small navigation table to plot the convoy, estimate its speed, and collect all the information to decide on the basic course the ships were traveling.

"Not as large as my last one, but big enough," said Kammerer. The last convoy had more than fifty ships, of which *Gruppe Apfelsine* eliminated fifteen.

The low profile of the U-boat and apparent lack of air cover now would let him go within eight kilometers of the targets. One destroyer moved back and forth at the head of the columns. Another paced along off the starboard bow. On the stern quarter, sturdy corvettes bounced along.

"Nine against six," said Graeber, forecasting optimistically. He added, "I think," to be safe. He guessed that the same number of escorts was on the other side of the convoy, with a destroyer astern.

"Uh-huh. But never be too sure," Kammerer replied. On the

last convoy attack, Kammerer underestimated the number of escorts by two. One had almost undone him. He kept studying the ship parade. Finally, an hour later, he said to Graeber, "Let's take her down and go in for a closer look," ordering submersion.

In a few seconds the bridge was vacated as bodies dropped through the hatch. Toes barely touched the aluminum ladder, and the electric alarm bell hammered a warning. All hands jumped to diving stations as red alarm lights winked.

Kammerer's feet had no more than reached the upper control room deck when *U-122* began to tilt downward. Hydroplanes angled to send her toward the bottom. Air hissed out. Water entered the diving cells. The diesels stopped abruptly on the bell sound. Battery-driven electric motors spun the propellers. She disappeared beneath the surface in bubbles and foam. Kammerer had trained his bridge watch to clear the conning tower in 1⅕ seconds per man.

With the diesels secured, a quietness, even calmness, settled as she dropped to a hundred feet and stabilized. Then Kammerer ordered her back to periscope depth when Fromm said she'd risen enough to allow a look around.

"Thank you," he said.

Trimmed and stable at less than fifty feet, electromotors slow ahead, the steel shark glided along quietly in the icy waters.

"Dreizehn Meters," said Fromm.

In the commander's control room, Kammerer bent at the waist, ready to press his forehead to the black rubber cups of the sighting piece. Though the basics of using the "*Spargel*," in U-boat jargon, had been taught at commander's school, mastery of this "eye" had taken hours of practice, right hand controlling the angling mirror, left operating the lever to make allowance for boat movement. A handle adjusted the lenses for magnification. There were two *Spargels*: the sea-sky type, which made the most of natural illumination (the model he was using), and the attack periscope, which had crosswires, range-scale, and bearings from the compass repeater. The latter had a saddle with pedals to train right or left. Both types, however, could be used for observation at underwater speeds of less than six knots. Increased speed would cause a problem.

The attack table, with its cams and graphs, was coupled directly to the periscope. Kammerer could fire at five different targets in a matter of seconds. The periscope and its adjuncts were wonders of German optical and computer engineering.

Kammerer hummed a few bars from *"Die Abend-glocke"*— "Bim, bam, bim, bam, bim, bam . . ."—a favorite. Then he laughed. He had a way of easing tension.

He raised the slender high-angle tube. A 360-degree check of the horizon was made. Then he lowered the *Spargel*, saying, "Increase speed to five knots." Meanwhile he relaxed, eyes closed, body limp, while *122* moved toward the convoy.

The whir of many ship propellers bearing dead ahead on the hydrophones indicated that the armada was where it should be. "Give me bearings every thirty seconds," he said without opening his eyes.

"Jawohl, Herr Kaleunt," said the hydrophone operator, Coppel.

✛ ✛ ✛

Sully came out of the chartroom with his sextant for the noon sighting. There was always competition to run up the ship's position with signal flags and compare it to the commodore's and other ships'. All the positions were averaged.

"Morning, Cap'n," Sully said. He'd woken up at eleven, eaten lunch already, and would relieve the third officer in a few minutes.

"Any bets today, Mr. Jordan?" Ewing asked, a more or less customary question when the sun was out. Otherwise the position would be dead reckoning.

"None, sir," he said, checking his watch against the two bridge chronometers. Aside from this exceptionally clear day, he'd had only two acceptable star sights since leaving Sydney.

"Get a good one, Mr. Jordan. This weather won't last more than three hours," the captain said. He nodded toward the north horizon. An approaching roll of thick nimbus clouds held rain or snow. A moment later Sully "shot" the sun, coming close to the *Mersey*'s navigator's position.

He had settled into the *Galveston*'s routines, which weren't that much different from the *Tuttle*'s or those of any other tankers he'd sailed in.

So far, he hadn't slept out on deck near the starboard boat, life jacket at his fingertips. No one else was doing it. But he was sleeping fully clothed, life jacket on the deck by his bunk; the survival suit, zipped down, was draped over the chair by the desk. He'd timed himself getting into it and zipping it back up at four seconds, timed getting up to the starboard boat deck at seven seconds. If he was asleep when she took a torpedo, it would take him another two seconds to awaken and scramble to his feet.

The clumsy-footed suit, which smelled like rubber and ether, had a powdery substance inside. He'd felt like a human sausage when he first tried it on. Two days out of Sydney he'd started taking it back to the saloon with him and up to the bridge for the watches. With the suit went his hope that he'd return to Maureen and the kids, and the *Galveston* would be no more than a good or bad memory.

The *Galveston* was one of five tankers headed for Londonderry, all of them riding inside positions, in Columns Four or Five, away from the flanks and "Hell's Corners," the four corners of the convoy. Ships on the outboard columns were the easiest for the U-boats to pick off. Tankers had some small protection simply because of riding the interior.

She was third ship in Column Four. Ahead was a squatty British Shell tanker, *Malay Prince*. On the beam was the white-hulled Norwegian *Lofoten*, a ship probably operating out of England since the Germans had taken over its besieged home country. The final tanker, *Texas Star*, two back in Column five, behind the *River Mersey*, was like the *Galveston*, lent to the United Kingdom.

Sully wondered where the subs were now that they'd edged into the Death Hole. Yesterday he'd seen the floating evidence—oil, boxes, pieces of wood, clothing.

"Have you ever been to Iceland, Mr. Jordan?" Captain Ewing asked.

"No, sir."

Couldn't this old man just be quiet?

"Wonderful birds over there, Mr. Jordan. Puffins, guillemots, kittiwakes, Arctic skuas."

"I don't know much about northern birds, Cap'n."

"Marvelous creatures. Have you ever sailed in the Denmark Straits?"

Sully's nerve ends were raw. "No, sir."

"Well, they aren't too far from here. I shipped out on a miserable vessel when I was about sixteen, and we steamed up the Denmark Straits. I remember that we ran into a field of floebergs, small icebergs, that thudded against the hull. Rather spooky, I'd say."

"I imagine."

Captain Ewing was showing his seventy years.

Pudney, the young helmsman, listening to the conversation, turned his head. "Was that during the last war, Cap'n?"

"No, Pudney, that was in 1905, '06. In an old collier. You don't know what luxury this ship provides. Back then each man had only twelve square feet of sleeping space."

The two of them should shut up. Sully turned his attention toward the stern of the *Malay Prince*. Suddenly she seemed to be dropping back a bit, for one reason or another. Maybe engine trouble?

The captain had noticed it as well. He murmured, "If she comes back any more, I'd suggest dropping five or six revolutions."

"I had that in mind," Sully said tensely.

"Did you get torpedoed in the last war, Cap'n?" Pudney asked.

Jesus Christ! God almighty!

"Yes, Pudney, I did. On a freighter, though. I was a second

officer, like Mr. Jordan. I remember the men swimming through coal dust and all the flotsam, some slipping under without a word."

"How did you survive, Cap'n?" the youth asked.

"I clung to a piece of hatch cover for about ten hours."

"That must have been awful," Pudney judged.

"It wasn't very pleasant at all."

Sully retreated to the bridge wing. Ten minutes later a life ring stenciled *Empire Gulliver* floated by. The body had slipped out of it.

✛ ✛ ✛

The closest propeller in the hydrophones was now the Flower class corvette on the port bow. Kammerer eyed the little workship through the attack periscope, thinking how easy it would be to blow it off the sea. He'd studied the British defensive ships and knew the 205-foot corvettes, whale-catcher types in civilian life, were all named after flowers—*Abelia* and *Azalea* all the way to *Zinnia*. They were anything but the sweet-smelling garden variety; they were tough and mean. Though tempted now with such a perfect target he knew a torpedo would alert both the ships and the escorts to his presence. He would wait for the night. Always surprise them, his instructors had said in his first weeks at U-boat commanders' school. Nothing had changed. Always wait for the big targets. Get into the middle of the convoy and turn it into a shooting gallery. That was Karl Dönitz's doctrine.

However, just for practice: "Bearing, mark. Range, thirty-four hundred. Bow angle, port sixty, speed eleven." He turned away from the rubber eyepiece and grinned. "We just notched a corvette." Theoretically, of course. The unsuspecting little ship plunged along in the gray light.

Rain threatened, but so long as it didn't get too heavy it was a lovely condition. He could hide. Moderate sea was a bonus enabling observation. The convoy had almost passed by. The last ship in the port outboard column was beyond the corvette, dim in the grayness but easy to identify by its bow curl.

The *U-122* slowly slid on southwestward underwater. At shadowy 1610, after another periscope look toward the rearguard destroyer and the two small rescue vessels in the wake of the convoy, Kammerer gave orders to surface. He'd had fourteen periscope sightings and knew a lot about this gaggle of ships.

The diving tanks were blown. When the conning-tower hatch was reported "free," and no longer under water, he quickly went up the ladder and spun the wheel, emerging into the late-afternoon gloom. The watch officer and three lookouts followed him up to the bridge.

After a quick check around he ordered, "Blow through." The electric motors stopped. Diesels were started, and the last bit of water was expelled from the diving tanks. Bilge pumps whirred. Clear, cold air was sucked into the steel sausage.

Bauer called down for the attack sight to be brought up, and the powerful binoculars, directly attached to the range finder, were mounted.

As *U-122* fell in behind the convoy, Kammerer scanned the outline of the weaving rear destroyer and decided to follow at a distance of about twelve kilometers. He ordered his latest reconnaissance information to be sent to Lorient, noting the convoy's change of course, approximate speed of seven knots, and disposition of still forty-plus ships including the exact position of the five tankers. He'd fulfilled his job as "shadower."

Twenty-five minutes later, using *Schlüssel M*, the navy's version of the Enigma Code, five-letter Hydra cipher groups, Heinze keyed Kammerer's message to Lorient. The boat's high-speed transmitter coughed it out in less than thirty seconds, hardly enough time, it would seem, for any listener to get a "fix" on a conventional radio direction finder.

Having finished with the blur of Morse dots and dashes and awaiting a "message received" response from Kernevel, Kammerer started transmitting the automatic homing signal to the other boats of *Gruppe Dresden*.

Come, gentlemen, join me.

As *U-122* motored on at seven knots with Bauer and the lookouts on the bridge in light rain, Kammerer dined on tinned corned beef in the tiny wardroom midships. "I have a good feeling about tonight," he said. "Such a good feeling that I will tell you about a treat I brought aboard."

Graeber and Dörfmann waited. Fromm wore a look of expectancy.

"Five bottles of Dom Pérignon."

"Nothing but the best," said Dörfmann.

"One for every two ships! If we get two tankers, we'll drink all of them. Then beer for all hands. My treat."

Dörfmann said, "If we get eight big ships, you'll get the Knight's Cross, eh, Kapitän?"

"Well . . ." It depended on tonnage.

The *Ritterkreuz* was awarded automatically on achieving a hundred thousand tons. Horst Kammerer had sixty-six thousand as of this late afternoon. What he really wanted some wonderful day was the *Eichenlaub*, oak leaves to be added to the Knight's Cross, for two hundred thousand tons. It would then be the equivalent of Britain's Victoria Cross.

Earlier, Kammerer had drawn forty-four small wedges, representing the ships of SC74B in nine columns, on a piece of brown butcher paper laid out on the wardroom table. "The tankers are here in Four and Five, right in the heart of the convoy, so we come in ahead of the last ship in Column One, port side, cut across the bow of the next to the last ship in Column Two, same for that one in Column Three, then motor right up the lane between Three and Four and make a fan shot . . ."

Graeber blinked. On the other boat in which he'd served, they'd always worked in the last two outboard ship lanes, never attempting to get into the heart. "Do you think we can do it?"

"Why not? Just keep your mind on shooting. I'll handle the boat, as usual."

Kammerer was well aware that junior officers were leery of boat commanders bucking for the Knight's Cross. The lure of the decoration sometimes led to foolish risks. Commanders who'd already achieved the cross were apt to be more careful and allow everyone to live longer.

Skinny Dörfmann said tentatively, "I just hope those diesels don't quit on us." He'd just turned twenty-one. Kammerer looked at him knowingly. "I'm always more worried about human failure."

"We'll be cutting across the bows of three ships?" the First asked, alarmed.

"They're moving at seven knots. We'll be going at seventeen."

"After we shoot, how do we get out?" Kammerer knew what Graeber was thinking: We're in the middle of all those ships, lit up by star shells. Every gun on every ship around us will be firing. Then we have to face their escorts.

"I'm gambling on confusion. Theirs. Not mine." He could also submerge and run for dear life, grit his teeth when the depth charges, the *Wasserbomben*, came down.

"There won't be any room for mistakes," the First said gravely.

"I'm not known for mistakes, am I?" Kammerer said with annoyance. In his mind's eye he could already see the *122* slide by the freighter at the rear of Column One on an angle, straighten out to run due south ahead of the next two ships, leave three hundred meters on each side, and then whip around to give Graeber easy shots at those oil carriers. Why weren't they excited?

He was plainly dismayed. "Look, the reason we're here is to take chances. We could play it safe and take potshots along the edge of the convoy. That's not why we're out here." He thought he'd made that clear back in Lorient. His first and second officers were staring mutely down at the wedges on the butcher paper. Didn't they get the same thrill that he got from seeing a ship, a whole ship, vanish stern-first or a tanker ablaze bow to fantail? Perhaps not.

What about that ammo ship he'd luckily hit on his last patrol, unaware of what it contained? A stern shot at fifteen hundred meters? It had blown a hole in the sea. The night heavens had turned gaudy red-green. Shock waves had knocked everyone down in the conning tower. Then pieces of steel had fallen. Some were as big as a man's arm, others not larger than a thumbnail. Deafened by the blast, he'd scrambled down the hatch to let out his victory yell. Emerging again in a moment, the whole convoy seemed to be gaping at the space in Column Six that the *St. Ives*, of London, had occupied. It had vanished without a trace. At dawn, racing away to spend a leisurely day before the next *Rudel*, a lookout had found a scalp impaled on an antenna and wanted to keep it as a souvenir.

Kammerer said, "Well, that's how we're going to do it." Whether they liked it or not. Via Dörfmann, word swept through the boat in minutes. Lang, the chief boatswain, blew out a breath and said, "Oh, Scheiss!" Same old Kammerer. When the *Maschinenmaat*, Freed, heard it he said in disbelief, "Into the middle of the convoy?" Goldbeck, the *Smutje*, standing by his small electric range only large enough for four pots at a time, said, "I want to get off this goddamn boat." Only Wendt, the chief torpedoman, clapped his hands. But Wendt was always bloodthirsty, as eager as the *Kaleunt*, the rest of the crew thought. Within a few minutes, every man awake on the *U-122* knew she was going to penetrate into the very center of all those ships, running like a fox.

✝ ✝ ✝

J. C. K. Haines wasn't particularly surprised to receive the Admiralty message at 1850 bearing the *OU* prefix, most immediate.

COMESCORT/COMCONVOY. BELIEVE
ENEMY SUBMARINE ATTACK IMMINENT.
ESTIMATE AT LEAST SEVEN BOATS INVOLVED.
ADVISE ALL PRECAUTIONS.

Neither was he particularly surprised that rain squalls marched across the convoy in sporadic bursts. The early night had all the texture of coal tar. Nine days out of Nova Scotia and eight days away from Londonderry, the rotten weather and the U-boats were right on schedule.

He read the message twice before conferring on UHF radio with the senior escort officer in the HMS *Spriggs*. The *Spriggs*, a Hunt class destroyer, rolled around somewhere out ahead, unseen. Only the *Spriggs* had the new surface detection device, radar, and she'd reported a malfunction during the day. During darkness she was blind except for sound detection.

In the late afternoon, on his gut hunch, the commodore's signal crew had advised all personnel to don survival suits during the night. Mere mention of the cumbersome suits was a message in itself. He repeated a previous order not to fire illuminating rockets until cued by the destroyers. Gunnery officers had been warned to take extreme caution in shooting at surfaced submarines to avoid hitting other ships. In the past, this mistake had met with tragic results.

His final advice was to maintain alert lookouts. Trying to peer through the rain seemed useless, but these were line squalls. Between them there was limited visibility. He'd changed course forty degrees at twilight, hoping it wasn't observed by any trackers.

Haines parted the blackout curtains, entered the quiet, darkened pilothouse of the *Mersey*, and waited for his eyes to adjust. A small cone of light came from the gyrocompass. The only noise inside was the soft click of the helm. He could make out the back of the man at the wheel; behind him were the ship's master, Captain Corkle, and the third officer.

The admiral joined them at the windows. Wipers fought back and forth to combat the peppering rain. "London has just informed me to expect attack. They estimate that at least seven boats are around us."

"Commodore, that usually means a dozen or more," said Corkle, a disagreeable bantam Yorkshireman. Capable master, though.

The admiral knew about Huff-Duff but wasn't at liberty to discuss it. "Oh, they've been pretty accurate lately. They said, 'at least,' so there may be ten at that."

Fast convoys could change course every hour, but ones like SC74B usually kept a slow, steady forward track because of wasted zigzag miles, collision risk, and stragglers. Instead, during daylight hours, Haines used "evasive" courses, wide changes of twenty to forty degrees over a three- or four-hour period.

Haines said, "If we can get by the next forty-eight hours, I'm optimistic we'll come through without too many casualties." In three days, air cover from the big Sunderland flying boats out of UK bases at Benbecula, Bowmore, and Bally Kelly would begin. The "Flying Porcupines" could carry a ton of depth charges.

The admiral was weary this night. Discipline had sorely lacked during the day. The Aldis lamps on the *Mersey* had blinked frequently at one ship or another.

"Number Nineteen, request you assume station and keep it!"

"Number Twenty-Seven, straggling invites torpedoes!"

"Number Eleven, your smoke trail endangers the convoy!"

Twice he'd sent the HMS *Dauntless,* the destroyer at the rear of the convoy, to persuade stragglers to catch up. Two had dropped several miles astern. Then at dusk, a diesel-engined ship started making sparks from her stack, clearly visible when the rain didn't hide her. He said wearily to Captain Corkle, "I'll be on the couch in the chartroom," and left the wheelhouse.

"Aye, Commodore," said Corkle, obviously glad to have the bridge to himself for a while. He hadn't asked for the *Mersey* to be a flagship and had extended no welcome when Admiral J. C. K. Haines and staff came aboard.

✢ ✢ ✢

With its slender bow sometimes buried into waves clear back to the 105-mm deck gun, the *U-122* matched the speed of the wallowing convoy. It traveled at about 6.5 knots, a pace any good distance runner could equal. The bridge watch was soaked and miserable. Kernevel had been advised of the convoy's forty-degree course change.

Down below, in dry warmth, Kammerer was on his bunk in the captain's nook reading *Donnerberg*, a German translation of Zane Grey's *Thunder Mountain*. A fan of both American Western novels and moving pictures, he always brought along several books. He liked Grey's stories and the films of Tom Mix, Ken Maynard, and Hoot Gibson. In another life he would have chosen to be a Texas cowboy.

Aside from the books, he'd brought little else aboard the boat—three changes of underwear, a half-dozen pairs of socks, sea boots, his watch shirts and pants, a leather jacket, and leather coveralls. His good shoregoing uniforms and other personal possessions were in a locker in Lorient.

What was good for the captain was good for the crew. Only seagoing clothes and photos of loved ones were allowed. Not even razors were permitted, in the interest of conserving fresh water. Only bucket baths were allowed, until the final seventh or eighth week when sailing home. By that time the shower stall, used to store food, was long empty. A lot of cologne was sprayed around the *U-122*.

Through the leather curtain that shut him off from the passageway, he heard the voice of the duty radio operator and rested his book. "Sir, there's high-frequency traffic between the escorts and the flagship." He'd been listening to the VHF monitor.

"What are they saying, Otto?"

Kammerer knew Heinze didn't understand English. His own was limited. He smiled to himself.

"I don't know, sir."

"I do. They're talking about us."

"The *U-122*, sir?"

"Any of us."

The other eight had all checked in by now, with Hans Remus, in *147*, in tactical command. They were already in position, ten miles out on either side of the convoy, waiting until 2300 to move in closer and observe the strike time set by Dönitz for 0100.

"Keep monitoring them, Otto."

The operator went back to his cubbyhole opposite the control room and the helm.

The chronometer told Kammerer it was 2100, time to catch some sleep before the 2300 awakening call. Though he wasn't unconcerned about the forthcoming attack, he didn't feel tense at all. The boat was sound; the crew was good and mainly experienced. The other captains had been on at least three patrols. Remus was a veteran of at least six, ready to step up a rank and command the base at La Pallice.

Dönitz had laid out attack techniques in his handbook for U-boat commanders, both submerged and on the surface. Any commander paying attention to *der Löwe* would likely have success.

Kammerer reached up and turned off his bunk light.

Two hours later, a hand pushed aside the leather curtain and touched Kammerer's shoulder, the voice behind the hand saying, "Time to awaken, Herr Kaleunt."

Kammerer was already sitting up before the speaker finished. On patrol, the slightest change in familiar sounds jolted him out of sleep. If one of the diesels shut down or a pump ceased to operate—any new or unusual sound—he'd awaken immediately.

He looked at his watch: a few seconds after eleven o'clock.

With some cold water splashed on his face and a cup of black coffee he was ready to slip on the foul-weather gear and sea boots, check the radio and sound rooms, and then climb up to the bridge.

Graeber was already up there. He said, "Good evening, Herr Kaleunt. Rain has stopped," as Kammerer emerged into the midnight dampness.

"Evening, so it has. Wind has dropped, too."

Graeber nodded.

Kammerer wanted to say, "Jesus Christ, it's cold," but he didn't need to remind the lookouts.

The sea had moderated a bit. Good shooting weather. "Our friend up ahead still behaving?"

"The destroyer? Can't see him or hear him, but I'm guessing he's there," Graeber said without much enthusiasm.

"All right, head north for a while, skirt our friend, and get abeam of the flock. Speed, fifteen knots."

In a moment, the diesels, which had been idling all night, began to roar. The *U-122* headed into the northerly chop, exhaust swirling in the murk, only her wake to mark the passage.

The boat awoke harshly and loudly: "Auf Gefechtsstationen!" Bells clanged.

✛ ✛ ✛

At a quarter to twelve, Sully came up to relieve the third mate. He'd already sat in darkness for ten minutes in his cabin to adjust his eyes. He dropped his survival suit against the after bulkhead of the pilothouse, near the chartroom door. The chartroom was dimly lit in orange. The usual course and speed information was soon passed on.

As Pudney took the wheel, Captain Ewing said to the now off-duty helmsman, "You might think about sleeping in your survival suit the rest of the night."

"Yessir," the sailor said. "Good night."

Sully stepped out on the port bridge wing to take a look into the blackness but couldn't even see the bow curl of the *American Exporter*, supposedly six hundred yards behind the *Galveston*. There was a faint phosphorescent track of the *Malay Prince* ahead. No signs of any ships a thousand yards on the port side. Then he went out to the starboard wing. The results were the same.

Tucked into the starboard bulwark was Gunner Congreve, in his survival suit with woolens beneath. He'd painted the suit red for easy spotting by the rescue ships. Like Captain Ewing,

Congreve did not sleep at night. He'd been torpedoed once. With a coffee thermos at his feet, he stood lookout either on the bridge wings or in the after gun tub, ready for action.

Breath pluming out, Congreve said, "It's enough to freeze yer cobblers . . ."

Sully agreed. He guessed what "cobblers" were.

Congreve said, "Nazi fuckers out there tonight, mate. I feel 'em. Like bloody sharks. I smell 'em."

"I hope you'll hit one."

"They show their arse, I'll fuckin' 'it 'em."

Sully almost wished they'd strike and get it over with. Now! He didn't know how much longer his nerve ends would hold out. Another night or two of this and he'd be quaking head to foot.

Congreve said, "You can smell 'em, mate. U-boat exhaust stinks like dead skunks."

Sully nodded and went to the end of the wing to look down. The seas were as ebony as Jusepin crude. At noon, the engine-room intake had recorded the water temperature at forty-eight degrees. Death water.

He reentered the pilothouse and said to Captain Ewing, "Everyone seems to be behaving." It wasn't what was on his mind.

"I pity lookouts on a night like this," said Ewing. "Here we are in this warm pilothouse, out of the wind and rain. We're lucky, Mr. Jordan."

"I'd say so, Cap'n." More maddening small talk.

"But I've stood my share of lookout in rain and snow and ice. I've stood crow's nest watches where you had to scurry up the rungs when the ship went down by the head and then hang on for dear life when she came back the other way."

Where in hell were the U-boats? That's what Sully Jordan wanted to know. Old Ewing was a pain in the ass.

"I remember once on a ship out of Southampton the door to the nest froze while I did my two hours. They had to send another man up the mast to chop it loose so I could come down." Ewing chuckled over the memory.

Sully's teeth were on edge. Every few minutes, he lifted his binoculars to try and find the stern of the *Malay Prince*. Captain Ewing was doing the same. The *Prince* seemed to be keeping station though her revolutions had been erratic all day.

"They're not putting crow's nests on ships anymore. I think it's a mistake. If you're in a low, low fog, a man high up comes in handy. And if you're coasting, Mr. Jordan, I find a lot of comfort to have eyes in the sky watching for reefs and rocks."

Was the skipper ignoring the U-boats?

Since leaving Sydney, Ewing had spent every night on the bridge, staying awake with cups of coffee. After the dawn danger period was over, he'd sleep for several hours in his sea cabin just off the chart room. He seemed to be made of iron and stone.

Sully walked over to the starboard side to look out again toward the column over there. Nothing. Then he went to the port side. Only blackness. Light rain hit the glass like handfuls of grain. He stood a moment.

Where were the fucking U-boats? Where were they?

When Sully returned to his position, to the left of the helm, Ewing said, "It's miraculous we haven't had one collision."

Sully knocked on wood. "We had that near miss in Column Seven yesterday."

"So far, so good," said Captain Ewing, yawning.

The ships still plugged along much the same as they had at nightfall. The dogwatch on each had settled in. Life-jacketed lookouts tried to keep warm in the after gun tubs and up on the bow. They sought any protection from the cutting wind and wondered what the hell they were doing out there with visibility no more than fifty yards. They couldn't see the ship ahead or behind, Sully knew.

✛ ✛ ✛

At 2400, judging that they were on the port quarter of SC74B, Kammerer turned due south, increasing speed to seventeen knots.

The lookouts—Graeber, Bauer, and himself—scanned for the corvette that was certain to be roaming around back there. Getting by the Flower class was the first step toward plunging into the convoy.

The eels were ready to fire. Kammerer always made sure his were treated like birds' eggs—removed from the tubes every few days, lubricated, and thoroughly checked for any problems. They lived sealed in their enclosures, watertight caps at either end, until time of use. Not too long ago there'd been a rash of faulty torpedoes and misfirings.

The effectiveness of any boat was often a singular thing, depending almost solely on the commander. If he was timid, scoring infrequently, he might live longer. If he was a Horst Kammerer, he'd score on every patrol. With every successful patrol the odds were higher that he'd perish along with his boat. Kammerer knew this; he accepted it.

"Where the hell is that corvette?" he shouted.

He always prided himself on his eagle vision and usually spotted a target before any lookout spied it. He'd met one of the tenacious little coal burners in the past and had suffered depth-charge damage. Their bite was a lot worse than their looks. He slowed down to make sound contact.

Seven minutes later, word came up from below: "We're picking up a single screw at zero-nine-zero; many of them dead ahead, faint."

The single screw had to be the Flower class churning away out there, and Kammerer aimed the high-powered glasses.

"Estimate twenty-one hundred meters on the single screw," said the hydrophone operator, Coppel.

No wonder she couldn't be seen in all this ink. "Let's go to one-seven-zero," he said to Graeber. Good-bye, Flower class! Now to find the path between those last two ships in Column One. He grinned at Graeber. "Hold on to your *Hoden*!"

Graeber didn't grin back. His pale face indicated that they all might need to hold on to more than their testicles before too long.

Kammerer felt the usual attack exhilaration as the boat

streaked toward the unseen convoy, his pulse quickening. That pitter-patter down in his gut wanted to make it all happen this instant. But he knew he would be successful only if he waited until they had the right targets at the best possible angle.

He shouted into Graeber's ear, "Until we get two of those tankers, I'm not interested in any other targets. I don't care if they're bull's-eye at five hundred meters ..."

This was always the worst time for the crew; they were locked in the bowels of the boat. If something went wrong, the lucky ones in the conning tower had a small chance of escape. They wouldn't be trapped inside the steel coffin. That was always their worst fear, the one they awoke with and went to sleep with. Convoy attack brought it up into their throats.

The following wind blew acrid diesel exhaust back over the bridge. One of the aft lookouts began to throw up, but the exhaust was only the trigger. Suddenly Kammerer spotted a white bow curl to the left. From it arose a dim shape—the last ship in Column One, the *Honfleur*, though he didn't know it by name. But he remembered the profile from periscope sightings of the previous day—big and bulky, with a low stack. On she came like a juggernaut, not a peephole of light showing from her. He switched the glasses to the right and picked up the white churn from the next ship in the column, again not knowing her name—the British *Peter Wells*, with tanks lashed down on her weather decks.

"Perfect," Kammerer murmured; he then ordered, "Steer one-seven-five," to slice the middle between the ships. "Add that extra knot, now!"

He counted on the rain, wind, and time of night to make the bow lookout on the *Honfleur* and the stern lookout of the *Wells* more concerned about comfort than vigilance.

His watch told him it was 0050. Ten minutes to go. He knew that Hans Remus, in the *147*, was on the starboard side of the convoy and would enter through Column Nine. Even though Hans was in tactical command, there was little need for communication at this point. The beauty of the *Rudel* was its combined attack with each commander more or less independent. It was almost impossible to say, "You take that ship and I'll take this one." The idea was to sink as many as possible. Sometimes attacking captains were robbed of targets by another U-boat just when they were ready to fire.

In the sound room, hooked to the hydrophone earpieces, Coppel said, "God almighty, I've got targets all over the place."

The *U-122* slid between the *Honfleur* and the *Peter Wells* unnoticed, splitting the roughly seven-hundred-yard avenue almost in the middle. The twelve-to-four bridge watch on the French ship had no idea a German submarine had just passed under their noses. It was truly the wolf among the sheep. Kammerer could kill two or three within sixty seconds.

He added another five degrees east to cut between the ships of the next two columns. He said to Graeber, "Get ready! Shoot when we pass astern of Column Three . . ."

Graeber nodded, sighting through the night binoculars mounted atop the target bearing transmitter (TBT).

Kammerer remembered his time as a First. It was far more exciting to shoot than to con the boat. There was that eternity between firing and the mushroom of water from the side of the ship, the explosion. The ship would stagger in the water or, in the case of a loaded ammo or tanker, a furious red half-moon would be followed by malevolent black smoke.

As they neared the stern of the third ship in the third column, Kammerer said, "Stand by." He glanced at his watch again, 0056.

There was a distant roar to the south. The *Rudel* had begun, four minutes ahead of schedule. Sound waves traveled quickly, and Coppel heard the roar even before Kammerer heard it. He shouted, "Here we go!"

Snowflakes, the two-million-candlepower mortar charges fired from the merchant ships, lit up the whole starboard side of the convoy like Fourth of July fireworks. Flaming debris fell from the parachutes, exposing both ships and the subs traveling the convoy lanes.

"Tubes one to six ready to fire," came up from below.

Dim white lights in the conning tower indicated that the bridge had control of the firing trigger.

"We're coming up on it," said Kammerer. He looked at the developing low-slung form of the *Galveston*, now backlit by the distant brilliance of the snowflakes.

Graeber shouted, "Open bow tube caps. Target angle right twenty, speed seven, range five hundred, torpedo depth ten. Stand by!"

"Tubes one to four ready for firing!" was the response from below.

A lot of breaths were held aboard the *U-122*. Kammerer withstood the temptation to order Graeber to fire. That was his responsibility, *to a point*.

Cross hairs of the attack binoculars lined up at midships of the shadowy tanker. Graeber called out, "Mark!" Gears in the computer rotated, digesting the information fed to it. Two red lights went out, telling Graeber, OK. Another light went on, indicating that the firing settings were being relayed to the torpedoes.

Graeber took one last look at the *Galveston* and shouted, "Tube one, fire! Tube two, fire!" He instantly pushed the button on the TBT. The *U-122* jerked twice. The eels were on their way.

Kammerer began counting aloud, "Twenty-two, twenty-three, twenty-four . . ."

Two separate explosions cleaved the blackness in the middle of SC74B. Then came a larger one as the *Galveston* erupted in red-and-black boiling flames. Shock waves swept across the bridge of *122*. Ears rang.

Kammerer let out his Tarzan yell. It would have pleased Johnny Weissmuller, the Hollywood chest pounder. Kammerer shouted, "Hard left!" to settle on a course straight up the columns, between Four and Five. Cheers rose from below.

Rapid-fire steering orders from Kammerer to the helmsman were blurted out.

+ + +

The *Galveston* heaved sideways. The twin explosions, almost simultaneous, were followed by the agony of shearing steel, then the thunderous roar of fire. At the same instant, the ship's whistle jammed and screeched.

The force of the explosions knocked both Sully and Captain Ewing to the deck. Pudney, holding on to the big wheel, was still on his feet.

The urgency to stay alive took over Sully. He got up and pushed the alarm bell while Captain Ewing, from his knees, rang down the engine-room telegraph. *Stop!* Red glare and black smoke filled the bridgehouse. One of the torpedoes had hit directly below them. Fire would likely envelop the structure within minutes if not seconds.

Coughing, Ewing shouted, "Stand by to abandon ship!"

Pudney was still grasping the helm.

Sully jerked him away from it, yelling, "Put on your survival suit."

The boy seemed dazed. Sully slapped him. "Do it, goddammit!"

Sully followed Ewing to the port wing, looking aft. The welldeck was ablaze. Flames were already twenty or thirty feet high. The other torpedo seemed to have hit just forward of the engine room.

Ewing shouted over the roar, "I don't think we can save her." He went back inside to phone the engineers, ordering an all-hands abandon.

Sully lingered a moment, trying to shield his eyes from the glare and spot the bow lookout. His vision was walled off by the fire and thick smoke. He returned inside to hear Ewing say resignedly, "The phone doesn't work ..."

Fire mounted the stairwell from the decks below, and Sully

thought he heard screams. The other mates and radio operator lived down there.

Captain Ewing said calmly, "Save yourselves. Now! Pudney! You, too, Mr. Jordan." He seemed strangely at peace with himself.

"You're coming, too," Sully said. "We can launch the starboard boat." There wasn't that much time, and they both knew it. Ewing nodded, saying, "I have to get my papers," moving toward the chart room and his sea cabin, disappearing into the oily smoke.

Sully shouted to Pudney, "Go out!" The young helmsman went out the starboard doorway.

It seemed to Sully that he'd been waiting for this moment all night, all week. He reached for his survival suit, reacting as rehearsed—spreading it open, right foot in, then the left, zipping it up tightly to his neck. The cork life jacket, with its waterproof light and referee's whistle, was by the door where he'd placed it night after night, ready to be scooped up. There'd be flotation in the suit from trapped air, and the jacket was extra insurance.

As he zippered up he remembered the *Tuttle*'s Chief Logan saying, "If you've got fire on the water jump into the discharge stream." The strong flow from the engine room would buffer the burning oil on the surface. "Then slide on back into the wake and try to stay in it. You may get fire on both sides."

Oil from ruptured tanks often caught fire and spilled into the sea, turning it into a cauldron. With a ship still making headway and moving like a giant torch, burning ribbons sometimes went five hundred yards astern. The engineers always tried to close down turbines after torpedo hits, but momentum could drive the hull another half-mile. Sometimes they failed to stop the propeller.

Sully knew the *Galveston*'s main discharge was on the starboard side well aft of No. 9 cargo tank, midway of the main engine room. He'd spotted it the second day aboard.

Hearing the roar and then the eerie and continued blast of the jammed ship's whistle, he knew what Ewing knew—the *Galveston* was finished. Even if they could get the fire out, ships weren't towed in North Atlantic sub waters.

He looked into the chart room and shouted for Captain Ewing—two times, three times—then broke into a spasm of coughing. Smoke was dense inside there. He turned back toward the bridge-wing doorway and stepped outside into the inferno, realizing that Ewing had no intention of leaving his ship.

He glanced out into the ship lane and saw a U-boat moving along, a big yellow-and-black leopard on its conning tower. The look lasted no more than half a second, a movie stopframe, but he saw it. Then a cloud of black smoke from below erased it.

+ + +

The *Galveston*'s pyre passed on the starboard side. The stench of her burning oil swept over the bridge of the *122* in hot waves, but Graeber was already concentrating on the other big tanker ahead, lining up to send a pair of torpedoes into the *Malay Prince*.

At the bow station, the *Torpedomaat* readied two greased reserve eels for insertion into the vacated tubes. They were on the rails, with block-and-tackle chains to lower them into place.

"Nice shooting!" Kammerer shouted. Usually, there were as many misses as hits. His opinion of Graeber suddenly elevated.

Star shells burst on the port side of the convoy. Then the closer parachute flares turned night into day to reveal the U-boat with the snarling leopards as it raced up the next to middle lane. Faces on her bridge were chalky white, with a reddish glow cast over them from the *Galveston*.

A fountainhead of oily smoke soared four or five hundred feet in the air from the tanker. Swords of flame came out of its base. Secondary explosions sent showers of fire skyrocketing upward as individual tanks blew. Yet the *Galveston* plowed on, roaring like a blast furnace. Kammerer looked at it in awe. "Get the other tanker, and we'll pull the plug!" Kammerer shouted to the First.

Roughly midway between the stern guns of the merchantmen

in both Columns Three and Four, the *U-122* was an easy target once they recovered from the surprise of the attack.

Graeber already had that in mind. He proceeded with the business of sending two torpedoes toward the *Malay Prince*, quite agreeable to having the *122* plunge under, the safest place of all.

The gun crew of the ship on the port beam of the *Prince* had collected themselves. The four-incher at its stern spat out a long tongue of flame, water erupting on the starboard quarter of the sub a few seconds later.

"Shoot, dammit!" Kammerer yelled to Graeber. "Before they get the range!"

He could hear other distant explosions from *Gruppe Dresden*.

Graeber hurried the process and finally yelled, "Tube three, fire! Tube four, fire!"

The *122* jerked again as the missiles left the boat, and Kammerer shouted, simultaneously, "Close tube doors!"

Alarm! Tauchen, dive, dive . . .

The alarm bell echoed throughout the hull as the bridge watch dropped down through the hatch. The first lookout barely got out of the way before the next man's boots hit the deck, almost beating the prescribed $1\frac{1}{5}$ seconds to clear the ladder.

Kammerer was last man down. He dogged the hatch shut. The main vents to the sea were opened. Diesels stopped. Electrics took over.

Speaking quietly to the two hydroplane operators from his post in the central control room as the boat slid downward, Fromm watched the depth and trim gauges. He'd already compensated for the firing of the first two eels and was in the process of compensating for the second pair when the dive order sounded, an order he'd anticipated. Eventually he'd add or pump out water by the gallon in the trim cells fore and aft to stabilize.

"All hands forward, all hands forward," came over the loudspeaker. Everyone without a duty post ran toward the bow, the weight helping the *122* to dive.

Air whooshed out. The boat began to glide under. Shells dropped on either side of the wash.

The bridge watch began to take off their heavy weather clothing, hearts still pounding. A lucky hit could cripple the boat at this vulnerable time.

✛ ✛ ✛

Wider tongues of fire licked out of the black smoke that rolled over the *Galveston*'s flying bridge as Sully reached the starboard boat deck. Another explosion on the port side, probably No. 4 outboard tank, sent flaming oil high into the air. He jumped back. He couldn't see Pudney. Maybe he'd gone overboard?

Sully looked aft. Fire was on the water over the entire left-hand side of the ship and over most of the main deck. The wooden planking of the catwalk blazed. The only route to the afterhouse was along the starboard side. Even there he saw pools of fire, some flowing into the scuppers and on overboard like trails of crimson icing.

Out of the corner of his eye he thought he saw movement on the starboard bridge wing and turned just in time to see a figure in a red survival suit climb the rail and leap, disappearing over the side. Congreve!

Another deafening explosion, further aft, sent a volcanic eruption high into the night. He made up his mind. Useless to stay longer!

He couldn't see Congreve, Pudney, or anyone else in the water, though the fire lit the night blood red. Still looking aft, he knew it would only be minutes until the starboard side was also totally engulfed.

He took a deep breath and jumped, remembering as he plunged down that he'd forgotten to take the stupid hot-water bottle, with the license inside, off his desk.

Bobbing up, breaking surface, and flailing with his arms to push away burning oil, Sully slid along the side of the ship. He kicked to hold himself near it and be carried back to the discharge stream. Seconds seemed like an hour before he reached the eight-inch outfall and ducked under it, allowing himself to be floated along in the warm flow into the wake of the ship.

The *Galveston*'s propeller no longer turned, though the ship still moved. There was no danger of being sucked into the blades. Right now, all he was thinking about was being picked up by the rescue ships. He hoped they were still back there, hoped they'd see him. He turned on his light and realized how tiny it was.

The night sky had first been turned crimson by the blazing, exploding *Galveston*. Now it was dazzling white.

The ship passing to his right—it had to be the *Exporter*—looked pink in the glare. It had turned, following convoy procedure, to steer around the *Galveston*, its tubby big bow no threat. As it passed he saw white faces staring at him from the stern gun tub.

Nothing seemed real as he floated along. It was as if he'd been dropped into a fiery surreal seascape of dazzling aerial snowflakes, star-shell bursts, and the boom of depth charges. He felt the concussion thuds, though the nearest charges were going down a thousand yards away.

In a moment he became aware that the survival suit was leaking. Cold water gathered around his feet. He wondered if the suit had been gashed.

And for the first time since the *Galveston* had been hit, he thought about Maureen and the kids. His chances of ever seeing them again weren't too good at this moment. The rescue ships would have a lot of customers.

Suddenly there was a shout behind him. Another bobbing light. He kicked that way and soon saw Congreve's pumpkin face and walrus mustache. In a few minutes a third light was seen. It belonged to Pudney.

Gasping in the chop, taking icy water in the face, they clung together. At 0150, all three men were caught in the *Dimmock*'s starboard boom net. The rescuers, holding on to the webbing with one hand, grasped them firmly. One shouted, "Ye're safe, mateys."

✛ ✛ ✛

The *U-122* was rigged for silent running. Just the submersion called for quiet, a welcome respite from the surface sounds. The big electrics in their casing of white enamel whirred softly.

Coppel, a blond sliver from Mannheim whose long legs had trouble fitting under the sound bench, had heard only one *boom* on the hydrophone loudspeaker, as did the whole crew.

Looking over at Graeber, Kammerer said, "Goddamn, we missed one ..." The First shrugged apologetically as Kammerer waited for the boat to level at thirty meters and then said, "Bring her up to twenty."

Three hits out of four wasn't bad at all.

They were almost abeam of the *Malay Prince* when the slender sighting mechanism projected from the water. Kammerer rotated until he could focus on the tanker. "Christ, you got her in the engine room! Lot of smoke coming out of the afterhouse. She's dead in the water. Stand by five and six ..." He'd try with the stern tubes.

Thick black smoke rolled down to the surface and suddenly hid her from view. He cursed again. He could gamble and fire into the smoke, possibly making a hit. But the eels were much too precious. Already in this initial strike on the convoy he'd wasted one.

Just as quickly, a fat bow emerged from the smoke. Another ship, a big freighter, had swung wide of the *Malay Prince*, going around her according to convoy procedure. She lumbered up on the *122* at her best speed. He could shoot down her throat, but the ideal angle would be on her port side, just forward of midships.

"Come left twenty," he ordered the helmsman.

In a moment, the necessary firing data, with the constantly changing settings, were being fed to the torpedoes.

"Go, go, go," the torpedo petty officer was saying, confirming that the data were being accurately transmitted.

Another ten seconds and Kammerer said, "Fire five ... Fire six."

A few more seconds and the boat shuddered, as usual, when the tubes were emptied—that sexual act that came to mind.

Finally Kammerer let out his Tarzan yell as the familiar sounds of steel grinding, shearing, and collapsing came over the hydrophones. Cheers went up again as Kammerer watched the big hull go down by the bow like a fighter going to his knees after a knockout punch. Headway drove water into the pair of gaping holes on the port side. It might take a while, he knew, but she'd sink and wind up ten thousand meters below. He gave a "well done" to the crew, lowered the periscope, and dropped the boat to a safer depth.

Kammerer said to Graeber, "We'll stay where we are, let the convoy pass by, then turn around and go after that crippled tanker. End her days forever ..."

Graeber nodded agreement.

"After that we'll go north, flank the convoy at five or six klicks, contact Remus, reload, and give everyone a little rest. Then get ready to hit it again."

Graeber nodded soberly again.

Kammerer sometimes thought of him as the "great sobersides nodder."

"And I think I'll go after that flagship tonight. I believe I spotted her yesterday afternoon, those Aldis lamps blinking message after message."

"The flagship?" Graeber repeated. He disapproved; obviously he didn't like the idea of going back into the center of the convoy.

Now it was Kammerer's time to nod.

He continued to have mixed feelings about the First. Technically, Graeber seemed to be capable and hadn't made too many mistakes. But there was a flaw in the man's makeup, and Kammerer hadn't been able to figure him out. He might be the first to break under interrogation in the remote possibility of the *122*'s capture. Better to go down with the boat, Kammerer thought. If the British managed to take survivors, a man like Graeber might well talk. But providing there was time, and if he himself were still alive, there were ways to prevent it. A Luger was in the safe.

"Yes, the flagship, Graeber."

At first light, Kammerer was examining the scene through the attack periscope: the *Malay Prince* was still afloat, and it appeared she might not be crippled after all. She was making headway. Two or three knots. The little rescue ship was closing in on the tanker. They were both within range.

He turned to Graeber. "How do I get two at once?" There was that mirth again in the brown eyes.

"That wouldn't be easy, Herr Kaleunt."

"Come now, we have this computer that is supposed to do wonders. Figure out the exact triangulation I need to fire two separate torpedoes almost simultaneously, each hitting a different target. I'd go down in the Dönitz record books, wouldn't I?"

"You would," Graeber agreed.

"Oh, well, I'll just take the tanker. I'll have to be satisfied with it, Graeber, won't I?"

"I think so, Herr Kaleunt."

As Kammerer had promised, the *U-122* killed another freighter before dawn.

"Do you know Shakespeare?"

"I had him in school."

"There is a line in the *Merry Wives of Windsor*: 'to bathe in fiery floods or to reside in thrilling regions of thick-ribbed ice ...'"

Graeber waited.

"That is the position of this exalted tanker now, between fire and ice." With that he turned back to the attack periscope and lined up the cross hairs to kill the *Malay Prince*.

Graeber's look said, This man is mad.

Thirty-six seconds later, two torpedoes struck the *Prince*, one forward of the midship house, one aft. A sheet of flame rose four hundred feet in the air.

✛ ✛ ✛

Five hours later aboard the *Faulknor*: "Asdic to bridge. I think I have a target at one-four-zero degrees. Range fifteen hundred yards ..." It was midmorning. The Asdic had been in a listening rather than pinging mode.

"Bridge to Asdic. You may be hearing the Flower class." Screw cavitations were possible.

"Asdic to bridge. Range to the corvette is more than fifteen hundred. I think I have a sub. She's turning faster than any ship out there."

"Bridge to Asdic. Hope you do. Give her the ping treatment."

The skipper of the *Faulknor* ordered general quarters to be sounded. The gong on the twenty-two-hundred-ton destroyer, painted in blue-and-white arctic colors, rang out. "Set depth charges at 150 feet." That was standard depth for the initial attack with the six-hundred-pound "ash cans" dumped over the stern.

The Asdic operator began echo ranging, seeking beneath the surface, reaching out for the target five degrees at a time: Ping and then wait for an answering echo. Ping again and wait. He was searching from 120 degrees through 180 degrees.

"Asdic to bridge. Contact. One-four-five!"

"Bridge to Asdic. Sensational. Get me range."

Ping-echo. Ping-echo. Ping-echo.

"Asdic to bridge. Range eleven-hundred-fifty closing ..."

The *Faulknor* suddenly jumped full ahead.

✛ ✛ ✛

At forty meters, Kammerer could hear the Asdic impulses bouncing off the hull—*tsst, tsst, tsst, tsst*—and then Coppel said, "I'm getting fast screw beats at zero-four-zero." Soon Kammerer could hear them without electronic aid.

A submarine is never ready to take a depth-charge pounding insofar as her men are concerned, but she's remarkably capable of surviving unless forced too deep.

Kammerer said quietly, "Let's go down another sixty meters."

He didn't need to say, "Stand by for depth charges." The crew already knew what was about to happen, even the nine hands on their first patrol.

Soon, the *122* was at a hundred meters, her propellers just ticking over, just enough to keep her moving and level. Old-timers were sitting down or lying down. They'd quickly put on felt slippers. No one was talking.

The first pattern exploded overhead, hitting the boat like giant fists. They were slamming, maul-like blows. They made *woopp* sounds, delivering what the enemy hoped would be knockout punches. Every inch of the *122* quivered. Light bulbs shattered. Glass tinkled on the deck. Loose parts crashed. Metal sawed and creaked. The boat was in agony. Ten *Wasserbomben* were counted.

Kammerer braced himself in the control room and quietly ordered course changes: "Twenty port ... thirty starboard." He listened as Coppel called off the position of the hunting destroyer. The pounding continued for fifteen minutes and then stopped.

He moved to the sound room, staring at Coppel. The soundman, his brow creased, eyes intent, and ears straining for the slightest sound from above, slowly shook his head. Nothing. The cat was quiet. Sometimes the enemy would stop engines and drift, hoping the U-boat commander would think the fight was over and surface.

After a few minutes of inactivity from the surface, Kammerer retired to his commander's nook, sprawling out on his bunk. In stockinged feet he read some more of *Donnerberg*. There was little he could do at this point except go deeper. But he didn't think the destroyer would stick around too long, not with the convoy moving ahead. The best thing he could do, as usual, was to show calmness to the crew. Everyone off duty had also bunked down per orders. No walking about, no dropping of a wrench, no talking.

Kammerer hoped that the fast-moving layers of water of different temperatures would create a sound barrier over the *122*.

It was as quiet as a cave, with only the stalactite dripping to be heard from the bilge. The ventilating system had been shut down, and every natural rotten smell of the boat was intensified.

The second pattern was closer. The *U-122* bucked and rolled, and anything not tied down crashed to the deck. Instrument glasses broke. The few pieces of crockery not properly stowed shattered. Lockers came open.

The destroyer was very, very angry, Kammerer thought. If she weren't on escort duty, she'd stay out here for a week to wreak vengeance. He got off his bunk to step to the control room. He quietly ordered all electrical equipment shut down except the hydrophones and gyrocompass.

He said to Dörfmann, who had the watch, "Mum's the word," then smiled briefly and went back to his bunk.

When he was a First on a five-hundred-tonner, stubborn destroyers had stayed above them for sixteen hours, throwing down canisters every ten or fifteen minutes, forcing them to a depth below five hundred feet. By then, they were all breathing with *Kalipatronen*, the air purification apparatus that absorbed carbon dioxide. After the attackers departed and she surfaced, the air in the boat was greenish yellow, stinking of sweat, urine, and fear. On that patrol the second watch officer had gone insane, poor fellow.

Between the explosions outside the hull, he heard sobs and guessed that one or more of his new men had cracked. Then he heard Lang, who'd made seven or eight patrols, berate the culprit, calling him a coward. It was not a time for sympathy. Though few men were capable of it, the best thing to do was to go to sleep during attack.

A half hour later, after another pattern had been dropped, causing a leak forward, Coppel announced, "She's going away," and there was wild cheering stem to stern. Kammerer yelled, "Quiet!" and then waited another hour before he sent the *122* cautiously to the surface. He stayed at periscope depth to take a look around, then broke clear into early-afternoon light. Engines half-ahead, he set course to follow the convoy again and recharge batteries. "Just for that discomfort we'll *sink* their exalted flagship tonight, eh, Dörfmann?"

"Yessir."

A few minutes later, he sent word to Lorient that the *U-122* had destroyed four enemy ships, two of them tankers. He was now approaching a hundred thousand tons and eligibility for the Knight's Cross; he knew that Dönitz would reply with congratulations. Half a dozen Kalbe channels, depending on time of day and season, were always open exclusively to U-boat traffic. Nothing was too good for the men of *Befehlshaber der Unterseeboote*.

Then Kammerer got on the loudspeaker to say, "Crew of *U-122*, we will share some champagne with the evening meal. Well done, all hands."

A little later, *BdU* radioed *Gruppe Dresden*, "Bravo. Dranbleiben. Weiter so." Hurrah! Keep it up!

Meanwhile, with a coffee cup at his elbow, Kammerer was at the wardroom table writing the war log, putting down the attack times and courses, conditions, and details of enemy counterattack. There were logs for almost every function of the boat, intently read in Lorient when the patrol was over.

✢ ✢ ✢

The *Dimmock* had plucked fourteen men from the Death Hole. Nine were now in the crew's messroom in various states of aftershock; of the five in the ship's hospital, two had third-degree burns and were not expected to live.

They'd all had a shot of brandy, had taken hot showers, and

had dried off. They were clad in Royal Navy seaman's issue and bedroom slippers, still not certain they were alive. Some sat in an almost catatonic daze.

Pudney said, "I saw the sub that got us." He'd been first to leap overboard. "He crossed over behind us and went up the starboard side. There was a big snarling leopard on the conning tower." He looked over at Congreve. "You see it?"

The gunner shook his head.

"A bloody big leopard, I tell you, plain as day. You see it, Mr. Jordan?"

"Yes." He'd seen it. He was still in a daze, but he'd seen it.

"I thought subs attacked underwater. That one was on the surface, bloody bold. I even saw the men in the conning tower before I jumped. There was one in a white hat. It looked like he was beating his chest. It got that close to me."

Bloody big leopard was right, Sully thought.

"Some fuckin' picnic," said Congreve. "I never got a shot off an' lost all my gunners."

The *Dimmock* had taken up station again and plodded along behind the convoy, waiting for the next onslaught. The *Southern Gem* had picked up seventeen survivors from other ships, retrieving eight in her boom nets, nine with her rescue boats.

More than either Pudney or Congreve, Sully was still stunned by the swift savagery of the attack. Though his feet and hands were no longer numb from exposure, he felt completely benumbed. What had been a living, breathing ship was now a funeral barge if still afloat; more than fifty sons, fathers, and grandfathers were all likely casualties, snuffed out by the second or third explosion, if not the first. There were only three *Galveston* survivors so far as he knew.

Pudney went from table to table, asking, "You see the sub with the leopard on it?" He either got blank stares or shakes of head.

After a breakfast of sausages and eggs, which Sully ate halfheartedly, he was shown to a bunk. Sinking down on it, he mercifully fell asleep thinking about Captain Roger Ewing and the grandkids he'd never see again, and about Maureen and his own children.

✤ ✤ ✤

As the customer departed, Hélène Dussac turned her attention to Sister Cecile, who was browsing over in the religious section. Approaching her, Hélène said, "Could I be of help?"

The nun turned. "I was looking for Heinrich Boehmer's *Luther and the Reformation*."

"I'm sorry. I don't think we have that one."

"I hear it's a very interesting work."

"I'm really not familiar with it," Hélène said, wondering what had occasioned this visit.

Sister Cecile again looked carefully around the store to make certain no one else was present, then said, "Our friends across the channel need information that may sound trivial to you—as it does to me. Yet they say they need it."

"What kind of information?"

"Anything to do with the shore activities of the U-boat officers and crew."

"I don't understand."

"I'm not sure I do, either. But they gave me an example—if the crew of *U-220* plays the crew of *U-440* in soccer at Quiberon, they want to know the score and who made the goals."

Hélène frowned. "For what reason?" Was she being asked to risk her life to report on athletic events?

"I don't know. They gave me other examples. A birthday celebrated. The news of a child born in Germany, especially anything to do with the officers."

Hélène shook her head. "How do I gather such information?"

"I don't know. You'll have to find a way. I can only think they're building dossiers on personnel for a reason."

The bell on the door rang as another customer entered, and

Sister Cecile said loudly, "Thank you for your help." She made her way to the front of the store and out.

Hélène was baffled as the nun retreated.

✝ ✝ ✝

She met Gobelins at Bar Raphael the next evening, still uncertain of herself and needing support. As usual Raphael's place was smoky and noisy.

"I have no idea how to do it." She'd told him about the strange request.

"Sporting events?" Shaking his head, he said, "I wish the bastards were using swords on each other."

"Birthdays, babies . . ."

"Have they gone crazy? You fight these people with a gun and knife. The way they fight."

"Sister Cecile thought they were building dossiers."

"I don't know what a dossier is. Only you college people know those big words."

"It's information."

Gobelins sighed. "It's necessary, I suppose. You know, I understand when they do things directly. They drop those leaflets from the bombers telling the U-boat sailors how to get extra leave. Pour sand into bearing grease. Those things make sense to me, but the name and date of a bastard's birthday doesn't fight the war . . ."

"Maybe this is part of that psychological warfare we hear about?"

Gobelins shrugged and sighed. He took a long drink of Raphael's house red wine. "I have a friend in Quiberon, and when I ask him to find out who won the soccer game between those bastards he'll think I've lost my mind."

"But you'll ask him?"

"Yes, I'll ask him."

LATE MARCH 1941

Bootsmann Lang had worked since dawn to retouch Rudmann's large leopard, scrubbed by wave and wind. The eyes and teeth needed some dabs. The faded body required a coat of orange. There wasn't time for the smaller leopards on either side of the conning tower with the paint that Rudmann had left behind. It was purely a matter of *U-122* pride that the bold symbols of combat success look as much like the original as possible. Lang had volunteered for the job.

Kammerer had notified Operations two days ago of his estimated arrival time in Lorient harbor. He now moved toward his rendezvous with three small *Räumboote* to escort him the last miles along the controlled approach. Booms spread as they sought any deadly eggs the British might have dropped. Approaches to Lorient were also mined by the *Kriegsmarine*. Sweepers were there to guard against self-destruction.

Rust-streaked and salt-encrusted, with her dark blue undercoat showing in places and green algae in spots along her main deck planking, the *U-122* would eventually motor slowly past the Citadelle, the ancient fort on the south bank, go through the narrow opening in the antitorpedo nets, and enter the harbor.

Two hours later, red-eyed, bone weary Kammerer was on the bridge with his watch officers, all as bearded as he was, all as tattered and scruffy as the crew. The enlisted men and petty officers were lined up on deck for the welcome-home ceremony, their moldy sea overalls stiff, grimy, and smeared with oil. Seven weeks in the rocking metal tube had exhausted them. Their faces were gray from being locked up. Dark circles were under their eyes. Some of them had not been up in fresh air since late February. For everyone aboard it was the first time in three days that they could stand in the open in complete safety.

A chill breeze flapped the red-and-black swastika, whipped the "kill" pennants that were now proudly displayed on the halyard strung from the extended periscope. Over forty thousand tons of merchantman had gone down on this patrol, easily qualifying Kammerer for the Knight's Cross. Nineteen torpedoes had been expended.

Soon, brass-band music was caught by the wind. The decibels wavered as they reached out for the conquering sailors. Kammerer said, "You know I always feel dead-ass coming home until I hear the music; then something happens. I get a spurt of energy from it."

Bauer said, grinning, "It just happened to me."

Graeber conned the boat, its diesels idling, as the clouds played a game with the sun overhead. A fine morning for arrival. No pesky bombers up there today.

There were shouts from the deck as the spirit of arrival caught on. Every man on board knew what wild times awaited ashore. First mail call, then some would head back to Germany and loved ones on the *Zug*; others would head to the *établissements* in the red-light district. Either way it was great to be alive. They would get thirty days leave!

Quite a few of the French people were surprisingly friendly, especially those who provided services, and Lorient, along with Saint Nazaire, was the most popular liberty port. The officers tended to inhabit Club Chez Elle, where the ladies of the night wore better dresses and more expensive perfumes but performed in a manner identical to those at Club Casino.

Soon, cheers rang out from the large crowd on the quay to which the old landing barge was tied.

✣ ✣ ✣

In a double-breasted, gold-buttoned longcoat of gray blue leather, Dönitz made a striking straight-backed figure. *Der Löwe* usually greeted returning boats personally, along with the flotilla staff and other officers in port—heartfelt camaraderie of brothers-in-arms. There was some cause to rejoice each time a boat returned intact.

Another *Gruppe Dresden* boat had come in the previous afternoon, its victory pennants announcing twenty-six thousand tons. Other *Dresden* boats had gone into La Pallice, Saint Nazaire, and Brest.

Dönitz nodded toward Kammerer, saying to Godt, "I think he'll be almost as good as Prien." The late Günther Prien had sunk the HMS *Royal Oak*, 895 dead. He was a national hero.

The chief of staff agreed. "With a little more experience."

Dönitz said, "I think he's just as smart and ruthless, a good man at tactics. He's aggressive."

"Shall we tell him about the children on the *Castle Innesberg?*"

BBC foreign-language broadcasts had made certain the world knew about the 106 children who had perished aboard the *Innesberg*. The British were using the incident for propaganda.

"Certainly not. Let his flotilla commander tell him. If he wants to discuss it with me, fine," Dönitz said.

The headquarters band was well into the Bavarian stein song, tubas oompahing the rousing *trinken* line. The admiral always wanted the arrivals to be light and carefree and departures patriotic. The crew of the *U-122* would be doing a lot of swilling as well as fornicating over the next month ashore.

Standing beside the band were *die blaue Mäuse*, pretty hand-picked secretaries imported from the Fatherland to take dictation during the day and sometimes spread their legs for the officers at night. Usually the "blue mice" were from good families and hoped to land a *U-boot* commander husband.

Next to them the nurses from the military hospital were lined

up, always assigned to meet incoming boats. They were holding
hothouse bouquets and smiling widely. Behind them were the
short-skirted hookers from the waterfront brothels. They laughed
and waved to the crew members and made sly remarks about the
blaue Mäuse.

Dönitz allowed the whores for morale purposes but was growing more and more concerned about them as security risks. Sooner
or later he knew he'd have to fence off the docks.

There were still and newsreel photographers present to record
Kammerer's being awarded his medal. All of Germany would
now see the boat with the snarling leopard, an idea that pleased
Kammerer immensely. Radio reporters were there with micro-
phones.

The *U-122* finally came alongside the crowded barge, and lines
were made fast. Graeber called down, "Finished with main engines!" Kammerer dropped from the conning tower and jumped
to the landing stage; he saluted and said to the admiral, "Sir,
U-122 has returned from patrol."

Glancing up at the nine triangular white kill pennants, Dönitz
said admiringly, "You did well." Beginning with the *Castle Innesberg*, there were eight more ships that had been attacked. Kammerer hadn't been able to identify two of them, but he had
estimated their size and tonnages. The pennants flapped.

Kammerer replied, "Thank you, sir. We could have used more
torpedoes."

He meant it, the admiral thought. He really meant it. Kammerer was indeed like Günther Prien.

Dönitz went aboard, saying, "Heil, *U-122*," to which the crew
shouted back, "Heil, Herr Admiral."

Then Dönitz shook each officer's hand, briefly addressed the
crew, and finally awarded the Knight's Cross to Kammerer. The
citation scroll that went along with it listed the tonnage of enemy
ships he'd sunk to date, something nice to take home to his father.
The Hamburg *Doktor* lived vicariously through his son's patrols.

Throughout the short ceremony, Kammerer's face remained

impassive as if what was happening to him was simply just and overdue. He had sunk more than a hundred thousand tons after three patrols. He'd earned the medal the hard way.

Though Kammerer was thinking of the decoration while the admiral's flag lieutenant placed the broad ribbon from which the Knight's Cross dangled around his neck, he was thinking more about leave: a few days in Paris at The Claridge, a quick trip to Hamburg on the *Zug* to see his parents, and a stop in Rotterdam to buy a big homecoming bouquet.

First, a long, hot freshwater shower at the Beauséjour. The thick beard would come off. Then the traditional homecoming dinner for the officers and crew at the *préfecture* at about six. After that, the crew would invade the bars, get sodden drunk, sing, and have their fill of girls. Kammerer was more interested in soapsuds and fresh linen for the time being, and a night's sleep without worrying about British escorts and the Sunderlands.

There was a routine for returning boats: dinner with the admiral and a few staff members, submission of the patrol report followed by a flotilla debriefing, and another conference after the report had been studied. Three or four days of procedures, then leave would begin.

As the flag lieutenant stepped back the admiral said, "Dinner with me tomorrow night, but I want to hear about the tanker kills now."

In the gray Mercedes on the road back to the château, Godt remarked, "Arrogant fellow. Did you see his face while he was being awarded the medal? His expression was 'I deserved it.'"

Dönitz looked over at his chief of staff. "He did deserve it. That's another thing I like about Kammerer. His arrogance and basic cruelty. He's a winner and a survivor. Give me a hundred like him, Eberhard. And a hundred new boats! We'll win this war despite Hitler and Goering! We'll force England to the peace table, I promise."

The next morning, in his dress uniform, the Knight's Cross around his neck, Kammerer posed in front of the conning tower by the leopard, for the customary formal photo. He was not smiling; he was grinning.

✛ ✛ ✛

"I just got in. I'm in New York ..."

Sully was calling from his room in the Hotel Henry Hudson, on West Fifty-seventh Street, where the company had put him up until the *Tuttle* arrived at Bayonne. She'd loaded in Caripito and was en route to Ambrose Channel. Traffic noises came up from the street below.

"You're safe?" Her voice was almost a whisper.

Maureen was using the phone in that dark hall at the Wilsons. "You're all right, Sully?" She sounded as if she couldn't believe it, as if his was a voice from the dead.

"Sure, I'm safe."

"Oh, thank God, thank God. I was so worried. It seems like I haven't slept in a month." She sounded relieved yet suddenly angry, too.

"I'm fine, I really am."

"Sully, for God's sake, you've been gone seven weeks! I heard nothing! Where did you finally go? Why didn't you call me?"

"Didn't get ashore, hon."

"I even called Consolidated Operations and asked where the *Galveston* was. They said she was at sea. That's all. That's all they'd tell me. Just at sea ..." Now she was almost in tears. "You've been with them five years; you'd think they'd tell me ..."

"I know, I know. Everything has to be secret with them nowadays. Pretty dumb."

Meddlesome wives were always a pain to Operations during peace or wartime.

"You sure you're OK? I kept having this feeling I'd never see you again."

"I'm OK. I'm sitting on a bed waiting for you to come up and get in it, stark ass naked ..."

"Where'd you go, Sully?"

She wasn't listening.

"Iceland. We went to Iceland." While deadheading back from England as a passenger on a Moore-McCormack ship, he'd had time to figure out what to say to Maureen. "Place called Halfjordure or something like that. Just a miserable anchorage. We pumped out offshore. Nobody got on the beach." He figured that telling her the truth would only cause more worry.

"You sailed in one of those convoys?"

"Hon, I'll tell you all about it. Now, listen to me. *Listen!* I'm going to be here five days until the *Tuttle* comes in, and I want you to come up. Do you understand? Take the kids to my mother's and then catch the train. Do you have any money?"

There was silence for a few seconds; then her voice changed as the anger vanished. "Are you serious?"

"Yep, I want you to come up here." He asked her again about money.

"Around thirty, I think." Suddenly she was excited and happy.

"OK, borrow fifty from my papa. Tell him I'll send it back with you. I got a bonus for that run."

"I've never been to New York, Sully. You know that?"

Sully laughed. Of course he knew. They'd gone to Miami on their honeymoon and later had a weekend in Washington. Otherwise they hadn't traveled anywhere together except a tanker ride when she got pregnant with Danny. Who had money to travel in the depression? "Now's the time," he said.

"I can't wait to put my arms around you. We won't leave the hotel." She sounded like the Maureen of old, the sexy one before the kids.

"Oh, yes, we will. We'll take in a play, go to Radio City Music Hall, even the Rainbow Room ..."

"Where's that?"

"On top of the RCA building ..."

"Oh, Sully . . ."

"There's a train out of Cape Charles at nine in the morning. Be on it." A ferry connected Norfolk to the Pennsylvania line on the Virginia cape.

"I have to do my hair, get packed. No nightgowns . . ."

"That a threat? Hug Danny for me. Tell him I'll see him soon enough . . ."

"We'll have four days together? Four nights . . ."

"I promise," he whispered.

✛ ✛ ✛

"I feel ridiculous even talking about this," Gobelins said. "*U-102* played *U-503* in soccer at Quiberon and *U-503* won, five to two. The leading scorer for *U-503* was named Aufhammer, and the scorer for *U-102* was Haupt. I'll spell them for you." Hélène was writing the information down.

"Leutnant zur See Fechner, *U-189*, had a birthday. He was twenty-four . . ."

"How did you find that out?"

"The baker who supplies the Beauséjour . . ."

"Spell *Fechner* . . ." Gobelins did so.

"Matrosenhauptgefreiter, what a mouthful. That means Leading Seaman Eckhardt, of Erfurt, has a new son. He's on the *U-702* . . ." Hélène looked up.

"That's it. And I'll be goddamned if I'm going to do this again unless someone tells me what it's for."

✛ ✛ ✛

Sully remembered the first time she'd wanted him to come ashore, just after Danny was born. They were sitting on the front porch in the swing, in summer. War hadn't even started.

"Can't you come ashore and work?"

"Do what?"

"I don't know what. Work on a harbor tug."

"For twenty a week?"

"They pay captains more than that, don't they?"

"I don't have that license, and those guys hang on to their jobs. Tug master for life. Then they pass it down, like harbor pilots. Father to son."

Then when she was pregnant with Julie, she'd talked about the war.

"Get a defense job. Go to work in the navy yard. They won't draft you if war does start."

"And sit on my ass here at home?"

"There are worse places. Yes, sit on your ass here at home with us. Safe! I don't know any tanker widows, but I don't want to be one, Sully." She had a point. Now she was coming to New York, and he planned to talk about it—finally talk about coming ashore.

✠ ✠ ✠

An amused look was on the face of Lieutenant Commander Ian Fleming as he sat in the chilled studio at Milton Bryan, near the village of Woburn, waiting for the first *Deutscher Kurzwellensender Atlantik* radio broadcast to begin on shortwave bands 30.7 and 48.3, which were almost the same frequency as the broadcast from Munich.

Fleming had taken the train to Brighton, coming by car to Woburn to hear this latest counterintelligence trick of NID 17Z, his own contribution toward defeating the enemy.

The studio was on the first floor of the brick building in the gentle Sussex countryside, a fine place for foxes and hounds. Local residents were curious about what went on inside the closely guarded house. Why the barbed-wire fence and the patrol dogs at night?

They might have been shocked to learn that several collaborating German prisoners of war resided there to read scripts in their native tongue. Authentic German dance-band music would be played for the pleasure of *U-boot* crews. "Vicki," the daughter of a Jewish playwright from Berlin, was the new sweetheart of the flotillas. She would broadcast the chatty personal news and gossip to those who wore the *U-boot* badge, inviting them into her bed.

Not far away at Crowborough was a powerful six-hundred-kilowatt transmitter standing by to inaugurate the *Atlantiksender*, a variety programme that would hopefully sound like it had been blessed not only by *der Löwe* but also by Dr. Goebbels himself. The "talent" had been rehearsing for two weeks.

Nearing 1900 hours central European time, the director, a former BBC employee, murmured, "Stand by," to the engineer, then pointed a start finger a few seconds later. A switch was flipped on the console, and the turntable began to spin with a snappy dance tune, which sounded as if it were being played by a Berlin ENSA band.

Then the director cued a former radio announcer from Hannover, who was captured recently while sweating with General Rommel in Africa. Albert Dietrich said, in flawless German, "Good evening, brave comrades of the Kriegsmarine, especially those serving in our glorious Unterseeboote. We bring you nightly music and news for your enjoyment wherever you may be ..."

Fleming understood very little German but was following the English script.

There was music, news, and finally romantic "Vicki" with her birthday and birth announcements, and personal chitchat for the "dear boys under command of the great Admiral Dönitz ..."

When *Deutscher Kurzwellensender Atlantik* signed off, Fleming was visibly pleased. He said to the director, "My only suggestion is to actually call up a U-boat at sea and play them a special request tune. Have the lads in Winn's shop tell you when one has sailed, wait a day or two, then dedicate a song to it. It'll drive Dönitz crazy."

✝ ✝ ✝

Sully couldn't remember Maureen ever having made love with such urgency, such abandon. They'd held hands in the taxi from Penn Station and kissed at every stoplight, and again in the elevator to the fourth floor. Maureen had almost been frantic to take off her clothes. She dropped them where she stood once they reached the room. She took off her glasses and suddenly looked beautiful.

Sully was slower; meanwhile her tongue probed hungrily into his mouth and licked his lips as her hands tugged at his belt and jerked at his shirt. Finally she pushed him to the bed half-undressed.

She kept saying, "Kiss me, kiss me," then covered his mouth before he could respond. Her fingernails dug into his shoulders. Her hips were already rotating, her bare skin on fire.

Then she rolled over, spreading her legs. "Do it, Sully, do it, oh, please do it . . ."

What had happened to turn this usually mild woman into a writhing animal? He entered her as a low muffled cry, almost a moan, escaped her lips.

In a few seconds he heard a different cry and knew she'd climaxed already, something she seldom did.

Then she breathed out, "Don't stop; please don't stop . . ."

And Sully, who had been stunned by his wife's ferocity, took command of her body. Maureen met his thrusts with tiny noises of pleasure. In a moment he climaxed; then she followed. He stayed atop her, momentarily spent, his cheek against hers.

Breathing heavily, she finally said, "I thought you were dead. I really, truly thought you were. I thought you'd drowned out there . . ."

"Hush."

"You don't know what hell I went through."

"Hush."

He dropped his mouth to a breast and circled it with his tongue, then went to the other side.

"I'm getting hard again."

"Do you need help?"

"Not tonight," he said and kissed her breastbone, the hollow of her throat underneath her jaw, and finally her mouth.

The lovemaking that followed was longer, gentler, and sweeter than any they'd ever had before.

"I didn't tell you the truth, Maureen. I'm sorry. I knew where that ship was going, knew she'd be in convoy. I knew she was going to England but didn't want to worry you."

Their heads were on the same pillow.

"I guessed that, Sully, and that's what made it so bad."

"And I didn't tell you the truth last night when I said we'd gone to Iceland."

"Where did you go?"

"We were torpedoed. After a few days at sea, I knew it was going to happen."

"Oh my God. The ship caught fire?"

"Yes. At a place called the Death Hole."

"Men were lost?"

"A lot. Nine survived. I was one of them. Six of the black gang jumped overboard the minute we were hit, and a rescue ship got them. Then three of us went over later, and another rescue ship got us ..."

He felt her shiver. "Everyone else was lost."

"I really feel sorry about the captain. I got to know him a little. Seemed like a wonderful man; he showed me pictures of his grandchildren. He was retired but came back to sea when his son was killed ..."

"The poor families," she said.

Sully nodded in the darkness. "I went on to England, was checked out in a hospital, and then they put me on a freighter."

"Why didn't the company call me when they knew you were safe?"

"They say the navy put the lid on."

"You were in the water?" she asked.

"About twenty minutes. If the rescue ships hadn't been there we all would have been fish bait."

"I'm glad you weren't burned. That's my fear."

His laugh was hollow. "Mine, too. No, only my eyebrows were scorched a little. They've grown back."

"Tell me exactly what happened; I have to know. I swear that thing they call telepathy was going on between me and that ship. I can't remember what night it was, but I woke up, heart pounding, thinking 'Sully's in trouble . . . '"

So he told her exactly what happened in the Death Hole. And while telling her he finally realized the extent of his own fear. He'd always had a true sailor's respect for the sea's power and rages, but until now he'd never been afraid of sailing tankers.

Maureen was totally silent as he spoke, but when it was over she finally asked, in a voice so small and thin that it seemed to come from a child, "Did it teach you anything, Sully?"

"Yeah, I thought I had brass balls before going on that ship. Now I know mine are just as soft and human as the next guy's."

Maureen's silence said more than words.

"That sub had a big leopard on the conning tower that looked like it was leaping. About two weeks later, deadheading back here, I had a dream. Guess what it was."

"You saw the sub again?"

"That damn leopard was chasing me along the railroad tracks back of the house."

Maureen said, "Sully, you've got to come ashore."

"I know. I'll finish this year out, then put in an application at the Navy Yard. I think I can be a rigger. That's what most guys try to do if they come off ships and go to work in the yard. I won't worry about the draft."

Maureen fell silent again.

"I'll make about the same, I guess, unless they take me as an apprentice. But we'll get by. We may have to put off renting a bigger house . . ."

She finally spoke. "Will it be hard to leave the sea?"

"Won't be easy. That's all I've done for fifteen years. I breathe it, I taste it."

"Are you doing this just because of me and the kids?" Maureen asked.

"I'm doing it because of me. I don't want to be burned alive, if you want the honest truth. That may happen to a lot of sailors over the next few years. So I'll take four or five more coastal trips and keep away from ships going across the pond ..."

"And?"

He laughed. "Screw your brains out three nights a week at 5 Vail Place."

"I'll go for four some weeks, maybe five ..."

✢ ✢ ✢

Godt closed the door to the admiral's office and said, "I learned they began broadcasting three days ago. They call the program Atlantiksender, and it's aimed at our bases, specifically for U-boat personnel."

"Does he sound like a German?"

"Absolutely. You'd think he was from Berlin."

"What does he say?"

"Gives the soccer scores here, names the boats, then slips in damaging information. There's a woman with a whore's voice who calls herself Vicki. She said Folkers of the *189* celebrated his nineteenth birthday and announced that a son had been born to a leading seaman on the *173*. Both true! That authenticates it. Last night the announcer said that you were most pleased with the broadcast ..."

"Where do they get the information?" Dönitz asked, sounding alarmed.

"I have no idea," said Kapitän Godt. "Informants, of course. But they give all these details, and you think for a minute that it is one of our stations, either at home or here in France. The music is German. Then this gossip is followed, very cleverly, by propaganda of one sort or another."

"What kind of propaganda?"

"Steel is inferior in boats coming off the ways and will disintegrate at 150 meters."

The admiral's frown widened.

"Yesterday he said that we were having trouble again with torpedoes and that four boats had been blown up when the eels homed on them."

"What?" There'd been a crisis with faulty torpedoes sometime back. Not now.

"He also said that the Royal Navy had a listening device so sensitive that a man's sneeze can be heard at a hundred feet. Imagine the enlisted personnel, if not the officers, hearing that kind of information spoken by a German . . ."

Dönitz said angrily, "Two things. One, we court-martial anyone who listens to that transmitter. Two, I'll call Canaris." Admiral Canaris was head of *Abwehr*, armed forces intelligence. It was of no use to call Himmler. The Gestapo would bungle it.

✛ ✛ ✛

The old brass bell on the door of Lorient Livres jangled. Hélène, at the counter, looked up to see that a young German soldier had entered. One of the garrison troops, she thought. He stood looking at her, hesitantly. A nice-looking boy, maybe twenty. That had been the hardest part, seeing boys near Christian's age.

"Yes?"

In faltering French he asked if they had any books translated into German.

She shook her head. "No."

Then he asked if there was another bookstore in town, or that's what she thought he asked.

"No."

He nodded and departed, obviously disappointed.

Max Goff would have just as soon made his store home to sewer rats if he had a choice between rats and *Deutsche* editions. Max had been gassed in the other war and was Jewish.

They carried some French translations of American writers such as Sinclair Lewis, Hemingway, Steinbeck, and Faulkner; translations of Italian authors Pirandello and Deledda; Norwegians such as Undset; and Shaw and Galsworthy from Britain. And of course, the works of many French writers, from Belgian Maeterlinck, Gide, and Gergson, to Albert Camus. But absolutely no Germans, not even Thomas Mann. If Max hadn't been seventy-four years old Hélène thought he would have joined Georges Gobelins in the *Résistance*.

Since the occupation a surprising number of enemy soldiers and sailors had come in to browse and ask for translations. Surprising to her, not to Goff. He said, "No, they've always been readers. It's not what they read, it's how they think." She knew many Germans appreciated literature as well as music and other fine arts. They were complex people.

About twenty minutes later the old brass bell sounded again, and Hélène looked up to see an officer entering. He looked to be in his early thirties. Hélène recognized the insignia and caught her breath. U-boat commander.

Smiling, he said, "Do you have Henry Miller's *Tropic of Cancer*?" He spoke fluent French.

Startled, she couldn't hide the instant hostility in her voice. "I'm sorry, we don't have that book in your language."

He continued smiling. "Mademoiselle, I read French as well as speak it. My mother is French, born in Auch, not far from Toulouse."

She said stiffly, "In that case, we have Henry Miller's *Tropic of Cancer*."

"May I purchase it?"

"Yes, of course." Her voice was purposely ice laden.

She felt his eyes follow her as she went to the shelf where American writers were displayed. As she returned, she knew she was blushing and looked away from his gaze.

"Do you know Miller?"

"I've read him."

"What do you think?"

She lifted her eyes. "He stands for liberty and freedom."

"So I understand. Don't we all?"

He was quite handsome, she had to admit, and his French was excellent.

He paid, tipped a finger to his hat, and departed, saying thank you and good-bye with a friendly smile.

Hélène remained silent as she watched him go and felt glad that she'd had the courage to say, "He stands for liberty and freedom." Gobelins would have been proud of her, she thought. Max Goff and Sister Cecile, too.

Then she raised a finger to her mouth. Wasn't she supposed to cultivate a German officer now? One had just walked into the store, and she'd done everything except kick him in the rear.

He returned the following afternoon, the friendly smile seeming just as genuine as the day before. "I stayed up most of the night reading Miller and was amazed that an American writer could handle sex so openly. I thought only we Europeans could do that. Don't you agree?"

Hélène, trying to be pleasant, smiled slightly. "I haven't thought about it."

He said, "Maybe we could discuss it sometime over dinner?"

"I'm very busy."

"Day and night? Even Sundays?"

"Day and night and Sundays."

He shrugged. "Well, perhaps I can find someone else who has read Henry Miller."

"Perhaps." Sister Cecile had said to be reluctant, yet Hélène was guessing that this officer would return, and next time . . .

"Do you have his *Tropic of Capricorn?* That's his latest, isn't it?"

Hélène nodded and again walked toward the shelf of American writers. His voice followed her. "You know, Henry Miller lived in Paris until rather recently."

Hélène turned. "Yes. He went home when Paris was occupied." Again, she couldn't resist.

"I doubt he'll write as well at home. Do you agree?"

"I haven't thought about it."

The officer laughed. "What *do* you think about, Mam'selle? Or maybe I do not want to hear that answer."

Though his smile was warm, there was a disturbing arrogance in his strong face and in his bearing, but that was a hallmark of high-bred Germans, wasn't it?

He paid, smiling wider than ever, and said good afternoon, again tipping that arrogant Nazi hat, with its eagle at the peak over the circled swastika and lip of gold braid on the brim.

He returned again the following afternoon at about three, saying he'd enjoyed *Capricorn* but not as much as *Cancer,* and asked for a biography of Jean-Paul Marat this time.

At that silly request, Hélène laughed. "The revolutionist who was murdered in a bathtub by Charlotte Corday?" she asked.

"Oui," said Horst Kammerer, straight-faced. He'd seen Marat's head, with a knife plunged in, at Madame Tussaud's.

"I don't think anyone has ever written a whole book on Jean-Paul Marat."

"I don't think so, either. Will you have dinner with me tonight at the Beauséjour and talk about him? Or any other place you name."

Hélène shook her head. "I'm sorry. I can't be seen on the streets or in any café with you."

Horst introduced himself, then said, "I understand. Do you live alone?"

Hélène nodded.

"Well, I'll come to your place, and we can talk. I'll bring food and wine if that would not insult you."

Hesitating again, but thinking of Gobelins and Sister Cecile, she finally said, "Tomorrow night."

She wrote down the address on rue le Coutaller, handing it to him. "Eight o'clock?" It would be dark by then. "I look forward to it, Mam'selle . . . ?"

"Hélène Dussac."

"I look forward to dinner with you."

As he departed, she knew positively that this was the boat commander she had to cultivate. Sooner or later she'd send him to his death, along with his crew. She thought of Christian again and that terrible day on town square, transposing the peach-hued skin of Kuppisch to that of the smiling officer who'd just walked out. But was she capable of causing *any* death?

✝ ✝ ✝

She told Sister Cecile that she'd finally made a contact. In late afternoon she bicycled to Gobelins's house. She wondered if she could pull it off. Already she was frightened.

The cottage on the road to Nantes was old and made of stone; it had probably looked neglected well before the war began. There was evidence from empty geranium boxes that a woman had once lived there. Weeds grew in the small yard, and there was a maritime junk pile in the back, of rusting anchors, boat tackle, and rotting nets.

Hélène sat down on the stone step and waited, thinking of what was expected of her.

At about six, Gobelins rattled up in his old truck. He swung off it and grinned at her. "Allo, allo." He came over and gave her a hug.

"I need to talk, Georges."

"I always like to talk to pretty girls. I can't tell you what a treat it is. Come in, come in . . ."

He unlocked the door, and she followed him in, looking around. The open kitchen was along one wall. The furniture was ancient. There was a smell of fried fish, fried onions, and fried potatoes. Claud had lived here with his father after the death of Gobelins's wife. A male smell dominated his home.

Hélène said, "Some Sunday I'll come by here and clean the place."

Gobelins said knowingly, "It's held together by cobwebs."

He turned on the gas burner. "I'll make some tea."

"I'm having dinner with a U-boat commander tomorrow night, and I'm scared to death."

Gobelins looked around. "Hmh. How did it happen?"

"At the bookstore. He came in three times, and this afternoon I agreed to invite him for dinner. I'm afraid I'll tremble—my mouth is already dry and my heart is pounding."

Gobelins nodded. "I don't blame you, but it might not be so bad. You must try to act natural, as if you were entertaining a Frenchman you'd just met. Don't try to charm him. Don't go to bed with him. Be beyond his reach for a few nights. Don't ask him anything about what he does ... not yet."

It was the same advice given her by Sister Cecile. "But will he see through me?"

"Not if you don't want him to. I think all these swine want companionship and they'll do almost anything to get it. Remember, French girls have a reputation around the world."

"He's half-French. He speaks the language fluently."

"Hmh. That may make it easier."

"I keep having doubts," she said.

"About yourself?"

Hélène nodded.

"You know how tough Tramin was—on the outside?"

She nodded again. Tramin had been executed in mid-March for an act of sabotage.

"Do you know he had doubts too, big ones? He kept asking me if I thought he'd give in to torture if he was captured. Would he tell on me and others? I told him, 'Tramin, if any man on earth would break, it would not be you.' When he was caught, after that silly fire bombing, they took him to the commissariat and gave him the 'charbon pelle.' Do you know what the 'coal shovel' is?"

Hélène shook her head.

"I was told he had to kneel on the end of a shovel blade. Then the blade was forced under his kneecap. Reach down and press the area under your kneecap. Do you have any idea of the pain Tramin endured? Yet he didn't speak. He went to his execution without saying a word about Duphot, Laennec, me, or you! Here was a brave man who had doubts. All of us do."

"Georges, I'm no Tramin," she said hesitantly.

His palms went up. "Look, all of us are human. Some will break, some will not. Don't think about it. Think about how heroic it is for ordinary people to fight back in their own way—teachers, nuns, bakers . . ." He smiled and added, "Fishermen and bookstore clerks."

She took a deep breath but didn't return his smile.

"Drink your tea, and let's talk about Tramin and Christian, Jean, Claud, and the reasons why we are doing this . . ."

She nodded and they talked a long time.

Finally feeling better, Hélène kissed his rough cheek.

"Good luck to you," he said as she climbed back on her bicycle.

✛ ✛ ✛

Hélène said to Kammerer, "Why don't you sleep with prostitutes like the others, or go to the whore bars?"

"I've never had to go with prostitutes. I meet girls like you in Hamburg, Berlin, and Paris. We have dinner, and enjoy each other," he replied quite confidently.

"Why me?" she asked.

"You're lovely; you're intelligent."

"That's not enough. You're all a bunch of bastards."

Kammerer kept smiling. "But I'm a nice one."

Hélène's look said that she was keeping her opinion to herself.

"I've talked to my friends and neighbors about what you've done—you've taken away our town from us, made us prisoners, killed our men . . ."

"I'm a professional military man. I was trained for this. I take my orders. I do my job and ask very few questions."

"But why Lorient?"

"We were trapped in the Baltic, and the North Sea is England's lake. We needed room to sail straight out into the Atlantic and save over four hundred miles. Your coast has given us that room. I hope we can give it back to you soon."

"All I see are drunken sailors. And drunken officers, too."

Kammerer nodded. "Do you have any idea what it is like to serve in a U-boat? Any idea at all?"

"I know it's dangerous."

Kammerer looked at her for a long moment, took a drink of wine, and said slowly, "It is no more dangerous than sailing on a ship until you meet an enemy destroyer. Then the danger is almost unthinkable."

Hélène waited. "Go on."

"I'm not sure I want to go on."

"All right." She shrugged.

"It's usually only the first few nights ashore. They get wildly drunk and go with every woman they can find—get it out of their systems. Then they go home on furlough, see their families, and return here for a different kind of drinking and lovemaking. The few nights before we sail are usually quiet. They know they might never get drunk or make love again. They think about it."

"Why do they stay in the U-boats?"

He took a while to answer. Finally he said, "Because we are special men and know it . . . and because of the thrill of sinking ships . . ."

Soft light turned her pale skin into a flawless ivory cameo. Her dark eyes examined him. She was trying to understand this man she hoped to kill. At this moment she would have made a fine model for Delacroix's *Woman Listening*.

But abruptly he said no more about U-boat sailors. "Ah, enough of that. Let's talk about Henry Miller or Paris or French food ..."

"You don't like German food?" she asked.

"Not at all. It's dull, tasteless, fattening ..."

"You prefer our food?"

"I'm half-French, Hélène. I'll remind you of that."

Not that it will do you any good, she thought, but she nodded just the same.

"My favorite place is a small one in Saint Germain, Café Geneviève, just by Cour de Commerce where Marat had his printing press and Dr. Guillotin lived in a loft ..."

"Marat again?"

"... it belongs in *Le Trésor Gastronomique de France* ..."

"I don't go to Paris nowadays."

"Well, you must dine at Geneviève sometime. I'll take you. Start off with a plate of snails in an emulsion of snail butter and puree of mushrooms and cream, then a scallop of salmon combined with sorrel ..."

Hélène had not had such a meal in almost two years but kept her composure. Nazi pigs, all of them, she thought.

"You know quite a lot about the French menu."

"I think so. The other dish I like there is the tiny medallions of lamb, topped with a thin vegetable crêpe placed around a traditional Provençal vegetable casserole. With that, you have a fine cabernet sauvignon ..."

"Have you had those dishes recently?" she said.

"A week ago."

"The war hasn't reached Geneviève then?"

"Hardly."

Hélène was wild with anger.

She did not sleep with him that first night. Nor did he pressure her. The third night, after five glasses of wine, she let it happen and enjoyed it. By then she knew the number of his boat; he'd told her the story of his Knight's Cross and how many ships he'd sunk; he'd even given her a framed print of his photo taken with the leopard by the *122*'s conning tower.

Two days later he sailed for patrol in the South Atlantic, though he didn't tell her his exact destination. But he had said he hoped to enjoy some sunshine rather than storms, a careless remark.

The same morning she took a long walk with Sister Cecile in the convent garden and told the nun everything she'd learned to relay to the OIC in London, especially the "sunshine" information. The photo of Kammerer in front of his leopard would be copied for the benefit of the sub identification section and sent to the British embassy in Lisbon for forwarding in a diplomatic pouch.

Just before Hélène went out through the old gate, Sister Cecile said, "Several months ago a British ship bound for America with many children aboard was torpedoed. All of them were lost."

"It was on the radio," Hélène said.

"I'm sure your German friend didn't know they were on that ship. I wonder whether or not it would have made any difference."

"Kammerer sank it?"

Sister Cecile nodded. "The British have made him a priority target. Your work has added importance even though they don't know who you are."

✝ ✝ ✝

Sully was back aboard the *Tuttle*, under way for Texas. He talked about the *Galveston* the first day or two in the saloon but then found he didn't want to talk about it anymore.

He'd joined the exclusive club of Captain Ryti and Chief Logan after being torpedoed. He was now regarded differently on the *Tuttle*, he knew. He could sense it, see it in the eyes of the crew.

They all wondered what it was like to be on a blazing tanker, and go overboard in frigid water.

Matkowski, unable to listen in the saloon, had asked about it on the first watch out of New York.

"It was a funny thing, Ski. I was scared shitless until it happened. Then it happened so quick I didn't have time to be afraid. All I had time for was to try and survive ..."

LATE JUNE 1941

From the bed in Hélène's upstairs apartment, Kammerer could see himself in the bureau mirror. After two weeks ashore, all the weariness from another patrol had departed his face. He now liked what he saw. He'd always been blessed with those good genes from the raven-haired lady from Auch and the handsome *Doktor*. He'd rightfully inherited their basic good looks. Beneath the eiderdown, he was as naked as the morning he'd entered earth, and he knew what couldn't be seen of him was just as pleasing. He had a trim, hard muscular body.

Hélène still had a radio—he was supposed to report her but had no intention of doing so—and the plaintive voice of Piaf was coming from Paris. Why not take Hélène to Paris on the train, hear Piaf in person, then make wild love to her in The Claridge? But he knew she wouldn't go as long as he was in uniform, and he had no civilian clothes at the Beauséjour. All of his civvies were in Blankeneese. He reminded himself to have a suit sent to Lorient.

She still refused to go out to dinner with him, even to the See Kommandant. The new German restaurant catered to U-boat officers and specialized in steamed lobster. She'd said, "Believe me, I can't be seen with you. The Résistance would kill me."

Kammerer now spent most of his nights in the small apartment on rue le Coutaller while the *U-122* crew rested and the boat itself was prepared for the next patrol. Food was bait, he knew. The occupying force had the first pick of everything that swam in the sea or stood on feet. He never came empty-handed. He often brought chicken, ham, smoked sausage from Guemene-Scorff, a bottle of Muscadet, or one of Gros-Plant.

She emerged from the bath sedately in a wrapper and went to her dressing table. She rubbed her head with a towel. Another woman was singing from Paris, and Horst asked, "Why are your songs always so sad?" He turned the radio off.

"They're thoughtful, not always sad," Hélène replied without looking over at him.

He studied her. She was petite, and her delicate unblemished skin was unlike that of overstuffed German women. At times, depending on the way the light struck her, she looked fragile. Yet there was nothing frail about her. Simply, she was small and weighed less than a hundred pounds. But the wiry childlike body seemed to erupt when they made love, draining and exhausting him. He almost thought she wanted to hurt him. In fact, she *had* hurt him. But his grinding explosion inside her offered the same sexual thrill he got from blowing up tankers.

He watched her dry her dark hair and drop the wrapper, and show him that doll's body.

She said, "I was insulted again yesterday while walking to work."

"Who insulted you?"

"Three of your bastard sailors. They made gestures and remarks. No naval police were in sight, as usual. And if they were they wouldn't give a damn."

"On behalf of the sailors, I apologize. I've told you before that they are blowing off steam."

She stopped the brisk massage of her scalp and turned her head. "Horst, do I look anything like a whore?"

"No. Never. At home, they would think you were a nice-looking girl."

"Why can't they do that here?"

He sighed. "Pressure of war, as I said before."

She stared over at him, her dark eyes big and searching.

"I repeat that U-boat phrase I said the first night I was here—'Eat, drink, make love, be merry, for tomorrow you may be on rocks at the bottom of the sea ...'"

She thought about all he'd told her and finally said quietly, "I hope the war will soon be over and all of you can go home."

"I hope so, too."

It was at moments like these that Kammerer thought he'd fallen in love with this pretty French girl. He knew his mother would approve if not his father.

Hélène arose from the dressing table and went back into the bath to hang up the towel, then came to the bedside. She said, "Turn off the light, and I'll open the window. There's a summer moon tonight." The heavy blackout curtains prevented even a sliver of light from coming out or in.

Horst said, "I'd forgotten about the moon. At sea, I sometimes use it to profile the ships."

She opened the window, letting in the pale shaft, and returned to the bedside again, saying, "The moon is always innocent." She thought of the *Castle Innesberg* and the dead children and remembered the BBC report that it had happened in moonlight. She didn't dare ask Horst about it.

He reached out and gathered her into his arms.

He was an expert lover, she'd learned, skilled with his lips, hands, and words. He was slow and gentle at first, as he kissed every part of her. When he finally entered her, she was always aroused, hungry for him, but still trying to channel her thoughts to Christian, Jean, Claud, and Tramin. She responded freely to Kammerer's heat but tried not to give herself mentally. She tried to tell herself that this was Jean inside her. But it didn't work.

Each time they made love she tried to deny to herself that she enjoyed sex with him. When his fingers were steadily caressing and their tongues were touching, she tried very hard to say to herself that it was purely mechanical, simply a response. Yet she knew it wasn't. When he was inside her and she was rising to meet him, she wanted more and more of him. Making love was to shut out cruelty and death. Yet she also knew that in another time she could have easily fallen in love with this man.

After he departed for the Beauséjour in the morning, she always took a shower in cold water and punished herself by using a hard sponge until her skin cried out for mercy.

✛ ✛ ✛

In Cradock, Danny asked, "Where is Daddy?"

"He's at sea, on his ship," Maureen answered.

"Where at sea?"

"Somewhere off the coast."

"What coast?"

"I'm not sure, Danny. He said the ship was going to Alabama for repairs."

"Where is Alabama?"

"That's a state south of us. Way over on the Gulf of Mexico. I do know that."

"When will he be home?"

"A few weeks, I guess. He has to take the ship into the shipyard."

"Then he's coming home?"

"Yes."

"Will he bring me something?"

"I'm sure he will."

The baby, in the crib across the room, had been making soft whimpering noises for a few minutes. Now she'd begun to cry. It was time for a feed.

"Let's kneel down and say our prayers, Danny."

"What will he bring me?"

"I don't know, Danny. Something nice. Now I lay me down to sleep ..."

Tucking him in, she said, "It won't be too long until he's home with us for good."

Book Three

LIFEBOAT
NUMBER TWO

DECEMBER 1941

The *Tuttle* had engine trouble due to the carelessness of a dozing four-to-eight oiler and possibly needed major parts replaced. Towed the last twelve miles in the Gulf of Paria, she was now anchored in Maturin Bay, at the entrance to Caripito, Venezuela. After her regular summer gasoline hauls from Texas, she was now on the winter schedule to South America.

Caripito was a dusty, mangy-dog oil port in which pigs wandered around unpaved streets and shoeless straw-hatted Indians lived in packing-crate huts. It was the kind of place few sailors ever regretted leaving. Tankers arrived, loaded, and departed as quickly as possible.

"Happy birthday," Sully said, rising from the breakfast table to hug his father on this December 7, 1941.

The Jordans looked quite a bit alike. Daniel was tall, ruddy, and blue-eyed. They had the same crooked, toothy grin.

As a birthday present, Dan was along for Sully's final voyage. Sully would soon be going to work in the navy yard as an apprentice rigger. It was Dan's first ocean trip. He'd retired from "The Yard," putting away his woodworking tools after forty years as a pattern maker.

Captain Ryti, Chief Kalevi, and Bob Cheney had already eaten, as had the engineers and Sparks. Nearing nine o'clock, it was time for One-Name Fong to secure food service until noon.

"I don't feel seventy," Dan said, with his crooked grin.

"You don't look it, either, Papa," his son said as he got a warm feeling from this new relationship. Dan was more of Sully's friend than father. "You've got a good tan; you look ten years younger. Wait'll Mama sees you."

White-jacketed Fong chimed in, "Happy birthday, Mr. Jordan," filling his coffee mug.

Sully said, spooning his cereal, "After you finish, how about we take a quick taxi run into Maturin, celebrate over there. I'll introduce you to goat tacos, let you look at the girls, no touchee . . ."

"Sounds good."

"If I find out we've got to stay here a couple of weeks, I'll take you over to Cumana, a place lots bigger than Maturin. It's my guess we're here for a while. That oiler really screwed up."

"Anywhere at all," Sully's papa said. Maturin was another mangy-dog place, though a step up from Caripito.

"Eggs, pancakes?" One-Name Fong asked.

"Both," Dan said. "Three over-easy."

"You'll get fat," said the flyweight Chinese. He was birdlike, not more than five-one or five-two. His legal name was Fong. He had no other name. He was from Seattle, not Hong Kong.

Dan couldn't figure out Fong. Nor, for that matter, could Captain Ryti or Chief Mate Kalevi or the third, Cheney. Sully had had the same problem when he first came aboard. They'd all been on the *Tuttle* for years.

For a long time, Sully had thought that massive Juho Kalevi, big in shoulders, arms, and belly, was one of those sailors who'd soured on women. He never went ashore. Yet there was a picture of an attractive woman on Kalevi's desk. Curiosity forced Sully to ask, finally, "Your sister?"

"No, girlfriend."

When the ship's mail came in, Kalevi always had a stack of letters from a little mountain town in Virginia. Then Sully found out that he saw her during his vacations and whenever the *Tuttle* went into the shipyard. He wasn't a ship hermit.

Dan had asked about Bob Cheney, too.

"Papa, that old man has a Rockefeller mind." He had stock and bond charts in his cabin. In Bayonne three weeks of the *Wall Street Journal* waited for him. He phoned his broker regularly from the dock.

✝ ✝ ✝

A chief petty officer and two other enlisted men were on Sunday duty on the fourteenth floor of 90 Church Street, in the financial district of downtown Manhattan, headquarters of the North Atlantic Naval Coastal Frontier. So far the day had been dull. The phone had rung exactly once. The Brooklyn chief's wife asked him to bring home bread and milk.

There were top-secret war plans in the safe. "Rainbow 3" had recently been reviewed by the new commander, Rear Admiral Andrew Ames. They projected enemy surface raiding forces; air raids conducted by shipborne aircraft and harbor penetration with motor torpedo boats.

Air raids on New York or Boston? Penetration of the New York harbor by torpedo boats? Come on! Even Ames didn't believe that. Yet all eventualities had to be considered.

Item C said, "Submarine activity may be expected with submarines operating against shipping with torpedoes, mines, and gunfire."

There, that one was realistic.

The teletype, which had been quiet all morning, suddenly came to life just after two o'clock with a Washington message. Chief Yeoman Appleton read the statement with an open mouth.

In his apartment on Riverside Drive, Ames heard the same message over WNEW and yelled to his wife, Eve, who was addressing Christmas cards in the dining room, to call a cab. He was already on his way to the bedroom closet where his uniforms were hung.

A stocky, thick-necked man with silver-gray hair and an Irish barhop complexion, Ames seldom touched the stuff. He'd acquired a reputation as an officer who got things done. He'd been a champion wrestler at the naval academy.

She said, "What's happening?"

"The goddamn Japs bombed us!"

"Where?" Her tone suggested disbelief.

He was in the process of changing his pants. He danced on one foot. "Navy Yard, Pearl Harbor. The sonsabitches. Call Phillips and Reston . . ." Captain Phillips was his chief of staff; Commander Reston was his operations officer.

"If he's home, tell Reston to call all the radio stations. Have them broadcast an order for everyone in the Third Naval District and the North Atlantic Frontier to report to duty . . ."

If the Japs or Germans really wanted to know, the Americans had goddamn *nothing* to defend themselves with, not even a pisspot to throw at them. He had seven Coast Guard cutters, the largest 165 feet, four patrol boats, four old subchasers, and three "Eagle" boats left over from World War I. There wasn't one vessel under his immediate command that an enemy sub operating on the surface couldn't outrun. He remembered that the Germans had sunk more than four thousand Allied ships in the last war. Dönitz could lay his new boats up against Coney Island this time, and Ames would have nothing to stop them.

The story in today's *Times* quoting the Secretary of the Navy was pure bullshit: "U.S. Navy Superior to All."

Within three minutes, Ames knew he'd made his first mistake of the day by taking a cab. At 110th and Riverside he said to the cabbie, "Take me to the subway."

+ + +

Dönitz was entertaining and debriefing two newly arrived U-boat commanders when Kapitän Godt strode into the château's dining room, his face flushed with excitement. On French clocks, the time was 8:45 P.M.

Godt bent over Dönitz and said in scarcely more than a whisper, "Japan has just bombed Pearl Harbor . . ."

"What?" Dönitz said, turning and looking up, stunned by the news.

"B-Dienst has confirmed."

Very matter-of-factly, Dönitz said to his wide-eyed guests, "America is in it now." They'd already overheard Godt.

One said, "That's good news, Herr Admiral."

"Perhaps. Excuse me," said Dönitz, rising, trying not to show his true elation. It would take a few minutes to get over the shock, though this moment had been inevitable.

In September he'd gone to Berlin to meet with Hitler for permission to send U-boats into so-called U.S. waters to harass convoys and be in a position to strike while the American antisubmarine defenses were weak. When he returned to Lorient, angry and frustrated, he'd said to Godt, "The answer was no. He listens to Keitel, Jodl, Göring, but not to Admiral Raeder or myself."

"So nothing has changed," Godt said.

Three months later Dönitz still simmered over that September meeting. What colossal stupidity! It would all boomerang, Dönitz had predicted. Now it had indeed boomeranged at Pearl Harbor, and there were no U-boats anywhere near America.

The admiral moved quickly toward the door. He knew the news would spread throughout the streets of Lorient within minutes. The attack would be greeted with joy by most of the French, he expected. They were a hateful people, anyway. He hoped there'd also be joy in the *U-boot* flotillas. The news would sweep across the Beauséjour, the raucous waterfront brothels, the smoke-filled smelly bars, and the enlisted rest camps at Quiberon and Carnac. He sincerely hoped that the men of the *Unterseeboote* would be challenged.

Dönitz questioned Godt again while they went down the hall to Operations. At the door to the *Lagezimmer* he paused to say, "In one way the Japs did us a great favor. We can now sink Roosevelt's ships. In another way, all those American factories will awaken. So I want to hit hard within the month. If Hitler had only listened . . ."

They went on in.

The minimal night staff was present. Ops was already celebrating as other sketchy reports of the attack came in via *B-Dienst*. There was complete destruction at Pearl Harbor, Tokyo said. Battleships had been sunk, and the navy yard was burning. Dönitz waved his hand for them to stand at ease as the senior watch officer spotted him and brought the staff to attention. The night lieutenant said excitedly, "Sir, they've sunk America's Pacific fleet."

The admiral, moving toward the U-boat status board, chided over his shoulder, "You know better than to believe everything you hear. We all tell lies." As of tonight, the board said that ninety-one boats were operational; fifty-four were awaiting repairs or service. He stared at it.

Then he moved over to the huge map of the Atlantic. He looked at the east coast of the United States, stretching from Canada's Cape Sable down to Key West. He'd studied that long coast for two years in anticipation and knew every contour. While he hated the British, he loathed Americans, especially Roosevelt, without whose help the British would have already surrendered.

Nodding toward the map, he said to Godt, "We'll hit between New England and North Carolina to start the campaign . . ." Looking at the maps was always frustrating for Dönitz. Too much ocean and too few U-boats. The enemy gathered strength each day.

The admiral, with Godt at his heels, crossed the room and went to his office, which was dominated by a large round conference table. Closing the door, Dönitz said, "I want to send twelve IXs over." They were long-range boats like the one Kammerer commanded. Twenty days to make the crossing, one or two weeks patrolling. Add a few days, always, for contingency. Then home.

"I'll begin tomorrow," said Godt.

"No, tonight. I want them under way within a week."

The admiral began to circle the table, thinking out loud as he walked. "I want them to strike simultaneously, all in the same day." He didn't want the first boat to trigger off a trap for the rest. He told Godt that they should be in American coastal waters for all the attacks and avoid contact on the way over. "No matter how fat a target presents itself, they must wait until they get off Boston or New York or Norfolk."

Godt frowned. "Their defenses are weak."

"I'm not counting on it," Dönitz said. "We can't afford to lose any more boats than we're losing right now."

There was no need to remind Godt of the losses. Twenty-six so far in 1941.

With America in action, it would be a matter of trying to sink ships faster than the Allies could build them. Still circling the table slowly, Dönitz said, "I still want them to concentrate on tankers. Stop those tankers coming out of Texas and the Caribbean and we stop their factories. We stop their freighters; stop the oil and we freeze the people . . ."

Dönitz suddenly halted in his path around the table, staring defiantly at his chief of staff. "If they'll give me enough boats, I'll single-handedly force the English to the peace table."

Godt believed him and went off to his own office to begin the night's work of preparing orders for the operations people to implement.

Dönitz went up to the sardine seller's master bedroom and got ready to sleep with a feeling of optimism despite the certainty that America would soon declare war.

✢ ✢ ✢

Sully and his father came back from Maturin at about half past six to find the dining saloon almost empty. The third engineer, McBain, sat at the long table alone, writing a letter.

"Where is everybody?" Sully asked.

"Up in the radio shack," McBain replied, looking up. "Haven't you heard? The Japs bombed Pearl Harbor."

"You kiddin'?"

McBain shook his head. "Go up and listen for yourself." McBain wasn't known for jokes.

Hurrying along the catwalk, Dan said, "FDR'll love this."

"I can't believe it. They came all the way to Pearl Harbor?" Sully said.

Dan said, "I'm not sure I know where it is."

"Hawaii."

They quickly climbed the stairway to the second deck on the port side of the midship house.

Sam Bessemer had never had so many guests in his radio shack. Captain Ryti, Chief Engineer Logan, Chief Mate Kalevi, Third Mate Cheney, Matkowski, Alvarez, the cook; and One-Name Fong.

In the doorway, Sully asked, "Is it true?"

Kalevi turned, nodding. "Sounds like they sank the whole damn Pacific fleet."

"Got two or three battleships," said Logan.

Sparks was copying as fast as the Morse dots and dashes flowed from the Associated Press wireless service. He passed another sheet of hand-scrawl to Kalevi, who read, "Reports of attack are coming in from Hong Kong, Thailand, the Malay Peninsula. Japan has struck on a line that stretches from the Gulf of Siam to Hawaii. Manila has been bombed . . ."

"God almighty, I can't believe it," Logan said angrily. "I'm too damned old for another war."

"So am I," said Ryti.

Sully was still standing in the doorway. He looked into the crowded room and listened intently, feeling anger as well as shock. Dan stood at his shoulder. Sully's mind was on the *Galveston*, ablaze as he'd last seen her.

✝ ✝ ✝

Horst Kammerer burst through the door with expensive champagne under his arm. In one swoop he lifted Hélène up and kissed
her. He swung her around then put her down. "Have you been
listening to the radio?"

"No." She'd been curled up, reading. She hadn't expected him
until later.

"You don't know?"

"Don't know what?"

"America is finally in the war. They were attacked an hour
ago by the Japanese."

Hélène felt like clapping her hands but said, "Doesn't that spell
trouble for you?"

"Not at all. It means that we can now sink their ships on sight."

"Have they already declared war?"

"They will, I'm sure. I was just starting dinner with another
boat commander when the news was sent from Berlin. Operations
called the Beauséjour."

Kammerer popped the champagne cork, then reached into the
cupboard for two glasses.

Soon he toasted, "To the Japanese ..."

Hélène repeated, "To the Japanese," but said silently, To the
Americans ...

No matter the cause, the champagne was good. She asked,
"What will this do to you?"

"I have no idea. But I hope the admiral will send me over
there."

"To America?"

"For two years they've been interfering, doing everything short
of declaring war on us. I wish the Japanese had attacked in 1940.
It might all be over by now."

"But America is a very powerful nation."

"So are we. Now Hitler will have to let us conduct the fighting *our* way. The U-boats can win it. The admiral is convinced of that. So am I. So are most boat commanders." He lifted his glass again. "To the end of the war."

She clinked and then asked, "Does this mean you'll leave right away?"

"No, no, no. We just arrived Thursday, and we'll need at least ten days to overhaul and resupply. I know where I'd like to go. Off New York!"

"Maybe you'll get your wish. Are you still hungry? We have some ham left, and I think there's still part of the chicken ..."

"I'm too excited to eat. Let's just talk, drink, and then go to bed."

She nodded, feeling a different excitement. There was hope now.

✝ ✝ ✝

Admiral Dönitz returned from Berlin the evening of December 11, the day Germany declared war against the United States. The United States reciprocated. As usual after a trip to the *Reichstag* city, he was in a foul mood. At the *Tirpitzufer* he begged the Naval High Command to release *all* long-range boats for the American assault. What good were they doing west of Gibraltar? Smaller boats were more effective for those waters.

"*Six!* They gave me six! My God. They say Hitler wants results, yet they tie my hands."

Godt stood silently in the admiral's office, waiting for the tirade to end.

"And do you know where the boats have to come from?"

Godt decided to let the admiral answer his own question.

"Out of my hat! Like rabbits."

Finally the exhausted admiral went behind his desk and sat down, then looked up at Godt. "We've got three IXs back from the South Atlantic ..."

"Three more will be out of overhaul this week," said Godt. The storm was over.

Dönitz sighed. "There's our six."

"We'll send the best commanders available. Schroder, Mueller, Holger, Langhans, Gergen—"

"Kammerer!" Dönitz interrupted Godt and said it as an order.

"Kammerer, of course," Godt quickly repeated. He was one of the best, Godt agreed. He deserved to go.

"I want them on their way within ten days."

"I don't think that will be a problem, Admiral."

"Try for eight and advise the flotilla commanders. Only on a need-to-know basis. I don't want it to be prattled about in the bars or at the Beauséjour. Only the flotilla commanders and the boat commanders are to know where they're going. Not even the watch officers."

Godt nodded, then asked, "What do you want to call it?"

Dönitz swiveled around. He looked up at the big wall map of America. The coastline ran forever. What would be appropriate? His loathing of all American things demanded a fitting Teutonic code name: something like a spirited bugler's call for a cavalry charge. He thought a moment, then swiveled back to look at Godt.

"Paukenschlag!"

He'd gone to his love of opera. The word meant a roll of the kettle drums; it also meant thunderbolt. Wagnerian. Godt smiled. Typical of the *BdU*. "Paukenschlag."

As Admiral Ames descended the stairs to the L-shaped room on the fourteenth floor, operating headquarters of the North Atlantic Naval Coastal Frontier, he asked Captain Phillips, "Any more phony sub scares last night?"

The chief of staff said, "No, sir. But we sure as hell can expect a couple today." They'd averaged two a day since December 7. This was the thirteenth.

"You think this city is blasé and sophisticated? Hah!" The admiral chuckled as he turned and started down the second flight. His heels cracked on the steel treads. "From the mayor on down, they're all pissing. La Guardia keeps talking about air raids. Our problem is what swims like a Dönitz fish."

They were headed for the morning staff meeting at which the admiral presided. The Joint Army-Navy Control Center was due to start business off to one side of the Ops room. First Air Corps and Northeast Defense Command officers plus Navy types would man it.

Navy Operations occupied most of the space. Ops' plots on merchant ships traveling off the coast were set up to be changed hourly once a system of keeping tabs had been established. All surface patrol vessels would be tracked and changed hourly. All air patrols, kind of a joke this day, would be changed half-hourly. Enemy sightings and contacts were to be changed instantly, updated constantly.

Ames and his staff had been busy sixteen hours a day. As of three days ago, mined areas covering approaches to New York had been established. Incoming vessels secured safe directions from the patrol vessel stationed off the Ambrose Channel entrance. Soon, Chesapeake Bay's approaches would be mined; then fields would be sowed at Boston and Portland. Then the southern ports.

As Ames and Phillips turned into the conference room where the staff waited, Phillips said, "It'll almost be a relief." Sub arrivals, he meant.

"I won't go that far," Ames muttered.

Captain Phillips would have finished his tour in two months, going on the retired list, if war hadn't begun. He'd been privy to false sub sightings for two years, including the one that Roosevelt reported in a press conference in 1939. The sub didn't exist. Fishing captains off New England had been seeing U-boats in their coffee cups since the seventh. All false.

As Ames sat down he asked, "What's the status of the sub

nets?" Steel nets were to be installed at major harbor entrances up and down the coast.

"Three months," said the officer who was supervising the civilian procurement man.

"We need 'em in two!" Then he looked over at the new army air representatives who had reported to the Joint Control Center. "Welcome aboard."

Operating from Westover Field, Massachusetts; Mitchel Field, New York; and Langley Field, Virginia, three AAC B-24 bombers from each field had made two daily sweeps over the ocean since December 9, looking for U-boats but finding none.

"Now we can have a little coordination around here, I hope," said the admiral. "Let me tell you briefly what we face." The sea lanes that ran up and down the east coast and into the Caribbean put nearly impossible burdens on any forces assigned to protect them. They were crowded with merchant vessels that ordinarily sailed alone. Most valuable of all were the tankers. "I can tell you right now Dönitz is licking his chops over these sea lanes. He can't wait to kick the shit out of us, and he has a good chance of doing just that ..." Ames stopped and looked at his navy group. "Any of you seen the figures prepared by ComAirDevlant?"

There were no takers.

"If a submarine sinks two six-thousand-ton freighters and one six-thousand-ton tanker, we've lost ammunition, stores, and gasoline that would require three thousand successful enemy bombing sorties to do the same damage."

Ames let them mull that over for a moment.

+ + +

Hélène Dussac studied the face of Horst Kammerer, wondering if there was any way he could possibly know what extraordinary playacting she had been doing here in the apartment since midsummer, besides in bed.

"Then you won't be here for Christmas?"

"I'm afraid not. I leave next week."

The temptation to ask, What day? Where are you going? was great.

"That's too bad. You Germans have such a wonderful time celebrating Christmas."

He smiled. "We'll have small trees on the boat, drink some wine and beer, and sing some songs."

"You almost sound eager."

"If the boat were ready, I'd be on the way tomorrow."

"Well, I'll think about you Christmas morning out at sea."

"And I'll think of you here in this apartment." He paused. "Hélène, my watch officers know about you. I've told them . . ."

"Oh? What did you tell them?"

"How pretty you are, how nice, how intelligent . . ."

"Thank you."

"You know, aside from what is available in the clubs, none of them have had contact with a local girl. Only one of them speaks any French at all, and it's difficult unless you can speak the language."

Where was this leading? She remained silent but tried to appear interested.

He reached over to take her hand. "As a special favor to me, and to them, would you join us for a farewell dinner at the See Kommandant?"

"The German restaurant?" It was an officer place, she'd heard.

"Tuesday night. I'm having a departure dinner with the admiral Wednesday night. I shouldn't say 'I'm.' He's having the four other boat commanders to the château that night as well. Originally there were six, but one boat can't go. Engine trouble."

"Then you'll sail the next day?" A friendly question. That would be December 17, she quickly figured.

"Yes."

So five boats would depart. To America, she was certain.

Hélène decided she'd need some persuasion to go to dinner. She withdrew the hand.

"I know what you're worried about—being seen with us."

No answer was best.

"I'll pick you up in one of our flotilla staff cars."

Still no answer.

"I'll make sure we have a table in the back ..."

She remained silent.

He shook his head in frustration. "Do you want a screen around it?"

"I'll go," she said quietly. "And a screen isn't necessary, but you do realize the danger." She added, "To me."

"I think that danger has passed."

"Not at all. It will never pass until you leave. There are men here who are ready to kill those of us who fraternize."

"Whether you deserve it or not."

She cocked her head over to one side to agree with him.

✝ ✝ ✝

"Papa, I'm buying you a ticket on PanAm to fly out of Caracas and on to New York. Then take a train home. I'll take you to Caracas."

Dan Jordan refused. They were having lunch in the *Tuttle's* saloon.

Captain Ryti said, "You should listen to Sully. I was sunk in the last war. You don't know how terrible the sea can be. I promise you don't know. Take my word."

Chief Engineer Logan, who'd been sunk 250 miles west of Ushant, concurred. "It isn't any fun, Mr. Jordan."

Dan hung in stolidly. If there was danger, he wanted to share it with his son.

Sully took a deep breath. "Papa, I didn't tell you, but I was torpedoed in the North Atlantic in March. Went overboard in fire ..."

Dan's mouth dropped open.

Sully continued. "You have no idea how bad it can be."

"You? Torpedoed?"

"Nine of us survived out of sixty-two. I wouldn't be telling you except that you're not listening to anyone."

Dan gripped the tabletop. His voice dropped. "I beg you to let me come back with you."

Sully sighed and looked over to Ryti and Logan helplessly.

All this had come up because the company had sent a message that morning instructing Ryti to route the *Tuttle* outside the usual ship track and use a zigzag course north of the Bahamas. He was to make a final check with the British navy in Trinidad on departure.

Two days later Sully was on the bridge deck supervising the swinging out of the starboard lifeboat, putting it into an immediate launch position from the davits and brailing it back against a make-shift spar.

Dan climbed the ladder and asked what was going on.

"So we can launch in a hurry. Now it can drop straight down into the water." Sully looked at his father and added, "We aren't having boat drills! This isn't for fun."

"I know that."

"I'm not sure you do," Sully said angrily, moving over to the port side to swing No. 2 boat out.

Twenty-two feet in length, with wooden sheeting in the bow and stern, the four lifeboats were standard for a ship of the *Tuttle*'s age—six thwarts and a capacity for twenty-five persons. They had the usual equipment: oars, sails, rudder, boat hooks, two axes, two water kegs, sealed tin boxes for provisions, a first-aid kit, pistol flares, and a mirror for signaling. Third Mate Cheney's chores included looking after the lifeboats, and he was diligent about it.

✦ ✦ ✦

As the car drew away from the See Kommandant, Kammerer said, "That was a bad idea."

Yes, it was, Hélène thought. "They were very nice."

"Why did I think they suddenly seemed juvenile?" Kammerer asked.

"The language difference, of course. How could they talk to me? How could I talk to them? But Hans spoke some French."

"Thank God."

During the meal there'd been a lot of smiling and awkward attempts at communication. Hélène wished she could understand the German cross talk. Except for Graeber, they did seem young. Early twenties, Kammerer said. They seemed even younger.

The Mercedes staff car was headed for the harbor, moving without lights. Hélène had not been in a car for months.

"Where are we going?"

"I promised I'd show you my boat. You can't go aboard, but you can see it. We've been loading stores the last two days, getting ready to go."

Hélène said to herself, Try to remember everything you see, everything he says. Don't think of anything as unimportant. Look at everything.

The sub pens were certainly no secret in Lorient. By day they could be seen blocks away, huge gray humps the size of Paris railway stations. By night they appeared to be low mountains against a shadowy horizon.

In a few minutes they loomed in the thin mist behind a high barbed-wire fence; lighted bays exposed the low shapes of U-boats. Everywhere were guards with slung rifles and glistening helmets.

She hadn't been down to this area of the harbor since the occupation began and felt an overwhelming menace from the grayness and the guards' uniforms.

Alighting from the car, they walked to the gate and were passed through. Faceless guards saluted Horst. "Guten Abend, Herr Kapitän."

Kammerer acknowledged them and steered Hélène by an elbow.

A paved roadway with trolley tracks on it was on the left-hand side of the bay. There appeared to be machine shops up against the left wall. Men were inside them at work. Overhead were more tracks for cranes with cables and chains hanging down. From one a steel plate dangled that moved forward.

Straight ahead were six submarines tethered in twos. Workmen moved around most of them. There were sparks from cutting torches. Hélène could see the blue flames of welding torches.

Remember and make a drawing, she told herself.

"We come in here soon after arrival and stay hidden until we leave. Whatever problems there are they're fixed here . . . There's my boat." He pointed.

It was in the second grouping, painted a light gray, with the leopards he'd talked about on the conning tower.

"You see, we're even loading stores at night."

She'd already been fueled and had gone on a trial run, Kammerer said. Ammunition and torpedoes were aboard. She was now taking on dry stores. A lorry was parked on the dock. Sailors carried tins and boxes aboard, stacking them around the galley hatch. Fresh stores would be last, he said. There seemed to be chaos on deck.

"They have to be carefully loaded according to a strict storage plan. If stored the wrong way, we can't keep trimmed when submerged. Worse if they shift. Sometimes I'll go down at a forty-degree angle, and all I need is to have a lot of food headed that way, too."

He pointed out the torpedo tubes, hydroplanes, conning tower . . . anything that could be seen from dockside. She really needed to know where he was going. Look at the other boats, she told herself. A pair of dice on that one, a unicorn on the other.

"Yours seems to be bigger than the one alongside it."

"It is. Frankly, I prefer the standard. It's easier to maneuver and quicker to dive. I didn't know you'd be this much interested."

She smiled up at him. "I've never been this close to a submarine."

"After the war, I'll take you for a cruise in one."

If you're still alive, she thought.

"Had enough?" he asked.

She nodded.

As they walked back toward the entry to the pen, he said, "Tomorrow we'll all move back aboard and take only the essentials."

He still hadn't hinted *where*.

They cleared the gate and got back into the car. Her apartment was the next automatic destination.

Time was running out. Where, specifically, was he going? He hoped for America! Did he know now? She wanted to be precise.

☩ ☩ ☩

Around the oblong table were the admiral, the five boat commanders, and Kapitän Godt plus two flotilla commanders. Usually, the boats weren't advised of their exact operational areas until they were at sea. *Paukenschlag* was an exception.

"Had the Japanese notified us, I would have had twelve boats available to open this campaign, even with High Command restrictions, but I have confidence that you five will have great success," Dönitz said.

"And I forgot something in yesterday's briefing. When possible I want you to direct gunfire at the bridge and wireless/telegraph cabins. That might prevent an SOS or SSS." Chase them off the bridge with gunfire and try to board the ship; recover routing instructions, codes, any confidential papers. "My suggestion is to use the deck gun to good advantage if the target is unarmed. The torpedo is your primary weapon, of course."

Heads nodded.

"Sir, what knowledge do we have of their defenses?" asked Kammerer.

"Very little, and even that is general." He told them that the main Atlantic naval base was in Norfolk but that the Americans had destroyer types in the Boston and New York areas; Charleston, South Carolina; and Key West. They had air bases scattered along the coast, he said. Dönitz didn't anticipate much opposition this early. "Later on, I expect very stiff opposition."

"Are their cities blacked out?" Gergen asked.

The admiral looked at Godt, who replied, "So far as we know lights are still burning. While operating close inshore, you should be able to silhouette targets easily. I talked to Intelligence this afternoon."

B-Dienst had monitored civilian stations constantly throughout the last week. Aside from news broadcasts America wasn't at war.

"Once you arrive you can have dance music on the New York stations."

"I like the band called Tommy Dorsey," Holger said.

There was laughter around the splendidly set table. The sumptuous fare for the night was lobster in a *coulis*, a rich hot sauce; oysters from Ille-Tudy; and *cotriade*, a Breton fish soup. Spirits, appetites, and calories were high on this eve of departure.

"Sir, what is the ratio of freighters to tankers in American waters?" Kammerer asked.

Dönitz said, "We don't know exactly, and it doesn't really matter. The latest ship count we got from New York was fifty departures and arrivals each day."

Norfolk, Boston, and Philadelphia had half that number; smaller ports such as Charleston had five or six a day. "Intelligence estimates two thousand ships a day moving along the coast and in the other areas."

There were surprised murmurs along the table. Schroder said, "We'll have a shooting gallery."

"I hope," said the admiral. "Kapitän Godt will brief you on the routes and assigned areas. I want the *122* to make a reconnaissance of the New York and Norfolk entrances." He looked at

Kammerer. "Go in as close as safety allows before you come home."
He had high hopes for Kammerer.

A large map of North America was set up on a stand, and
Godt went over to it, holding a pointer.

The coastwise shipping lane began in the Saint Lawrence River,
going out into the ocean at Cabot Strait. It went along the coast of
Nova Scotia, passed outside Georges Bank and Nantucket Shoals
to New York. There it was joined by ships from New England
ports that came through the Cape Cod Canal and Long Island
Sound. From New York the lane went south to Cape Hatteras,
with breaks up into the Chesapeake and Delaware Bays, then on
to Florida.

"Gentlemen, I'm offering you a veritable feast," said the admiral, lifting his glass of Dom Pérignon.

✛ ✛ ✛

With his white capcover freshly starched and a sprig of hothouse
camellia in his left leather coat lapel, which he'd received from a
pretty *blaue Maus* along with a kiss, Horst Kammerer stood confidently on the bridge of the *U-122* as she backed down into the
river on her electrics.

The crew members, looking as trim and alert as their commander, were lined up on the deck, save for the engine ratings.
The band on the quay played "Deutschland über Alles." Flotilla
officers smiled and saluted; whores shouted and waved to boyfriends of the past two weeks.

Nothing was more uplifting than stirring band music, superiors
to say good-bye and good hunting, and women to remind the
sailors of what delights awaited them on their return, Horst
thought.

Twenty-two torpedoes were nestled below along with rounds
of 105-mm, plus the antiaircraft ammunition. Food was jammed
into every nook and corner, even filling one of the toilets. Hams

and sausages hung from pipes, bags of potatoes were in nets, bread was in hammocks, and hundreds of tins of vegetables and fish were poked into engineering spaces.

As the boat slid past Île Saint-Michel and came opposite Kernevel, Horst ordered the engines started, aware that Dönitz and his staff were most likely watching from the windows of the château. The admiral sometimes attended the farewell. Obviously he had more important duties this morning; he had to plan other strikes against America. Kammerer nodded across the channel toward the stately building. "He was in a good mood last night. Very optimistic," he said to Graeber.

Diesels coughed and roared. Dark, acrid smoke rolled across the deck, pushed by the light southerly breeze. On each bow were two minesweeps. The RAF had occasionally planted mines in the Lorient area. British submarines had laid them outside. Sweeping operations were constant, and subchasers tried to keep Limey U-boats from having too much fun in the approaches. The *U-51* had been torpedoed last year while nearing home and safety. There'd been other underwater attacks. There was nothing scarier.

"Where are we going?" Graeber asked, his expression indicating he'd already guessed.

Kammerer looked over. "I'll make the announcement as soon as we dive."

Rocking gently in the light swell, the *U-122* motored steadily west. When the buoy line ended at Banc des Truies, the ratings were ordered below to assume duties, excepting the bridge watch. The escorts still plugged along on the forward quarters. The Brittany coastline had begun to fade.

"Enjoy yourself at home?" Kammerer asked Graeber.

The First had gone back to Wuppertal. "I had a wonderful time. You stayed here throughout?"

Kammerer nodded, thinking of the happy nights with Hélène Dussac, and wondered how to persuade her to come back with him to Hamburg after the patrol. His mother was anxious to meet her. His father still hoped he'd marry a German girl.

With the low headland of Morbihan turning gray, the senior escort commander signaled an *auf Wiedersehen* and *viel Glück*; Kammerer replied with a *Danke*, and the little vessels peeled off to return to harbor.

"Full ahead, both engines," Kammerer ordered.

There were a baker's dozen of French trawlers, in rainbow colors, approaching port with the night's catch. Graeber easily conned the boat through them. No greetings were exchanged; the fishermen were always a surly lot in Kammerer's opinion. Well, they'd better get used to our presence, he'd often said. We'll be around for the next century. He glared back.

Thirty kilometers west of Île de Groix, the largest island off Lorient, Kammerer ordered the bridge cleared for the obligatory test dive. Along with Graeber and the lookouts, he dropped down into the pressure hull. The *U-122* soon vanished from the dirty, weed-littered surface of the Biscay. Some nine hundred feet of water was now below her keel. She'd stay submerged, conducting trimming trials until "U-boat Alley," the RAF hunting grounds, was cleared. The boats were required to send a short signal back to *BdU* when they'd safely reached fifteen degrees west longitude. She'd surface at nightfall to recharge batteries.

As soon as she trimmed level, Kammerer got on the speaker system to say, "Men of the *U-122*, we are going to America—" He had expected instant approval. What he got was tumult. The whole boat erupted. He waited as the cheers subsided. Extra combat pay was assured.

"—Along with four others, we have the honor and privilege to be the first to attack American shipping in their front yard. The zone will extend from Boston to Cape Hatteras, in North Carolina. One by one you can all come to this station and look at our chart. We'll operate independently off Hatteras in Carolina. With your help, the *U-122* will kill a dozen Allied ships . . ."

There were more cheers as she groped slowly westward, eventually to take a Great Circle route, the sound of her electrics a pleasant hum within the steel tube.

The next few days would be extremely busy with the usual practice drills for every department on board. Without warning, Kammerer would order deep emergency dives, and "attacks" with the torpedo mates simulating the real thing. All vital equipment would be tested, especially hydroplanes and pumps. A boat that couldn't dive was a sitting target; a boat that couldn't resurface was a coffin.

Though Cape Hatteras was thousands of miles away, he planned to have the *122* in top fighting condition by arrival.

✛ ✛ ✛

Hélène said, "He left a half hour ago along with another one after a big celebration. A band was playing ..."

Sister Cecile said, "I thought five boats were going."

"Not all of them from here."

"Maybe Brest or La Pallice ..."

Hélène shrugged. "I don't know."

"Do you know their numbers?"

"I know his, the *122*. It has that leopard on the conning tower. The other boat has a dancing girl. I watched them go."

"Who commands the other boat?"

"I don't know. For a moment last night he seemed ready to tell me. He was a little drunk and excited. He'd just come from a dinner with his admiral and hinted that he was going far away, then suddenly he wouldn't even talk about it anymore. He said it was a top secret, that not even his watch officers knew. But I'm certain it's America."

Sister Cecile said, "Perhaps London will agree. Did he talk about the dinner?"

"Only to say that his admiral was in a good mood and optimistic about the patrol."

"Think hard, Hélène. When he hinted that he was going 'far away' was there any indication how long he'd be gone?"

Hélène nodded. "He said he'd see me again in seven or eight weeks and tell me all about it."

"That means America."

"He left me at about three o'clock, going straight to his boat. Everyone moved back aboard on Thursday."

"Did you go to the U-boat base?"

"He wanted me to, but I made an excuse. I didn't want to be seen there in daylight. But I watched the boat move down the harbor from the fishing port."

"Anything else?"

"Not that I can think of."

Sister Cecile smiled. "You did very well. It hasn't been so difficult, has it?"

"Sleeping with him has been very difficult. I enjoy it."

The nun's smile vanished.

✝ ✝ ✝

At 7:42, a Bletchley Park teleprinter pecked out a decoded message from Hennebont, via Sevenoaks, Kent: Five U-boats departed from Biscay bases having loaded stores for eight-week operations. One boat had a leopard insignia, another a dancing girl. Destination unknown but agent thinks U.S.A.

As soon as the transmission was completed, the civilian in charge of monitoring six of the teleprinters, which carried messages and intercepts from around the world, neatly stripped the nine single-spaced lines coded from Sister Cecile and walked them over to her section chief for the four-to-midnight watch.

Lieutenant MacPherson, pale as a corpse in the harsh light, studied the wire transmission from Hennebont and said, almost to himself, "They're headed for the United States."

He looked up at the civilian. "Where else?" The civilian shrugged.

"Copy and route this on to Tracking."

From there it would be disseminated routinely and presented at the OIC staff meeting in the morning and then become part of the weekly "Most Secret" Special Intelligence Summary for the First Sea Lord and other higher-ups, including the prime minister, who was now en route to Washington aboard the battleship *Duke of York*. Pearl Harbor had brought about an emergency meeting with FDR.

+ + +

Admiral Ames studied the priority dispatch from COMINCH, new title for Ernest J. King, commander-in-chief of the U.S. Navy, and stared out of the spattered window of 90 Church Street. He was weary. Rain had been falling on New York all night, and the weather was as grim as the blunt advisory from Washington: Five U-boats on their way; more certain to arrive. COMINCH didn't mention the source: the alert warwise Brits, the miserable Limeys that COMINCH so despised.

Ames buzzed his secretary to put himself squarely on formal record and tell ball-buster Ernie King what King already knew. He was totally helpless for the time being. But just in case King or any member of his staff ever forgot that circumstance, Ames wanted it down on paper. *Don't blame the Commander North Atlantic Naval Coastal Frontier when Nazi torpedoes start to hit.* Otherwise, give me defensive ships! Christ, give me destroyers! Ames knew for a fact that there were at least twenty sitting in Atlantic ports, yet King had not ordered them to sea. What the hell was he waiting for?

Matronly Mrs. Jennifer Cinelli, whom he'd inherited from the last commander, thank God, entered with her notebook, asking with a gentle admonition in her voice, "Admiral, did you sleep here last night?"

"Not quite," he replied, pleased with her concern. He'd gone back to Riverside Drive shortly after one, and returned to the office just after seven. He'd rolled and tossed and sighed and beaten his pillow until Eve said, "Andy, why don't you just get up?" It was 5:00 A.M., chill, and wet. She said it sympathetically. He'd looked over at her in the darkness. "A ship leaving Bath, Maine, can be sheltered in Boston before evening. Boston to New York is a daylight run. From New York to Delaware Bay is another day run unless the ship goes like a turtle. Between sunrise and sunset a ship can steam from the Delaware Capes to the Chesapeake Bay entrance, from there south . . ."

"Is that what you've been thinking about all night?" Eve asked.

"Yep." He got up.

"Do I look that bad, Mrs. Cinelli?" he said, cutting short his reverie. He had a meeting at 10:30 A.M.

"No, sir," she said. Then quickly she took it back. "Yes, you do."

"I'll use some Murine. Send this priority back to COMINCH."

Should enemy submarines operate off this coast, this command has no forces available to take adequate action against them, either offensive or defensive.

Mrs. Cinelli wrote the message in shorthand and then asked, "Is that all, sir?"

Ames nodded.

"Is it really this bad?" she asked.

"*Adequate* means the ability to stop them."

Nothing had changed in two weeks, grand declaration of war or not, nor did he expect the situation to change any time soon. Atlantic Fleet destroyers were leaving Norfolk daily for the Pacific. King wasn't about to make them available to defend the East Coast.

"Surely, they'll give *us* help." She was frowning.

Ames smiled slightly. *Us.* She'd been at the Frontier longer than any admiral; she knew more about the inner organization than he did and was privy to twenty years' worth of 90 Church Street. Yes, she was part of the Frontier team, a very knowledgeable, efficient part.

"They can't give us ships they don't have."

He didn't know her exact age but guessed she was in her

midforties; her dark hair was beginning to gray. He knew she had a grown daughter and son. The day after Pearl Harbor she'd announced proudly that Anthony would soon be heading for boot camp. He'd joined up.

"What about the Army Air Corps? First Bomber Command?" she asked.

He didn't want his low laugh to sound wry and caustic. "They don't have the right aircraft, or enough of them; nor do they have pilots trained in antisubmarine warfare. Neither do we, as a matter of fact."

"Why does it always have to happen this way? We're never prepared."

"Well, it's too late to ask Congress, isn't it? They controlled the dollars ever since the last one. Those mealymouthed sonsabitches are interested in only two things—their pork barrels and getting reelected."

She nodded and left the office; her son Tony was likely on her mind.

The admiral arose, put on his raincoat and hat, then went down the stairs to Operations to check with Captain Phillips for any late important messages.

"I've got that meeting with the oil people but should be back by noon. Mrs. Cinelli knows how to reach me," Ames said.

Captain Phillips said, "I thought you were going to try to duck that one, Admiral." His eyes were inquisitive.

Ames nodded. "Better judgment now tells me I may need those barracudas on my side."

Phillips nodded and agreed. The white-haired chief of staff, a submariner, hadn't been tested so far, but Ames already liked what he saw and heard. A good chief of staff went a long way to make a command tick, as did a good secretary.

Ames went out to the elevator bank. If the oil barons wanted to know what plans he had to protect their tankers he'd have to dance on hot coals, then use "security" and say apologetically that he couldn't discuss defensive measures. Hell, he didn't know exactly what to say to them. That's why he'd told Phillips he'd like to duck the meeting. Ames wasn't in the habit of lying.

The staff driver was waiting; he saluted smartly and led the admiral outside into the downpour. Off they went, fighting the usual wet-weather traffic toward midtown.

☩ ☩ ☩

Late in the afternoon, Admiral Dönitz wished all the boats at sea a very merry Christmas in a long *Sondermeldung*, transmitted on the Allouis station. He praised them for their courage and sacrifice. He also announced a Christmas Eve gift to the Third Reich: *U-154* and *U-455* had just stuffed a freighter and a tanker into their stockings off Rockall Bank, Ireland. They were likely convoy stragglers steaming for the North Channel. Cheers went up in *U-122*.

"Well, you know what I'd like for Christmas, but I'm willing to wait for a year," Kammerer said, lifting a spoonful of fish soup.

Graeber looked over and asked, "What?"

"A big, fat American troop transport with twenty thousand soldiers aboard. What a sight, huh? Twenty thousand dumped into the sea? Pandemonium!"

They were crammed into the wardroom, having the traditional *Heiliger Abend* meal of goose, potatoes, vegetables, and Christmas pastries. The boat was submerged for the celebration, gliding along at four knots and tucked a hundred feet below the dark Atlantic swells. There was barely any movement on the golden surfaces of their coffee mugs, which were filled with *München* liquid, a special all-hands treat from the commander. There were small trees fore, aft, and midships, perched between machinery. Carols were sung over the loudspeakers before the meal, which was served in two sittings. "O, Tannenbaum" competed with the melody of the electric motors. There were packages and bags of treats.

The *U-122* lacked a roaring fireplace, family, and a bowl of rum punch, but considering the circumstances Kammerer had done his best to make the evening a festive one.

Dörfmann said, "Troop transport, huh? They go too fast I've heard."

"If only I could get a bow shot," Kammerer mused, as if he could see it. "Hit it near the chain locker, either side, open it up enough to stop it, then slide around to put two or three more into it midships . . ."

Dörfmann said, "In school they told us that a bow shot was the most difficult of all, not to even try it."

"Rules are made to be broken," Kammerer advised. "Troopships do travel fast and bow shots *are* almost impossible to make, but if I saw the *Queen Mary* and could line up on her in time, I'd sure as hell try it. To shoot a spread down her throat would be worth it."

The look on Graeber's face suggested that they should be talking about home and family this particular evening, not the killing of troopships. He lowered his head.

"You're serious, aren't you, Herr Kaleunt?" asked Dörfmann.

"Absolutely. Soon they'll be using her to run to America. She just brought twenty thousand Aussie troops to London. She steamed around Cape Horn and came up the coast of Africa like she owned it. The *Gneisenau* went to intercept her, but no luck. Wouldn't that have been a show with no air cover around?" He shook his head in wonderment. "Battleship one-on-one with the *Queen Mary*, matching her in speed and able to outmaneuver her—"

"Slaughter," said Dörfmann.

Graeber cleared his throat.

Kammerer sensed the First's distaste and decided to change the subject. Dinner was supposed to be merry, after all. "Graeber, tell us who'll be at your house tonight."

"My mother and father, my sisters, and any other member of the family living in Wuppertal. Hans might be there, too." Brother Hans was in the Luftwaffe, Kammerer knew. Graeber sank into sentimentality.

Then he prodded Dörfmann and Fromm to talk about their

homes and family, another mistake. The mood in the wardroom turned solemn, and Kammerer wished he'd kept on talking about battle.

He remembered his own "family" Christmases of the past. The doctor always took them to a lavish dinner at the Alster, then home to light candles on the tree and exchange gifts. But he'd envied the families with many members and felt lonely at Christmas.

His thoughts turned to Hélène. He wondered what she was doing this night. Was she alone in the small apartment on rue le Coutaller? Was she truthful in saying she had no boyfriends? Pretty as she was, it didn't seem possible that there was no current romance in her life. Who were her other friends? There were some mysteries about the pretty French girl that needed to be solved before he asked her to be his war bride.

Graeber proposed a toast to family and loved ones with the beer they had left, and Kammerer joined in, adding his own *Prosit* to the future success of *U-122*.

At 2000 hours he said to Graeber, "Let's get back to business," and soon the slender steel tube pierced the ocean, emerging into a starless night. Kammerer climbed into the tower, feeling a lot more comfortable on the bridge than he did below. Saying little to the duty watch, lost in thoughts of Hélène, he stayed up there for an hour with the wind and cold increasing as they plunged and rocked westward.

Telephone connections out of Caripito, via Cumana and Caracas, were less reliable than jungle drums. The Jordans decided on a Merry Christmas cable to Maureen, the kids, and Mother Jordan just in case the Bell system didn't work. They knew everyone would be at Papa's house. They tried phoning Christmas Eve and again Christmas morning but gave up around noon.

Dinner aboard the *Tuttle* was as festive as any ashore. The steward had found turkeys in northern Venezuela. Champagne corks popped. Fong put on a bow tie for the occasion and served as if they were in Longchamps.

The saloon was crowded with the addition of the seven engine mechanics flown in to Caracas, then bused over to Caripito. They'd promised to get the *Tuttle* under way, fully loaded, by December 30.

Yet the mood in the mahogany-paneled room was somber. The booze, after a while, only made it worse.

Sully listened to his father and Sparks ramble on about past Christmases for a while and then walked out to the fantail. Two other tankers were in port, partially loaded. They were scheduled to sail in the morning, and their crews had a break; they spent the holiday hooked to land.

Sully thought of Maureen, Danny, and Julie; he also thought of the *Galveston*'s eight other survivors and the families of the men who didn't make it past the Death Hole. He thought of Captain Ewing's grandchildren and of the distinguished gentlemanly convoy commodore. He'd heard in Liverpool that SC74B's final death toll was 306. He looked over at the two old tankers nearby, and wondered if they'd still be afloat in six months.

World War I had come along when he was six. When he was nine or ten he remembered digging trenches with the neighborhood kids. They played Germans and Yanks, and shot at each other with wooden rifles, strips of inner-tube rubber stretched to fire blunt-headed "arrows." But he hadn't really thought much about war not being fun until he was in his twenties. He read Remarque's *All Quiet on the Western Front*. A young soldier was killed after the fighting had stopped while the politicians and generals were arguing about armistice. Even now, Jordan could quote the next to last paragraph verbatim:

He fell in October 1918, on a day that was so quiet and still on the whole front, that the army report confined itself to a single sentence: All quiet on the Western Front.

Sully stayed out on the deck a little longer and then decided he'd go back into the saloon and get pass-out drunk.

✝ ✝ ✝

Fifty hours later, the Atlantic ignored the holidays. She began to provide her own activities for *U-122* and the other four boats that crept toward America. Gales raged back and forth between northwest and southwest, attacking the hull with sleet, snow, and hail. They tore the tops off waves that rose up thirty or forty feet and sheeted them over the conning tower. The bridge watch struggled to keep from being washed away, harnesses straining.

The slender hull, creaking and groaning, surged upward on each new crest, hung a few seconds at the top, and then plunged downward on the back slope. Screws beat the air frantically until submerged again in white water. The *U-122* was charging batteries and trying to make miles westward.

Clad in oilskins, Kammerer strained against the steel-wire tethers that held him between the periscope and the bridge coaming. Razorlike wind threatened to rip off his goggles.

Down below there was chaos. Glassware and crockery shattered. To move about required hand-over-hand; even then, feet couldn't stay on the floorplates. Water sloshed down when the hatch was open, adding to the clamminess, the smell of oil and vomit.

On the radio a dozen signals from the mid-Atlantic could be heard. Ships were in distress from the storm, not from U-boat attack.

In the late afternoon, after two straight hours of battling the storm, Kammerer sent the beaten-up watch below. He remained alone on the bridge like Ahab.

Graeber asked Dörfmann, "Why are you being relieved?" helping the Second out of his wet gear.

"I don't know."

Graeber quickly pulled on his oils and climbed the ladder. He stuck his head above the deck level and peered around. In the meager gray light he saw the commander defiantly yelling into the howl of wind. He'd taken off his goggles and sou'wester and was letting the sleet pound his face. In his safety belt, he was riding the boat like it was a wild horse.

Graeber watched for a moment in alarm and then dropped back down, saying guardedly to Bauer, "He's mad, I tell you."

"Just angry at the storm," said Bauer.

As darkness settled, the heaving ocean still streaked with wide phosphorescent veins and foam, Kammerer descended from the bridge; his cheeks, forehead, and nose were fiery red from the cutting spicules. He shouted hoarsely, "All hands to diving stations."

U-122 went to the basement, stabilizing at 150 feet, riding almost motionless horizontally, peace and quiet enveloping it.

The Atlantic gales lasted another three days, Kammerer ducking *122* under when it became almost unbearable for the crew.

✝ ✝ ✝

The *Tuttle* sailed early morning December 30, as scheduled, with a partial load of Jusepin crude. Caripito harbor was too shallow for ocean tankers to take on a full load. She lifted up to the safe mark inside Maturin Bay and then went outside to top off at Guiria, on the Paria Peninsula.

She now had her full 78,000 barrels aboard and, riding low in the water, proceeded in the Gulf of Paria toward Trinidad to find out what courses the British navy suggested north and what sub warnings were posted, if any.

She'd cleared Guiria at noon. Sully was on the bridge with his father, and Matkowski had taken the first hour at the wheel as usual. Dan said to Matkowski, "I was too old to be a doughboy in the last war. But I was ready to go if they asked me, wasn't I, Sully?"

Sully said, "Yeah," not knowing whether it was true. He was eight at the time and didn't remember how his father had felt.

He walked out to the starboard wing of the bridge. He now realized how much of a mistake it had been to bring the old man along. Daniel Jordan had been wearing thin on the *Tuttle* for several weeks. Maybe he felt he had to talk. Maybe he didn't understand that silence was part of going to sea.

Several times Sully had been on the verge of saying, Christ's sake, Papa, shut up! His own nerves, he knew. Or perhaps it was the sudden tension that had gripped everyone else, and fear of what was slopping around beneath the decks. Ever since December 7, Sully had noticed a difference in the crew, the mates, and the engineers.

None admitted to being scared, but there were the same indicators he'd seen and heard on the *Galveston*. When Fong dropped a plate in the saloon, half the diners came out of their chairs. When a wrench hit the grating in the engine room the black gang on watch froze.

Sully stepped to the door of the wheelhouse. "Come left ten degrees."

✛ ✛ ✛

"Did you celebrate last night?" Admiral Ames asked Mrs. Cinelli.

She laughed. "No, we had linguini and a bottle of red and went to bed. How about you, sir?"

"We had split pea soup and went to bed."

He joined in her laughter. "Anyhow, Happy New Year."

"The same to you, Admiral."

An hour later, Captain Phillips brought up the COMINCH reply to Ames's request for help and then stood by silently as the admiral read it.

"I fully realize the weakness of the forces assigned to defend your command, but a review of the situation indicates that it will be inadvisable to detach any vessels from their present duty with the Fleets . . ."

Ames looked up. "Answers my request, doesn't it?"

"I think so," said Phillips, bleakly. He held another sheet of paper in his hand, also marked secret. "Since we can't expect any help from the sea, I have the aircraft availability as of this morning."

"Read it to me."

"Naval Air Station, Salem: None available. Squantum, eight Kingfishers (Pontoon Observation Scouts, carrying two Mark VXII depth charges); Quonset, two Kingfishers; New York, ten King-fishers; Lakehurst, three ZNP (blimps, each carrying four depth charges); Cape May, none . . ."

"Jesus . . ." Ames frowned. The Kingfishers moved like lard.

Phillips droned on. "Fleet Air has fourteen patrol bombers, seaplane types, but six are out of commission . . ."

Ames shook his head woefully. "Happy 1942."

"Carnival time," said Phillips.

"You're an old submariner, Tom. What would you do if you were a German U-boat commander?" Ames asked earnestly.

"Well, I'd know that ninety-nine percent of the American merchant vessels have no guns." Phillips then said he'd know their skippers disregarded blackout and didn't pay much attention to engine smoke; he'd know that their radio operators were on the air night and day gossiping about weather, speed, ships' positions, and arrival times.

"I'd know that the goddamn civilians are too selfish and greedy to turn off their lights ashore." He'd come into the shipping lanes and pick 'em off one by one, tankers being the priority. He'd shell some, torpedo others. He'd lie on the bottom of the Continental Shelf all day and sleep; then he'd come up at dusk like an alligator, see the ships outlined against the shore lights, and go to work.

"That's how you'd do it?"

"That's how," Phillips said.

The admiral slumped back in his chair.

A few minutes later, Phillips returned to advise Ames that there'd been an update from Washington on U-boat movement to the west.

"Seven supposedly left Biscay bases within the past week."

"He intends to kick our asses," the admiral said.

"That's a good assumption, sir," replied Phillips. "And there may be many more." It took three or four hours for Washington to decipher the British code.

✛ ✛ ✛

"Damn!" said Sully, wiping his eyes on the afternoon of January 7. They already smarted from the strain of peering into the light and the intermittent snow though the watch was less than two hours old. The bridge thermometer read twenty-eight degrees.

"Would dark glasses help?" Matkowski asked.

"Then I wouldn't see *anything*," Sully said.

In steadily worsening weather, the *Tuttle* steamed north at nine knots about sixty miles northeast of the Virginia capes. Matkowski steered a zigzag pattern as ordered by the navy. With a base course of 354, he changed fifteen degrees every fifteen minutes—over to 341, back to 354, over to 009, back to 354. Sparks hadn't had any sub reports, and the zigzag courses were precautionary. Ryti had ordered Logan to give him every possible revolution.

The stiffening wind blew a mixture of sleet and snow in sheets. Visibility was up to a half mile, closing again at several hundred yards. White water washed along the welldecks as the deeply laden hull, down to her load marks, bit into long gray rollers four or five feet high. Soon she'd be burying her bow as the wind and rollers mounted, Sully knew.

"Wouldn't you think this stuff could have held off for another forty-eight hours? Just our luck." They'd pick up the pilot off New York by then and move on slowly to Bayonne.

"Pretty nice down in Venezuela after all, wasn't it?" Matkowski observed.

Sooner or later, the young helmsman would understand that you *always* paid for good weather. No matter where you sailed, highs and lows always caught up and made life miserable. This cold front had descended earlier, just as they put Cape Hatteras and Diamond Shoals on the distant beam. Navy routing was taking them outside the eastern edge of the Gulf Stream.

"Uh-huh."

Captain Ryti was catching a nap in his sea cabin off the chart-room after having been up all night. Sully's father was last seen back in the mess playing checkers with Fong. Except for those on watch, the ship was secured from deck work. Both officers and crew were in the sack or playing cards. All the reading material had been exhausted in the Caripito stay. A day like this was welcomed by most aboard the *Tuttle* though not by the mates.

Down in the radio shack, Sam Bessemer was half dozing when his receiver awoke:

SSS SSS SSS DE LDDI
POSITION 41.51 N 63.48 W TURNBULL TORPEDOED
NEED ASSISTANCE HURRY

That position would be somewhere off Nova Scotia. Sparks noted the time as 1351 eastern standard time and had no sooner written it down when the receiver crackled again with another SOS, this one from a ship southeast of Montauk Point, Long Island. Then another off Delaware.

Sparks quickly typed out the messages, put the receiver on automatic, and began to climb the inside stairway laboriously to Ryti's sea cabin. The subs were now definitely in American waters, not out in the middle of the Atlantic.

✛ ✛ ✛

Admiral Ames was dictating a letter to Mrs. Cinelli when Captain Phillips strode into the office without knocking, saying, "They're here! Three of them hit within thirty minutes; the first off Nova Scotia, the second off Montauk, and the third off Delaware."

The admiral said, "Oh, shit," then quickly apologized to Mrs. Cinelli. "Notify all commands. Set *Condition Red*."

"We're already doing that, Admiral."

Then he accompanied Phillips down to Operations. The sub reports were being positioned by a yeoman on the huge new wall map of the Coastal Frontier, stretching to Key West. COMINCH was about to change the name to Eastern Sea Frontier, with Ames's responsibility from the Canadian border to the end of Florida.

"OK, let's go to war," he said to Captain Phillips with a frustrated look.

Phillips issued orders for a destroyer, a Coast Guard cutter, a minesweeper, all available aircraft from Salem Station, and a navy blimp to get under way.

✛ ✛ ✛

Just after receiving Dönitz's "roll the drums" go-ahead from Lorient, Kammerer had stumbled onto the unsuspecting tanker at 1335. Coppel nailed her first on the hydrophones. The thrashing of her single screw said she was unmistakably a merchantman. Then he closed on her enough to read the name: *E. D. Tuttle*, Wilmington, Delaware. A big tanker for his first *Paukenschlag* kill. Kammerer was delighted.

Heinze quickly looked her up in the ship's registry and reported, "She's 9,750 tons."

"Hurrah!" Kammerer yelled down.

The *U-122* had tracked her for almost half an hour; they ran alongside her at a thousand meters, hidden from her by the snow, staying roughly opposite her amidships. Kammerer saw her now and again through the target binoculars, ghostly in the boiling whiteness. She had no stern gun, and no guns up forward either.

"Let's try to get her without a torpedo," he said to the skeptical

Graeber. With all the targets easily available along the coast, no sense wasting an eel on an unarmed ship in this weather. But the snow was letting up, and visibility cleared.

The gun crew, on standby below, was ordered to the deck as the *U-122* started closing to three hundred meters. "Use incendiaries," Kammerer shouted down to Dörfmann. "Hit her forward so the fire will carry back."

Ammunition handlers stood by to pass shells up through the conning tower, then down to the gun crews. Gunnery from a submarine in any sea conditions except dead calm posed a hazard to the men on deck. They were tethered on safety lines. Aiming and firing even in moderate seas was tricky.

Kammerer had never shelled a ship. Guns were of no use in convoy attacks, but he'd talked to other commanders who had combined armor-piercing with phosphorus shells.

At 1410, Dörfmann hung on as the boat rose and fell; a mixture of spray and fine snow doused him, and he waved up that his crew was ready. Kammerer yelled, "Open fire!"

The 105-mm boomed hollowly, and cordite fumes swept up over the bridge. Kammerer watched a spurt of flame from the hull just forward of the midships house. A clean, clear hit.

"Perfect!" he yelled to Dörfmann.

✛ ✛ ✛

Sully was saying, "This keeps up, and we'll have ice—" when the first shell hit not thirty feet from his shoes. He yelled, "Good God!" and moved to his left to stick his thumb on the general alarm button.

Sparks was bent over Captain Ryti to tell him about the sub attacks when they both heard the bang and felt the impact. Ryti jerked erect and ordered Sparks to get a message off.

Chiefs Logan and Kalevi awoke instantly in their cabins and grabbed for their shoes.

In the engine room, the Second, Evans, felt the jar, heard the bell, and moved toward the steam-smothering valve. He turned it to activate the system and blanket the tanks.

In the saloon, Daniel Jordan heard the explosion forward then the alarm bell trip-hammering. He arose and asked Fong, "What's happening?"

Not taking time to answer, Fong plunged out into the passage-way to go below.

Dan followed him out, running for the catwalk to the midship house.

Sparks went down to the radio shack, his strong hands grasping the rails on either side of the stairway, his body airborne, and his artificial foot not touching the treads. Inside the room, already filling with smoke, he disconnected the auto alarm, shifted the main antenna from auto reception to transmission and from the main transmitter to emergency. Another shell slammed into the side of the ship and, feeling heat, he sent an SSS with the *Tuttle*'s position that Ryti had given him. Each word was sent twice.

He shifted to reception and awaited acknowledgment, yelling at the receiver, "Talk to me, talk to me . . ."

Nothing! Not a click.

He pressed the key down to check the antenna current. There was still plenty of juice, and he transmitted the message twice again, slowing the word rate. SHIP BURNING. PLS. HURRY . . .

Coughing, gagging from the smoke, he finally screwed the key down to send a continuous signal, then put on his sheepskin jacket and lifebelt to climb back to the bridge.

Fire rose from the tanks just forward of the bridge, and Sully bolted outside, pulling on his jacket and telling Matkowski to hold his course. There was another red flash through the light snow, and the *Tuttle* reverberated again.

Raising his binoculars he saw the submarine, its bridge crowded and a knot of men, the gun crew, on deck. Though he focused on the gun crew, he saw the snarling leopard on the conning tower from the corner of his eye and shifted his binoculars. God, could it be the same boat that got the *Galveston*? Though it had faded, the animal was definitely a leopard, spots and all. That's what he and Pudney had seen at the Death Hole. The leopard boat!

Suddenly, the *Tuttle* heaved as No. 3 tank blew. It sent a dark red wall of flame and burning oil high into the air over the bridgehouse. Sully ran for safety inside. This was a repeat of the *Galveston*. That memory was still fresh in his mind. He thought of his father back in the afterhouse. Another hit or two, and in a few seconds the after welldeck would be a sea of fire. Yet his duty at the moment was on the bridge.

Captain Ryti shouted on the phone to Chief Logan in the engine room: "Shut the engine down!" He was looking through the inferno ahead. Thick black smoke funneled into the blown-out bridge windows.

Seeing Sully in the dense swirls, he yelled, "What's it like aft?"

"Fire all along the starboard side back to No. 7."

Just as he was saying it, his papa emerged out of the smoke with an ashen face, mouth open, lips moving. No words came out.

Then a direct hit slammed into the flying bridge, with the impact knocking everyone down. Matkowski bled instantly from shrapnel. He stayed on his knees, bent over.

Sully helped his papa off the deck as Kalevi entered from the chartroom, Cheney at his heels. Both men had pulled on lifebelts. They carried oilskins.

Ryti yelled to the first mate. "We have to save the crew. I'm abandoning ..."

Kalevi nodded and moved out toward his lifeboat station on the port side.

Sully was on the phone to Logan, shouting, "Abandon ship, abandon ship!"

The chief would pass word to the black gang on duty, then have an engineer check crew's quarters and the mess.

Sully yelled to Cheney, "Get Papa into the boat. Don't leave him ..."

Cheney's job was to check the status of the midship's boats. He ran back into the wheelhouse: "No. 1 is full of shrapnel holes," he announced. Then he moved across toward the port side to stand by and man the forward falls.

Sully lifted the groaning Matkowski off the deck and followed Cheney out. The boy was in shock; his face was paper white where it wasn't covered with red. He had a head injury.

Ryti shouted, "I'm going down for my skins." Like Kalevi and Cheney, Ryti knew that his survival would depend on staying warm.

The *Tuttle* was still moving ahead, roaring stem to stern. The roar was punctuated by explosions. She was like the *Galveston* and hundreds more. Creaking, moaning, and dying.

✛ ✛ ✛

Ames had come down from his office to Operations and was reading the teletype:

SSS DE KGRE
36.55 N 75.42 W SS PLYMOUTH TORPEDO ATTACK
AT 1422 EST

SSS DE KPSI
38.53 N 74.03 W SS E D TUTTLE SHELLED NEED
ASSISTANCE
1428 EST

SSS DE KPSI
TUTTLE BURNING PLS HURRY 1436 EST

Ames watched, feeling ill, as the *Plymouth* and *Tuttle* were posted on the wall chart, noticing that the *Reliance*, the nearest Coast Guard cutter, was about 90 miles from the *Plymouth* and 130 miles from the *Tuttle*. Two other vessels also under attack were closer to the cutter and would likely get first assistance.

For the time being, the survivors of the *Plymouth* and *Tuttle* were on their own, God help them.

Shaking his head at his own helplessness, he returned to the fifteenth floor.

✝ ✝ ✝

"Cease fire!" Kammerer shouted, seeing that another tank had exploded.

He'd used fourteen rounds. The target was now almost totally engulfed in flames, aside from a section of her bow and part of her afterhouse. The SS *Tuttle* would never carry another cargo of oil for the Allies. Everyone topside on the *U-122* watched her death silently, a fascinating sight, somewhat akin to that of a stricken bull in a Madrid ring. Bauer was taking pictures.

A lifeboat was being launched from the starboard side, aft. Men slid down the knotted ropes. He presumed the port-side boat was also being lowered.

"Secure the gun crew," Kammerer said. "Well done!" he yelled down to Dörfmann.

Then he said to Graeber, "Let's crank up and go take a look around on the other side of her. All ahead full."

He wondered what had happened to the bridge personnel and the ship's master. The starboard side of the bridge had disappeared behind the curtain of flame.

The *U-122* scurried ahead to go out in front of the derelict, which scarred the entire seascape around her with red and black. Oily smoke coiled into the low clouds. The crimson reflected angrily against the snow drizzle. She was still sliding forward. Heat radiated from her.

"See how easy it was," Kammerer said to Graeber. "I had no idea it would be this easy. We saved ourselves two torpedoes. I don't think one would have killed her."

Circling the *Tuttle*'s bow, he saw the midship's port boat being lowered to the water and a half-dozen life-jacketed men poised to enter it. Smoke swirled around them. Probably master and mates, he thought.

He leaned over to the speaking tube to tell Heinze to draft a message to Lorient: *Have destroyed SS* Tuttle, *10,000-ton U.S. tanker north of Virginia Capes. Gunfire. Many targets available. Am proceeding Hatteras. U-122.*

✢ ✢ ✢

"Lower away, lower away!" Chief Kalevi yelled to Sully, manning the forward fall himself. Sparks helped. The lines had been splashed with oil when the No. 3 tank blew. They were slick as well as frozen, complicating handling of the bulky lowering gear. The tricky part was to keep the prow high as it touched the water, letting the stern go in first so it wouldn't swamp.

Sully had the afterfall in hand. He slacked it off around a cleat, his knuckles white. Captain Ryti was his backup.

Unless No. 4 tank, which was partially under the midship house, exploded, they had a few precious minutes to spare. No matter how much experience any sailor had—peace or war—launching boats in a seaway was always difficult and dangerous. Lives were lost just getting down on a wild day like this one. Bodies were crushed against the side of the ship, legs and arms broken, and men drowned.

Sully glanced over his shoulder at his father; he was frightened for Dan's safety and still angry because he had been needlessly aboard. He'd sent him below to wear a jacket over his sweater. Beneath smoke smudges, Dan's face was as white as his son's knuckles. He stood there, appearing dazed and disoriented. Over his shoulder, Sully yelled worriedly, "I'll tell you when, Papa."

The smoke, growing thicker, twisted down over the boat deck. The noise from the fire was almost deafening. Everyone was coughing.

Out of the smoke appeared One-Name Fong. Thinly clad, he hadn't thought about the weather. He was still wearing slippers.

Kalevi yelled at him, "You'll freeze to death."

Fong's expression didn't change. He clutched a small black bag. That he'd gotten forward through the fire was a miracle.

Ryti shouted to Cheney to be first. "Go on down."

Cheney lost his grip on the second big knot of the lifeline and plummeted, slamming heavily on a thwart on his spine. He screamed out in pain. He wouldn't likely be of much use.

Shaking his head, Kalevi yelled at Sparks, "You go down," and Bessemer released his grip on the fall. He swung out on another lifeline, swaying but managing to hang on until his good foot touched a thwart. The artificial leg dangled. He'd always resented it when people called him a cripple.

The stern of No. 2 boat skimmed the surging waves, bouncing on them drunkenly. It rode like an out-of-control sled, swerving against the hull. Metal screeched. Sparks flew. Spray shot up in the space.

Ryti, Kalevi, and Sully were all thinking the same thing: *Oh, God, don't screw us up; help us launch and not swamp or turn over.* Both were distinct possibilities, and there was no way to get back to the boats on the afterhouse. They couldn't even see them. No. 2 was *it*, the one chance to survive.

Ryti shouted to Fong, "You go!" The messman rammed the handle of the bag up over his wrist and swung down on a lifeline, landing on his feet.

Then Sully shouted to his father, "Papa, you go . . ."

The elder Jordan stood staring at the bucking boat, looking as if he were hypnotized by its movement. His eyes were wide.

"Goddammit, Papa, grab a line and go down," Sully shouted in exasperation. "Now, dammit, now!"

The elderly man was like a marble statue.

Captain Ryti moved quickly to his side, placing the rope into his hands. He yelled, "Do it now!"

Dan's hands fell away. He couldn't move and looked helplessly at his son.

"I'll take him down," Sully shouted to Captain Ryti, and lowered away on his fall until the stern of the boat was solidly in the water, skidding and bucking even more. As the fall sagged, Sparks unhooked it.

Long ago they'd rigged out spare painters forward and aft attaching the boat to the ship. Ryti called down to Sparks to cut the stern line. They needed a rope to lower Matkowski, who was still bleeding and unconscious.

Sully tied him under his armpits and then took a turn around a stanchion. He and Ryti sent the ordinary down into the arms of Sparks Bessemer.

Ryti yelled to Bessemer, "I'm going to drop the medicine chest." He'd need it for Matkowski. Cheney was groaning as if his back were broken.

Trying to balance himself on his good leg, Sparks had his hands outstretched when the boat pitched heavily to the left. The medicine chest hit the starboard gunwale, bounced, and then dropped overboard.

Ryti closed his eyes. What else could go wrong?

He opened them a second later and grasped a lifeline, sending his sixty-nine-year-old body down the slick rope, landing on his feet with the spryness of a teenager.

Three more to go and only pure luck would let them get off before No. 4 caught fire and blew.

Sully shouted to Kalevi, "I'll take Papa down now."

Kalevi, with his massive strength, was still holding the boat's bow out of water, the sea reaching up and grabbing at it hungrily. The big mate nodded, his bloodshot eyes barely visible in the smoke. He'd be off last.

Dan stood on the boat deck between the swung-out davits. He was a zombie figure in shock. Sully put his mouth close to his father's head and shouted, "Listen to me, Papa. I'm putting your arms around me. I want you to hold on to me. You understand me? If you don't you could kill us both. Understand me?"

Dan nodded. Sully took his limp arms, placing them around his shoulders. Then he reached out to grab a lifeline, seeing that

Ryti and Sparks were holding the other end. Suddenly the arms fell away, and his father was dead weight.

"Hang on," Sully yelled frantically.

Kalevi yelled, "We don't have all day . . ."

Sully nodded and quickly pulled the lifeline up, took a hitch around his father, and literally shoved him out over the boat, heaving back at almost the same moment, bracing his feet for the jerk.

Ryti and Sparks caught him and Papa Jordan was finally safe in the boat.

Sully followed him down. Then big Kalevi swung out and landed; Sparks and Sully tried to push off from the side of the *Tuttle* as Ryti chopped the forward falls away, not even attempting to unhook them.

The boat crashed against the hull. Kalevi unhitched the sailing mast to help fend off. The mast snapped in two. Kalevi used the stub as a ram to prevent another collision.

As the heavy boat was finally pushed away, an icy wave broke over the bow, cascading in and drenching everyone. The water in the boat was knee-deep. It washed over Cheney and Matkowski, who were on the floorboards. Cheney groaned. There was no sound from Matkowski.

Pulling on his oar, Sully looked at his father. Dan sat hunched, head down. He held his hands in an odd position, with his palms up. Fong shivered beside Jordan.

A moment later, the sub passed brazenly nearby the wallowing lifeboat. Sully saw the snarling leopard on the conning tower and the black-bearded officer with the white capcover.

Could it possibly be the same U-boat that had killed the *Galveston*? The one they'd talked about on the *Dimmock*? Was this the same black-bearded skipper who was staring at them? Sully thought so. Pudney had said he had a black beard.

Enraged at losing his ship, Captain Ryti shouted over, "You son of a bitch!" but his words were flung away by the wind. No one on the leopard U-boat did more than stare.

Sully got a last good look at the sub and her commanding

officer as it motored on south, finally disappearing as another curtain of snow swept over the sea.

+ + +

Admiral Dönitz was ecstatic—five successful attacks against four tankers off the United States were accomplished within three hours. He could not have asked for more, and those five subs still had plenty of kill time and plenty of torpedoes left.

After the last messages were decoded, he called Raeder in Berlin to give a glowing preliminary report of *Paukenschlag*. There'd be an immediate phone call to Hitler. The führer basked in the news of victories. There hadn't been too many lately.

Dönitz said, "If we can keep this up for any length of time, it can cause chaos not only from the loss of ships and cargoes but from the long-term manning effect." They knew the Americans could put new hulls into the water. But if the sailors were too afraid to man them, those ships wouldn't get under way. "It's something I want to stress to my commanders."

"Good idea," responded Raeder.

Dönitz was tempted to point out to Raeder that had he been allowed twelve boats, the success of *Paukenschlag* would have been twice what it was already. He decided that that was futile and perhaps even harmful. Raeder didn't take kindly to the possibility of his staff making mistakes.

"Keep me informed, Admiral," said Raeder, as stiff and unemotional as ever.

Dönitz said he'd do that and scribbled a message to all boat commanders who dealt with enemy merchant ships, especially ones sunk close to shore. *Survivors may only be rescued when interrogation may be of value to the U-boat. Be severe! Remember that while bombing German cities the enemy has no regard for women and children.*

Despite previous orders, some commanders had offered first aid, brandy, or food, and even towed lifeboats for a distance. But no more.

That settled, Dönitz said, "Did you happen to notice that Kammerer took that big tanker with gunfire? He saw that it was unarmed and did not waste a torpedo on it."

"He's fulfilled your faith, all right," Godt replied.

✠ ✠ ✠

"My God, Papa, why didn't you tell me?" Sully said, looking at his father's raw palms. The flesh was torn away. They'd blistered and peeled. No wonder he couldn't grab the lifelines!

"I burned them going down to the cabin. The ship lurched. I grabbed a red-hot railing."

"You should have told me," Sully said.

"Too much was going on."

Dan was hunched on the thwart he'd occupied after getting into the boat. He looked gray and in deep pain, with every one of his years showing.

"We'll put something on your hands," Sully said. He wondered if his father would survive. Dan's shoulders quivered. "They're numb now." Having said that, he began to throw up.

The wind had increased. Sully, Sparks, Kalevi, and Ryti manned the oars but fought a losing battle to keep headed into the waves. Broadside, they could easily flip over.

Ryti, clad in a wool jacket, had given his oilskins to Fong. The messman shivered head to foot, grasping his black bag. The skins provided little warmth.

Cheney and Matkowski had been lifted up out of the swishing water in the bottom of the boat. They were stretched across the thwarts. Cheney moaned each time the metal hull banged. Matkowski was still unconscious, though the bleeding had stopped.

They spotted the other two boats from the *Tuttle*'s afterhouse and saw that most of the men aboard them weren't clothed to battle the winter weather either. One was in shirtsleeves. The other boats were less than thirty yards away, wallowing in the swells.

Captain Ryti shouted to Chief Logan, "Stick together!" but the wind and water drowned his voice.

Ryti had asked Sparks at least three times if he'd gotten the SOS messages off. Sparks had assured him they'd been sent. So Ryti was convinced that the navy or Coast Guard would soon respond.

"The main thing is to last until tomorrow," he said.

Now, with darkness unavoidable, they began to prepare for a long night ahead. They stopped rowing, and Kalevi dropped the sea anchor overboard to slow the drift by keeping the bow into the waves. But the canvas cone carried away, leaving just the steel frame. Kalevi cursed the obviously rotten canvas, but it had been his own job to make sure Cheney inspected equipment for each boat. Too late for curses.

"Let's rig the keg," Sully suggested.

Sparks had hit the spigot on the wooden water keg with an oar when trying to fend off, busting it. Soon it was dropped over the bow on a spare painter. The boat swung around to head into the wind. Snow had begun to fall again.

First they bailed the water out of the bottom. Next, they rigged the sail over the center thwarts where Cheney and Matkowski were sprawled. Sully moved his father beneath the shelter. "Papa, all we have to do is last the night out. There'll be a cutter out here by daylight. We're less than a hundred miles from Norfolk."

Ryti opened the small first-aid kit and drew out a tube of salve, spreading it gently over Dan's palms. He fulfilled the traditional master's role as ship's doctor.

The standard supplies of hardtack and chocolate were in the galvanized waterproof survivor box. For eight of them the emergency food could last for weeks if rationed out. There was another keg of water intact.

No one was hungry. Even Sully felt seasick as they huddled beneath the sail and sat close to each other to keep warm. Drying out was impossible. Wind flapped the canvas, getting under it, invading with icy blasts. They were freezing already.

Captain Ryti, huddled against Sparks, said, "The last time this happened to me the chief officer was a Welshman who said the way to survive in a lifeboat is to talk. He was right. We only lost two men out of seventeen, both injured before we left the ship."

"What'd you talk about?" Sully asked.

"We talked about the hottest women we'd ever slept with. We talked about the hottest curry we'd ever had . . ." Though his teeth were chattering, he forced out each word and was doing exactly what he should have done as a leader to keep up morale. But soon they were all too seasick to talk.

The boat climbed the waves, hung for an instant, then slid down the other side through veins of foam.

At twilight, Cheney began to moan louder, finally screamed, and then convulsed. Sully and Sparks held him down while Kalevi shone the light on his face. His eyes were open and bright. The screams stopped as abruptly as they'd started.

Sully looked at his watch as Captain Ryti took the third mate's pulse. The time was 1720.

"If I had to guess I'd say he broke his back or his spine."

Then he leaned over to check Matkowski, who was so still that he looked deader than Cheney.

"There's a faint pulse. He's trying to live."

Sully remembered telling Ski that he should stay on the *Tuttle*, not go back to freightships. Now he was dying. Taking another look at the wrinkled, peaceful face of the third mate, Captain Ryti said to Sully, "Use his jacket and cap."

Sully reached over to remove them from Cheney and strangely felt no emotion. He placed the bobcap on his father's head and gave the jacket to Fong. His father seemed to have shrunk in the last half hour, Sully noticed.

The *Tuttle* lifeboat No. 2 plunged and bucked on its makeshift sea anchor as Sully and Kalevi moved Cheney's body forward.

✛ ✛ ✛

Just after six o'clock, Hélène heard the sharp knock, then Gobelins's voice. She moved across the room to let him in. He'd come
to the apartment only once before. She immediately thought something might have happened.

"Is he coming here tonight?" Gobelins asked, as soon as the
door was closed.

She presumed he was talking about Horst Kammerer. "No, he
went out on patrol two weeks ago. I think he was going to America.
Why?"

Gobelins took off his rain-sparkled beret and sat down. He lit
up one of his awful-smelling cigar stubs, staring at her.

"I didn't want him to walk in on me."

She moved across the room to turn off the Vichy evening news
broadcast. Though it was filled with propaganda, she always listened.

" 'Ici Londres' will be on soon." The news from London was
on in French at 6:30.

"You get it on that old radio?"

Hélène shook her head and stepped a few feet to open a panel,
revealing a new radio. "It's German. He gave it to me. It's very
good."

"He knows both of them are illegal?"

"Yes."

Gobelins shrugged.

"Would you like some coffee? Fine Colombian. He brought it
for me. He never comes empty-handed."

"Coffee? I should say no simply because the bastard had his
hands on the bag, but I'll say yes because I haven't had any for
months." Hélène stepped into the kitchen area, feeling that Gobelins's visit wasn't social.

"You are not falling for all these gifts, are you? Softening up?"

Hélène laughed softly. "No danger of that." She felt him staring at her and turned.

"Don't fall in love with him," he warned paternally.

She laughed. "No chance of that, either."

Waiting for the water to heat, she asked, "How have you been?"

"I can't say I'm fine. What I catch I have to sell to them at their price."

As soon as she served the coffee, she sat down opposite him; he looked up and said gravely, "Hélène, I was in Raphael's this afternoon and heard this fellow talking about a girl on rue le Coutaller who entertained a German officer, and guessed immediately that it was you."

Her heart began to pound.

"I know him and went up to him. I asked him to come over in the corner. He knows about me and knew whatever he told me would be safe. He described you and gave your apartment number. I then asked him what he planned to do. His reply was, 'You know already.' "

"I then told him you were one of us, swearing him to secrecy."

Hélène's voice was tight as she asked, "Can you trust him?"

"I think so. He was talking to two other men, and there was nothing to do but have him explain to them. Otherwise ..."

"We've gone out only once. I swear it."

"But people watch every German officer. You know that. They see him turn in here and disappear."

The cup jiggled as she lifted it to her lips.

"I got you into this but don't know how to get you out. Maybe you should not see this Nazi bastard anymore? Do you have relatives away from here?"

"An aunt in Marseille."

Suddenly she wanted to leave Lorient desperately—go farther than Marseille. Every tortured day, France was more a place of hatred and death. Gobelins sensed her fear, rose up, came over, and put his arms around her. Then he dug into his coat pocket and came out with some notes for the *Atlantiksender*. Flotilla soccer scores, officer and rating birthdays. Gossip.

A moment later, he departed; she stood against the door, her back to it, her eyes closed.

✢ ✢ ✢

After full darkness Sully came to think that they all might die out there before help arrived. With the wind blowing hard, icy spray penetrated under the canvas cover. His feet were already numb.

Teeth chattering, clothes plastered over them, the occupants of No. 2 shivered, hunched, and surrendered in silence. Matkowski was still lashed on the middle seat. They'd quit talking despite what Ryti had said. They weren't doing anything to save themselves now. Not a single thing. And Sully thought he knew why. When darkness descended shock had settled in, even on Ryti and Kalevi, who'd spent their lives out here. They knew as much about the sea as any man alive; they had spent a hundred years between them fighting it. They were already giving up, he thought. He had great respect for them, but he also knew that shock was eventually as much a killer as the elements.

The darkness alone was terrifying. The roar of the sea, the plunging of the boat as it rode the waves added to the terror. Each roller-coaster plunge sent shovelfuls of water back over the bow. Four hours after abandoning ship they all squatted there as helpless, sodden, half-frozen lumps. They pitched forward, then backward. They would all surely die.

At a little after six he yelled in contempt, "Goddammit, let's bail again! If we sit here on our asses we'll drown! You hear me? This boat is filling up . . ."

In an hour or so, they'd be waist-deep in water, with only the buoyancy tanks keeping them afloat. In the dimness, he could see heads lifting.

He yelled at them again. "I don't know about you guys but I'm too goddamn young to drown out here . . ."

Age. That was part of it. Except for poor unlucky Ski, who would probably die anyway, they were all older than Sully and Sparks by at least twenty years.

"Give me the flashlight!" he shouted at Kalevi.

The chief mate, who was bent down in defeat beside Captain Ryti, passed it over obediently. He looked bewildered.

Sully crawled forward and located a bucket and three wooden scoops, getting doused on his head and shoulders though it mattered little now. Crawling back, he hung on to the thwarts, slid under the canopy again, and pushed a scoop each to his father, Fong, and Ryti. He gave the bucket to Kalevi. "Use 'em!" he ordered, as if speaking to children. Sparks was already bailing with his cap.

Then he crawled aft and found another bucket near Cheney, who was awash, banging back and forth in the bilge water. In the glow of the light, his eyes and mouth were open in a bloodless corpse face. He was already stiff.

When Sully got back to the center of the boat, they were all bailing. He joined in with his bucket but saw that his father was having trouble holding the scoop. He'd forgotten about the blistered, raw palms. "Papa, I didn't think about your hands."

The elder Jordan didn't answer but kept moving the bailer toward the floorboards with his right hand.

Sully looked away. It was no time for sympathy. If they could last the night there might be help after daylight. The way to last the night was to keep hope alive and bodies moving. A little warmth was creeping back into him because of arm motion.

Finally Sully said, "Papa, you don't have to . . ."

Dan answered tersely, "They're numb now."

A little later Sully yelled at them again. "I don't know what you guys are thinking about, but I'm thinking about home." He hadn't been reminiscing but did now as he filled the bucket and sloshed it over the side. He made himself think about the little house on Vail Place, the warmth of the coal-fired furnace in the kitchen, and the glow from it. He made a picture in his mind.

Sparks volunteered, "When I was a kid the sand got so hot at Daytona Beach in July I'd wrap a wet towel around my feet to dance across it . . ."

That was what Ryti had prescribed. Talk about heat.

"Hottest I ever got was in the Persian Gulf. We loaded in Abadan in 135 degrees and had to wash down the decks even to walk on 'em . . ." That was Kalevi.

Finally his father said, forcing words out, "We had a spell in the Tidewater back in 1912 when you . . . couldn't cross the streets without getting into melting tar . . ."

By nine o'clock, when the snow finally stopped, they were winning the battle, staying even with the sea that invaded the bow. Water only skimmed the floorboards.

By midnight, the front had almost passed. The wind died down to a thin whisper, no longer sweeping the wavetops angrily. But it seemed even colder now, and ice was sheeting up on the thwarts and over the gunwales in the vicinity of 37.53 degrees north, 74.03 degrees west.

Sully knew the hours until dawn would be sheer cold agony. After that . . .

✝ ✝ ✝

Admiral Ames stared at the night's logs at 90 Church Street with equal despair. He'd gone home just before 8:00 P.M. What was new began after that time. Nothing encouraging, to be damn sure. Four more ships either attacked or sunk within the four hours to midnight. Two after. Then he recapped the action of the previous afternoon, the two close in and the *Tuttle*, which reported her position eighty miles out.

Weather had hampered search-and-rescue operations of the cutter even on the ones close in. It was rough and mean from Halifax south at 6:00 A.M. Typical January.

Salem Air Station. V-185. Proceeded to vicinity 40.28 N, 70.45 W. Sighted raft containing four men about twenty-five miles north of derelict. Later sighted lifeboat containing about twelve persons. Made radio report to authorities.
That would be the *Norness.*

Lakehurst. LTA K-3. Arrived over raft and lifeboat. Lowered coffee, cigarettes, and sandwiches.

The blimps would be useful after all, Ames thought.

He noted with satisfaction that a cutter had finally reached the scene and had carried out the rescue mission. Sixteen lives saved out of perhaps forty or more. Even sixteen was a triumph.

Then he called down to Operations, asking the duty officer what was being done to aid the *Tuttle* lifeboats. They'd now been in the ocean twelve hours in rain, snow, and high seas. The memory of that tanker meeting at 30 Rockefeller was still fresh, in particular that acerbic fellow, J. D. Pyle, of Consolidated Oil. The *Tuttle* was a Consolidated ship.

"Sir, a cutter was dispatched last night from Norfolk at 2010 but then diverted an hour later."

"Where to?" The admiral was livid.

"Another tanker was under attack twelve miles south of Oregon Inlet."

Oregon Inlet was above Hatteras.

"Who the hell ordered that diversion? They've got small craft to handle anything that close, for Chrissakes." He knew there were motor lifeboats stationed at Oregon and Hatteras inlets, with experienced crews, even at Ocracoke a little farther south. They could pick up survivors.

"Senior Coast Guard Officer, Fifth Naval District, ordered the diversion, sir. He wanted to go after the sub."

On second thought, the Coast Guard was exactly right, Ames decided. Get that goddamn sub if at all possible. Motor lifeboats couldn't do that job. A big cutter, with depth charges, could.

"OK," the admiral sighed. "But what have we got to help the *Tuttle* people?"

"The *Clayton* was sent out there at 0500. From Norfolk, sir."

"What is she?" Not a lousy tugboat, he hoped. He wasn't familiar with the *Clayton*.

"Destroyer, sir. Mahan class."

OK. Mahan class. A two-stacker built in the midthirties. She could handle it easily enough. But in those big seas off the Virginia Capes, even at fifteen knots, she wouldn't arrive at the *Tuttle*'s position for another four hours. They could all freeze to death in the meantime.

"Let me know any signals from the *Clayton*."

"Yessir."

Ames hung up, looking again at the logs.

0012: Submarine picked up on listening device south of Hussey Sound. Telephoned Captain Phillips. Closed Boston, Portland and Portsmouth to all shipping. Then began to receive reports along the coast on the same subject. Listed below.

Ames read all eleven signals. Most seemed to be figments of imagination. That would occur a lot, he knew. Which were which?

0511 EST
SS Chester Swaine sighted submarine 32-25N; 76.25W. Swaine proceeding to Wilmington, N.C.

Ames's laugh was low and tinny. "Proceeding" had to be a gross understatement. *Hell, she was running for her life.* It was going to be a long day at Headquarters, Eastern Sea Frontier.

✛ ✛ ✛

Sully had no idea of when he finally fell asleep or how long he'd slept. Not very long, he thought. The night had seemed forever, but he was aware now that daylight wasn't far off. Stars were dimming and it was yellowing to the east.

As he sat there trying to clear his head, he vaguely remembered a dream and being chased up Fifty-seventh Street by the leopard. Maureen yelled from a window of the Henry Hudson, "Run, Sully, run!" Another leopard nightmare to cap a nightmare night.

And he was slowly aware again of the savage cold. He had no feeling in his hands or feet. His face felt frozen, and his eyes stung from salt burn. He checked his hands. They were claws. He moved his legs. They felt hinged. His whole body felt sore and numb.

In the dawn dimness, he looked around at his shipmates under the ice-stiffened boat cover. Except for Matkowski, still prone, and Kalevi they were all swaying with the boat's motion, like weary dozing passengers on a grotesque midnight subway. Horse plumes were coming from their mouths and nostrils. They shivered in their sleep, rocking back and forth at the same time. It was a scene better suited to another dream. But the ocean was real. The boat was real. The bitter cold was real. Nor had any of them dried off. He banged his hands together to get some feeling into them.

Papa Jordan sat next to him, as he had throughout the night, hunched over but leaning toward Sully. Cheney's blue bobcap was pulled below his ears. He was asleep but apparently still alive. Though his mouth was hidden behind the folds of his jacket collar, puffs of vapor came out, thank God.

Captain Ryti was on the other side of Matkowski's still body. He had his arms folded, hands drawn up inside his armpits, and head down facing aft. He and Sparks, who sat beside him in almost the same position, breathed in unison. But Kalevi was down on his knees in the bilge as if he were praying, with his cap tilted over on his curly head and his cheek resting on the rimed thwart. No breath from him. He'd frozen to death already.

Sully stared at Kalevi but made no effort to touch him, feeling strangely removed from the kneeling body. It was unlike Kalevi to die so quickly. He'd thought that Kalevi, with that big gut and those hammy arms would outlast them all. Here he was another corpse, and, more than grieving for him, Sully wearily resented him for dying. He'd taken the easy way out, going off in his sleep. Sully had counted on Kalevi.

Even in the first gray light, Matkowski's innocent face shone. Tissue thin spray had congealed on it. Matkowski might still be alive if I hadn't told him that tankers were the greatest, Sully thought again. Tankers were actually deathtraps. He saw that Fong was still miraculously alive. But his parchment skin was bluish gray. Tiny as he was, he looked even smaller this dawn. Fong hadn't spoken a word since he'd dropped into the boat.

Sully shifted his body to look out from under the canvas hood and realized his buttocks had frozen to the wooden floorboards. No wonder they made them of wood, not metal. Had they been galvanized he'd have ripped his pants getting free. He rocked himself to escape the icy grip.

The other *Tuttle* boats were not in sight as it got light. Had they managed to put up sails? All those engineers? Then he stood erect to get a better look around the entire horizon. He saw just a bird or two winging over the frigid yellowing waves. He'd always wondered how they managed to survive out here especially in winter.

Sully noticed that the makeshift sea anchor was still doing its job, keeping them headed into the swells. But the bow pointed eastward toward the rising sun. If they kept moving in that direction they'd reach the Azores or Portugal. When everyone was awake, they could row awhile, turn west again, but that wouldn't last more than a few minutes, given the shape they were in. Maybe they'd be better off conserving energy and praying to God for a ship to pass close by. They were in the north-south track, usually loaded with hulls.

He felt movement against his leg. Then Sparks rose up from beneath the cover, asking hoarsely, "See anything?" He breathed as if he had asthma. His reddened face was a salt-crusted oval in the jacket hood. His eyes were bloodshot. Sully knew his own were the same or worse.

"No, not even our boats ..."

His jaw felt rigid. It hurt to talk.

"I think Kalevi is dead ..."

Sparks nodded. He looked under the cover to view Kalevi. When his head came up he said, "You knew he had a heart condition."

"No." Maybe he didn't freeze to death, after all. Didn't draw on all that walrus fat to stay alive. Hell, what was he doing out here with a heart condition?

Sparks, shivering head to foot, looked around again. "Christ, it's cold. Worse than yesterday."

Sometime during the night Sully had thought about starting a fire, using one of the buckets for a stove. At least they could warm their hands.

"I'll start a fire."

Sparks began to laugh insanely.

Sully stared at him. What was so goddamn funny?

"Whatta you gonna burn, Sully?"

Wood, you idiot, Sully thought but didn't answer. Instead he ducked back under the cover to check on Captain Ryti, his father, and Fong.

His father was awake but sat there in an almost catatonic state. Fong seemed to be asleep, his right hand still clutching the bag.

Sully knelt down beside Dan, saying, "Papa, I'm going to warm you up."

Jordan turned his head. Finally his lips moved, and he asked, in little more than a hoarse whisper, "Are we going to be rescued, Sully?"

"Yeh, Papa. I'm going to make a fire in a bucket and get everyone warmed up ..."

Dan repeated vacantly, staring at his son with dull sunken eyes, "Will someone rescue us today?"

Sully put his arm around his father's shoulders, wanting to

weep for the first time. Why in God's name had he ever wanted his papa to take a tanker trip?

"Listen to me, Papa. The sun is coming up. It's going to be a clear day. They'll send aircraft out and spot us."

"We'll be rescued?"

"Yeh, Papa, we'll be rescued." Surviving was believing you'd survive, he'd always been told.

"When, Sully?"

God knows when. "Soon, I hope."

Captain Ryti, who had also awakened, said in a croaking voice, "You see the other boats?"

"No, Cap'n. There's nothing out there. Maybe later on when the sun is higher."

"We should have stuck together."

In yesterday's bad weather that was impossible, and what Ryti said was wishful thinking.

"Matkowski's dead, Kalevi's gone, Cap'n," Sully said gently, as if Ryti couldn't see the corpses.

"I know," Ryti answered, his dimpled chin suddenly quivering. Like the older Jordan, he seemed to have aged five years in less than twenty-four hours. He seemed a shriveled old man for the first time. He'd lost his beloved ship and at least three crew members, perhaps many more. That had taken a terrible toll on him. Worst of all, he'd given up tough Juho Kalevi.

"Finest mate I ever had," he added sadly, not glancing over at Kalevi but studying Sully instead. "At my age, I should have gone first."

"He was a good man," Sully agreed, then was silent a moment before suggesting that Kalevi, Matkowski, and naked Cheney should all be put overboard. Three cadavers in the stern weren't of much help to the living, in Sully's opinion.

Ryti slowly got out from under the boat cover, each movement painful and arthritic. "All right, we'll do it tonight if we're not picked up . . ."

Sully felt he had to say something upbeat. "Cap'n, I'm going to start a fire in a bucket. We can burn everything except the rudder ..."

The thwarts were planked, as were the stern and bow sheets. They could even burn the oars.

Ryti, hanging on to the gunwale to stay erect, simply nodded, then turned to Sparks. "When you sent that SOS message off, you reported our position?" Ryti was just making certain that help was on the way.

Sparks said he did.

"Noon position yesterday?" Ryti questioned.

"The one you gave me, Cap'n. 38.53 north; 74.03 west ..."

Ryti's mouth dropped. His breath sucked in. "I said 37.53 ..."

Sully looked back at Sparks with alarm. A degree mistake was sixty miles. Any search aircraft or ships would be scouring the ocean approximately sixty miles to the north of the lifeboats.

Sparks frowned widely. "No, sir. I remember distinctly, you gave me a 38-degree latitude."

Ryti scanned over at Sully. "Which was correct?"

"37.53 north; 74.03 west ..."

He'd not only laid it out on the chart, extending the course line from the previous day, but he'd written it out on the usual slip of paper at the top of the mercator. Without anger Captain Ryti said, "Sparks, you might have given us a death sentence."

"Now, dammit, Cap'n, I heard you distinctly. I'm not to blame if they don't find us."

Ryti ducked back beneath the cover, and Sully busied himself using an axe to pry up the boards that were bolted to the sternsheet frame.

Sparks yelled after the captain, "I'm not to blame, you hear me!"

A few minutes later Sully poured kerosene from the emergency lamp over a board and used sulfur matches from the survival kit to light the wood.

They should warm their hands, try to dry out a little, and have something to eat, was what Sully thought. Then strip the clothes off Kalevi and Matkowski, divide them, and set up lookout watches fore and aft. He planned to suggest that to Ryti, who seemed to be retreating totally from command, looking more and more helpless.

Sparks stuck his head under the cover to yell, "I sent the message you told me to, Cap'n . . ."

"OK, OK," said Sully. It didn't matter much who was to blame. The problem was to stay alive.

Fong suddenly arose from his stupor. He yelled deliriously and flailed around.

✝ ✝ ✝

Kammerer had killed the *Esso St. Louis* at 0417 off Hatteras, a single-screw vessel of seven thousand deadweight tons, with a single torpedo and then twenty-five rounds of 105-mm. He now watched her burn from a quarter mile away. Clouds of black smoke mixed with swatches of violent red coiled up into the dawn sky. He was close enough to hear the growl of the fire.

They'd been up all night, having destroyed a freighter at 0115. A tanker, likely a fast new navy vessel, doing eighteen knots, had outrun them an hour later. Then the elderly *St. Louis* loped along. If another target didn't show up soon they'd slip down to the sandy bottom, get some sleep, and come up at sundown, rested, fed, and ready to hunt again.

But the sexual thrill of hitting the target grew with each attack. Kammerer thought that most of the *122*'s crew felt the way he did. They felt like invincible true warriors in these waters. The gunners, for instance, never saw action in convoy fights. On this patrol they were kings and could watch the fruit of their work—fireballs and oily smoke.

"Do you know anything about the Gulf Stream?" he asked

Graeber while watching the tanker die through his binoculars. Three lifeboats were hove-to several hundred yards from the stern of the blazing hulk.

The First said that, unfortunately, he knew nothing about it. The *U-122* drifted on the east edge of the stream. Kammerer wanted to hang around for a while and wait to see who might come along and attempt to rescue the survivors.

Four pairs of weary eyes searched the horizon north, south, east, and west for any mast tops that might emerge above it. Three pairs were on aerial lookout. The radio operator had monitored the *St. Louis* SOS, so there was nothing secret about her plight some fifty miles east-northeast of Diamond Shoals Lightship, off Cape Hatteras.

Each man had a ninety-degree sector that overlapped with the next lookout, scanning with the seven-by-fifty binoculars. The antiaircraft guns were fully manned with gunners on lookout as well.

"It's a remarkable current that comes up out of the Gulf of Mexico, around six hundred feet deep, and flows up to four knots northerly. Ships have been taking it north since Vespucci. They take it until it veers east. Why, here we are in light clothing, as if we were in the tropics. A day ago we were in freezing cold. The last time I looked at the intake water it was sixty-five degrees centigrade. Can you imagine that, Graeber? Warm enough for a bath?"

"Remarkable," said the first officer, looking at the sky, antsy at being exposed on the surface so near a fresh kill.

Kammerer viewed the eruptions of the *St. Louis*. "We go north and we're in the Labrador Current, maybe thirty-four degrees air temperature. It crashes head-on into the Gulf Stream. You hear about Hatteras being the famous 'Graveyard of the Atlantic.' That's why. The Diamond Shoals are so tricky that even fish don't appreciate them."

Graeber finally cleared his throat nervously. "Herr Kapitän, do we know about enemy air bases near here?"

Kammerer took the binoculars down to look at the First. "Not a thing. That's why we have lookouts, Graeber. But this is not the British coast, so we have more leisure in what we do. Correct?" Disdain was in his voice.

"Yes, Herr Kapitän."

Kammerer's eyes returned to the more satisfying view of the *St. Louis*. He continued his education of the first watch officer. "Exactly where we are right now is the world's best U-boat hunting ground. Fifty or sixty ships pass here every twenty-four hours, and I, for one, plan to take advantage—"

Just then, Schoenleber, the young seaman from Lüneburg, sang out, "Smoke dead astern!"

Heads swiveled; Kammerer looked south to confirm the slim telltale smoke. Most likely another merchantman. "Let's go meet it," he said to Graeber; then he said into the speaking tube, "Both engines ahead full." He soon brought the *122* due south, and they raced toward the new target.

✛ ✛ ✛

Admiral Ames stood in the doorway of Captain Phillips's office, his wrestler's body filling it, a wide scowl on his face. "How many goddamn subs are down at Hatteras? Five ships in twenty-four hours. Now, a sixth under attack . . ." He'd seen the *Esso St. Louis* SOS.

The light down on the street level of Manhattan's financial district was gray and fleeting. The big clock in Operations read 1652. The working day for downtown stock-and-bond people was over, but the navy four-to-twelve watch at 90 Church Street had just begun on a discouraging note.

"I suspect it's just one sub," Phillips replied.

"How so?"

"Two of those ships have identified it as having a leopard on the conning tower. Except for the *Tuttle*, which was well to the north, the other attacks were within a few miles of each other. It's likely he got the *Tuttle* off Virginia and then steered straight into the Gulf Stream shipping track."

"A one-sub task force? What the hell will happen to us when Dönitz sends over a dozen?"

"*Hell's* the right word, Admiral."

"If this was the Old West, I'd put a bounty on that son of a bitch with the leopard sub."

"And he'll be back, Admiral. When a good commander finds a good hunting area he works it for all it's worth. That one down there is probably a very good sub commander. I'll guarantee you he'll be back. He'll go home, rest for a couple of weeks, load his torpedoes, and return to Hatteras."

"I hope we'll have something out there by then to take him on. We damn well better have something."

The Hatteras activity had been checked just after dawn by a pair of Catalina flying boats. They found the *Esso St. Louis* and the *Samuel Sinclair* on fire, survivors in lifeboats. One of the Cats had flown out to the position where the *Garborg*, a Norwegian freighter, had sent an SSS. They saw no trace of her, no lifeboats. Neither did they see any submarines.

Ames moved from the doorway to walk over in front of the huge chart of Frontier waters, Maine's Grand Manan Channel down to Florida's Key West. Phillips followed and stood beside him. Markers indicated the six confirmed kills, from off Maine's Jonesport down to the Chesapeake Bay entrance, with the *Tuttle* unconfirmed but probable, as well as the ships clustered off Hatteras. There were four additional unconfirmed attack reports and seven sub sightings, also unconfirmed.

"As of this minute, how many of these vipers do you think are actually here?" The admiral had his own guess.

Phillips answered as if he were positive. "I've been thinking about it all day. If even half of the attack reports and sightings are legitimate, more than the five COMINCH predicted."

"That's my hunch, too. All right, the British tell us this class boat can operate over here for two weeks, based on average fuel consumption. So we're facing a minimum of ten more days, maximum of fifteen, until they go back to France and are replaced."

Captain Phillips said, "Correct."

"And we may lose five or six ships a day based on losses so far?"

"Yessir."

His mood changed to pure gloom as the admiral stared at the ocean from New York to the North Carolina border. Games at the War College said it was potentially the most dangerous shipping sector in the western world. The inner belt was the coast itself; the outer extremity was seventy-five west longitude. Fifty or sixty thousand square miles of playground for Dönitz.

"Jesus Christ, Tom, the American people will want our necks, and they'll be right. Caught red-assed with our drawers down again ..."

Phillips remained silent.

As Andrews turned away he asked, "What's the latest on the *Tuttle*?"

"The *Clayton* went out to her reported position, and the last we had from her, at 1430, was not even signs of debris. A search plane went off from Norfolk at 1000. Fifth Naval District is trying, Admiral."

Ames nodded and left Operations to return to his office.

✛ ✛ ✛

The dark green Gestapo sedan was parked in the château lot at Kernevel. The driver dozed inside while Kuppisch was in Kapitän Godt's office, paying an in-person visit with what he thought was some interesting information.

"You have a waiter spying on my officers?" Godt said, with an incredulous frown.

"I prefer to say 'protecting' them, Herr Kapitän."

"Does this mean that when I come into the See Kommandant your waiter is likely to write down my name?"

"No, Herr Kapitän. This girl is under suspicion, and when she comes into the restaurant with one of your boat commanders then we take notice."

"Are you certain it was Kapitänleutnant Kammerer?"

"Quite certain. He is known there."

"Why do you suspect the girl?"

"She goes to Bar Raphael, which is a hotbed of the Résistance; she goes to the convent where we suspect there is an agent. She works at a local bookstore that is owned by Max Goff, a Jew. He is currently under investigation in Paris. He didn't register and has denied being Jewish. Whether or not he is, we discovered Goff contributed money to an underground newspaper. Add up all these and I think that Herr Kammerer should be very careful in his relationship with Hélène Dussac."

Godt sighed. Operating U-boats was often cleaner and simpler than dealing with human problems. Men would always go with women. There was no way to stop it, and the wise commander didn't try. There was never a way to know that a girl was an agent or in the *Résistance* until it was too late. Damage control, at sea or on land, was the only answer.

"He's on patrol at the moment. When he returns I'll advise him of your concern." He'd written down the girl's name.

"Thank you," said Kuppisch. "And please give my regards to the admiral." Godt nodded. He'd do no such thing.

Rising, Kuppisch said, "You have a very nice place here. Quite elegant."

"It serves," Godt said, rising too; he moved from behind his desk, saying coldly, "I have an officer waiting; you'll excuse me."

✢ ✢ ✢

They'd spent most of the glittering ice-cold day on lookout. Just before noon there'd been a smoke trail against the clear blue sky to the southwest. For a while there was hope. The weather was ideal for rescue; visibility was almost unlimited and the winter sun shone—its irony did not escape them. Any aircraft within ten miles would have seen the mirror flashes. A ship even five miles away might have seen the reflective stabs.

But the ship to the southwest remained hull-down on the horizon. Ryti remarked glumly that she was inviting torpedoes. Sully didn't even bother to flash the rectangular metal. Aside from the pencil of smoke, the sea and sky had been agonizingly empty and their spirits fell again by late afternoon. They'd mostly dried out from the dazzling winter sun and the bucket fire, but they knew they'd meet the brutal frozen night soon enough.

In the morning, Sully and Sparks had stripped Matkowski and Kalevi, and divided their clothing five ways. They dragged their bodies aft, placing them with Cheney by the sternsheets. All day, they'd tried not to look over at the naked, warped blue-white cadavers.

"Papa, you've just got to believe that tomorrow they'll find us. You know how many ships and planes the navy has in Norfolk. You've seen them."

The elder Jordan nodded but without much conviction.

"You've seen them!"

Sully's arm was around his father's shoulder again, comforting him.

"They searched in the wrong place today, but they'll come south tomorrow."

Dan nodded again. He hadn't said twenty words all day; he'd only moved off his seat to urinate, eaten a few bites of sea biscuit, and had a taste of the square chocolate.

"All we've got to do is last the night out."

Papa Jordan turned his head toward his son. He was fading fast. Faster than Ryti, who wasn't in good shape either. Dan's watery eyes were those of an old sick man. "I'll try, Sully," he said. His bewhiskered gray chin quivered. "I'll try."

"You have to, Papa. What would Mama do if I didn't bring you back in one piece?"

Dan nodded again and closed his lids, retreating back tiredly into his shell of misery.

Sully had wrapped his father's festered hands and feet after tearing up Kalevi's woolen shirt. He'd also given him Matkowski's jacket and pants.

"Mama would never forgive me. We love you! Stay alive."

His father nodded once again.

The boat, with its three dead and five living occupants, the latter bundled like Mongolians in their borrowed clothes, continued to wear across the moderate swells as light faded. The sun dropped into cloud folds to the west, turning them saffron. The dreaded cold crept in again, and Sully thought it was time to give up the dead.

It was a chore that had to be done, in his opinion, even though the cold would preserve them. There might not be a rescue for days. Just seeing them hour after hour was a path to madness. Disrespect for them or next of kin was not involved.

"Cap'n, I'd like to put them overboard, for everyone's sake."

Ryti lifted his head and nodded.

"Do you want to say a prayer?"

Ryti labored up and painfully crossed the two thwarts to reach the bowsheets.

Sully had an idea that few masters could recite the traditional prayer, burials at sea not being common in peacetime. But Ryti seemed to know it, though his words of commitment were in Finnish. He spoke them and quickly turned his back. He crawled forward again to his place in the middle of the boat and hunched over in dejection.

"All right?" Sully said to Sparks.

The radio operator took a deep breath.

Steeling himself and trying to think that he was handling an inanimate object, not the distorted remains of a human, Sully lifted Cheney's stiff right arm. Sparks grabbed the left. They slid the third mate over the stern. Then they sent Matkowski and Kalevi behind Cheney.

"Don't ask me to do that again," Sparks said, not looking at the bobbing heads in the wake of the boat.

Sully preferred not to answer. He climbed forward to replace the sail cover for the night. He'd already chopped all the remaining wood with the exception of two oars, the tiller, and the rudder. Maybe there was enough wood to last until daylight. He'd let the fire die out in midmorning. It was time to relight, nurse it while they huddled around, and try to combat frostbite.

✛ ✛ ✛

"Heinz Bonartz," said the familiar voice. "How are you, Admiral?"

"I'm very good," said Dönitz to the head of *B-Dienst*.

"First of all let me congratulate you on the sinkings in American waters. We can hardly keep up with the distress signals off the east coast over there." *B-Dienst* had increased the wireless monitoring after *BdU* signaled *Paukenschlag*.

"I must say I'm delighted, Kapitän. And we're doing it with only five boats. I have more on the way, however."

"Well, I'll anticipate even greater action, then," said Bonartz.

"Yes, and please keep Headquarters informed."

"I assure you I will, Admiral."

"I need all the friends I can get on the Tirpitzufer."

Bonartz laughed. "You have many."

"I'm not so sure," said Dönitz, carefully. If he'd had more friends there'd be a dozen boats off America instead of only five.

"Admiral, another reason that I called is to tell you of my concern about a major security leak in Lorient. Today we finally decoded a group of three-week-old messages from Intelligence in London to Washington. One of them estimates that five U-boats were headed for coastal waters of the United States and gives the precise date and time of their departure."

Dönitz frowned. "Only two departed from here."

"I'm sure that many people see them depart, but to say flatly that they were headed for America is more than a guess, I'd say."

"I agree." Yet most intelligence was piecework and guess.

"Additionally, the two boats that departed from Lorient were identified by their insignia. A snarling leopard and a dancing girl ..."

Kammerer and Gruppner, Dönitz knew. That was precise enough.

"What alarms me the most is the fact that London knew the departure time *from the harbor*. They usually learn it when the boat reports to you that it has cleared the bay ..."

"Correct."

"Someone is going a step ahead. I suspect an agent."

"Have you told anybody?"

"No, sir. I wanted to talk to you first, Admiral."

"I'm glad. Let me handle it, Heinz. I'll inform Headquarters after we investigate locally."

In Berlin, there were enough loose tongues and suspicions to create deadly problems of all sorts. Better to attempt to solve them in Lorient.

They chatted a minute longer, Bonartz saying he envied the admiral for the peace and quiet of France if not the fine food and wine. Dönitz had known Bonartz for years. The communications expert was trustworthy, a man of his word.

After he hung up, Dönitz sat for a moment in thought before summoning Godt. He had misgivings about bringing that oaf Kuppisch into further confidence. His opinion of the Gestapo started in the cellar and went down. Yet Kuppisch had warned Godt about Kammerer's seeing a French girl.

✜ ✜ ✜

Off and on as Sully fed the bucket fire and held his father, encouraging him, lifeboat No. 2 drifted northeast in the early evening. It continued to plunge and pitch and flounder drunkenly across the swells. Though they'd mostly dried off during the long day, they were now soaked again. What little food they'd had at sundown had come up.

Sully and his father faced Ryti, Fong, and Sparks in the center of the boat, all bundled like mummies. Their feet were on the bucket, and their hands extended toward it.

Sully tried to keep up the conversation, but aside from Sparks they sat there silently. With their eyes closed, they swayed and rocked around. He knew they were dying. "All day I've been thinking about that bearded son of a bitch in the white hat and the way he looked at us. You ever see such an arrogant son of a bitch?"

Sparks didn't answer.

"You know, he didn't need to keep shelling us. A half-dozen would have done it. He was using that pyrotechnic kind to see how fast he could get us burning. I just wish to God we'd had a gun to shoot back with."

That subject exhausted, Sully sighed and then said, "We'll be picked up tomorrow. We're too close to shore not to be picked up. There's too much traffic out here, isn't that right, Cap'n?"

Ryti didn't answer.

"It's not like we're out in the South Atlantic or down in the South Pacific. Hell, we're right in the middle of the greatest ship highway on earth ... a hundred a day go by here." Where are they? he asked himself.

"We get another clear day like today and an aircraft'll spot us," he continued.

They were paying for the clear skies now. It was at least ten degrees colder. Skim ice was already forming on the bilge.

"We still haven't used our flares ..."

Sully suddenly realized that Sparks was no longer talking. He'd succumbed to fatigue and dozed off. The wind and savage cold had sapped and weakened them to the point they had no resistance. No one talked. They were giving up; perhaps even Sparks was.

After what seemed to be endless hours, he looked at his watch. The radium dial said it was only 8:42 P.M. To be honest, he knew that if they weren't rescued tomorrow he'd no longer care. With salt-caked mouths and lips and their throats afire none of them could eat anything. He knew that his feet, nose, and ears were bloodless, probably frozen. It seemed that only his brain and breathing functioned; the rest of him was numb.

A little later Sully closed his eyes. Soon the fire died out.

The boat kept heaving and lurching northeast behind the keg as the temperature fell again.

✣ ✣ ✣

Hélène opened the letter from Paris addressed to Lorient Livres. The sender did not identify herself. It said, "Max Goff was arrested for failure to register and was taken to Gestapo headquarters for questioning. He was also accused of forging a false ration card and contributing to an underground newspaper. In the afternoon, he was seen being pushed into a prison truck, manacled. I heard later that he was taken to the camp on the Dordogne River near Bergerac. I would not attempt to contact him. Be careful."

Hélène felt ill.

The ration card charge was ridiculous. It had been used before by both the Vichy *judiciaire* and the Gestapo when they wanted to jail someone. But she knew that Max had purposely failed to register as a Vienna-born Jew. Why entrap himself when he had false proof he was a Catholic? Why not gamble?

She was close to tears as she read the letter again. Poor, harmless old man—what had he done to deserve this? But that was a foolish question to ask nowadays almost anywhere in Europe. Since there was no way to help him at Bergerac, though she planned to ask Sister Cecile, how would his arrest affect her? Would the Gestapo now go after her simply because she worked for Goff?

+ + +

At 0912, the USS *Clayton* machine-gunned lifeboat No. 2 of the *E. D. Tuttle* so that no other vessel would stop and investigate it, and become a torpedo target. Shortly it would sink two thousand fathoms to the bottom.

The *Clayton*'s captain, a lieutenant commander, watched the gunnery as her executive officer, a lieutenant, walked out on the bridge of the destroyer. "Cap'n, the doctor says we need to go full bore for Norfolk. He's not promising anything. They're only half-alive, suffering from severe frostbite and exposure, good candidates for pneumonia ..."

The skipper turned to the watch officer. "Tell gunnery to cease and desist. That thing's got more holes in it than the cook's sieve." Then he turned back to the exec. "What about the other three?"

The exec shook his head. "I knew they were dead when I looked under the sail. They were all huddled around a fire bucket."

"A fire bucket? What were they burning?"

"Any wood that was in the boat. They were all frozen, but the old men were like icicles. They literally cracked like ice when we got them aboard. You wouldn't believe what they were wearing. It looked like they'd robbed clothing off other guys. I have an idea that boat held more than five at one time."

"The two that are still alive, can they talk?"

"No, sir ... They're unconscious. They look younger than the dead ones. One of them has had an amputation. We brought his artificial leg up. We also brought up a black bag that one of the older men was holding. He looks Chinese. Doc said he would probably have to use wire cutters to get that bag out of the guy's hand. His fist has a death grip on it."

"Tell Doc to keep me posted." Then he turned to the watch officer again. "Have Communications tell Norfolk we're heading home at twenty-five knots with two survivors and three dead. Estimate three and a half hours. Need the medicos to meet us ..."

Forty-five minutes later, the exec visited the bridge again to exhibit a black bag. "You know what's in it, Cap'n?"

"Don't make me guess."

The exec opened the catch, revealing stacks of green. "U.S. currency—thousands!"

"Good God. The Chinese guy?"

"Yessir."

"Count every dollar of it, with two witnesses standing over you, and then it goes into the safe. Just goes to show you. You can't take it with you . . ."

Book Four

THE Q-SHIP

parks and Sully were still in the merchant marine hospital in Norfolk. Sully's cheeks, forehead, and the back of his hands had lost some of the purple hue, but the tip of his nose was a crimson-black scab. Even hardened nurses winced.

"Sorry I haven't been able to come down until now," Jack D. Pyle said, taking a chair across from the beds after removing his expensive topcoat. His fingernails were manicured, but his scarred hands were those of a roustabout.

"That's OK," Sully replied, as he studied Consolidated Oil's burly president. He'd heard about Pyle but had never seen him except in company photos. He knew Pyle had worked the fields of Texas and Louisiana and had gotten his share of dry holes as well as lucky ones.

"Well, we really didn't expect you," Sparks added.

"I'm very sorry about your dad," Pyle said, addressing Sully directly.

"I picked the wrong trip."

"What happened wasn't your fault."

Sparks said, "I've told him that a dozen times."

Sully ignored Sparks.

Pyle, a smooth-shaven portrait of rosy health and wealth, was visibly uncomfortable at seeing the abrupt ending of Sam

Bessemer's amputated legs beneath the covers and Sullivan Jordan's wrecked face. He shifted around on his chair, his stubby fingers rotating his hat brim. "We've been pretty busy the past two weeks. First the *Tuttle,* then the *Beaufort* and the *Churchfield* ..."

Sully and Sparks knew both ships.

"Sunk?" said Sparks.

"Within two days of each other. Everyone got off the *Churchfield,* thank God. Twenty died on the *Beaufort,* so far as we know. Nineteen known survivors."

"Where?" Sully asked.

"*Churchfield* off the Delaware Capes; *Beaufort* off Diamond Shoals."

"What happened to the *Tuttle* people? We know about our boat. How about the rest?"

"No one told you?"

Sully shook his head.

"Two survived from boat No. 3, Larsen and Macready. They were picked up by an Argentinean reefer the day before you were rescued. They died before the reefer made it to New York."

"Boat No. 4?" Sparks asked.

Chief Logan had been in that one, along with most of the black gang, Sully remembered.

Pyle shook his head. "No trace as yet. We still hope for them." His eyes said otherwise.

"Did anyone on the *Beaufort* see the sub that got them?"

"I don't think so. It happened just past midnight."

"Well, if anyone has talked to them I'd appreciate knowing if they saw a sub with a leopard on it."

Rolling his eyes, Sparks said, "Sully is hung up on that sub."

"It got the *Galveston* and the *Tuttle* ...," Sully explained to Pyle.

"I'll ask Operations for you," Pyle said.

"I'd appreciate that," Sully said.

Finally Pyle asked, speaking to both men, "What are your

plans? If you don't want to go back to sea, we've got office jobs for you."

Sparks admitted, "I think my seagoing days are over."

"We'll find a place for you," Pyle promised and then looked over at Sully, who was fully clothed and propped up on pillows. "When will you get out?"

"Tomorrow, they said."

"Take some time off, Sully. You're on the payroll at sea wages, and you'll stay that way for the time being. If you want a shore job, I'm sure we can use you in Operations or at a terminal . . ."

"I've been thinking about the navy, Mr. Pyle."

Sparks broke in. "He wants to get that sub." Sparks circled his index finger at his right temple. The guy's looney, his finger said.

Pyle cast a baffled look at Sully as if he hadn't heard right. "You mean you want to get into combat?"

"I have a reserve commission as a lieutenant. They offered it when I made chief."

Pyle frowned. "If you want to stay at sea, Sully, you're needed on *our* ships." He added quickly, "But it's your decision, of course."

"I'll make it soon."

Pyle nodded, appearing even more restless than when he entered. "Now is there *anything* you need? Just pick up the phone."

"We don't need anything," Sully said.

Pyle arose, saying, "Well, fellows, I've got a plane to catch." He lingered a moment longer before saying good-bye. "I know that both of you and everyone else did the best you could out there. I'm grateful. That goes for everyone at Consolidated." His tone was awkward and apologetic.

After Pyle departed, Sparks urged, "Take one of his shore jobs, Sully. You'll be home every night."

Sully's eyes were still focused on the empty doorway. "If I hadn't let that fire go out . . ."

"Chrissakes, Jesus Chrissakes, they were all old men, and there wasn't that much wood left," Sparks said.

The rebuke from Sam Bessemer mattered not. All Sully had to do was look in the mirror.

✝ ✝ ✝

Admiral Ames stood in Operations at 0530 on murky January 20, looking at the *Enemy Action Diary* for last night and up to 0400 this morning.

2320—Received from Duty Officer, Phila. via Tuckerton Radio: SS PAN ATLAS sighted submarine 0900 GMT at 37 30 N; 75 60 W. Course 30 T. speed 11.5 knots. Dispatch forward to OpNAV, COMINCH, CINCLANT.

Ames scanned the rest of the night's reports and didn't see a single hopeful sentence anywhere in the diary. January 20 wasn't starting out any better than the nineteenth.

0400—EST—Burning tanker seen by fishing vessel 20 miles ESE of Wimble Shoals.

A few minutes after nine, Mrs. Cinelli hurried into the admiral's office, speaking softly, as if God were calling. "Admiral King is on the phone." She'd been around the navy long enough to know when God, as represented by COMINCH, was going to orate.

Ames picked up the black instrument, knowing that one of a half-dozen voices would usually preface the conversation, so he said casually, "Admiral Ames here."

The voice he heard belonged directly to the ball-buster himself, Old Blowtorch. King said, "Andy, I just came back from the White House."

An impressive enough opening, Ames thought.

"The president is appalled at what's happening, and so am I. *Slaughter!* He doesn't understand it, but we do."

"What does he want, Admiral?" Ames asked.

"Q-ships."

"Good God!" said Ames.

"That was exactly my reaction. I told him that the British had already tried them, and they weren't successful. He said, 'Try them now!' So that's what we're going to do, whether you or I or anyone else in this whole goddamn navy likes it, we're going to have three Q-ships."

King said he'd arranged for money outside normal channels so they wouldn't have to go through General Accounting. "We're going into the privateer business, and I don't want to hear anything about it until you go out and sink a German sub."

"Yessir." Q-ships. Just like that, Ames thought.

"The president said we should hang our heads in shame. I don't hang my head to anyone, but we better damn soon get ourselves a German submarine. Whether we do it with a Q-ship or the Staten Island ferry I don't care."

The phone was hung up with a crack.

Ames laughed brittlely. "Q-ships!"

"What are they?" Mrs. Cinelli asked.

"Warships disguised as merchantmen. So far as I'm concerned, they're useless. However, in this case we're going to use them."

"Why, if they're useless?"

Ames gazed at her over the rims of his reading glasses. "Because Franklin Delano Roosevelt told us to use them."

"Oh."

He pressed the intercom button to summon Captain Phillips. A moment later he asked the chief of staff what he knew about Q-ships.

"Not a thing. I know what they are, that's all."

"Well, we're going to be operating three of them, so we'd better learn. We're going to buy three, arm three, crew three, and send them to sea with orders to become targets, then sink a submarine ..."

Captain Phillips whistled softly. "Ernie King?"

"Go higher. FDR!"

"When do we start?"

"Five minutes ago. Get Reston and Hedley on it."

Lieutenant Commander Rollins Hedley was assistant operations officer, an ex-Academy man recalled to duty.

"I'm assuming it's 'need-to-know' classification."

"Don't even tell your dog."

With raised skeptical eyebrows, Phillips departed.

Ames sat back for a moment, contemplating Q-ships. You invite the enemy to kill you and then try to kill him first.

A coded dispatch from COMINCH arrived within the hour, making it official and informing the few parties to be involved, from OPNAV (Naval Operations) down to navy yard commandants, of top-secret Project RQ: *R* for FDR and *Q*, of course, for the phantom ships.

✢ ✢ ✢

Rusty Hedley, a graying bandbox-handsome Annapolis graduate of the class of '26, had opted for civilian life when his young wife was diagnosed as having lung cancer. He wanted to be with her, so he came ashore to work as a stockbroker, commuting to Wall Street every day from fashionable West Nyack. His good looks and Ivy League manners helped make him a lot of money, but his heart was still with the navy. He volunteered when things began to heat up. He'd been a destroyer gunnery officer previously. He'd reentered as a lieutenant commander and still turned female heads.

"As far as I can determine, Admiral, the British sank eleven subs and damaged two by Q-ship action in the last war," Rusty said. He'd gone to Washington for research.

Ames asked, "How many Q-ships were lost?"

"Twenty-seven."

"Ouch. How about this war?"

"They commissioned eight. One was blasted on its first sortie. Then another was sunk. The other six were dearmed and are now hauling cargo again," Rusty explained.

"What about us?"

"We commissioned the *Santee* in the last war. A U-boat promptly sent her down."

Captain Phillips said, "Doesn't speak a helluva lot for them, does it?"

"Hardly. I think we're talking about fish bait. However . . ." The admiral let the "however" hang in the air like a falling kite.

Rusty continued, "I'll smooth draft this tomorrow and add more detail if you agree generally."

"Read it," said Phillips.

Hedley pointed out that a Q-ship should have as much buoyancy as possible to remain afloat after being torpedoed. In the case of a tanker it could be accomplished by filling her tanks with empty oil drums.

For armament he proposed four 3-inch, .23-caliber guns on the broadsides, fore and aft. They were readily available, could be installed in a few days, and had a fairly high rate of fire. He recommended a heavier 4-inch, .50-caliber gun on the stern and passed a rough drawing of the hidden gun positions on a small tanker. K-mountings to hurl three-hundred-pound Mark 6 depth charges would go on the stern.

Aside from standard items, the other equipment would include underwater sound gear, a range finder, and small arms and hand grenades for possible boardings.

Phillips said, "Crew."

"I've covered that, sir." Two crews—one for gunnery, five men per gun, and one to man the ship plus carry out "abandonment." He'd learned in his quick British research that the whole thing hung on how realistic the "abandoning" looked.

"Officer complement?" the admiral asked.

"Two qualified gunnery officers. One for battery control on the bridge, the other for battery control aft." One or the other could well be a casualty on the torpedo hit. "We need to make certain one can function at all times in a sustained gun battle."

"Ship's company?" Ames asked.

"Streamlined. Commanding officer, gunnery officers doubling as watch officers, communication, the usual . . ."

Ames said, "It has to be a volunteer situation!" He'd sent a letter to Ernie King yesterday to that effect. "Volunteers only. Assign them, but then tell them this will be a high-risk operation."

"Absolutely," Phillips said.

Rusty nodded that he understood. "The attacks have mostly been at night and at close range against tankers, so it makes sense that we use a tanker as one of the decoys." It would follow the coastal routes between New York and Charleston, proceeding south unloaded, then taking on ballast to appear loaded on the trip north. "She should pass the most dangerous areas at night—Hatteras, off the Virginia Capes, and off New Jersey."

"Appearing as if she's on a regular run?" Phillips asked.

"Yessir. If and when she's torpedoed, the usual high degree of confusion should take place; boats should be launched with eight or ten men getting into them . . ."

"Suppose the submarine commander opts to take her with gunfire?" the admiral questioned.

"The same abandonment drill applies; battery control officers should hold fire until such time as the sub is in easy range. At least, that's my solution," Rusty said.

"Probably the only solution," Ames agreed.

"I forgot one thing—everybody aboard will be dressed as merchant seamen. Everyone. Not a single naval uniform should be seen once they clear the harbor."

Ames nodded. "Then I recommend we commission them as regular naval vessels. They revert to being merchantmen at the sea buoy."

Hedley nodded.

"Security," said Captain Phillips.

"It's obvious that shipyard workers will suspect something is out of the ordinary when we put this many guns on a merchant ship. There'll be talk. But we just have to risk it," Rusty went on.

Admiral Ames took another look at the arming sketch. "Draft it smooth and have it ready for my signature this afternoon."

Hedley slipped a photograph out from under his note sheet. "One more thing, sir." He passed the photo to the admiral. "That's the tanker I recommend. *Esso Dolomite.* She's 375 feet long overall, and forty-one hundred tons. Diesel powered, she can make nine knots loaded. She's used only on coastal runs. I took a look at her yesterday in Philadelphia. She's in good shape."

"Where the hell did you dig her up on such short notice?" the admiral asked, examining the photo.

"Mrs. Cinelli gave me the name of an Esso tanker contact you had, a Mr. Patrick Carroll."

Ames snorted, "I knew I went to that meeting for a reason."

"I called him the day before yesterday. He called back at Main Navy yesterday morning, and I caught the Pennsy to Philadelphia at noon. We can charter her bareboat as a special favor from Esso. All they want is standard insurance."

"You didn't tell him why?" Ames inquired.

"He didn't ask."

"Good. Call the Bureau of Ships, have them send an inspection team up. Let's lock the deal if she's seaworthy. *Esso Dolomite.* I'll be damned."

Rusty Hedley departed in high spirits, saying thanks to Mrs. Cinelli as he passed her desk. Now to scramble around and find a couple of coastal steamers. He had a lead with McGill Lines.

Four-year-old Danny stared at his father wide-eyed. His face tightened in a grimace as if he'd just been administered bad-tasting medicine.

Maureen held the sleeping baby in her arms. She said quickly, "I told you that Daddy was frostbitten in the lifeboat. It's healing now."

They were in the living room. Sully had limped into the house a moment before.

Sully said to his son, "I look like a Halloween mask, but I'll be fine. You should have seen me the first day in the hospital."

"The end of your nose is gone," Danny said, still wearing the grimace.

"It looks funny, but once it's healed the doctors will make a new end, I promise."

"What happened to your ears?"

"They were frozen, Danny, but I can hear just the same. They just look bad now."

Danny pointed to Sully's left hand. "What happened to your hand?"

The left hand was bandaged. "Three fingers were frozen. But the rest of them are fine." Sully figured he'd put his right hand under his armpit before he'd fallen asleep. The left had been exposed all night. The doctor couldn't explain why only three fingers had been frostbitten.

"You should have seen him two weeks ago, Danny."

"I look a hundred-percent better," Sully assured his son.

"Mommy said you lost four toes. Can I see where you lost them?"

Sully frowned at Maureen. Did she need to tell him? The boy was looking down at Sully's feet. A nurse had cut out the ends of his slippers at the hospital. There were bandages beneath the white socks. "You'll see them when I change bandages."

That seemed to satisfy Danny. He said, "Come and look at my new goldfish."

Maureen said, "Oscar died, and I bought him a new one last week at the dime store."

Oscar? How long had Danny had a goldfish bowl?

There was that feeling of strangeness for a few minutes every homecoming, as if he didn't belong. This time was worst of all. Two weeks ago he had been unconscious in boat No. 2. Now he had to connect back to them as if he hadn't gone away, as if nothing had happened.

He followed Danny into the children's room. "This is Oscar the Second."

"Good-looking fish," he said.

Maureen said, "Would you like to hold Julie?"

He took the baby. He had her head cupped in his good right hand, with her tiny body against his chest, but he didn't realize he was still transfixed by the swimming fish.

Maureen broke through. "You have the funniest look on your face, Sully. What are you thinking about?"

"I let the fire go out. I let it go out."

"Stop punishing yourself," she demanded worriedly.

He'd told her some of what happened in boat No. 2.

The N & W coaljack clanked and pounded by the house a little after eleven, shaking it as usual, but Maureen didn't wake up. Perhaps she only woke up when he wasn't home.

Unable to go to sleep, Sully slid out of bed and went to the john. While washing his hands, he again stared at the distortion in the mirror.

✢ ✢ ✢

After the obligatory appearance at the crew's arrival dinner, Kammerer went straight to Hélène's apartment. He put down the food parcel and champagne bottle and gathered her into his arms. He kissed her with the hunger of almost eight weeks. There were only a few hours that he hadn't thought of her.

He'd brought the *U-122* into Lorient just after daylight to a noisy, triumphant welcome—he had sunk eight ships, forty-eight thousand tons. Late that morning, he'd sent a messenger to Lorient Livres to tell her he'd returned. He'd see her at about 8:00 P.M.

She was on his mind even during the arrival ceremonies. Now

she was returning his kisses and frantically meeting his tongue. She wore nothing beneath the robe. Within seconds his hands were grasping her small firm buttocks.

When their mouths weren't joined, he kept repeating, "I missed you, oh, I missed you," and she said the same. He finally did what he'd been thinking about doing for almost eight weeks; he carried her into the bedroom and spread the robe open, then got out of his coat and uniform in a frenzy.

They both climaxed early, almost simultaneously, then spent themselves again. Finally, after tender, mutual kisses, he rolled away from her and got up to put on his own robe. He'd bought it the last time in port.

He opened the chilled champagne and brought it back to the bed with two goblets. They sat up, side by side, as domestic as any couple could be, and he told her about the patrol off America. He wanted to talk about it. He'd tell Dönitz and the others about it in the morning. But he wanted to tell her about it tonight.

"There is a cape called Hatteras, in North Carolina. It sits at the very end of a string of narrow little islands called the Outer Banks." He told her it was like the middle of a drawn bow, sticking far out into the sea, and the ships had to go around it. "I blew up six of them off Hatteras." Then he told her about each attack beginning with the *Tuttle.*

"I'll go back there next time and get ten. I'll make a bet with you tonight that I'll get ten off Hatteras next time . . ."

After they finished the bottle of champagne they made love again. Sex, not food, was important this night for both of them.

✣ ✣ ✣

Charts of the sea area from New York's Sandy Hook to Diamond Shoals Lightship, off Hatteras, were laid out on the oblong table in the *Lagezimmer.* Admiral Dönitz, Kapitän Godt, and the usual day operations group gazed at them. Pointing to Ambrose Channel, Kammerer said, "We penetrated to approximately here. I was close enough to the lightship to ask for coffee without using the megaphone."

There was laughter, but Dönitz didn't join it.

"New York's lights appeared just as bright as Berlin's three years ago. Every ship was outlined against the glow. You stay to the east of them and shoot."

A yeoman was taking shorthand.

"Navigation lights are still on, though they may have dimmed them a bit. Ships move along the buoy line, and all you have to do is lay off it and fire. Incredible."

Godt said, "B-Dienst has said they haven't even restricted radio traffic."

"They are doing everything but calling their wives to ask what's for dinner." Kammerer felt jubilant. There was more laughter.

The admiral finally spoke. "What about defensive measures?"

"Meager and amateurish. Single destroyers move up and down the ship lanes. All you have to do is time them. You know when they'll be back. The few aircraft they sent out flew around without a search plan. They crisscrossed the traffic routes hoping to stumble on us." Kammerer had already briefed the admiral and staff on the kills.

Dönitz said gravely, "I assure you that their amateurism won't last too long. Any boat commander who becomes careless will wind up on the bottom."

Kammerer said, "I didn't mean to imply we should be careless."

Dönitz nodded and glanced around at his staff. "I hope the lights farther south and down in the Caribbean are glowing as strongly as over New York." Boats would shortly be off Florida, in the Gulf of Mexico, and near the Caribbean oil ports.

The debriefing continued another half hour. To conclude, the admiral again expressed his appreciation to Kammerer for the fine patrol and excused himself.

Godt lingered by Kammerer for a moment, saying, "When you finish here, please come to my office for a moment."

There were more staff questions in a relaxed atmosphere; then Kammerer walked the few feet to the chief of staff's office, carrying the charts under his arm.

"Please close the door," Godt said, waving the *U-122*'s commander in to take a seat. "I wanted to talk to you alone about a very delicate matter."

Kammerer was mystified.

The Kernevel skies were thick and gray this morning. They darkened Godt's office, giving it a foreboding look.

"I'll come to the point. You're acquainted with a French girl named..." He paused to check a note on his desk. "Hélène Dussac."

Kammerer frowned, answering slowly, "Yes, I am."

"You've seen her a number of times?"

"Yes, I have, Herr Kapitän." His frown grew deeper. "Last night, in fact."

"Do you know anything about her?" Godt asked.

"She's a very nice and an extremely intelligent girl."

"The Gestapo has an interest in her."

"What?"

Godt chose not to reply immediately. His desk light formed an oval over his sad face, lighting it theatrically.

"Are they prying into my personal life?" Kammerer said, completely outraged.

"Not your life. Hers. They suspect she's an agent."

"An agent. That's ridiculous!"

"I'm certain you're right," Godt said, though his expression was open to interpretation. "But to be on the safe side both the admiral and myself would appreciate your cooperation."

Kammerer felt sudden perspiration oozing on his forehead. His heartbeat elevated. *Hélène, an agent?*

"The Gestapo believes she has a motive. Has she ever told you that her younger brother was executed here last year?"

"No, Kapitän, she's never mentioned that."

"Has she ever told you that the bookstore she runs is owned by a Jew?"

"She's never mentioned that, either."

"Or that the Gestapo arrested him not too long ago for failure to register and for supplying funds to an underground newspaper?"

Kammerer shook his head, feeling the heat in his temples.

"All of these things may simply be that they are building a web of suspicion, at which they're expert. But there also may be indications that Hélène Dussac is not what you think she is," Godt said cautiously.

Kammerer felt all the elation from the successful patrol and the warmth and wonder of last night slipping away. He knew how to fight a U-boat but didn't know how to handle intrigue, if indeed there was intrigue.

"The British seemed to know far more about *Paukenschlag* than the usual operation. They knew the exact number of boats that were going, knew your 'leopard,' knew Gruppner's 'dancing girl.' They had the correct time and departure date. The operation seemed to be an open book to them."

"It isn't much of a secret when we sail, Kapitän. Many people seem to know. The workers, the suppliers . . ."

Godt replied, "We're aware of that, but we must always try to withhold information. You know about the Atlantiksender?"

Every commander knew about *Atlantiksender* by now.

"Any officer or enlisted man caught tuned in to Atlantiksender can be in great trouble."

"I'm glad you informed me," Kammerer said.

"It is a vicious campaign set up to undermine this command specifically. The admiral calls it 'poison kitchen Atlantik.' We know that the men believe some of the lies that are told."

"How is Hélène Dussac entangled in all of this?"

"The Gestapo isn't certain. They simply suspect her. But you can help prove her innocence."

"How, Herr Kapitän?"

"Part of the so-called authentication is the broadcasting of sports scores and personal gossip from the flotillas. Casually mention an officer's birthday to her. If we soon hear it again on Atlantiksender then we know who's responsible for feeding British counterintelligence. If we don't hear it, we know that your Hélène Dussac is innocent and the Gestapo closes her particular case. For the sake of the command and your own sake, will you do that?"

"Without the slightest hesitation," Kammerer replied.

"Good!" Godt finally smiled. "And would you please do us another favor? Kuppisch would like to talk to you at your convenience." He wrote down the address on rue de la Patrie, handing it across his desk.

"I have nothing to hide," Kammerer said.

"I'm quite certain of that," Godt said, sincerely. "And you aren't the only commander being asked to cooperate. There are four others who have developed, let's say, close relationships with local girls."

Kammerer knew about two. "There's a file on all of us?" he asked, outraged again.

"I'm afraid so. But there's nothing to worry about, is there? We understand the need for female companionship, but security always takes precedence over companionship, as you well know . . ."

"But, Kapitän, there must be at least five hundred French girls in this town who are fraternizing . . ."

"Perhaps more. But Kuppisch said he wanted to start at the top."

"I see," Kammerer said, rising.

"Again, congratulations on a superb patrol."

Kammerer departed Godt's office both angry and apprehensive. Yet he was certain that Hélène Dussac was not a pipeline to the enemy.

✝ ✝ ✝

The Bureau of Naval Personnel had recruiting desks at all the major facilities; Sully sat before Lieutenant Commander Steinbrink at the Norfolk Naval Operating Base. He'd brought his reserve commission as a lieutenant along, as well as his mate's license.

When Sully limped in, Steinbrink, a reserve himself, had raised his eyebrows as if to say, "Buddy, you're in the wrong place." But what he'd said was, "How can I help you, Mr.—uh . . ." He glanced down at the form Sully had filled out.

"You can give me a physical and swear me in," Sully said. He hid the three empty spaces on his left hand.

Steinbrink, in his midforties and formerly a personnel executive with General Electric, took another look at Sully's face and hardly knew what to say.

"I'm a little beat-up from frostbite, but physically I'm fine," Sully said. He told Steinbrink what had happened with the *Tuttle* and lifeboat No. 2.

Steinbrink listened sympathetically but finally said, "Mr. Jordan, I think you'd be better-off in the merchant marine. I can't even recommend you for a physical."

"Why not?" Sully bristled.

"Well, you limped in here, and I noticed you've got three fingers missing. We've got standards. They're lowered in some cases, but physical impairment is not one of them. I appreciate your desire to help and your, uh, patriotism, but I'm sorry, Mr. Jordan . . ."

Sully argued for a while, then departed Norfolk NOB angrily, feeling humiliated.

"You said to call if I needed anything." He was in a Bell booth by a drugstore. He didn't want to phone New York from the Wilsons'. They always listened in.

"I did indeed," Jack Pyle answered from his spacious office above Wall Street. "Good to hear from you, Sully. How are you feeling?"

"There's a war going on."

"How well I know. You ready to go back to work? We've got a ship for you. What can I do?"

"I went over to the naval base today to ask for active duty. If you remember, I told you they gave me lieutenant senior grade, inactive, when I got my chief's papers. Part of that program is to recruit reserves for their cargo fleet."

"I remember."

"They rejected me, Mr. Pyle. Turned me down flat." He told Pyle about the interview. "What they didn't say was that I looked too hideous to be a naval officer. They don't want anyone walking around in a lieutenant's uniform with biscuits for ears."

There was thoughtful silence from Manhattan for a moment. Then Pyle said, "Sully, you'll make a greater contribution by staying with us. We need experienced men more than they do. We've got a chief's job waiting for you."

"I appreciate everything you've just said, but I want to get into combat."

"Sully, there's enough combat between here and Texas to last a hundred years."

"I know that, but I want to be able to shoot back. I don't want to stand up on the bridge and have a goddamn sub lob shells at me, and not be able to shoot back."

"Every ship in the tanker fleet will soon have guns and gun crews."

"I'm sure that's true, but I'm asking you again . . . Will you help me? You must have some Washington contacts."

There was another deep silence. Then Pyle said, "In the hospital, Sparks said you wanted to get that sub with the leopard on it. I don't blame you, Sully, if that's the same one that got both the *Galveston* and the *Tuttle*. But if it's the only reason you want to go into the navy . . ." Unsaid was, *Jordan, you're nuts!*

"Any sub, Mr. Pyle, any of them. I told that guy I wanted destroyer duty. I just want to be in on the killing of a U-boat. Isn't that a good reason?"

Silence again. Finally Pyle agreed, with resignation. "I know an admiral here. Come on up. I hope you'll change your mind by the time you get off the train."

+ + +

On rue le Coutaller, Hélène held Kammerer's hand. "You said last night that you saw the skyline of New York and the Empire State Building—how close did you go?"

Was that a leading question, was it something that British intelligence would want to know, or was it simply something innocent Hélène was asking? Kammerer asked himself. "About twenty kilometers."

"With the naked eye?"

"You could see it much better with binoculars, of course." What earthly good was it to anyone to know how far he'd penetrated? It was just a matter of innocent curiosity with her, he was certain.

"I've always wanted to go there. I hear it's the most exciting city on earth."

Innocence! "I think Paris is. I prefer Paris or Vienna or Rome. And Berlin, of course, before the war."

"Everyone secretly wants to go to America."

How could they possibly think this vivacious, enchanting girl was a British agent? Over the past ten hours, since leaving Godt's office, he'd tried to remember every question she'd asked him concerning the boats or what he did. He was beginning to realize that she hadn't asked *anything* of importance, that he'd volunteered what little information he'd given her. In fact, Berlin urged them to talk about ships they'd sunk!

Other commanders, in their cups, had probably given out vital information. Enlisted men bragged to whores in the Casino or Krazy Kat. Kammerer was satisfied that he hadn't breached security.

He'd planned to spend all his leave time in Lorient with Hélène instead of taking the *Zug* to Hamburg to see his parents. The

Gestapo's suspicions had now marred that decision. He fought against the temptation to question her.

This night they'd dined luxuriously on Saint Brieuc scallops and *andouillettes,* the small chitterling sausages from Quimperlé prepared for him at the Beauséjour, cauliflower, and mixed fresh fruits from Spain. A bottle of Muscadet and candlelight completed the celebration. He knew she hadn't eaten like this for two months.

After dinner that small, strong body again provided intense delight, and now they were in the warm afterglow, close to each other under the eiderdown. His right hand gently stroked the dark hair on the pillow. Dance-band music came softly from Rennes.

"You have any air raids while I was gone?"

She said, "We've had one a week. The same token raids, usually at night. Very few planes and not much damage."

"They're still concentrating on our cities. I've told my parents they should move to the Alps for safety. But my father says he must stay in Hamburg."

"I went to the Swiss Alps one Christmas, but never to the Bavarian," she said.

"I'll take you someday. You know I thought about you at Christmas, all alone here."

"I spent some of the day with a friend."

"Male or female?"

"Male."

"Young or old?"

"Fiftyish. He's a fisherman. We had dinner here. I cooked."

"Well, I'm glad you weren't alone. With no father, mother, sisters, brothers, boyfriend . . ."

Hélène remained silent.

"You told me your brother was dead but didn't tell me how he died."

"An accident."

"What kind of accident?"

"I'd rather not talk about it."

"All right. How's the store going?"

"I'm closing it at the end of the month. There's not enough business, and no new books are being published."

"The owner agree to that?"

"He suggested it."

"I hear he's Jewish."

"I've heard that, too."

"You told me once he lived in Paris. Is he still there?"

"Most of the time."

"What will you do?"

"Try to find another job as a clerk, but they're very scarce. I may go to Marseille."

"I hope you don't. Enough of this small talk," he said, his voice turning husky suddenly.

His tongue went deep into her mouth, and the palms of his hands slowly circled her nipples. Her fingers responded, gliding over his belly.

In the early morning, just before he returned to Flotilla Operations to brief two skippers about to sail for America, he said, "I'm giving a little party for Hans Dörfmann at the Moulin de Rosamedec on Tuesday evening. He's turning twenty-three. Would you come?"

"It's still too dangerous, Horst. I could be beaten or killed."

Kammerer said he understood.

✤ ✤ ✤

"I wonder what it'll be like to live in a big city, in an apartment building?" Maureen said. Her excitement bubbled through. They were at the breakfast table on Vail Place before daylight. She'd fixed eggs and bacon while Sully dressed.

He was about ready to catch the first trolley to Portsmouth, then the ferry to Cape Charles and the Pennsy on north.

"Maureen, nothing is certain about working in New York." He hadn't told her why he was going.

"But you said you'd been offered a job in Operations."

"Pyle mentioned it along with a terminal job while I was still in the hospital. That doesn't mean a job is open." He now regretted telling her about New York.

Maureen frowned. "Then why are you going?"

"To talk to them. What they'd like me to do is go back to sea." That was true!

"On a tanker?"

"Of course. Consolidated only runs tankers."

"But you already said you won't go out on tankers again."

"That's right."

"Well, it seems to me that you could just talk to them on the phone without having to go up there so soon."

"I may not even go back with Consolidated."

Maureen shook her head and let out a frustrated sigh. "You know what you're doing . . ."

"That's right. I do."

✢ ✢ ✢

Rusty Hedley took the paper into Admiral Ames. Standard Oil had signed the *Dolomite* over to the Maritime Commission.

UNITED STATES MARITIME COMMISSION
RECEIPT FOR DELIVERY OF THE TANKSHIP
ESSO DOLOMITE
PHILADELPHIA, PA
FEBRUARY 11, 1942

The Secretary of the Navy hereby accepts from the United States Maritime Commission delivery of the tankship *Esso Dolomite* at 0900 E.S.T. on February 7, 1942, at Philadelphia, Pa., pursuant to and in accordance with the provisions of that certain agreement between the United States of America acting by and through the United States Maritime Commission and Standard Oil Company (New Jersey).

For the Secretary of the Navy
Rollins Hedley

Admiral Ames examined the hurriedly typed document. "We're in business?"

"The *Dolomite* left Philly this afternoon for the Norfolk Navy Yard. Conversion work on her will begin in the morning."

"Who said we can't act when action is necessary?" The admiral was pleased. "What about the two cargo ships?"

"We take possession tomorrow morning in Boston, and they'll get under way for Brooklyn in the afternoon," Rusty said.

"I'll advise OpNav," the Admiral noted.

"I thought about having the camouflage bulkheads fitted in the yards, then letting the crews install them once they got out to sea. But that's a bad idea, I think. The crews wouldn't know anything about the mechanics of it, and if the camouflage didn't work, the whole thing would have been useless."

"Think you're right," the admiral said. "Second question—what's your estimate on conversion and personnel?"

"Three weeks if the yards go night and day."

"Make sure they do, Rusty. I'd rather see them out in two weeks. Tell BuPers we want crews within the week. And Rusty, use my name at the first eye blink. And if that doesn't work, don't hesitate to say 'Admiral King.' " BuPers was the Bureau of Personnel.

"Yessir."

✛ ✛ ✛

Jack D. Pyle had called 90 Church Street to say he wanted to see the admiral for a few minutes without divulging the purpose to

Mrs. Cinelli. Now he was introducing Sully to Ames. "I have an employee here who wants to join our navy, though I'd damn sight rather have him sail with us. Chief Mate Sullivan Jordan."

The admiral's first reaction was a visible doubletake at Sully's appearance. His second reaction was one of quick annoyance. He was much too busy to be involved with recruiting. Before he could courteously direct Pyle and his disfigured employee to personnel, the oil man said, "Sully is a survivor of the *Tuttle.*"

In a split second, Ames's attitude changed. He moved out from behind his desk and extended his hand. "I wish we'd been able to get out there to you sooner."

Sully said, "I'm sure you tried, Admiral. We gave you the wrong position."

"It must have been pretty bad."

"It was."

"Sully lost his father in that lifeboat," Pyle said.

"So I heard. You have my deepest sympathy."

"Thank you."

"Now what's this about you wanting to throw in with us?"

Ames couldn't recall ever having met a merchant sailor before. Navy people had always viewed them as either romantic trampship figures or generally loathsome, drunken, brawling real-life characters. But a merchant sailor stood here wanting to join up.

"I have an inactive commission as a lieutenant, senior grade. I'd like to go active. I tried at the Fifth Naval District but was rejected."

"Why?"

Pyle answered, "Because your picky people down there didn't like his frostbitten looks."

"The official reason was because of some missing fingers and toes, although I wasn't examined by a doctor. The officer I talked to said the navy's policy was to reject anyone with missing limbs."

"Peacetime policy. Fingers and toes aren't limbs, in my definition."

"I'll soon be walking without a limp, and my left hand functions almost as it did before. I really think it was because of my face."

Ames said, "All we need are qualified people."

Pyle said, "Sully's qualified. Fifteen years on tankers. He'll be a master soon. In fact, I'm a fool in trying to help him get into a uniform. I need him worse than you do."

"Tell me, Mr. Jordan, why do you want to get into the navy? We've got good health and death benefits, but the money's better where you are. We don't pay hundred percent bonuses for war zones."

"Admiral, I've been put into the water twice by submarines in a year's time. Some pretty good men died out there while I lived."

Pyle interrupted again. "Sully was also on the *Galveston* that went down in SC74B."

"So I'd now like to take a few shots at them myself."

Admiral Ames moved back behind his desk, pushing his intercom button. He asked Mrs. Cinelli to summon the district personnel officer. "If you're physically OK—forget the fingers and toes—I think we can upgrade you a notch. How old are you?"

"I'll be thirty-three in May."

The personnel commander soon entered the office. Ames ordered him to take Jordan in tow, get him a physical, and process him to active duty without delay. "I want this man with us, and if there's a problem have the doctor call me."

The commander frowned at the sight of Sully. Ames caught it. "We're not in the business of beauty contests here! Get him started!"

After they'd departed, the admiral said to Mrs. Cinelli, "Get Rusty up here."

As soon as Hedley came through the door, Ames said, "I may have a commanding officer for the *Dolomite*. He's a tankerman, survived SC74B and the *Tuttle*. He has a score to settle. Right now, the medics have him for a physical. Tell that chief corpsman to let you know as soon as Sullivan Jordan is through in there, then come back here with him—and I'll warn you in advance he looks like he's had a fight with a meat grinder. Try not to react the way I did . . ."

Just before noon, Hedley returned with Sully.

"You pass?" Ames asked.

"I think so, Admiral. They're doing the blood and urine now. The doctor said I was in good shape."

"Take a seat, Mr. Jordan, I have a proposition for you, although I don't think I'm doing you any favors. You know what Q-ships are?"

"Vaguely."

"They're peaceful-looking merchant ships armed to the teeth for the purpose of sinking submarines."

"Some were in the last war," Sully said.

"Correct. The British had them, and they did destroy a few subs. But I have to be honest; more of them were lost than the submarines. My question is—are you interested in being the commanding officer of a tanker Q-ship? If you're not, tell me now and forget I mentioned the subject."

"I'm interested."

"Frankly, we don't expect it to last more than one cruise. Every last man on board will be a volunteer. The chances that you'll return alive are no more than fifty percent. Are you still interested?"

"I am," Sully said without hesitation.

"We won't ask you to 'fight' the ship. You'll have trained gunners." Ship handling and abandoning the ship after enemy attack would be Sully's primary role, the admiral said. "*I want that ship to look and act like a merchant ship under a merchant captain.* If the sub is crippled, you maneuver to kill her with depth charges. I'm simplifying all this, and Commander Hedley will brief you fully if you decide to volunteer."

Sully nodded. He wasn't worried about the ship handling.

"Do you have a wife and family?"

"Yessir."

"Well, by all means think it over."

"I don't need more time, Admiral. I volunteer."

"Something else, Mr. Jordan. If you get into trouble don't expect any help."

"I understand."

"You and every other crew member can back out up until the time you drop lines and sail. Is that clearly understood?"

"It is, sir."

Ames nodded to himself in satisfaction, then asked, squinting at Sully, "I take it this is a personal vendetta, this debt you want to repay."

"You could call it that, Admiral." Sully paused to look from Ames to Hedley, then back at the admiral before he continued. "I believe that the sub that shot up the *Tuttle* is the same one that got the *Galveston*. It had a big leopard on the conning tower. So, yes, I guess you could call it a personal vendetta."

"I'll be goddamned! That same son of a bitch," Ames said. "He just played hell with us off Hatteras."

"So I heard," said Sully. "The intelligence officer that came to the hospital said he thought he got a total of eight ships, including us."

Ames glanced over at Hedley. "See if that new OpNav liaison section has anything from the British on that murderous bastard."

"I'll try to find out, Admiral," Hedley said.

Speaking to Sully, Ames said, "The Admiralty has a sneaky outfit called Submarine Tracking. I've heard they know what Dönitz had for breakfast yesterday. Maybe they'll tell us when that SOB sails out of the Biscay."

The admiral gazed at Sully a moment more, then arose and offered his hand. "Thanks for coming by." To Hedley he said, "Take him back to personnel, Rusty; get him sworn in if the doctor OKs it. He's all yours."

✛ ✛ ✛

Partial London transcript of broadcast, *Deutscher Kurzwellensender Atlantik*, 17 February 1942: "...*falls Ihr noch nicht gehört haben solltet, vor zwei Wochen eroberte Feldmarschall Rommel des Afrika-Korps Agedabia von den Engländern zurück...entledigte sich letze Woche seiner Kleidung in der Astoria-Bar in St. Nazaire? Smutje Hagen, of the* U-85, *has a birthday this week and the same for Leutnant-zur-See Dörfmann, of* U-122, *with a party at Lorient's Moulin de Rosamedec next week...*"

✛ ✛ ✛

"I don't understand, Sully. Consolidated offered you a job, didn't they? You told me they did." Maureen was furious.

"They did."

"Then you go into the navy? I don't understand."

On the way back to Norfolk, as the Pennsy coach swayed and bumped its way down the DelMarVa peninsula, rolling past small farming towns and winter-dried fields, Jordan thought about how to explain himself, what he did and why.

"I had to."

"You didn't have to, Sully. You wanted to."

"I guess that's right."

"Did you even think about us?"

He'd waited until after dinner to tell her. The truthful answer to that, he thought, was *no*. He sighed, "It was the kind of decision you couldn't be part of."

"I'd like to know why not."

"Look, we're in a war. I have to be involved."

She laughed harshly. "Haven't you already been in a war? You're lucky to be alive, Sully. Why try to get yourself killed again?"

"Maureen, several of the guys on the *Galveston* had been torpedoed three times, and they were still going to sea."

"Aren't they dead now?"

It was an argument he couldn't win. "Yes."

"You still haven't told me why you did it."

"Merchant ships aren't fighting ships; you know that. After what happened, I wanted to be on a fighting ship."

"And risk getting killed on a different type of ship?"

"I suppose so."

"What type of navy ship will you be on?"

"A warship that fights submarines."

He couldn't bring himself to tell her that it was the leopard boat he needed to find and destroy. If not that one, then another one to take its place. He would be at peace with himself only after he saw it slide under in bubbles, and belch oil and debris. He could then sleep at night and go for days without thinking about the *Galveston* or boat No. 2. Until then . . .

Coming down on the train, he'd even thought of what would happen after the *Dolomite* had done its job. He was a cargo man, and the navy had a cargo fleet.

"A destroyer?"

"No, another type. But it has guns and depth charges."

Maureen was red with anger. "I guess I should be proud you're going off to war again and tell everyone my husband is in the navy. But I don't feel that way, goddammit. I feel robbed!" She stopped the tirade and sighed. "At least you're not shipping out on another tanker."

Sully wasn't about to tell her that the *Dolomite* was also a tanker but wouldn't carry stuff that gurgled. In fact, he knew she was at sea this day steaming tanks, getting ready for the shipyards. He said, "Hon, stop worrying about me. I'm probably the most durable husband you'll ever have."

Maureen's laughter was both futile and hollow. "Yeah, probably. Just when do you go in?"

"I'll buy my uniform tomorrow. There's a shop down near the navy yard gate. I'll report day after tomorrow."

"Where?"

"The navy yard."

She rose from the table, repeating, "The navy yard." Casting another frustrated look at him, she muttered, "Dammit, Sully," and walked out of the kitchen.

✛ ✛ ✛

Kapitän Godt said, "B-Dienst is monitoring the Atlantiksender for Abwehr, and I have something for you to read." He passed over two sheets of paper. "I underlined what is important on page two."

Kammerer took the stapled papers as if they were dipped in acid, already guessing why the chief of staff had summoned him. He glanced at the underlined sentence about Hans Dörfmann's birthday party at the Moulin de Rosamedec.

"I feel like a fool. I had no idea," he said, his cheeks flushing.

"It happens all the time, unfortunately, but as long as you didn't reveal anything . . ."

"I've tried to think of everything I told her, and I don't believe I compromised anything important."

"Then it has served as a lesson. I hope you'll be quite honest with other boat commanders. We can turn this incident to good purpose."

"What will happen to her? I was with her again last night but carefully did not talk about anything concerning operations."

"Did she ask any questions?"

"No."

"What will happen to her is in the hands of Kuppisch. He was notified this morning. I suggest you have no further contact with her. Under the circumstances if she were to leave this area for any reason you might be blamed."

"I won't see her. When will the arrest be made?"

"This afternoon, I'd guess."

"Will that be all, Herr Kapitän?"

Godt nodded. "Kammerer—you weren't the first. You won't be the last. Luckily, we caught this before further damage was done. Now they'll have one less ear to feed Atlantiksender. Foolish girl. She'll pay for it."

Kammerer saluted and then left Godt's office. He wondered what, if anything, would go into his official record concerning Hélène Dussac, and whether or not Admiral Dönitz had been told. Did Operations staff know? He purposely skirted Operations as he hurried out of the château toward the sedan he'd drawn from the motor pool.

Hélène! It didn't seem possible. His stomach was in knots. Godt had seen his shocked face as he scanned the underlined sentence about Dörfmann. How could he have thought he was in love with her? Yet he knew he had been even if it was only sexually. And he'd thought she felt that way, too. He'd seriously, yes seriously, thought about marriage on the last patrol. How could he have told everyone at the Beauséjour what a wonderful girl she was? He'd bragged about her. They'd all find out now. The Gestapo would make an example of her.

As he started the Mercedes, he thought about going to Kuppisch and asking to be allowed to take care of this himself, quickly and quietly. *A single bullet.* That would be the compassionate way compared to what the Gestapo would likely do. He was in agony.

He stopped by the roadside before reaching the Lorient checkpoint to vomit.

✛ ✛ ✛

Sully felt as if he didn't rate the glistening gold stripes on his sleeves. He'd felt uncomfortable returning the salute at the navy yard main gate earlier in the morning, certain he wasn't performing it the right way; he'd been uncomfortable meeting the yard's planning officer, a silver-haired engineering captain.

As they approached the *Dolomite,* tied up on the Elizabeth, Captain Copley said, "We could have put a fence around it and posted sentries, but that would have only attracted more attention in my opinion."

A crane dangled a gun forward; another was landing steel plating. Workers were everywhere.

"We just have to depend on the patriotism of everyone involved. If you put this many guns on a merchant vessel, you ask for questions. My answer, Commander Jordan, is short and to the point—she's an experimental ship."

"That'll be mine, too," Sully said, as they climbed the ramp to go aboard. Being called Commander rattled Sully. "Mate" suited him better.

The yard had always been a special place for him. He'd ridden by it a thousand times or more as a kid on a bicycle. He'd entered it on special occasions, Navy Day or Visitor's Day, going aboard ships and to the foundry to see his papa at work. Now here he was in a fancy uniform, a part of it. Maureen hadn't commented about how he looked. She was still angry.

From dockside, the *Dolomite* appeared to Sully to be a sturdy, well-kept little tanker. He thought he'd seen her before chugging along the coast.

On the deck Copley said, "I hope you're going to be satisfied with the placement of the guns and throwers."

"Captain, if you haven't been told—I'm a chief mate, a tankerman. I put on this uniform yesterday. I know nothing about guns. All I'm supposed to do is handle the ship. I'm leaving gun placement up to you professionals."

Copley smiled. "Welcome into the navy. I was wondering about you but afraid to ask. Looks like you got bunged up recently. Torpedo victim?"

"Frostbite victim."

"First I've ever seen. Anyway, welcome aboard. I have a lot of things to do, so why don't you just wander around. Get me later in the day if you have any questions. And, by the way, I'm open to suggestions. You don't know the navy; I don't know tankships.

One problem is expanding crew's quarters from fifteen to well over a hundred. Lunch at the 'O' club?"

Sully smiled back. "Thanks. Should I salute you?"

"Hell, no. I save my right arm to carry blueprints." With that Copley strode forward to where the gun was being landed.

Sully made his way to the mahogany-paneled master's stateroom in the bridgehouse. He changed from the fancy uniform to a pair of coveralls he'd brought from home, the smartest thing he'd done all day.

For the next four hours he explored every accessible square foot of the *Esso Dolomite*. Unlike larger tankers, her bridgehouse was forward over the bow. Finding an emergency light in the engine spaces, he explored her tanks. They still smelled faintly of heating oil—the *Dolomite*'s last cargo, though the dominant smell was from welding torches. The main work going on at the moment was strengthening the deck where the guns were to be mounted. Tankers were never intended to be gun platforms.

Thinking he wouldn't feel comfortable in the officers' club surrounded by all the braid, he lunched in the civilian employees' cafeteria and then went back to the *Dolomite* to make some calculations. Somebody had probably figured out how many empty fifty-gallon steel drums could be fitted into the tank spaces for buoyancy. Sully wanted to know exactly how many for himself.

✢ ✢ ✢

Hélène was naked, spread-eagled on a battered table in the basement of the *commissariat de police* with four Vichy officers holding her down by the wrists and ankles. She'd been under interrogation for more than three hours, denying she was an enemy agent, and refusing to name any contacts. A few minutes ago she'd been stripped and stretched out, reduced to quivers and a whimpering "Please, please, please . . ."

The blood-stained room was lit by a single fly-specked bulb.

Many others had been tortured down here since the autumn of 1940. It was a chill, dank room of pain and death.

A poker was being heated by the flame of a plumber's torch, and Kuppisch chatted with the French interpreter while waiting for the tip to turn pink.

"Is it the salt pasture that makes your mutton different?" Kuppisch asked.

"Yes, I think it is the salt grazing that gives it the different flavor. Sheep grazed in other parts of the country don't have it," said the interpreter.

"I like leg of lamb, but I'm not normally a mutton eater. I do like yours," said Kuppisch. "At home, I dress the lamb with crème de menthe as it roasts. The green gives it a beautiful patina."

"Herr Kuppisch, the iron is ready," said one of the Vichy cops.

"Ah, so it is. Stretch her legs wider."

Then he said to the interpreter, "Tell her she has ten seconds to give us the name of her contact here in Lorient." It was the same question they'd been asking all afternoon.

The woman spoke rapidly, but the only response was the whimpered "Merci, merci, merci . . ."

The glowing poker sizzled as Kuppisch spit on it, moving it toward Hélène's vagina. He touched it against her inner thigh; a piercing, almost deafening scream filled the room.

"Five seconds!" He moved the iron within a half inch of the opening. Her singed pubic hairs smoked.

Hélène whispered, "Sister Cecile."

"Who?" Kuppisch shouted.

"Sister Cecile."

"So we thought," Kuppisch said, handing the poker to the Vichy cop who was holding Hélène's ankles. "Have some fun with her and then throw her back in her cell."

As the major and the interpreter were leaving the basement room, the policeman who took the iron placed it back in the torch cradle and began dropping his pants.

✛ ✛ ✛

Rusty Hedley shuttled between New York and Virginia. He spent a day or two at the Brooklyn Navy Yard with the conversion of the two small freighters, then forty-eight hours with the *Dolomite,* then back to Brooklyn. "We have to determine the limits of train and approximate depression and elevation of each gun." He stood by Sully as the forward starboard 3-inch, .23-caliber gun was being welded to the reinforced deck. "Damn little room to do it. On paper, it works."

"I can't help you," Sully said apologetically.

"You're not expected to," he said. He checked Plan NNY-D7-5, a hurried blueprint of necessary structural changes to accommodate the gun. "We're all making educated guesses." The plan indicated the doors or "shutters" that would hide the weapon until time to drop them. He muttered to himself, "If I'd only picked a bigger ship. I wasn't thinking . . ." The bigger ones were needed to take cargo to England.

He'd told Sully he was afraid the doors would jam, not fall, or have other mechanical problems. They were designed to drop down and hang on ropes. "I get the 2:00 A.M. shakes about that," he said. The doors had to be sufficiently rugged to withstand repeated gun crew training yet still function for combat. "The real joker may be sea conditions." Rough weather could quickly stop Operation RQ.

Thinking about sea conditions, Sully said, "I do have one suggestion. If we get into it at night, I'd like to send some flares up. Light her up like Broadway." He'd seen the *122* in the chalk-white glare over SC74B.

"Good idea. I'll put mortar tubes on each wing," Hedley said.

Sully followed him back through the bridgehouse to the welldeck, where Rusty stopped by a tank hatch and bent over to measure it. Straightening up he said, "You're going to be hauling pulpwood."

"What?"

"I can't get enough fifty-gallon steel drums to fill two tanks, much less all of them. I'd need six thousand. So we're going to fill them with wood. Chunks of it." He stretched the tape. "None longer than four feet."

"A tanker full of wood? Well, that's something new."

"It floats, doesn't it? That's what I hope you'll do."

"And I pump in ballast?"

Hedley nodded. "BuShips says it'll work. You'll have tanks of water and wood. Without loading the centers, you'll be down nearly to your marks."

Sully laughed and shrugged. "Whatever you say. After that torpedo hits, we may be picking out splinters for a month." He was suddenly amused at the thought.

"You may," Hedley acknowledged.

After a week's work the ship was well masqueraded even to those permitted to board her. The fake blended with the real. There were dummy sections of the bridgehouse and the afterhouse. Within the past twenty-four hours, passageways had been cut through the center tanks—holes just large enough for a man to race through—to facilitate movement of the enlarged crew without being seen on deck.

The pumproom was now equipped as an "armory"; there were five tommy guns, the same number of sawed-off shotguns, twelve Colt .45s, fifty hand grenades, and some tear-gas canisters, all needed for boarding parties. The paint locker, already equipped with stream-smothering apparatus, was now the space for ammunition storage.

Telephone circuits to the gunnery positions fore and aft were being laid out. Emergency lighting was being strung, even in the tanks, and was supplemented by portable dry-battery lights attached to bulkheads throughout the hull. An emergency radio room was being equipped in the afterhouse.

Lights burned all night since the *Dolomite* was expected to meet the three-week delivery date by Admiral Ames. Captain Copley had not been home since she arrived in the dirty Elizabeth. What little sleep he got was at the yard's BOQ.

Meanwhile, all Sully could do was stand around and watch as the civilian workers made the changes according to the specifications of Copley and Hedley. He felt useless. The gunnery officers and supply warrant, assigned by a Washington desk, were due to report in two days; the crew, also assigned out of the Bureau of Personnel, would arrive next week.

He wondered how they'd react to a merchant marine commanding officer with lilac-colored biscuit ears and a tipless nose.

✛ ✛ ✛

Gobelins first heard about Sister Cecile through the secret network—one was operating in almost every city, town, and village—but he did not learn about Hélène Dussac until a day later. He'd been at sea with Duphot, fishing for sole north of Santander.

After cleaning the boat they'd gone to Raphael's, and it was there that they were told that the Gestapo had arrested the nun. It was shocking news yet not surprising. Sister Cecile had been involved for almost two years. Someone at the convent had turned her in, Gobelins thought. No place was safe. There were rats in Notre Dame de Victoire as well as in the *préfecture*.

But it was not until the following day that Laennec said, "The girl was arrested, too."

"Which girl?"

"Hélène Dussac, your friend."

Gobelins sat on the side rail of the *Vaincre* denying what Laennec had just said. He was shaking his head, saying, "No, no, no."

"They got her before they got the nun."

"Are you certain?" Laennec nodded. "It is in *Le Nouvelliste* today. Kuppisch announced they'll be executed tomorrow for espionage." Heartsick, he felt the strength ebb out of his body; Gobelins put his head down and wept.

Duphot and Laennec walked up the dock a way to let him grieve with dignity. They knew Georges well enough to know he wanted privacy. When he finally rose from the side rail, they returned to the boat.

His eyes were red and puffy, and he looked drained and lifeless. He said, "I'm getting out, dear friends. I've caused so many deaths. I recruited her. I caused her death. Tramin's too ... "

He wiped his cheeks.

Duphot said gently, "Sit down, Georges."

Gobelins took a deep breath and did as commanded.

"None of us can 'get out,' " Duphot said. "We can't give up."

Gobelins looked at Duphot. "It's useless. The Germans meant what they said. They've always meant what they said ... "

Gobelins was talking about the announcement in *Le Nouvelliste* in June 1940.

"*Les Résistance et les actes de sabotage ...,*" the proclamation had begun. Acts of sabotage were useless and would be punished in a most severe fashion. That had been the first of warnings. Lately they didn't warn; they just killed.

+ + +

Sully had never shot off anything bigger than a rifle or twelve-gauge shotgun—"crackers" on the Fourth of July. Not wanting to be entirely ignorant of what warships were all about, he'd asked Hedley to arrange a three-day crash course in gunnery, depth charges, and sonar.

He was turned over to "chiefs" aboard a newly commissioned Benson class destroyer. They taught ninety-day wonder "boot" officers as a weary, normal course of events. As Ames and Hedley had said, it was the legendary chiefs who actually ran the navy.

A dry, bespectacled chief sonarman from Pennsylvania began the course. "What we've got here is sonar, an ear on the bottom of the ship. It's in a retractable dome. It can listen for a sub's prop noises, or you can 'echo-range' with it; it can 'ping' off a sub hull, and its time of return gives you the sub's range and bearing..."

Sully had heard the hollow *ping* echo in the Portsmouth picture show, in a submarine movie.

"We're talking about frequencies above the audible range of fifteen to sixteen thousand vibrations per second. Is it any good?" the chief asked.

Thrown by its thousands of vibrations *per second,* Sully said, "Supposed to be, I guess."

"Depends on the operator! The echo comes back with varying degrees of pitch depending on the nature and movements of the target. The variation in pitch, the 'Doppler effect,' should tell a trained operator if he's listening to a ship or a whale, whether it's a stationary or moving target, and its speed and direction. OK?"

"OK."

"Not OK. This piece of equipment has more tricks than Houdini..." Sully spent most of the day asking questions and listening to a training recording.

Next was a cram course in depth charges conducted by a chief gunner's mate from Florida: "The old Y-gun, which fired two cans in opposite directions, had to be mounted on the ship's centerline; but you can put these new K-guns, single-arm throwers, anywhere along the sides. They've got three hundred pounds of TNT. You set the firing device at whatever depth you think the sub is. It fires by hydrostatic pressure down to three hundred feet..."

"At what distance is it lethal to the sub?" Sully asked.

Chief Stubbs replied, "BuOrd tests tell us twenty-one feet. So I'd suggest you drop it on the conning tower."

✛ ✛ ✛

"Wednesday night and Sunday night," Edwige said.

Gobelins had just asked the whore when Major Kuppisch paid his weekly visits.

"At what time?"

"Eight o'clock. Always promptly at eight o'clock."

"Does he bring anyone with him?"

Edwige shook her head. "He's always alone."

"Is he armed?"

"Yes, he carries a pistol. He is usually half-drunk. He brings a bottle of schnapps." She made a face.

"He drives himself here?"

"No. His driver parks out in front, and he comes up alone."

"Where in front?"

Edwige walked over to her third-floor window, and Gobelins joined her. Pointing down, she said, "There."

Her finger was aimed at the opposite side of the street near a lamppost.

"And how long does he stay?"

"About an hour."

"Never longer?"

The chunky dentist's assistant and part-time prostitute said, "Never. Sometimes shorter." Her Rubenesque face broke open in a wide grin. "He is a one-time man," she added, holding up her thumb to indicate the size of his penis. "Tout petit."

Gobelins wasn't interested in Kuppisch's measurements. He looked out of the window again and then turned back. "Edwige, if you want to live to be an old woman you better forget I ever came up here."

No longer grinning, she swore, "I'll forget. He was a good customer, but I'll forget."

"Be certain you do."

His hand was now on the doorknob; he sniffed the air. "What is that I keep smelling?"

"Lavender sachet. Don't you like it?"

He said, "I guess it smells better than fish."

+ + +

MAILGRAM

061310 CR 853 U.S. NAVY YARD
SECRET PORTSMOUTH, VA. DATE MARCH 11, 1942

FROM: COMMANDANT, NAVY YARD, PORTSMOUTH, VA.
TO: OPNAV
SUBJECT: COMMISSIONING VESSEL
1. USS CATAWBA placed in commission at 1430, March 11,
1942.
Lt. Comdr. Sullivan W. Jordan, D-V (3), USNR,
Commanding.

✛ ✛ ✛

Chill light rain hissed as it hit the tin reflectors of the strong work lights on the deck of the USS *Catawba/Esso Dolomite*. Night-shift workmen moved around the topside in rubber coats. That's the way Sully had left her an hour ago. "Most of the crew'll be coming in tomorrow so I'll move aboard in the morning. I won't take much. It's just to show my face, let them know I'm on the ship," Sully said.

"Hedley suggest that?" Maureen asked.

"He didn't need to. Some things work the same on all ships, merchant or navy. There's no such thing as an absentee captain on a good one."

"You said you liked the officers."

"They seem fine."

A lieutenant senior grade, two lieutenants junior grade, and two ensigns had reported in the last two days. The commissioned supply warrant had been delayed a day. Except for the warrant they were all reserves. Klein, the lieutenant, was on his way to a new destroyer. All the deck officers had gone through gunnery school recently. Klein was also executive officer, number two in command.

"Thank God they've given me some experienced petty officers. The chief machinist mate has had twenty-two years with diesels. The chief gunner's mate taught at the Fleet Training Command. I got a break."

"Sully, I know you've been going to sea for a long time, but for the life of me I don't know how you ended up commanding a navy ship."

"I'm there to handle the ship. I can take it out and bring it home. Hedley said to let the navy system work. Go by the book. That's what I'm doing."

"You sound like you're enjoying it. You seem to be getting a kick out of it."

"It's something new, Maureen."

How could he tell Maureen? That morning two K-guns were being welded to the fantail deck. The job foreman said, "Cap'n, you better be goin' full speed when you toss your ash cans, else you'll blow your butt to bits. These things are usually mounted on the side. I'm puttin' 'em where they told me to."

"I'll remember that," Sully replied.

How could he tell Maureen?

Each day was new. The guns were all in place including the .50-calibers concealed on the bridge wings, to roll out on tracks. False bulkheads now covered the three-inchers in the fore- and afterhouses; the four-inch ones were bolted and welded behind the K-guns. What had been an open fantail was now a false extension wrapped around the stern with the dummy airports, painted to match the gray of the afterhouse.

"I think Papa would be getting a kick out of all of this, don't you?"

"I suppose so."

He really wanted to tell her what each day at the yard was like, what he was doing, what he was going to do. He wasn't worried about her keeping the "secret" of the *Dolomite*. His only worry was how she'd act if he did tell her the truth.

"You won't be home tomorrow night, or any night after that?" she asked as an afterthought.

"Probably not. We'll be going out early Friday or Saturday."

It was Monday. He'd go a few miles off the coast into a navy training area, out of the normal ship track, to "shake down"—practice abandoning ship and boat drills under oars, and dropping the gun disguises and working the gun crews in pointing, setting, and training. They'd practice for two weeks, coming back to anchorage in the "roads" every night; then they'd load ammunition and go sub hunting.

"Hold me, Sully."

They were side by side in bed. The only sound they could hear was the drip of the gutter. Few cars ever looped down into Vail Place after ten o'clock. The kids were asleep in the next room.

He gathered her into his arms and gently caressed her temple and cheekbone. He felt her anxiety. His arms could say more than words. That wouldn't change either.

Sully awoke well before dawn but didn't get up. His sleep had been shallow and restless. Though they weren't touching, he could feel the heat from Maureen's nude body and hear her soft breathing. He assumed she was still asleep.

He stared at the ceiling, thinking of the *Dolomite* and what it might face in ten days or so.

Suddenly he had the urge to tell her. She deserved the truth. If this was the last night they would ever spend together she had to know why he felt so strongly about joining the *Dolomite*.

He reached over.

"I'm awake," she said instantly. "I've been awake for an hour. I thought *you* were asleep."

He took her back into his arms. "I have to tell you something and know I can trust you not to tell *anyone*."

She remained silent, waiting.

"This ship I'm taking to sea is a decoy vessel. It's a tanker, all right, a coaster, but we'll be carrying a load of wood."

"I don't understand."

"We hope to lure a submarine to attack us, then sink it."

As it became clear to her, Maureen sat up, wrenching free. "Sully, you volunteered for it? My God, you volunteered for that? I can't believe you. You didn't need to volunteer."

"I had to."

"Why, Sully? Why?" She turned to look down on him in the darkness.

"I have to try and kill one."

Maureen was silent awhile; she was stunned. But she finally said, "You're not a naval officer, Sully. You don't know anything about fighting subs."

"There are men on board who do know. My job is to take it to sea and make sure it looks and maneuvers like a merchant ship."

"If a torpedo hits the ship, you could all be killed."

"I don't think so. That's why we'll be loaded with wood."

"But why you, Sully?"

"You know why, Maureen."

"I don't know why," she stormed.

"The leopard sub. That's why. I have to try and sink it once and for all . . ."

"Is this because of your papa?"

"It's because of all the people on the *Galveston* and the *Tuttle*."

"Suppose you don't find him, or he doesn't find you?"

"Then, hopefully, I'll find another one."

"You seem determined to get yourself killed."

"I promise I'll try my best not to, and that goes for every man on the ship."

"I wish you'd promise me something else."

"What's that?"

"Get out of the navy! Just get out!"

"I can't do that. There's a war going on."

"How well I know! I'm surprised they let you in. You're already a war casualty."

She sank back down by his side. "We always end up fighting about this same thing. I may never see you again, but we're still fighting about it."

"I shouldn't have told you."

"Yes, you should have. I just think you're insane now that I know."

"Well, you're not alone. Sparks thought the same," he admitted.

"Sully, for the sake of *us*. All of us, do something for me. Tell the navy you want out as soon as you bring that ship back to port."

What did he have to lose? Hedley would laugh. So far as he knew you just didn't *ask* to leave the service in wartime. You were carried out or stayed in. But he'd ask. "OK."

"We have a deal?"

"We have a deal. I'll ask."

"Sully, I want you to remember this. *You'll give up the sea?*"

"I'll give it up if they'll let me," he promised solemnly.

Maureen's brother, Ed, a 4-F because of asthma, came by in his pickup truck at seven o'clock to take Sully to the navy yard. Two suitcases and a sea bag went into the back of the truck; then Sully went out to their car-less garage to get another bundle.

"What's that?" Ed asked, nodding to whatever it was wrapped in a bedspread. It was oddly shaped.

"Hobby stuff," Sully replied.

The evening before, Sully had gone to his mother's house to say good-bye to her. While he was there, he borrowed his father's favorite crossbow and the best high-powered 30.06 rifle he'd ever made. It was fitted with a Bausch & Lomb scope. Dan had gunsmithed as a hobby.

Back in the house he said his good-byes to the children, held and kissed Maureen. She watched the truck drive off from the doorway.

✛ ✛ ✛

Gobelins and Duphot worked side by side with shovels at the Cemetière de Kerentrech with the only gravedigger who hadn't fled Lorient. He was a grizzled old man and had nowhere to go. They worked silently.

The executions of Sister Cecile and Hélène Dussac had taken place in the morning at the *commissariat de police* yard. Nuns had taken them by horse cart to the convent, where Gobelins and Duphot claimed Hélène's body. It was in a plain pine box that sat nearby.

Tears welled as Gobelins shoveled, but his rage prevented him from weeping openly. Kuppisch would pay for their deaths, pay for many deaths, Gobelins had again vowed. He had not decided how to kill the Gestapo major but Kuppisch would suffer as Hélène and Sister Cecile had suffered. He'd heard that even the nun had been raped by the guards.

Finally the old gravedigger nodded that the space was deep enough, and Gobelins turned to look at the pine box. He murmured once again, "Forgive me," and then moved the few feet to help lift the box and slide it into the hole. They quickly filled the grave and went away.

✛ ✛ ✛

In the morning Sully called Rusty Hedley from the shipboard phone on the *Dolomite,* catching Hedley before he took off for Brooklyn.

"I know this sounds impossible, but I have to ask you. If I get a sub for you, can I get out?"

"Out of what?" Hedley sounded puzzled.

"Out of the navy."

"You just got in."

"I said it may be impossible. I understand that."

"We're in a war, and you get out on the casualty list or dishonorably discharged. There's no in-between, Sully. I don't understand why you'd want out."

"I told you about Maureen. She doesn't think I'll survive many more ships, including this one."

There was a pause.

"She may be right, at that. Tell you what, let me talk to the admiral. You get a sub, any sub, and I'll see if I can guarantee you a shore job until the shooting is over. Maybe that'll help her go to sleep."

"Try for me."

"Look, I'm sympathetic. Wives are catching a different kind of hell from all of this. Call you back."

Twenty minutes later, Hedley was on the phone from 90 Church Street. "Ames said if you get a sub he'll station you ashore for good! The only time you'll pull water under your keel will be on the Norfolk-Portsmouth ferry. You can tell Maureen that."

"Thank him for me," Sully said and hung up.

Then he called the Wilsons, thinking it was about time he put a phone in. They'd skimped long enough! They had no car, no phone, and Maureen had to run next door to call. Saving for a down payment they'd denied themselves too much.

Maureen said, "I didn't think you'd ask," when he told her of the shore job promise. "I thought you'd be too proud."

"We made a deal," he reminded her. "I'll be back in three or four weeks. We'll get a phone, a car . . . "

"It's about time, Sully."

"Long overdue," he admitted.

"You take care of yourself. We'll pray for you every night." *God bless Daddy; keep him safe.*

"I know you will. Check on mother now and then, and make those kids behave. I love you."

"Take care of yourself, Sully. I love you."

✣ ✣ ✣

The new crew of the *Esso Dolomite,* known of course for official paperwork as the USS *Catawba*, AOG 77 (fleet auxiliary gasoline tanker), was assembled in an old navy-yard building not far from where she sat, pallets of stores being craned aboard her. The doors of the former sail loft had been closed and locked.

Jordan was finally doing what he'd almost dreaded for the last four weeks—facing "his crew," the 136 sailors who would man the Q-ship. He knew that some of the petty officers had already guessed the mission. How many others had also figured it out was anybody's guess.

He told them to "stand at ease," a term he'd learned from watching several navy movies. There was no such order in the merchant marine. "I'm Sullivan Jordan, commanding officer of the *Catawba*, and I wanted to introduce myself." He hoped his nervousness wasn't showing. He felt uncomfortable as all those eyes zeroed in on him.

"First of all, two months ago I did not look the way I do this morning. I suffered frostbite when the tanker I was on was attacked by a German submarine. I was in a lifeboat for only a few days, but a few days in an open boat in winter can be a death sentence. Secondly, I'm not a navy man although I have a commission in the reserve. I've been a tankerman for fifteen years..."

Although he'd never made a speech before, so far, so good, he thought. The faces in front of him showed interest.

"You've all been assigned to the *Catawba*, but I'm here to tell you that you must now agree to volunteer for service aboard her. We'll operate after several weeks of special training, in hopes of killing a German submarine. This ship will be a target for a U-boat. We'll attempt to destroy it." He told them there'd be no disgrace if anyone didn't wish to volunteer. Simply step forward. "But I order you to regard this meeting as top secret. Tell no one what the ship's mission is. It could cost lives including your own."

Jordan paused as heads turned up and down the ranks to see if anyone declined. No one stepped forward.

"I'm required to ask you to sign a piece of paper indicating you've volunteered, but I would also like to qualify that by saying you can back out at *any time* up until we finally sail for the operational area. Any questions?"

The chief boatswain's mate raised his hand. "What about shore leave between now and the time we get under way?"

That was an easy one. He'd already discussed it with Harry Klein. "Sorry, we'll be too busy."

With that he said, "Thank you, gentlemen," wondering if he should have used the latter word with enlisted men. The hell with it, he thought, walking toward the door.

He heard Klein taking over. "I have some things to say..."

✛ ✛ ✛

Anxious to get under way and redeem himself after the Hélène Dussac debacle, Kammerer signed for the *U-122.* The Keroman maintenance officer declared her ready for action after a three-week overhaul. Kammerer was ready for patrol and certain he'd be allowed to operate again off America.

The *affaire de Mlle. Dussac* had been discussed in the Beauséjour and in the Préfecture Naval, sometimes raucously. If he'd kept his *Wurst* zipped up, it wouldn't have happened. Poor Horst. At the same time, those skippers who hadn't been entrapped were lucky, he thought.

After a hurried trip to Hamburg to spend a few days with his parents, Kammerer had returned to Lorient, making few appearances at social events, staying mostly around the boat, dining alone at bistros that seldom had officer clientele, and counting the days until he could cast off lines from the pontoon barge.

Hélène had come up only once in Hamburg. Giselle asked, "What's happening with your romance? The pretty French girl?"

Kammerer replied stiffly, "I've found she really didn't like Germans."

His mother laughed. "Neither did I before I married your father."

The *Doktor* also laughed.

Godt had told him that Hélène had been executed while he was away, probably tortured as well. Godt reminded him she *was* an enemy agent; she could cause boats to be sunk. He'd been duped. Despite all that, Kammerer felt sorry for her.

Graeber had returned from his short leave and in the midst of dinner at the Pescadou on a side street, Kammerer asked the First if he'd heard about Hélène.

"Yes. I'm sorry for you and her."

He was too embarrassed to ask Graeber what he'd heard. The only possible way to regain face, and career for that matter, was literally to slaughter ships and get himself back in Godt's and Dönitz's good graces. He would make every torpedo a hit and then attack with guns. If he could sail home with sixty thousand tons of pennants strung from the periscope, there'd never be another mention of Hélène Dussac, at least not to his face. Sixty thousand would also put him well above the Oak Leaves mark. Diamonds were next.

Kammerer said, "We're going all-out on this patrol."

Graeber thought they'd gone all-out the last time. Kammerer's individual score, his first boat included, was 148,000. What more did he want?

"My goal is sixty thousand this time."

"That's a lot!" Graeber was startled.

"There's no reason to believe there won't be just as many targets. We'll shoot anything larger than four thousand tons with a torpedo; under that, we'll use the guns. I've ordered extra ammo."

"I thought the admiral was still basically against attacking with guns."

"He saw what we did with the *Tuttle*. His only comment to

me was, 'you got by with it. You just better make sure you don't attack one that is armed.' I'm not that foolish, Graeber, am I?"

The First said no but clearly meant yes.

"I heard yesterday that Topp just got a big collier with gunnery."

Graeber hadn't changed, Kammerer thought. He was still faint-hearted even after two very successful patrols. But it was far too late to ask for a replacement. Besides, he was in no position to ask favors of Kapitän Godt.

"Wait and see! After this patrol, I'm certain you'll have your own boat. Then you'll make these decisions."

Graeber said, "I've learned much from you."

The launch came alongside the USS *Catawba* at dusk. Stars were already punching through the cold March sky. There were a half-dozen other ships at the anchorage, all in training status with their lights dimmed according to the new port regulations. But the *Catawba* was by herself, purposely in the farthest west corner, fifteen hundred yards from any eyes interested in the nearest vessel.

Lieutenant Commander Hedley hurried up the accommodation ladder and identified himself to the armed watch personnel. They were bundled against the chilly breeze that blew across Hampton Roads. He went directly to the commanding officer's cabin, forward, bringing operation orders.

"How's it going?" was the first question he asked Sully.

"OK, I think. They're getting used to me; I'm getting used to them. They were pop-eyed at first. I haven't shown them my toes."

Hedley laughed and then repeated his question.

"I'd like a little more controlled confusion in abandoning ship. Nothing goes right when you do it for real. This has to look for real, like we hadn't practiced. Whoever is on the bridge of that sub has to be convinced it's real."

"That's for damn sure."

"When we're hit, and I hope to God we are, they'll screw up. But I hope they don't screw up too much."

He broke off talking to Hedley to finger the intercom: "Lieutenant Klein to captain's quarters . . ."

"I want Harry in on this," he said.

Hedley nodded.

Klein came through the door a few minutes later.

"Anybody opt to go ashore?"

"Not so far. Oddly enough, they seem to think it's a big adventure. They're excited. They can't wait to get hit. Little do they know. But you should have seen them drilling today."

He'd rung the alarm bell twenty times. The PA system bleated, "Action stations! Action stations!" Gun crews raced through the passageways cut into the bottom of the tanks to man their guns. The abandon-ship personnel manned boats fore and aft. The depth-charge personnel rehearsed at the K-guns.

Klein said, "What they lack in knowledge they make up for in enthusiasm. I'm satisfied but wish we had another week."

"Sorry," said Hedley.

Klein, a year younger than Sully, had been a naval ROTC instructor at Purdue whose request for sea duty had been honored the year before.

"How's the equipment working?" Hedley asked.

"We've had some problems, but the chief carpenter and machinist's mates swear they can solve them." The false bulkheads over the forward guns had hung up several times. "If we get lucky and a sub hits us I've ordered the gun crews to simply cut the ropes, drop everything in the ocean, and fire away. At that point our disguise is worthless."

Hedley nodded. "I have some news for both of you. The leopard boat sailed."

"Really?" Sully felt a spurt of adrenaline.

"Ten days ago. The British notified us that she was headed for

Hatteras. No great surprise, but it's confirmed. It wasn't something we wanted to put in a dispatch. Their Submarine Tracking chief attached a personal message, a kind of for-whom-it-may-concern . . ."

Sully waited, then said, "And it concerns me?"

"In a roundabout way," Hedley answered. "Two French agents, a nun and a young woman, reported the Hatteras destination. It was probably the last thing they did. They were caught, tortured, and executed."

"God," Sully said, shaking his head.

Klein said, "Oh, no."

"It's added incentive if you need one."

After handing over the sealed orders, Hedley unrolled a nautical chart of the Hatteras area. "Take a look at this. He got three in a few hours the day after he got you. All of them within a few miles of each other. At 0915, the *City of Auburn,* at 35.42 north, 75.20 west; at 1420, he got the *S. W. Parrish,* at 35.22 north, 75.24 west; and at 1640, he got the *Empire Cathay,* at 35.39 north, 75.19 west. Three ships within eight hours. He couldn't ask for more."

"Oh, yes, the son of a bitch could."

"He has a name, Sully. Sub Tracking provided that as well. Kapitänleutnant Horst Kammerer, winner of the Knight's Cross. You see, they'd like to nail the bastard as much as we would. He torpedoed a ship last year with 106 children aboard. All of them were lost. Two were grandchildren of the commander, Western Approaches. So they have a deep interest in helping us."

"I'm glad."

"Another thing Tracking told us—this fellow has an obsession with tankers. Over half of his known victims have been tankships."

"I'm well acquainted with two."

Horst Kammerer. So the man with the white cap and beard had a name. What was startling to Sully was the fact that they knew his name.

Hedley tapped the chart, illuminated with a circle of ivory light. "If I were you, I'd go by that middle position, 35.22 north and 75.25 west, on a wild chance, in ten days."

"Why do you say ten days?"

"Tracking has a well-used table on it. Kammerer has to cover thirty-four hundred miles; let's say it takes twenty to twenty-two days for that type of boat to go from Lorient to Hatteras, subject to weather conditions and how much trouble he has getting out of Biscay waters."

"He only makes ten knots?"

"He saves fuel for when he needs it. If it were me, I'd be there at first light five days in a row."

Sully nodded, looking again at the chart. "Is any of this realistic?"

The stockbroker shook his head. "No, but we have to try. Hell, he could start action three hundred miles east of Hatteras. You know that ship track better than I do. He might find a half-dozen targets out there and not show up off Hatteras until April 3, 4, 5, if ever. Look, Sully, kill any sub you can find. Any. Don't wait for that son of a bitch. If you find one sooner, sink it."

"I understand."

"Now, let me run over radio procedure with you. If you're challenged by a friendly ship, use the *Dolomite* call letters. If by remote chance a submarine should challenge you, use CWBT. You'll be the SS *Douro*, Portuguese registry. D-o-u-r-o. In general, guard 355 kilocycles."

Jordan was writing.

"I talked with the admiral last night, and he said to make doubly sure you understand that you attack *only* when you're close enough to ensure destruction. You already know that, but I'm passing it along from the man with the wide stripe, as ordered."

"Well, if it's the leopard fellow, he comes in close. He was less than 150 feet from the lifeboat."

"Your officers OK?" Hedley asked the exec.

"They seem to be." Klein nodded.

"Not much choice at the moment."

Hedley glanced at Sully. "Any resentment because you're from merchant marine?"

"Can't see any. I've made sure they know I've sailed these things before."

"Your guns OK?"

"We'll know tomorrow. They've got a tug with target rafts scheduled for us. That's Harry's department. All I'll do is conn the ship," Sully said.

"Well, if you need anything let me know. I'm headed back for New York in the morning. I've got your sister ships to look after." Hedley looked around the stateroom. "Nice digs, huh?"

The mahogany-paneled room was far superior to the captain's quarters on the average navy ship.

He saw the crossbow hanging on a bulkhead. "Is that what I think it is?"

"It is. Belonged to my father."

"You don't see many of them around. What in the world are you doing with it here?"

"I amuse myself. Use it for target practice."

Then Hedley noticed the 30.06, the Bausch & Lomb scope sitting on the barrel. "And what's that for?" It was strapped up near the crossbow.

Klein said, "He's an old bear hunter."

"Good-looking stock," Hedley said admiringly.

"Walnut. The forend tip and pistol cap are rosewood. I'll bet Papa hand sanded that wood for a week."

Hedley looked back at the crossbow. "As an old gunnery officer I have to ask what the range of that thing is."

"Depends on who's shooting it. I used to be pretty good at forty yards."

Hedley turned his eyes back toward Jordan. "Why do I suddenly have the feeling you intend to use it on Horst Kammerer?"

Jordan smiled.

"You think you'll get 120 feet from him?" Hedley asked.

"I hope to ram him."

Hedley said, "I'll be goddamned. You're probably the only human alive going to war with a crossbow."

"Maybe not. Maybe there's a Yugoslav or a Turk out there tonight with a quiver full of quarrels."

"I don't care how you do it," Hedley said.

"If he's more than forty yards, I'll try the rifle."

Hedley nodded.

"Thanks for stopping by."

Hedley took another long look at Jordan. "You know, you're getting prettier by the day. Good luck."

He said good-bye to Klein, then said, "See you, Cap'n," and returned to the waiting launch for the ride back to the Naval Operating Base.

By now, except for her ship-at-anchor lights, the USS *Catawba/Dolomite* was a vague shadow on the calm roadstead.

Sully went up to the chart room and opened the drawer to extract 1232, which covered Hatteras from just below the Oregon Inlet south to Ocracoke. He'd looked at it before, making crosses where ships had been sunk so far.

Horst Kammerer. He could almost smell the diesel fumes again as the sub passed by their lifeboat, and see that bearded skipper with the white capcover.

✝ ✝ ✝

Duphot hit Kuppisch's driver in the back of his skull with a heavy wrench and then grasped him by the collar, dragging him out to the ground.

Gobelins grabbed an arm, and together they towed him to the fish truck parked a hundred feet away. They heaved him in, covered him with tarred netting, and then with tarpaulin. They walked slowly back to the shadows of the old building on Chaussee de Trèfaven.

The dentist's office was on the ground floor, and Edwige's apartment was above it. The major had been up there almost a half hour. Tonight was Wednesday, and they'd seen Kuppisch arrive a few minutes after eight for his twice-weekly romp with the whore.

Driving toward de Trèfaven, Gobelins said he wanted Kuppisch alive. He didn't care what they did to the chauffeur or how. He wanted the major alive and had made a sandbag to aid that goal.

Aside from an RAF nuisance raid taking place, orange bursts around the Merville district, the spring evening was pleasant enough. There was little traffic, a car or truck headed now and then toward Kerdual. No one was walking. Blackouts and air raids had a tendency to keep people at home.

Police station secrets were hard to keep, especially during the occupation, and Gobelins knew Hélène had been tortured with a sizzling iron as well as raped. He would have enjoyed repayment in kind but had other fisherman's plans for Kuppisch.

A few minutes after nine Gobelins heard voices from above. A quick sword of light cut the darkness upstairs as Kuppisch began to descend, humming, on schedule. He was half-drunk, as Edwige had predicted.

As his feet touched the final step, Gobelins moved out of the shadows and sand-bagged him. Kuppisch fell with a grunt and was soon in the back of the truck.

While Gobelins trussed Kuppisch, Duphot moved the Mercedes three blocks away to remove suspicion from Edwige. He heard the all-clear signal as he returned.

The route skirted the Keryado and Ville Neuve districts. They drove at a leisurely speed, taking back streets to the fish docks. The headlights of the Citroën cast dim yellow beams.

By half past eleven Kuppisch and his late chauffeur were at sea on the *Vaincre,* headed for the fishing grounds west of Île de Groix. Gobelins and Duphot were having a sandwich and tea as the boat bobbed in the low chop, the engine purring as if it were brand new. Stars were overhead; it was still a pleasant night.

A few feet away Kuppisch, bound hand and foot, was stretched on ropes between the winch, normally used to haul up the nets, and the towing bitts at the stern. He was moaning, "Bitte, bitte, bitte," and "Mein Gott, Mein Gott," in the same way Hélène probably had pleaded for mercy in the bottom of the *commissariat de police.*

At Gobelins's convenience, the winch would be started and Kuppisch's flabby body would explode like a hawser under great strain. His remains would be washed overboard like tunny entrails.

✝ ✝ ✝

Only Harry Klein, a tall hollow-cheeked Missourian, and Radioman First Dubrow knew about the leopard boat. Dubrow knew because he'd seen the reference in two coded dispatches from COMEASTSEAFRONT. They were messages from Hedley. He'd asked, "What's this leopard stuff, skipper?"

Jordan had made light of it. "A sub we'd like to meet."

Klein was not even the most experienced officer. Klarfeldt, the "jaygee," had been a warrant boatswain. Ensigns Cromatty and Scalsi had graduated from college a little over a year ago and were fulfilling their naval ROTC contracts. They'd gone on two midshipmen cruises aboard cruisers and destroyers during summers.

Having moved into the tiny captain's sea cabin just off the chart room behind the navigation bridge and given up his usual quarters to accommodate his entire complement of officers—five bunks had been built in—Sully had hung his crossbow on the forward bulkhead of the *Dolomite*'s bridgehouse. Alongside it was the 30.06.

He'd gone over several possibilities with Klein. He respected Klein's knowledge of gunnery. "What happens if he decides to shoot us up instead of using a torpedo? That happened with the *Tuttle* and a half-dozen more I know about."

"We already know the range of his guns. They aren't any

more than ours." The "he" meant any German sub commander operating in the Atlantic.

"So he has no advantage there?"

"Sure he does. We don't want to get in a duel with him. He'll submerge and blow us out of the water." Hopefully, he'd hit them with a single eel—not wanting to waste more than one on a ship that size—and then come in close to finish them off with his guns. "That's when we sock him. If we're talking guns, we've got six times his firepower broadside..."

Sully nodded. "What'll you be aiming for?"

"Any piece of him. Penetrating his pressure hull is sketchy, but if we can put a couple of holes... who knows? I'd like to make it so he can't dive. If he can't dive, he's in trouble. But he can still maneuver and use his tin fish..."

"Cripple him, Harry. Give me a shot at ramming him."

"Big order, Captain. Now let me ask you a question. How will we look to him?"

"I can't get her down to full load, but we'll open enough valves to make her look like she's three-quarter loaded."

"What happens if we don't catch fire or blow up?"

"Not all of them catch fire. The *Thalia* didn't until she got hit with incendiaries. The *Clark* went down with a full cargo of heating oil. The only smoke from her came from the stack until it was sucked under. The *Esso Nashville* broke in two but didn't catch fire," Sully explained.

✢ ✢ ✢

The British had turned up the heat on the Bay of Biscay, with continued mining of the approaches and bombers scouting dawn to dark on the usual tracks of the submarine ports, so Kammerer had stayed submerged during the day on the first forty-eight hours away from the Brittany coast. Now after seventeen uneventful days under way, he found the North Atlantic more congenial on this trip.

The *U-122* headed directly for Hatteras. The only target he'd sighted had been an east-bound troopship type, likely carrying Canadians, at twilight on the thirteenth day. Her speed was an estimated twenty-two knots, and she was zigzagging. She was as much a target as a bounding antelope.

The weather, though chill, was sunny and practically cloudless this late March Wednesday, wind three knots. Visibility was unlimited to the horizon. Though he'd spent a lot of time in his bunk resting for battle, Kammerer was now mostly on the bridge as the boat neared America.

Forenoon, he lectured young Kalisch on the composition of the sea floor. "Try to picture the land free of trees and houses but with ridges, slopes, and low mountains. You've got the Mid-Atlantic Ridge running from the Demerara Abyssal Plain all the way to the Reykjanes Ridge below Iceland; you've got the Bermuda Rise over there ..."

Stahlman, the lookout covering the port bow sector, broke into the lecture sharply with, "Herr Kaleunt, there's something bearing one-four-zero ..."

Lifting his binoculars, Kammerer said, "Well, it's about time." His beard was full again. His depression from the Hélène Dussac incident was lessening each day. His confidence was back. He was ready for action.

A tiny patch of white marred the blue off the port bow. It bobbed up and down. All five pairs of eyes on the bridge were momentarily studying the puzzling dollop of ivory.

"A sail," Kammerer said with disappointment. Lookouts guarding the stern quadrants went back to their search sectors.

Surely no pleasure boat was out this far. It had to be a lifeboat, and he decided to investigate. They were bearing down on it, anyway. Even without a course change, they'd pass it within a quarter kilometer. He knew four ships had been sunk within the past ten days in the area.

He made a slight course adjustment, increased speed to fifteen knots, and then summoned Graeber to the bridge, ordering action stations. The crew needed sharpening.

As soon as the First reported, rubbing his eyes, Kammerer said, "Lifeboat," nodding off the port bow. "We'll find out when the ship was hit and give them direction to land." Where was it hit? He was curious.

Graeber looked a little surprised. He could understand the skipper's being curious, but it was unlike Kammerer to aid the enemy. He certainly hadn't aided the *Castle Innesberg*. Dönitz's instructions were clear: Do not rescue survivors! One less merchant seaman was one less person to man the next ship off the ways!

Kammerer read Graeber's face. "Don't worry. Telling them which way to sail is not much help."

There was a lazy swell, and soon the *122* bridge occupants could see there were two boats, one being towed by the boat under sail. They could make out eight or ten men in each boat.

"Man the guns," Kammerer ordered as they approached within fifty meters.

Bauer was the only one aboard who spoke any English. Kammerer regretted he'd forgotten what he'd learned in school. "Ask them when and where they were hit. What kind of cargo were they carrying? Then give them the current position and the course to steer to shore."

"Should I ask if they need any supplies?"

"No. Offer nothing."

The *U-122* dropped revolutions until she was gliding at five knots; then finally Kammerer ordered, "Stop engines," conning the boat to the left, narrowing his distance to the survivors.

They stared across the water in sullen silence at the gray hull with the leopard insignia. They were sea whipped and haggard. Salt crusts lay on their eyebrows and whiskers, and their backs were bent from the ordeal. Two men in the first boat did not even raise their heads. If there were any dead, they were in the bilges. Kammerer guessed they'd been out there several days. Luckily for them the weather had been moderate. He noted the name stenciled on the prows, SS *Houston Reefer*. American, he also guessed, and leaned to the speaking tube to tell Heinze to check it, spelling it out. Perhaps *B-Dienst* had heard her calling for help. He'd log it. Every scrap of information aided intelligence.

Kammerer asked for enough engine revs to keep the *122* alongside the *Reefer* boats as Bauer used the loud-hailer to ask if the captain were present.

No one responded.

Only the wet puttering of the diesel exhausts, the flap of the lifeboat sail, and the soft splash of water against the gray hull could be heard. "When were you torpedoed?" Bauer asked.

Still no answer. The angry stares continued.

Kammerer gave up. "Tell them to steer zero-nine-five to nearest land." Then he shouted, "Auf Wiedersehen!" at them.

The words had barely left his lips when an elderly man in a gray fedora, perhaps the master, stood up. His arm extended. A spot of red grew from it. The bullet ripped Bauer's neck open. Blood sprayed over Kammerer. Bauer collapsed, clutching his throat.

Dörfmann waited no more than another second. He aimed the 20-mm, made expressly to penetrate the metal skins of aircraft, at the first boat. The gun crew reacted to Dörfmann's shout, "Achtung! Feuer! Feuer!"

Kammerer shouted, "Both ahead, hard right!" as the heavy bullets tore into the people in the lifeboats. The tattered sails turned pink. At point-blank range few or none could survive.

Graeber yelled at Dörfmann, "Feuereinstellung! Feuereinstellung!"

The chunk-chunk-chunk of the ack-ack gun died out.

Kammerer turned the *U-122* sharply away from the shattered, half-sunk boats. Bodies were already floating. Those who survived were paralyzed by what just happened.

Graeber shouted to Dörfmann, "My God, why did you shoot?"

"We were being attacked!" Dörfmann shouted back.

"Enough!" Kammerer yelled; he had already made up his mind to get rid of Graeber.

He looked back at the lifeboats. He had two choices: He could circle around and finish the job so that no one could ever report the leopard boat, or he could continue on the course to Hatteras and put the incident behind them. But if he left no survivors, someone in his own crew, perhaps even Graeber, might testify in Lorient, and accuse him of cold-blooded murder. What would Dönitz say, or do?

Meanwhile, Bauer was carefully lowered down the hatch ladder. He was bleeding profusely.

Dönitz would be professional about it, Kammerer decided. The *U-122* had been shot at, and he had returned enemy fire. That was all.

He looked back at the boats and made up his mind. Most were already dead. "Stand by to fire," he shouted to Dörfmann, ordering a course change to make another pass at the *Houston Reefer* boats. The 20-mm mount soon barked.

Then he said to Graeber, "Continue on the original course. I have to go below and try to help Bauer."

Graeber said, "Jawohl, Herr Kaleunt," but closed his eyes and swallowed as Kammerer left the bridge. He looked as if he wanted to throw up.

✛ ✛ ✛

In Submarine Tracking, Roger Winn bent painfully over the "billiard table" of U-boat activity. He gazed at the pins that marked the latest invaders of the American theater.

He paid special attention this week to the western waters because of continued agitated interest from the prime minister. Churchill had almost forgotten about all the other coasts and seas. He was very upset about the sinkings off the United States. Was the U.S. Navy defenseless? Most of those ships were bound for Liverpool, London, Bristol, Plymouth, and other U.K. ports. He was inclined to be protective of the British-flagged ships, of which sixteen had been sunk.

There were the usual pieces of daily evidence to be decoded by station X—reports of sinkings, sightings, and intercepts between individual boats and *BdU* that had to be dealt with.

He knew six U-boats were returning home from the Caribbean to end *Operation Westindien,* flying victory pennants. Others were moving along Florida and in the Gulf of Mexico. Winn's staff played croupier with all the symbols.

The leopard boat continued to be of special interest. He checked the position.

The *U-122* had inadvertently provided some clues through Kammerer's message to *BdU*; he reported what he thought to be a troop transport scurrying northeast toward England, giving his exact position. Perhaps Kammerer had thought it deserved a few Kondor bombs somewhere off Ireland. At any rate he'd magnanimously divulged himself on March 13, and now it was established, by dead reckoning, where he'd generally be on March 30, give or take a day. He was burrowing toward Hatteras.

✟ ✟ ✟

Bauer, shrouded in canvas, was buried at twilight. He slid into the sea aft of the conning tower.

Kammerer lingered a few minutes on deck; if only he hadn't stopped to question the lifeboat survivors . . .

He finally went to his captain's nook to draft a message to *BdU* reporting Bauer's death. Any elaboration would wait until they returned to Lorient. Was he to wireless, ". . . killed in incident with lifeboat"? Kernevel would react with disbelief. His already tarnished reputation didn't need to be destroyed any more. What was happening to his career?

✟ ✟ ✟

The *U-122*'s short requiem for Wolfgang Bauer was duly received in Lorient, and in Torquay, not too far from Plymouth, England.

It was teleprinted to Bletchley Park for decoding. It was also "fixed" by a pair of Huff-Duff listeners; the first by a Brit in Hamilton Harbor, Bermuda, and the other by the U.S. Navy, in Wachapreague, Virginia, on the DelMarVa peninsula. A nice cross was formed, soon much appreciated by Commander Winn.

Winn said with delight, "This fellow is giving us a road map, isn't he?"

Winn concluded that it was a freak accident of some kind. Oh, well. One less *U-bootsmann*.

✛ ✛ ✛

MARCH 27, 1942   1840 EST
WSC-COASTAL RADIO STATION TUCKERTON, N.J.
WSC DE SQIB SS GUATEMALA
SS HOUSTON REEFER AGENTS IN NYC RESCUED
ONE SURVIVOR HOUSTON REEFER THIS DAY X
OTHERS MACHINE-GUNNED BY SUBMARINE
WITH LEOPARD INSIGNIA X REQUEST AGENT
CONTACT UNITED FRUIT FOR BERTH
ASSIGNMENT AND ARRIVAL TIME NYC.
MASTER.

Rusty Hedley was perplexed by the wireless/telegraph copy from the SS *Guatemala*. "Why in hell didn't he give us his position?" he said aloud. Another nail in the iron coffin of the leopard. The son of a bitch was machine-gunning lifeboats!

Then Hedley wrote out a message to the master of the *Guatemala*: REQUEST IMMEDIATE EXACT POSITION YOU RESCUED SURVIVOR HOUSTON REEFER.

It was sent priority within the hour.

✛ ✛ ✛

The *Dolomite,* five days at sea in an operational status, hammered along at seven knots, puffing up the usual balls of diesel smoke along with a few sparks now and then, waiting to be torpedoed.

She was on her own; butterflies zoomed around in the bellies of the "merchant" crew. Sully had his own *Galveston* and lifeboat No. 2 butterflies.

He'd gone as far south as Georgia, his old stomping ground. Within the hour he'd swung the *Dolomite* 180 degrees, heading north toward the scene of Kammerer's last crimes in January.

He was satisfied that he looked authentic. It was an unarmed oil carrier, laker size, too big for the inland waterway but useful for hauls along the coast and up the Chesapeake and Delaware. The *Dolomite* was a juicy target—worth a single torpedo, then ten or twenty shells.

He was bridge walking, though with a slight limp. His toes were still gimpy. The bridge wings were each twelve feet; the distance across the pilothouse was twenty-one feet; the deckways to the afterladders, port and starboard, twenty-two. Add it up and he had eighty-nine feet in which to exercise and think.

The *Dolomite* was riding the inner edge of the Gulf Stream off Savannah; Sully was admiring its deep blue and startling clarity. In the bright sun, the water sometimes looked painted. He'd always wondered about the lack of phosphorescence at night in the stream. Perhaps a scientist could tell him someday. Well south of here the Antilles Current joined it, adding its warm, salty indigo blue. Together they were remarkable phenomena.

Dubrow caught him as he made a turn on the starboard bridge wing, handing him a decoded priority dispatch from COMEAST-SEAFRONT:

STRONG INDICATIONS *U-122* KAMMERER STILL PROCEEDING
YOUR INTENDED MARCH 30 POSITION

Sully read the slip of flimsy paper, frowned at it, and then looked back over the side. "Dubrow, you ever notice that shallow debris tends to drift to the eastern edge of the stream—never to the western side? I haven't been able to figure it out."

Now it was Dubrow's time to frown. "No, sir."

"Show this to Mr. Klein," Sully said.

Dubrow departed for the radio room, and Sully returned to his pacing. He felt shooting would soon begin.

✟ ✟ ✟

At 0110, the SS *Penn Lube,* a new vessel 461 feet in length, built to haul high-grade lubricants with special cylindrical tanks and special pumps, proceeded north toward Philadelphia at 11.3 knots under a brilliant full moon. With a crew of thirty-eight, mostly asleep, she also skirted the inner edge of the stream.

Directly abeam of her, sixty-one miles away, was Kitty Hawk, on the narrow Outer Banks, site of the Wright brothers' flight. Her residents of late had heard the booms of navy depth charges dropped on phantom targets. They had seen red glows on the horizon. One day they picked up two oil-soaked bodies on the beach. Then a battered unoccupied lifeboat drifted ashore, over-turning in the surf.

Though attached to the United States by a single bridge and ferries, the Outer Banks, with only sand tracks for almost a hundred miles beyond Bodie Island Light, were nearly foreign. The sparsely populated villages had names such as Rodanthe and Chicacomico. Whalebone fences were around the cottages of fishermen and Coast Guard lifeboatmen. Violent deaths in this area weren't uncommon.

The *Penn Lube* was lit by the moonlight. Almost every feature of her—from the rounded stern, white afterhouse, and white bridge structure to the band of white on her forecastle—was visible, though she was entirely blacked out. The Americans, at last, had learned that lesson.

Kammerer studied her. No guns. He lowered his binoculars and said to Graeber, "All yours!"

At 0155, the torpedo blew open the bow of the *Penn Lube,* shearing the wall of No. 1 tank and causing more than five thousand barrels of fine machine oil to gush into the water.

But the *Penn Lube* kept ploughing on, her bow an open cave, pushing the sea against the bulkhead of No. 2 tank. She looked like a whale with its jaws open.

"Verdammt," said Kammerer disgustedly, viewing her again through his glasses. The torpedo had been aimed to hit midships. But torpedoes weren't perfect. Neither were the intricate electronics aiming them, not to mention their human mentors.

He was close enough to see she'd been heavily damaged. The giant orange-red rosette had told him a few seconds earlier they'd made a hit, though not where he desired. In fact, another thirty feet and they would have missed the bow altogether.

But the target was slowing steadily, and he decided to take her by gunfire rather than waste another torpedo. She was the perfect example of a wounded hippo though not capable of attack herself. She might well limp into Norfolk. He ordered Dörfmann to go to work. "Hit the bridgehouse first."

"Jawohl, Herr Kaleunt."

He'd already sunk two freighters earlier in the night. This big tanker was a bonus.

The first salvo of the foredeck gun was directly on target. It hit the starboard side boatdeck, bursting into orange flames, with white whiskers spurting from the burst.

A few minutes after 3:00 A.M., Kammerer called for a ceasefire; the *Penn Lube* would never ever sail again. He set a course west toward Kitty Hawk, passing the gaping bow of the furiously burning target. The silvery sea had turned dull red in her vicinity. Thick smoke slowly rotated into black mushrooms in the starlit sky once again.

He considered one last hunt before the night was over but then decided the crew, though exhilarated, was as exhausted as he was. Just before dawn he submerged, dropping the *122* to the bottom, landing with a thump on the soft sand at thirty fathoms. It was time to sleep.

Operations were secured at 0620. Kammerer congratulated the officers and crew for beginning the patrol with three successful attacks: one torpedo each, a total of twenty thousand tons for the night's work.

"If we continue this way, we'll head for home in less than ten days. Sleep well."

There were cheers stem to stern.

On nights such as this he sometimes played Brahms's cradle song, "Das Wiegenlied," at bedtime. Some of the married men resented it because it evoked memories of their little ones, but the young bucks laughed about it.

Soon the *la-la-la, la-la-la, la-la,* a scratchy rendition from a Stuttgart music box, came over the loudspeakers. Even before it ended there were snores. Lights had been dimmed. All but the vital machinery was shut down. The engine-room and control-room duty watches fought to stay awake.

The *U-122* slept on the sandy bottom like a garfish without gills while navy planes and Coast Guard surface craft circled around the burning *Penn Lube* fifty miles away.

✛ ✛ ✛

The *Dolomite* poked northward. Sully made her as attractive a target as possible. Above decks sailors chipped and painted. The abandon-ship off-duty crew played cards and read. Gunners drilled behind the false bulkheads at 0900 and 1400.

The crow's nest, the original eye-in-the-sky, a steel cylindrical pod with a pie-pan roof, was manned night and day. Forty-five feet above deck it added another four to five miles of sea search during the day, probably two on moonlit nights.

Shortly after sunrise, Sully cut the speed to steerage way and hoisted two black balls to indicate a breakdown. What more could a submarine commander ask for than a helpless ship? Until late afternoon, the *Dolomite* barely covered twelve nautical miles. No takers.

No further messages had been received from COMEASTSEA-
FRONT, but tension had mounted steadily since Dubrow monitored the night's attacks. The nearest was the *Penn Lube*.

Sully had stayed on the bridge all night, certain that sooner or
later, in that bright moonlight, he'd feel the German fist slam
against the hull. It was a moment he'd found difficult to describe
to Klein.

The exec was up and down a dozen times, coming out on the
bridge wing to talk and stare out across the milky sea. Last time,
about 0300, he'd rasped, "I can't sleep. Why doesn't the son of a
bitch shoot?"

"Give him time, my papa used to say, when we knew there
was a big bass around a lily pad..."

Klein grunted, then said, "Sully, I've thought all day about
where to hit him. Common sense tells me to get the conning tower.
That's the easiest target. But aft is really where we should stop him
with the 4.50. Blow the ass end off that thing..."

Sully smiled. "That would be nice."

Klein left the bridge, and Sully suddenly realized he'd been
thinking more about putting a bullet into Horst Kammerer's chest
than about destroying the sub.

Dawn came in quietly. Too quietly.

The day passed without event.

Now it was another twilight; the sea was calm, and the air warm
and hushed. The *Dolomite* still probed northward at seven knots.
She'd buttoned up except for several blackout violations. A port at
the afterend of the bridgehouse was cracked open; the blackout curtain to the hatch off the main deck, aft, was sliced to reveal another
careless slit of light. General quarters for all hands was set.

✛ ✛ ✛

It was evening when the *U-122* rose from the bottom. She went to
periscope depth so that Kammerer could scan both the sea and sky.

He carefully searched the brown dusk for signs of patrol craft and then took a turn at the sky periscope. It wasn't wise to stay on the surface for any length of time during the day this close to shore. So far as he knew, enemy aircraft had no night capability as yet, but with the bright moonlight...? He carefully scanned the sky sectors and then ordered a "blow through."

The *U-122* emerged after almost twelve hours of quiet and sleep. Lookouts were established, and she went back toward the Gulf Stream. Her speed was twelve knots.

Moonrise was 2010.

Twenty minutes later she crossed behind a menhaden boat headed south, running with full lights as if to say, "Hey, I'm only thirty meters long. Don't shoot..."

At 2150, the bow lookout for the starboard quarter said, "Target bearing zero-nine-zero..."

Kammerer said, "I see it," and ordered five degrees to starboard.

Three pairs of binoculars were trained on it, a shape again too small to be of interest. It was showing a red running light to port. A trio of red lights from the foremast indicated a tug and tow. The eyes moved on behind it to take in two barges, also marked with running lights.

"Go in peace," he murmured.

✠ ✠ ✠

Twenty minutes before midnight, Dubrow came up to the bridge. His face was shadowy, tense. "A freighter's under attack. It's near here, I think." He handed Jordan a copy of the SOS message with the ship's position.

Sully and Klein went immediately to the chart room to plot it. The soft red light over the chart table made them look surreal, elongating Klein's nose, and deepening the light purple hue on Sully's cheeks.

He took the dividers and stepped off the distance to his own estimated position. "Fourteen miles," he said, looking over at Klein. "We're about here."

The needle-sharp divider point stuck in the Mercator chart east of Diamond Shoals. The distance between the positions occupied less than an inch.

Still staring at Klein, he said, "Hour-fifteen, hour-twenty minutes."

"They usually hang around a fresh kill, don't they?" Klein said.

Sully replied, "They want to make sure they've got a kill."

They returned to the bridge, where Sully ordered all hands to battle stations. Alarm bells clanged. The guns and depth-charge stations had been partially manned since sundown.

The sea was again a sheet of silver.

"With this much light we ought to be able to spot him, whoever he is," said Sully.

"He's got a low profile, Skipper. He'll look like a big snake crawling along," Klein said.

"You ever do much fishing?"

"Not much."

"There are fish that nibble or suck at the bait. You have to be patient. When you judge they've got a mouth over it, you jerk back enough to set the hook. Those are the smart ones. The dumb ones, like mackerel, barrel along, hit your bait without a second thought, and swallow it. They really hook *you*, Papa taught me."

"What kind of fish do you think that sub is?" Klein asked.

Sully dropped into his Virginia drawl. "I reckon he's a smart 'un."

Klein was thoughtful a moment; then he said, "So it behooves us to be patient."

"That's how I'm thinking."

"Skipper, you've been sunk twice, so you know more about this than anyone else, but I suggest you put on that helmet hanging there. I'm putting mine on."

Down below, all hands had on their helmets and life jackets. The quartermaster first class, who had just relieved the second class at the sound of battle stations, was wearing his. The navy was always particular about fighting stances.

In the crew's mess, aft, the three enlisted medics had set up their "hospital."

Meanwhile, the *Dolomite*'s *ker-chunking* engines were driving her twin screws steadily toward the attack scene at eight knots, now and then flinging a handful of sparks up her stack.

✛ ✛ ✛

The *U-122* slowly circled the stricken freighter, whoever she was. The torpedo had hit directly below the bridgehouse on the port side, square in the middle of the ship. A fine shot by Graeber. She'd gotten a message off, but there was a problem with identifying her call letters. The international ship's registries were now outdated, and this one looked new. Kammerer was guessing seven or eight thousand tons, a good start for the night.

Broken in the middle, like a bridge span, her stern and bow both tipped up. She had guns all right, but they were rendered useless by the angles of the platforms. Air spaces fore and aft kept her partially afloat.

He decided to go in closer to attempt to pick up her name or at least get a better estimate of her tonnage. Operations always wanted as much factual information as possible. But it was pride as well that drove Kammerer to make positive IDs on the ships he sank. His ego was stroked when he could list the name as well as accurate tonnage on the victory pennants for arrival back in Lorient. Though names had been painted over, sometimes a life ring could be picked up. Cleaning fluid would reveal the name.

So he stayed around the sagging hulk, identified only by GKUP, another twenty minutes, shining his light over her sagging superstructure and sky-pointing bow and stern. A single lifeboat was in the water with men in it, and he saw several life rafts, but he stayed well away from them. He'd learned his lesson. He had no desire to converse with the seamen.

"You think she'll ever sail again?" he asked Graeber, facetiously.

"No, Herr Kaleunt."

"I'm of the same opinion, and the night's young. Maybe Heinze will figure out who she is. Tell him to keep listening."

The *U-122* set off south and east, the crew savoring the Gulf Stream not only for its delightful water but also for the abundance of targets. Get rid of the torpedoes and go home to Lorient.

Ten minutes later Matrosengefreiter Schoenleber, a seaman with exceptional night vision, said, "Target eight degrees off starboard bow . . ." He was guarding that sector.

The bridge clock in the control room stood at 0403 Greenwich mean time.

Kammerer and Graeber trained their binoculars in that direction and confirmed Schoenleber's spotting. It wasn't large, but it was definitely a ship. Not a tug or a purse-seiner.

Kammerer altered course to swing out and approach the target midships, look it over, and decide whether or not it was worth a torpedo.

✛ ✛ ✛

In the crow's nest of the SS *Dolomite,* Seaman Michael Crosetti, one of the abandon-ship personnel, who also possessed excellent night vision, was sweeping around with his binoculars. He'd been ordered to cover beam to beam.

Suddenly he saw movement ahead, not particularly a wake, but a low dark object, maybe a fishing boat. He estimated two miles. It was coming toward the *Dolomite* but was at least a mile off the course his ship was steering.

He whistled into the speaking tube.

"We've got something off the port bow about two miles ahead."

Sully asked, "What's it look like?"

Crosetti replied, "It could be a fishing boat."

Sully and Klein exchanged looks.

"Low and dark," Crosetti added. Words always came out of the speaking tube as if filtered through a tinny tunnel.

Klein left the bridge as if his tail were on fire, took the short ladder down to the foredeck in almost a leap, ran to the foremast, and began shinnying upward.

Reaching the crow's nest, he hung on the ladder. "Gimme the glasses. Where?"

Crosetti pointed.

Klein stared at the "low dark" object for a moment. "Christ, that's a sub."

He practically slid down the ladder and returned to the bridge.

The moon that had lit the *Castle Innesberg* was now profiling the *U-122.*

✛ ✛ ✛

Studying the tanker, Kammerer said, "I'm tempted."

He saw no guns.

He judged her to be 350 feet, maybe more. A coaster obviously. She could carry heating oil north from Texas or Louisiana. Thirty-five thousand barrels perhaps. Four thousand tons, he guessed. Some ship would have to be built to replace her, and that's what this Dönitz-brand war was all about.

He looked at Graeber. "You have my express permission to send her and everyone aboard down the River Styx."

Graeber quickly responded.

It took a few minutes to set the mechanics for a single torpedo to be aimed at the coaster.

Meanwhile, Kammerer said, "I'm amazed. She's blacked out, but I see four cracks of light. The captain should fire the engineer. Look at the sparks."

In a moment, Graeber gave the order to fire. The torpedo

streaked toward the exact middle of the target. Flame whooshed skyward seconds later, followed by a boom.

✛ ✛ ✛

On the *Dolomite* anyone not seated or somehow braced was knocked down by the explosion, though Sully had warned moments before, "Stand by for a hit! Brace yourselves!" But the impact was far greater than anyone had expected. The size of the ship was a factor; a baseball bat had been used to kill a fly. The *Dolomite* was swatted sideways at least thirty feet, wood splinters showering down.

In the drills Sully had said repeatedly, "Do not abandon ship until I give the order. Stay at your stations and wait. Do not wear helmets into the boat."

He was now on the port bridge wing staring at the sub through the glasses, waiting for it to begin closing.

Klein had repeatedly told his gun crews, "I'll let you know when to drop the bulkheads. Fire the very second you drop them when you find the target. *Do not fire until then* ..." He was aft with the big gun, the four-inch, .50-caliber; the three-inch, .23-caliber batteries; and the depth charges, the biggest sock the *Dolomite* had.

Over the last two months Sully had rehearsed this in his mind over and over. Wait until Kammerer got into range; wait until he started to fire.

The first shell screamed in, aimed, as usual, at the bridge. It was the *Tuttle* all over again. It hit the after part of the house, tearing steel and wood, immediately filling it with smoke.

Sully yelled at the young quartermaster, "Steady, steady," and then got on the PA system. "Abandon ship, abandon ship ..." He hoped the Germans would hear. Suck them in. He repeated the order.

Klarfeldt had the forward batteries, with ensigns Cromatty and Scalsi handling the secondary guns, the three-inchers aft. The latter two, so new to the navy, seemed to have more confidence than anyone.

Sully went to the port wing as the boats were lowered.

Another shell whined in and hit forward of the afterhouse, in the tanks, its incendiary load throwing up a fan of flame.

A third slammed into the afterhouse itself, near the stack. Smoke plumed up.

"Stop engines but stand by for immediate start," Sully ordered the engine room. The *Dolomite* drifted.

Two boats were in the water, he saw. Oars were broken out. It was working, so far.

The U-boat came closer, lobbing shells about every thirty seconds.

Jordan focused the glasses on her again. This time the shadowy outline of a leopard was held in the circle of vision. *U-122!* Third time around. His heart beat faster. Was the same commander still aboard her? He lowered the glasses to pay attention to the *Dolomite*.

The after lifeboat, port side, had spilled as planned. It was canted, bow down, hanging from the davits. Sign of a very normal abandonment. There were screwups, confusion.

Sully reached for the 30.06 and took the safety off. He had loaded it long ago. Earlier in the day he'd cocked the crossbow, warning each watch not to tamper with it.

There'd been three direct hits on the target's tanks but no fire as yet. "Hit the tanks! Hit the tanks!" Kammerer yelled down at the foredeck position. "We can't stay here all night."

He was worried that destroyers from Norfolk would come at flank speed after the last unidentified ship got off its SOS. Set this one afire and get out!

Graeber said, "Maybe it's loaded with molasses."

That wasn't at all funny, Kammerer thought, using the seven-by-fifty binoculars to study the coaster. God, Graeber was irritating.

She'd messaged as *Esso Dolomite* under sub attack. *SSS*. Heinze had looked up her call and reported her name. The Americans had odd names for their ships.

"There, she's burning," Kammerer muttered.

+ + +

Jordan was on the phone to Klein, who was watching from a crack in the false bulkheads. "I hope he comes closer. You ready? We're burning . . ."

Phony fires. Oil-soaked rags were blazing in barrels midships in the tank area.

Klein said, "I'm ready. But give me a count to thirty so my guys can drop the bulkheads." Cut the ropes with their knives.

Another shell flashed in, hitting No. 3 tank.

Thank God the cargo was wood this time, Sully thought.

Another two minutes, four more shells, and Sully began the "thirty" count, his eyes pinned on the conning tower of the leopard boat. He thought he could see a white cap but wasn't sure. The main thing now was to attack before the sub cruised away.

He finished the thirty and yelled into the PA system, "Drop bulkheads! Open fire!" Then he ordered the parachute flares sent up.

The abandon-ship crews had been told to row out of danger. He saw they didn't need further urging. Their oars were flashing.

+ + +

Kammerer turned away to call down to Heinze and ask if he'd been able to identify the previous target. He uttered only, "What's the—" when tongues of flame came out of the new target, fore and aft. Almost instantly the *U-122* staggered from a direct hit aft. Then the sky lit up, exposing the boat. Chute lights floated down.

Stunned by what had happened without warning, every man

topside, including Kammerer, was frozen for a moment. Then Kammerer shook it off, realizing what was less than five hundred meters away; a goddamned Q-ship! He'd been suckered. The *Esso Dolomite* was U.S. Navy.

On deck, Dörfmann shifted his fire from the target's tanks to the flaring of the forward battery, hoping to knock it out. He scored a direct hit.

The *Kanonier* mate of the *122*'s aftergun opened fire on the Q-ship's afterbatteries. His gunners were all veterans.

They were suddenly involved in the worst of all U-boat nightmares. A duel.

Machine-gun tracers poured out from the enemy ship.

Kammerer shouted, "Clear the bridge. Dive! Dive! Emergency! Dive . . ." Then: "Prepare for torpedo attack . . ."

The gun crews were already scrambling past him for the conning tower hatch. The bridge watch had cleared.

As Kammerer looked at the target and waited for the men to get below, the enemy guns winked again. Another shell burst against the hull above the forward torpedo room.

Fromm had heard the dive order in the engine spaces, which were now filled with acrid smoke, but he also knew there was a slice ten inches wide over the engines. "Wasser einbruch!" Then he discovered his phone was dead.

He ran to the control room, shoving bodies aside, to inform the *Kaleunt* that the *U-122* was crippled. There'd be no diving. Meanwhile, damage control!

A few seconds later, breathing hard but in control of himself, Kammerer dropped to the deck of the conning tower, away from the shrapnel for the moment. He stood by the periscopes. Bridge watch faces around him were pale with fright. Every eye was on him. Calmly he said to Graeber, "We'll fight on the surface while going away." Then he gave orders with the same calm: "Gun crews back on deck; resume firing. Prepare for surface attack, stern tubes . . ." The engineers were ordered full ahead.

He said to Graeber confidently, "We'll get her!"

Q-ship trickery was unspeakable to submariners. But even as he spoke, another 4.50 shell hit the *122* aft, in the engine spaces.

He returned to the bridge.

✛ ✛ ✛

Sully had the *Dolomite* moving again, having no idea how badly the U-boat was damaged. He knew Cromatty's battery had been hit just below the bridge; he had felt the shock and heard the screams. Now there was silence down there.

Another hit had silenced the chattering of the 20-mm just behind the port bridge wing.

Though firing steadily, the leopard boat didn't seem to be moving. She was still broadside. He'd expected it to dive or run away at full speed.

✛ ✛ ✛

Kammerer yelled frantically, "Why aren't we under way?"

The *122* drifted.

Word came up from below: "Engine room took two hits. The diesels are down . . ."

"Shift to electric!" Kammerer raged. "Use your heads down there . . ."

Turbulence soon developed under the boat's stern.

He could see the target beginning to turn. Maybe it was trying to run? Once he got into position on the electrics, he'd blow this fucking coaster over the moon, then head out to sea, lick his wounds, and make repairs. How in God's name had he allowed himself to be trapped? A heavy price to pay for four thousand tons.

Both vessels were turning, each as slow as the other, the U-boat turning inside the Q-ship radius.

The engineers reported they needed a half-hour to put one

diesel on line. Kammerer was already thinking how he could get out of aircraft range by daylight on half power. The main thing now was to destroy this *Schwindler,* with all hands, even those in the boats.

Graeber had orders to torpedo the *Dolomite*'s engines.

✛ ✛ ✛

The pale night was lit with red gun flashes and the stark whiteness of the parachute flares. Sully ordered the sailors at the flare tubes to keep the sub lit up so the gunners could make hits. They rocketed up every few minutes, trailing smoke as they floated down.

Klein's voice pierced the noise. "Get the goddamn thing around so I can use the four-inch! You're goin' the wrong way."

Sully yelled back. "Give me a minute."

The ship didn't make thirty knots. *Anywhere!* It didn't turn fast. "You got it hard over?" Sully yelled at the quartermaster, knowing it was.

He focused again on the sub's bridge. In the harsh light he could plainly see the white-hatted captain. He had a black beard. Sully had last seen him from a thwart in lifeboat No. 2.

He watched as the *U-122* got slowly into its turn, puzzled that it hadn't jumped to full speed if it was trying to run. Seventeen knots was what Rusty Hedley had told him. Enough to leave the *Dolomite* far astern.

Then it occurred to him that maybe the sub couldn't use its diesels. He'd seen the flashes aft when the 4.50s hit. Maybe Kammerer was having to use his electrics. Rusty Hedley had said they could make seven knots underwater. He couldn't remember if Rusty had said anything about the surface speed. What he was seeing was very slow movement.

Klein's voice broke into his thoughts. "For Chrissakes, get this thing around . . ."

Only the aft port-side 3.23 was still firing because of the turn.

As if lightning had struck, it also occurred to him that Kammerer was attempting to put the sub's stern into position for a torpedo shot, even a spread of them.

He murmured to himself, "Gotcha!" and yelled to the quartermaster, "Keep it hard over!" He'd turn with the sub, parallel her, edge closer, and then use his extra two knots to ram. He knew ship handling. All these explosives were not of his experience.

The *Dolomite* took another hit aft as he stepped out on the port wing. He jumped back inside as machine-gun fire laced the bridgehouse.

✣ ✣ ✣

Kammerer shouted, "Direct all fire at the bridge . . ."

Whoever that American captain was he knew ships. He was also a *gottverdammte Bulldogge*. He wouldn't let loose. "Destroy the bridge!" he yelled to the ack-ack gunners. The captain had to be killed.

The Q-ship kept coming, edging closer, and in a fit of rage Kammerer jumped to the nearest twin-barreled ack-ack gun, shoved the gunner aside, and began raking the already smoking bridge.

✣ ✣ ✣

Through the bullets ricocheting off the steel housing, Sully glanced out the farthest port toward the *U-122* and saw that the white-hatted skipper himself was firing at the *Dolomite*.

He grabbed the 30.06 and did something no ship's master is ever supposed to do in emergencies. He yelled, "Keep coming hard port!" and left the bridge.

He raced down two ladders to the main deck and stood over tank No. 1, shielded by the afterhouse bulkhead. He took careful aim through the Bausch & Lomb scope and fired two rounds from the rifle his papa had made.

Kapitänleutnant Horst Kammerer fell away from the ack-ack gun, a surprised look on his face.

Sully was too busy to feel anything one way or another. He climbed the ladder back to the bridge in a few seconds.

✛ ✛ ✛

Graeber saw Kammerer on the deck, gasping, blood oozing from his chest. He saw the bow of the *Esso Dolomite* bearing down. He yelled into the speaking tube, "We've lost! Bring up a bedsheet . . ."

In the remaining moment of his life Kammerer saw Graeber waving the bedsheet and tried to speak. Only red bubbles came out of his mouth. He'd been right about Graeber all along.

✛ ✛ ✛

Sully spoke into his mike. "I'm going to ram her, Harry."

Klein didn't answer. He was too busy to talk, Sully thought. Or he was dead.

Sully lined up the *Dolomite* to hit the *U-122* at the conning tower and yelled over the speaker system, "All hands, prepare to ram; prepare to ram . . ."

In about sixty seconds the blunt bow would crunch down on the submarine.

"Steady as she goes."

He felt a great calmness. He'd never purposely hit another ship in his life. It was against everything he'd ever been taught.

He saw someone waving something white from the *U-122* bridge. It was too late for that.

A shell from her foredeck gun hit the bridgehouse, peeling back the overhead, lighting it with a thunderous clap, and Sully felt himself flying backward.

He was on his hands and knees when he felt the jolt, like a thousand sledgehammers hitting the bow at once, and heard the crush of steel; he felt the *Dolomite* lifting and seesawing;

and he heard the muffled screech of the *122* as it went under the keel.

Shaking his head to clear he weaved out to the port bridge wing to see the U-boat roll over, exposing its rudder and still slowly turning propellers. In the moonglow it looked completely harmless, and he realized that it *was* completely harmless. Never again would it kill.

Some bodies floated free, and then it sank, with eruptions of oil and air making horrible gurgling noises. Debris from it bobbed up. *Never again would it kill. Never again would Horst Kammerer stare over at a lifeboat.*

He went back into the mangled bridgehouse and realized that the quartermaster was on the deck. He knelt down and tried for a pulse. There was none.

As he went to the PA system to secure from general quarters, he found himself weeping. There were a lot of things to do: pick up the abandon-ship crew from their lifeboats, get the damage-control party to put out the fire aft, take care of the wounded, take care of the dead, and check the bow for damage.

Wiping his cheeks and trying to get hold of himself so that he could talk, he knew what he wanted to say, but he didn't know how at the moment. All he knew was that the leopard boat was dead.

The *Dolomite,* eighteen dead and thirteen wounded, limped toward Norfolk at four knots, her fires still smoldering and the sea washing in and out of the house-sized hole on the port side. Jordan was afraid she might break up. He'd shone a light down in the hole to augment the moon, but it was difficult to assess the damage. If the keel was broken they'd be lucky to reach port.

He'd radioed COMEASTSEAFRONT priority:

SANK LEOPARD U-BOAT 45 MILES ENE DIAMOND SHOALS X EIGH-
TEEN DEAD THIRTEEN WOUNDED THIS VESSEL X RECOVERED
FIVE ENEMY X REQUEST IMMEDIATE MEDICAL ASSISTANCE X THIS

VESSEL BADLY DAMAGED FROM TORPEDO AND SHELLFIRE X RE-
QUEST TUG X AM PROCEEDING NORFOLK X MY POSITION IS 35.11N
75.17W. MASTER DOLOMITE

Sully knew he should be elated about Kammerer, but he was too weary to feel anything but sorrow for Harry Klein, Ensign Cromatty, and the sixteen dead enlisted men. He hardly knew them, yet they'd had the brief but everlasting bond of shared danger.

All he wanted to do at this point was get the *Dolomite* safely behind the antisubmarine boom, hand her over to the navy, and sleep for a week.

With shaky knees and trembling hand he stood by the port nearest the wheel as the light began to broaden on the east horizon. The bridge was a shambles and smelled of gunpowder and death. The bridge clock put the time at 0545.

He was headed home to Maureen and the children. Ashore, forever.